Holtondome

BY RYAN SOUTHWICK

The Z-Tech Chronicles
Book 1: *Angels in the Mist*
Book 2: *Angels Lost*
Book 3: *Angles Fall*
Book 4: *Angels Found*

Z-Tech Chronicles Stories
Zima: Origins
Once Upon a Nightwalker

ryansouthwickauthor.com

HOLTONDOME

Timeless Keeper Saga
Book 1

Ryan Southwick

ISBN: 978-0-9998342-7-5 (Hardcover)
ISBN: 978-0-9998342-5-1 (Paperback)
ISBN: 978-0-9998342-6-8 (Ebook)

Any references to historical events, real people, or real places are used fictitiously. Names, characters, and places are products of the author's imagination.

Front cover illustration by José del Nido.
Front cover design by Sentinel Designs.

Printed and bound in the United States of America.
First printing, 2022.

Wick's Words
Pacifica, CA

Visit ryansouthwickauthor.com

1

Seg

SEG YANKED HIS STEERING WHEEL to the right and slammed the gas. Performance off-road tires, backed by a monster all-wheel-drive powertrain, responded with authority. The vehicle swerved right, throwing a rooster tail of dirt and gravel in its wake. The wheel jerked and shimmied in his grasp like a wild beast. Seg redoubled his grip, muscles straining.

A pothole the size of his racer loomed just ahead. If the beast won at this speed, he was a dead man.

His front-left tire dipped a toe into the gorge-like pothole, skirting its edge. Instead of fighting death, Seg cranked the wheel left and met the pale horseman head-on. All four tires grabbed the dirt. The back-left tire hooked the pothole's edge like a train on a railroad track. The racer whipped around the outside of the crater like a rollercoaster car and shot out the other side.

Wind teased his hair like a rough lover. Seg drank it deep, then let out a soulful "Yeeeehaaaaawwww!" that surely rattled the windows of Mars Colony a hundred and thirty million miles away.

Heavens above, it was good to be alive.

But Seg wasn't done yet. The racer had more to give, and he'd be hogtied if he let even one of the seven hundred and eighty-six horses under the hood go unridden.

With a grin bigger than Jupiter, Seg mashed the gas pedal. The engine roared, flattening him back against the custom racing—

A loud electric *pop* snapped Seg out of his daydream. He jerked his foot off the accelerator.

1

The hauler had overloaded—again—protesting his mistreatment of its aged electric powertrain. Apparently, sixty-four kilometers per hour on a dirt road with a full wheat harvest was too much to ask from the vehicle that had served his great-grandfather.

Saying a silent prayer to Odin that he hadn't broken it, Seg eased the throttle back up. The electric motor warbled, then settled into a steadier hum. Seg wiped his brow in relief—

—and nearly poked his one good eye out when the hauler lurched sideways from another monster pothole. He wrestled the monstrous vehicle back under control, then swore under his breath.

That was the third pothole in five kilometers that he'd misjudged the distance. Seg was only glad no one had been present to witness his mistakes. He was in no mood for a lecture on how his lack of depth perception meant he had to drive more carefully than others.

It was quite the opposite. As far as Seg was concerned, having only one good eye meant he needed to practice more—push himself harder to overcome his deficit.

Still, they'd be reluctant to let him near a vehicle even as slow as the hauler if he damaged it.

A glance in the rear-view mirrors showed he hadn't lost any bags of wheat, which was a relief. Harvest was terrible this quarter, as occasionally happened, so they needed every kilo they could get.

Fortunately, the hauler's bumpy ride hadn't worsened, either, which meant he hadn't broken the suspension. The monstrous vehicle had evidently survived three generations of Holtons for a reason.

And if the hauler doesn't live to see a fourth generation, Peg will kill me.

The irony made him laugh. His mother, Peg, was also Seg's inspiration for racing. Not only was she a great mechanic—inasmuch as Providers were allowed—but her stories of the days before The Fall, when combustible fossil fuels powered most of the world, were so full of passion and vivid imagery that Seg longed to get behind the wheel of one of those extinct vehicles and experience the roar of its engine for himself.

Reluctantly accepting reality, Seg relinquished his racing daydream, slowed down, and concentrated on hitting as few potholes as possible.

The sun was high—or so he imagined, since the ever-hazy gray sky made it impossible to tell its exact position. Not for the first time, Seg wondered what their star, Sol, looked like. Not the splotch of amorphous light hiding above layers of chemical gasses and who-knew-what-else, but how it must have appeared in the twenty-first century, when Earth's sky was purportedly crisp and blue.

Seg shook his head. He couldn't imagine it anymore now than when his parents used to tell him those stories at bedtime as a child.

No one alive remembered the sky the way it used to be. They would have to be three hundred years old at least, and people just didn't live that long. Well, maybe in the City they did, but certainly not in Holtondome.

We're lucky to be alive at all, Seg thought, looking around the countryside.

Sharpgrass grew waist-high in large clumps as far as the eye could see, its wide, pointy leaves painting the landscape dull-green between barren patches of dirt and rock, interspersed with winding streaks where acidic rain had carved brown troughs in the terrain.

Maybe "lucky" is the wrong word…

Stories claimed that towering trees used to grow in the wild, along with grass that wouldn't slice flesh open if you walked too close. And they grew on their own, outside the weather-protective domes.

Living outside of a dome…

Seg laughed at the idea. Violent lightning storms and acid rain ensured nothing but sharpgrass and insects could survive outside of the domes for long. He wouldn't be out in the open now, nor have even attempted this trip, if there were any signs of a storm coming.

Suddenly paranoid, he surveyed the horizon. The sky was gray, but not storm-gray. The winds, too, were stiff, but carried none of the musty smells of a dust storm, nor the caustic stench of an acid downpour. With Holtondome just three kilometers ahead, even the hauler's leaden pace would have him home before Mother Earth could smite him.

Thunder peeled in the distance.

Or she might fry me with lightning just to prove me wrong.

A glance in the rear-view mirror showed dark-gray clouds where there hadn't been just a minute before—which meant they were moving in fast. Seg stepped on the accelerator.

The old hauler lurched forward with a few electric pops.

Then it died.

Oh no.

Seg mashed the pedal a few times, but it was no use; the instrument panel remained dark. The battery meter showed fifty percent charge—more than enough power to get home, which meant there had to be a short-circuit somewhere in the ancient wiring.

The question was whether he could find it and return to Holtondome before the storm fried him.

He pulled a lever under the dash to pop the hood, folded the passenger seat down, grabbed a toolbox, and jumped out of the hauler.

A glance inside the electric motor compartment showed nothing unusual. Seg pulled on a pair of long gloves from the toolbox and fastened a wire from each to the metal chassis. Back when he was a teenager and Peg was teaching him how to care for the hauler, he'd once foregone the grounding gloves, thinking himself above the laws of physics. The hauler had punished him with an electric jolt that had almost stopped his heart, and earned an earful from Peg on the importance of electrical safety. He'd never skipped that step again.

Five minutes later, the thunder was loud enough to rattle his teeth, but he was no closer to isolating the short. The wind had picked up from a casual breeze to a whipping gale. Rain smacked his face like tiny punches. The sky above was light, but behind the hauler, a torrential wall of gray moved toward him with frightening speed, streaked by frequent lightning flashes. Even if he managed to fix the short now, the hauler was too slow to outrun the storm.

Seg slammed the hood closed and made for the cab. He'd have to buckle down and pray the lightning passed him by, and that the winds didn't blow the hauler over and destroy the wheat harvest, and…

A black shape appeared within the storm, low and close to the road like some sort of vehicle. Seg rubbed his eyes, unable to believe anyone would be stupid enough to drive through a lightning storm, but the longer he stared at the emerging shape, the more defined it became, until its conical nose and windshield were unmistakable.

The vehicle was unlike any Seg had seen. Long and sleek with a polished black finish, the body was shaped like a giant teardrop, as if built for pure speed.

And speed it had. A rooster tail of water ten meters high flowed behind it. How its tires could take such punishment from the dilapidated road was beyond him. The hauler would have shaken apart at half that speed, but the sleek vehicle, if anything, seemed to be accelerating.

And it was on a collision course with the hauler.

Seg waved his arms. "Hey! *Hey!*"

His warning should have been unnecessary, given the mountain-sized hauler beside him, but the approaching vehicle showed no signs of slowing. The road was too narrow for both vehicles, and swerving off road at that speed would be catastrophic.

Rain slid from the strange vehicle's windshield as if repelled by an invisible force, giving Seg a clear view inside. Slicked, graying hair placed the driver in his forties, if Seg had to guess. He wore tinted glasses, a fashion that had disappeared centuries ago along with the sun. The glasses also made it difficult for Seg to tell whether the driver had seen him, or if he was even awake.

Seg waved his arms higher. "Hey! Slow down! You're going to…"

The driver lifted two fingers from the steering wheel and casually gestured toward the hauler. He apparently had no intention of slowing and wanted Seg to move.

Crazy bastard!

Seg wasn't going to argue, however. With the sleek vehicle almost on him, he scrambled into the hauler and shut the door just in time.

The vehicle glided off the side of the road, plowing through the stiff sharpgrass with ease. Road spray smattered the hauler like a hail of pebbles. Seconds later, when Seg could see through his window again, he expected to find the sleek vehicle tumbling out of control over the rock-strewn terrain, but it pulled back onto the dirt road with ease, leaving Seg far behind.

Thunder rumbled. Wind rocked the hauler with increasing authority. Seg rolled his windows down a few centimeters on each side. Rain would soak the interior, making for an uncomfortable wait, but leaving them up meant the glass might blow out. With the harvest as bad as it was, they would barely have enough to barter for essential repairs for the dome, let alone to replace glass for the hauler, and Seg would certainly never hear the end of it.

Of course, broken glass would be the least of his worries if lightning struck the hauler—which was very, very likely.

Ahead, the speeding vehicle skidded to a halt. To Seg's surprise, it turned around and headed back toward him.

Seg rubbed his arms against the chill. Anyone with a car that nice must be from the City, and City folk could care less about a farmhand like him. What could they want?

The vehicle made a wide U-turn through the sharpgrass and pulled alongside his own. Its curved passenger window silently rolled down.

"Get in," the graying driver said.

Seg glanced at the hauler's cargo. It was a lot of wheat. If he left it unattended…

"Get. In." The driver punctuated each word, as if explaining to a dullard. "That is, unless you want to be barbecued alive in that mammoth lightning rod. Offer expires in ten… nine…"

Seg opened the hauler door. Gale winds yanked it from his grip. He wrestled it closed, then slipped soaking wet into the sleek vehicle's passenger seat.

The driver didn't even glance at him before hitting the accelerator.

G-forces flattened Seg back against the plush leather seat. A grin crept over his face. Acceleration like this shouldn't even be possible on a dirt road, but at that moment, he didn't care. Seg had never experienced a more glorious feeling in his entire life, and he was going to enjoy every second of it.

Is this what riding in a spaceship is like?

It couldn't be far off.

"Thanks for the ride," Seg said.

"Wasn't my idea. But if you insist on thanking me anyway, you can start by not touching anything."

"Oh."

Seg self-consciously pinned his hands between his knees, making himself as small as possible. As with the exterior, everything about the interior came straight out of a science fiction story. Brilliant displays with letters Seg couldn't read littered the dashboard. The steering wheel was a ring of polished black so enticing that he had to clamp his knees tight to keep from grabbing it.

They definitely didn't have anything like this at home.

"Where are you headed?" Seg said more as a distraction than anything, since there was only one logical answer.

"Holtondome."

Of course. "Me too. Happy to show you around when we get there."

"You can show me to the bar, if you have one, kid. But apart from that, I'm good."

Seg rankled at the "kid" remark. He was twenty-eight years old, which made him practically a senior by Holtondome's standards.

"You already have a place to stay, then?"

It seemed unlikely. If the driver's visit was expected, everyone in Holtondome would have known about it, and Seg hadn't heard a thing.

"I'll sleep in the bar," the driver said. "That way I don't have to sober before I leave that piss—" He coughed into his hand and left the sentence unfinished.

"'Pisshole,' you can say it. Well, in front of me, anyway. I'm not as patriotic as some. I know Holtondome doesn't hold a candle to the City."

"Been to many Cities, have you?"

Seg ground his teeth. He'd never been to a City, and this prick knew it. He'd also never talked to anyone from a City before without the Feds monitoring his conversation, so he let his annoyance slide in favor of getting information.

"No. Which City are you from?"

"Would the name mean anything if I told you?"

Temper down, Seg... "It might. Our geography knowledge is a few generations out of date, but we do our best to pass information down through storytimes. How much could City names have changed in three hundred years?"

"You really don't want to know. And I could get arrested for telling you, so do us both a favor and stop pumping me for info."

Seg nodded. Any and all information about the outside world had to come from the Feds, which he well knew. Still... "Can't blame a guy for trying."

"I can't at that."

Seg let the silence drag, hoping against hope the driver would break protocol and throw some tidbit to satisfy his imagination, but he kept his eyes fixed on the road, which whizzed by at an alarming speed. The car's suspension glided over the potholed road as if it were a white fluffy cloud.

Determined not to let his first—and perhaps only—ride in a modern car go to waste, Seg let his eyes roam. With the exception of the steering wheel and a few components, every surface was leather. Not the rough leather they cured in Pigdome, this was smooth, supple, and flawless in ways that would make their leather master break his tools over his knee and cry. The glass was so clear that Seg had to tap it with a fingernail to make sure it was actually there.

He twisted around to examine the back—

—and gaped when he found a woman staring out the driver-side window. The woman didn't react; her black-rimmed eyes watched the landscape pass without interest.

"Sorry," Seg said, although he remained facing her.

The driver mentioned that turning the car around hadn't been his idea...

"Thanks for going out of your way to pick me up."

"Mm." The woman twirled a blonde ringlet of hair around her finger, but didn't take her eyes from the landscape.

"Lightning storms are deadly out here. You might have saved my life."

"Mm." Her voice was soft and dreamy, as if she was hardly paying attention at all.

Not the talkative type, I see.

"Well," Seg said, "if there's anything I can do to thank you while you're in Holtondome, just ask. I know everyone and everything there is to know about that place. I'll hook you up."

"Mm."

7

The driver cleared his throat. Seg turned to find a reproachful glare waiting. The driver started to speak, then froze. His tinted glasses made it hard to know for sure what he was staring at, but Seg had a pretty good idea.

"My eye's been this way since birth," Seg said.

"You mean… it's real?" The driver shook his head. "Looks like glass. Never seen an eye that white before."

"Doc hadn't, either."

Seg tried to contain his excitement—and his disappointment. The driver had inadvertently shared information about the outside world, but he'd also confirmed what Seg had feared his entire life: his birth defect was a true anomaly, which meant there may also not be a way to fix it.

He sighed. It had been wishful thinking. Even if a treatment existed, it would be expensive, and would require going to a City—which in itself wouldn't be permitted even if his life depended on it, and having sight in only one eye didn't qualify as life-threatening, anyway.

"You should wear a patch," the driver said.

"With that slicked hair, you'd look better in one than me."

The driver cracked a smile. "That wasn't an insult, kid. Eyepatches create an air of mystery. They're like sunglasses, only better, because people's imaginations go wild dreaming of all the horrible things that might be underneath. Get a patch, and people will be standing in line to talk to you. Then you can make up whatever crap you want to lure them in."

"Lure them in for what?"

"Whatever you want. Selling them a piece of land on Mars, getting women in bed…" He glanced in the rear-view mirror. "Sorry if that was inappropriate, ma'am."

"Mm."

Seg looked around to find her still staring out the window. He lingered to give her a chance to gawk at his white, glassy eye, like everyone did, but she didn't even twitch a muscle on her high cheekbones. He couldn't decide whether to be relieved or insulted.

Another "ahem" from the driver made him turn around.

"My client is doing you a favor," the driver said softly. "Do her one and treat her with respect. That means not staring."

"Let him stare," the woman said. "Most people do."

Although he knew he shouldn't, Seg turned around anyway. "Why?"

In answer, she finally pried her gaze from the window and looked him head-on.

Every story Seg had ever heard about the beautiful sky of old seemed to come alive in the woman's eyes. A blue he'd only dreamed of stared at him in vibrant pools—crisp, wild, serene, infinite. If he looked hard enough, he'd bet he could see the wispy white clouds and glorious sun that existed now only in stories. Thick black lines ringed her eyelids, like his sister's eyeliner applied with too-heavy a hand. Even her hair, he suddenly noticed, wasn't pure blonde, but tinged with vivid green, as if she carried the last vestiges of Earth's lush past on her very shoulders.

"Enchanting," Seg breathed. The word had escaped before he could catch it, but it was true. Combined with her high cheekbones, she had an exotic look he found enthralling.

If the woman was pleased or offended, she gave no indication, and simply turned back to the window.

Seg faced front again with a silent curse. After a lifetime of being gawked at himself, he should have known better. Peg would have rightly cuffed him, and he had half a mind to let her do so when they returned.

"Sorry, miss," Seg said.

"Mm."

2

Holtondome

RETURNING TO HOLTONDOME IN ONE piece always gave Seg a sense of relief. At one hundred meters high and a third of a kilometer across, the opaque white dome was visible from all five of the surrounding agricultural domes, beyond which he had never traveled. The prismatic sheen of Holtondome's solar panels, which covered every inch of its surface, lent a welcome dash of color to the otherwise drab landscape.

Everyone was preparing for the oncoming deluge when they neared the western entrance. Lightning storms meant clean water. There hadn't been one in weeks, which didn't help the harvest one bit, and even their drinking reservoirs were running dangerously low.

People dotted the outer dome's curved shell, cleaning runners that would guide the rainwater down to one of four retractable collection ducts that directly fed the underground reservoirs. Many also took the opportunity to scrape grime from the solar panels, still caked from yesterday's dust storm.

Understandably, work stopped when the sleek car approached. It glided through the western entrance with silent grace. Inside, Seg's father, Hap, pulled himself together and gestured the driver to an empty spot between a broken-down tractor and a stack of empty wheat sacks.

"Thanks for the ride," Seg said to the driver.

"Like I said, don't thank—"

"Right, I forgot." Seg turned to the woman in the back seat. "Thanks again."

"Mm."

He'd hoped she would grace him with her eyes once more. Here in the car might be the only time he would be close enough to fully absorb their wondrous mystery, but the woman kept her gaze fixed on the window, as she had for most of the ride. With a sigh, Seg bade a silent farewell to her and the car's plush interior, neither of which he was likely to see again, and stepped out into the gathering crowd.

Surprised chatter met him. Seg would have been surprised, too, if he'd seen someone from Holtondome step out of a City car.

Troy pushed through the crowd, his eyes wider than the rest. "Seg! Where's the hauler?"

"Busted on the road."

"What about the wheat?"

"In the hauler." Seg ground his teeth to keep from adding a "dumbass" that would surely have started a fight between him and his brother. Any other day, he might have welcomed the boredom relief, but fighting in front of the woman with the enchanting eyes would be poor hospitality.

Troy shook his head, throwing his sandy curls around like a hair tornado. "It'll be ruined! Traders are coming tomorrow, Seg. Tomorrow! We need every scrap this quarter."

"I know! Everyone knows! What was I supposed to do? Carry it on my back through a lightning storm? Ask the City folk to throw it in their trunk? I was lucky they even gave me a ride."

"You could have not broken the hauler in the first place! You were racing it again, weren't you?"

Seg couldn't bring himself to deny it, so he set his jaw and met his brother's glare. A fight was brewing as sure as the coming storm, whether he wanted it or not.

"Of course you were."

Troy stepped closer until Seg could feel his breath. Troy's upper lip twitched, a sure sign he was ready to swing. He was thirty-one, three years Seg's senior, but the extra years hadn't tempered his aggression—especially not against the younger brother with whom he seemed at constant odds.

"I don't know the last time you bothered to check, but Fen's getting worse," Troy said. "And she's almost out of medicine. We barely have enough food to trade for dome repairs as it is. Without that wheat, we won't have enough to barter for medical supplies, let alone replacement parts for the hauler. Remember that the next time you think about taking our livelihood out for a joy ride!"

Troy tensed, clearly expecting Seg to hit him.

And boy, did Seg want to. He balled his fists so tight that his nails bit into his palms.

The rear driver-side door opening—followed by a fresh round of chatter —was the only thing that stopped him.

The woman swept her enchanting eyes over those gathered with the same interest she'd shown Seg, which was none at all. In contrast, the crowd gawked at her, bewitched, just as Seg had been when he'd first seen her.

Hap shuffled forward with a warm smile. "Welcome to Holtondome. Hap Holton, at your service."

In an un-City-person-like move, the woman extended her hand in greeting. Hap's smile faltered, but he took it just the same.

"Fi," she said. "Thank you for having me in your dome."

It was as strange a name as Seg's own, rhyming with "hi" rather than "he," as he might have expected. Hap registered it with barely a blink and nodded.

The contrast between them was, in Seg's opinion, depressing. Fi's black silk blouse was sharp and unblemished, as if it had just come out of the factory, while Hap's hand-woven shirt, grimy from the day's work, looked like it might have been used to clean the machinery. Although his hands were clean, no amount of scrubbing could erase a lifetime of hard labor and chemical burns from crop fertilizer. His hand looked ragged and ruined while enfolding her fair, untainted skin.

The only thing that didn't contrast was their height. At one-point-eight meters tall, Hap was average for a Holton male, but a half-head taller than any woman in the dome. Fi, however, matched him centimeter for centimeter.

Hap recovered his warm smile. "Miss Fi, it's a pleasure. If there's anything you need while you're here, just let me know, and I'll make sure you're attended."

"Thank you, but in compensation for his ride, your son has already offered his services during my stay." She arched a brow at Seg. "Isn't that right?"

All eyes turned to him.

"O-of course, miss." Seg briefly wondered what he'd gotten himself into —or how she knew Hap was his father—but soon dismissed the concern. Fi's demands couldn't be worse than the death-by-lightning she'd saved him from.

She probably won't be staying long anyway, he thought. If Seg owned a vehicle like that, he wouldn't stay one minute longer in this go-nowhere Provider dome than necessary.

Hap eyed him before returning his attention to Fi. "And how long will you be staying in Holtondome, miss?"

"Three weeks."

Seg's gasp joined everyone else's. City folk rarely visited rural domes, and never stayed more than a day or so, only long enough to conclude their business so they could return to the comforts they were used to—whatever those might be.

"Ah," Hap said. "And what…"

The question burned on his tongue. Seg could see it. He silently urged Hap to ask why she had come, but in the end, propriety won; her reasons for visiting were no one's business but her own.

Hap nodded with a sigh. "Will you be needing any special accommodations, miss?"

"A room with two beds should be all."

Everyone glanced at the driver, who emerged with a stretch.

Hap cleared his throat. "So… just one room, then."

"I don't have enough luggage to fill another, so yes, one will do. The driver will probably want his own room, though."

"The driver will be perfectly happy with a bar stool and a drink," the driver said. "The need for a room will depend on how comfortable the stool is and the strength of your drinks." He ambled to the rear of the vehicle and popped the trunk, where three bags sat. He hoisted two out with a groan. "Now, if you would, someone point me to Fi's room so I can get to business."

"Nonsense! You're our guest, too," Hap said. "Seg, Troy, take their bags and help them get settled. Whether the gentleman uses his room or not, he shall have one all the same."

Troy shot Seg a threatening glare, then retrieved the last bag from the trunk. He undoubtedly blamed Seg for reducing him to servant status, and would just as certainly exact punishment later.

"That's mine," the driver said to Troy. He handed the two bags he was holding to Seg. "These are Fi's—just like you are."

"Come on, Seg," his sister Jen said. "I have the perfect room for Miss Fi."

Jen bowed to Fi like a servant would, her brown eyes downcast. Seg could hardly believe his eye. Jen had just this morning chewed him raw for forgetting to charge the hauler, which had put him behind schedule by a good thirty minutes. Seeing her subservient to anyone felt sacrilegious.

"Miss Fi, if you would, please follow me," Jen said.

Without looking to see if she did, Jen turned with a flip of her black ponytail and walked toward the staircase leading up to the living quarters.

Fi followed closely, towering over Seg's older sister by a full head.

Fi's enchanting eyes roamed Holtondome without interest, and Seg couldn't blame her. The dome's first story had a higher ceiling than the rest, almost six meters tall, and was primarily used for agricultural processing and storage. The floor was more dirt than metal from constant vehicle and foot traffic from the outside, plus the occasional dust storm. Wooden crates filled with apples stacked the far eastern edge of the dome. Next to them was the large refrigerated storage where packs of cured pork waited inside for shipment. Walls of wheat sacks stood nearest to them, filling his nose with the familiar scent of sweet decay.

Seg shook his head. Why Fi would want to spend one day—let alone three entire weeks—in a dirt-crusted Provider dome in the middle of Wyoming was beyond him. Cities had to be a better choice by far. They *had* to be.

So why is she here?

They paused for a forklift to pass, then ascended the wide metal stairway curving up along the inside of the dome wall.

The room Jen had chosen was on the fourth floor, which was low enough to grant easy access to the second-floor common areas, but one level removed to reduce the noise from lively nightly gatherings. She opened the door and, still not meeting Fi's eyes, gestured her inside, where the two promised beds awaited.

"You can put my bags anywhere," Fi said to Seg. Then to Jen, "Would you help me unpack while your brother fetches clean clothes?"

Seg and Jen shared a confused look.

"Miss?" Jen said.

"He's had a rough day, and I imagine he'd like to freshen up. The shower in this room should work as well as his own."

"It does, Miss Fi," Seg said. "But it will only take me a minute to go use mine."

"Why? If you're going to be living here, you may as well use this shower."

"I... W-what?"

Jen snapped her mouth shut with a *click*. "Miss Fi... we will, of course, do everything within reason to make you feel comfortable during your stay in Holtondome. But holding my brother against his will as a... a *concubine* is, well..."

Fi laughed softly. "I haven't heard that word in a while. As for holding your brother hostage... I have no power over him, so he may do as he will. But I haven't heard him object."

"Because he hasn't had a chance to!"

Fi's heavenly blue eyes turned to Seg. "Do you object?"

Her tone was so bored—so certain he *wouldn't* object—that Seg had to laugh.

"I don't."

Jen's mouth worked soundlessly, then closed with another *click*. "I see. Miss Fi, Seg is my younger brother, and… forgive me for saying, but he doesn't always think things through. For instance, he may not have considered how sleeping in the same room with an honored guest—who he's known for all of ten minutes—might affect his marriage prospects."

Seg knew what Fi was going to ask him before she uttered a sound.

"Have you considered how staying with me will affect your marriage prospects?"

"I have." With only one working eye, his marriage prospects were already abysmal, which Jen well knew. A scandal like this could hardly make his prospects worse.

Oblivious to Jen's dagger-stare, Fi swung her large suitcase onto a bed and opened it, revealing an array of women's garments, then began arranging the piles into a dresser drawer with precision.

Jen's scowl lasted only until she realized she wasn't going to win the argument from either side. She sighed and walked stiffly to the bed.

"May I hang these dresses for you, Miss Fi?"

"In the right half of the closet, please, facing left. Your brother can have the other half." She looked at Seg. "I'd like it if yours faced right."

"Whatever you say," Seg said, not caring if they faced right, left, or were piled at the foot of his bed. "Back in a minute."

He closed the door behind him with a smile.

Life in Holtondome had just become much more interesting.

3

Pot Pie

THE SHOWER WAS RUNNING WHEN Seg returned to Fi's room—or to *their* room, rather—a few minutes later, carrying a small armful of clothes. Jen stood by the bed with her back to the bathroom door, hands clasped in a white-knuckled grip. Seg arched an eyebrow at her.

"Since you took your sweet time returning," Jen said, "Miss Fi decided to take her shower first."

"And you're still here because…?"

"She asked me to remain in the room until you returned. Now that you have…" Jen stormed past, nearly knocking him onto the bed, then spun at the door to face him. "Enjoy this little fling, Seg. When word gets around about your… *promiscuity*, no woman in Holtondome will come near you."

"Unless nothing actually happens between me and Miss Fi, of course."

Jen snorted. "Good luck convincing anyone of that."

"Including you?"

Her jaw firmed. Seg braced for one of her famous tongue lashings, but her eyes softened along with her voice.

"Be careful, little brother. Unlike Miss Fi, Holtondome is the only home you'll ever have. Don't let her ruin it for you."

With a last look, she left and closed the door.

Seg breathed a sigh of relief… followed by an unexpected silence.

The shower had stopped running.

He turned to see Fi emerge from the bathroom. A towel wrapped her hair, but nothing else. Thick black markings, similar to those around her eyes, circled her breasts, swirled down around her womb like flowing scrollwork, and disappeared into the fuzzy patch between her legs, which was the same blonde-green color as her hair up top.

17

Seg tore his eyes from her beautiful, athletic body and made a hasty about-face. "Sorry, Miss Fi. I'll leave you to dress."

"Or you can remove your clothes and take a shower."

Drawers opened and closed behind him.

"Am I in that much need?"

"I've smelled worse."

Seg grinned. "Do you always do that, Miss Fi?"

"Mm?"

"Give orders that aren't orders?"

"If I don't voice my wants, they won't be fulfilled. You should try it."

"How do you know I haven't? You barely know me."

"Feel free to correct me if I'm wrong."

The closet slid open behind him, followed by *clinks* of hangers rattling together, and the rustling of fabric.

"Speaking of wants," Seg said, instead of admitting she was right, "why do you want me to stay with you?"

"I hate being alone."

"Then why not choose Jen?"

"Because I like sex, occasionally, and for that I prefer men." Cloth rustled again. "So, would you like us to stay here all day, or shower so you can show me around?"

Seg risked a glance over his shoulder and was relieved to find her fully dressed, though part of him wished she wasn't.

"I'm surprised," he said. "You don't seem the type to ask rhetorical questions."

"It wasn't rhetorical. You can shower first so we can leave, or we can take our clothes off right now and get into bed."

Seg gulped, feeling his face flush. "That seems... promiscuous, like Jen said."

"'Promiscuous' implies 'indiscriminate,' which I'm not. You and I are compatible."

"But... we've only just met. How can you possibly know that?"

"I'm a pretty good judge of character. Like I said, though, I have no power over you, so do whatever makes you feel comfortable." Fi laid on the bed nearest the bathroom, smoothed her leaf-green dress over her legs, and busied herself with her short fingernails.

Seg sighed. "Comfortable" would be moving his stuff out of her room right now.

But Seg didn't want "comfortable." He never had.

After filing his clothes neatly away in the dresser and closet, he stood at the foot of her bed, where she was still playing with her nails, and stripped his shirt.

Fi never looked up.

As a test, he focused a hungry stare on her, as if his will alone could make her feast him with her eyes—make her crawl across the bed and run her hands over his flat stomach.

She flicked a nail as if he weren't there.

So that's how it's going to be...

Seg tossed his shirt on the empty bed and headed for the bathroom to remove the rest of his clothes. From the corner of his good eye, he caught Fi stealing a glance at his bare chest before he went inside.

He closed the bathroom door with a chuckle.

The game was on.

Seg felt much better after showering. Dressing in front of Fi had set his pulse racing—not from excitement, but from the same anxiety contestants in the Mr. and Ms. Holtondome pageant must feel on stage, silently awaiting judgment on their strengths and flaws.

He'd chosen his fanciest outfit: a fine-weave green shirt with a loose collar, close in hue to Fi's dress, and leather pants dyed dark brown. A few scratches marred the left thigh, but they were still the least-worn-looking garments in his wardrobe. He ran his fingers through his bowl-cut black hair, giving it just enough fluff to not look a complete mess, and nodded.

Fi never spoke a word, nor looked at him again until he was fully dressed. Neither did she seem disappointed that he hadn't accepted her casual offer for sex. She simply went to the door and waited.

"The... the dress suits you," Seg said, desperate to break the awkwardness that, apparently, only he felt. It wasn't a lie; her dress' rich green tone complemented the green tinge of her blonde hair perfectly, as did her gold-laced bodice. Her simple outfit reminded him more of hand-knitted textiles found in Holtondome than the fine fabrics of the City.

"Thanks, it's one of my favorites," Fi said. "Where are we going first?"

"Tad's Tavern, in the Commons, two floors down. I don't know about you, but I could use a bite to eat."

"Mm."

Taking her less-than-enthusiastic response for assent, Seg led her down the wide staircase. Fi walked beside him, closer than he would have expected of a stranger, but not lovers-close, solidifying his suspicion that her earlier come-on had been purely casual.

And why wouldn't it be? Seg thought.

What did he have to offer a City girl?

Not an Odin-blessed thing.

On the other hand, Fi could have chosen anyone in Holtondome when she'd stepped out of that car—but she'd chosen *him*. Fleeting or not, their relationship would stir a veritable shitstorm, which, as far as Seg was concerned, made Fi worth her weight in medicine.

Seg was smiling like a dog with two ham bones by the time he entered the tavern, where it seemed half of Holtondome had gathered. Conversation dipped when Fi followed him in. Knowing stares chased him all the way to the bar: many surprised, some disgusted, and more than a few were plain jealous.

The only person not staring was Fi's driver. The graying man occupied a spot on the far end of the bar, nursing a glass of dark liquid. He swayed gently on his stool. Evidently, it wasn't his first drink.

"Afternoon, Miss Fi," Tad said from behind the bar. He shot Seg a congratulatory wink, then returned his attention to Fi. "We don't have the sort of fine food you're used to, I'm sure, but if you make a request, Nin will do her best."

"Thank you, but I didn't come all the way out here to eat City food. I'll have whatever you recommend."

"Well, now, that's right sporting of you." Tad set the mug he'd been cleaning under the counter and smoothed his bristly mustache. "As you may know, our main exports are apples, wheat, and swine, though we do grow other crops just for the locals. Nin's pork pot pie recipe has been perfected over six generations. I know for a fact she'd be tickled up the... That is, she'd be humbled to have an upstanding lady like yourself nibble her prize."

"Why, bartender, it sounds like she's peddling more than just her cuisine."

Tad looked distant, then chuckled. "So it did. Apologies, miss, it's a hazard of the trade. Around here, boys and girls alike appreciate a raunchy poke. I hope you took no offense."

"Only if the offer to nibble her prize wasn't real," Fi said without a hint of amusement. "I'd like to meet her."

Tad's jaw almost hit the bar. "W... ah... w-well, I could certainly ask, Miss Fi. Nin's an adventurous soul, b-but I..." His eyes narrowed on her, then his robust gut shook with a hearty laugh. "By Odin's beard! You had me. No easy feat, that."

Seg watched her closely. Fi betrayed nothing, just as she hadn't when she'd offered herself to him in their room, making it impossible to tell if either had been genuine, or merely a tease.

"Glad I could help," Fi said with a nod. "Even bartenders need to be kept on their toes. I'll have her famous pork pie, please, but I can't promise I won't be thinking of her while I eat it."

"I'll tell her you said so, Miss Fi. She'll be tickled up the... well, you know." He poured two waters for them and retreated to the kitchen.

Seg looked at her. "Are you this merciless with everyone, or just us rural folk?"

"That was nowhere near merciless."

"Oh?"

"He wasn't crying, was he?"

Seg blinked. "You wouldn't..."

Fi sipped her water, then turned to the kitchen. "Bartender!"

"That wasn't a dare," Seg said under his breath. "Miss Fi, please don't —"

Tad poked his head between the swinging doors. "Miss Fi?"

"Bring the cook out with the pot pie."

"Oh, o-of course. It'll be a few minutes yet."

"I hope so, otherwise I might think you're serving me someone's canceled order."

Tad's laugh was less hearty this time. He slipped quietly back into the kitchen.

Seg gulped.

What have I done?

"Look... Miss Fi, I'm sorry, I didn't mean to insult you. Please don't take it out on Tad or his wife. Nin's as nice as they come."

"Mistakes are how we learn," Fi said, studying her water glass. "The most powerful lessons come from those with real, personal consequences."

"You're going to hurt them just to teach me a *lesson?*"

Fi sipped her water.

Seg clenched his jaw. He wanted to say more, like how Fi could take her lesson and shove it right up her pork pot pie, but he was pushing the boundaries of hospitality as it was. There were laws, after all.

Minutes later, Tad emerged from the kitchen, followed by his equally plump wife. Nin's smile faltered on seeing Fi, but eased into the welcoming show of teeth Seg was accustomed to seeing on her round face. She carried a plate with a steaming pie over as if it were a newborn and set it gently on the counter. One whiff of her masterpiece was enough to make Seg's stomach grumble with neglect.

"I hope you enjoy, Miss Fi," Nin said, wringing her hands. Beside her,

Tad nodded.

Fi didn't even give the courtesy of meeting her eyes. She looked at the pot pie with disinterest, as if Nin had set a slice of plain toast in front of her instead of a delicious meal inside a flaky pastry shell. She unfolded her cloth napkin, gave it a precise flick, and, to Seg's surprise, stuffed a corner down her gold-laced bodice, then meticulously arranged it to cover her dress.

"You like stories?" Fi said.

"Of course," Nin said. "Literacy laws forbid us from reading and writing, so telling stories is our only means of preserving our heritage."

"Then I'll tell you one."

Fi gathered a utensil in each hand. Curiously, she held the fork in her left hand, index finger pressed to the back with the tines facing down, and the knife in her right. Seg had never seen someone from the City eat, but he hadn't imagined it would be far different from how they ate in Holtondome. He'd been wrong.

Tad's smile faded. "Are you sure that's wise? We've no Feds among us now, but they'll be here tomorrow with the Traders, sure as acid rains in autumn. If they discover you've passed unsanctioned information—and they *will* question us—they'll make life difficult for everyone. Even you, Miss Fi."

"This story is of Holtondome's history, so it's safe. The Feds won't uncover anything you shouldn't already know."

Fi's timbre assumed a resonant quality, as the more skilled storytellers' did when telling a tale.

"One hundred years after The Fall, after humanity had scraped itself from the brink of self-extinction from the most devastating global war in history, after the scant survivors around the world united under the governance of the Federated Nations, Grand Chancellor Chang the First enacted a set of laws and programs designed to prevent humankind from destroying itself ever again. These programs called for smaller societies and isolated social structures that would, by their very nature and the laws enacted upon them, eliminate the harmful, global groupthink Chang believed responsible for The Fall.

"These programs, along with a decimated planet no longer capable of sustaining its inhabitants, led to the creation of the domes."

Seg nodded. Everything she'd said so far was part of the Federated Nations' yearly education program.

The tavern had gone quiet. Almost every eye was on the woman with the blonde-green hair—hundreds of souls as eager for new information as

Seg.

Fi continued as if the water glass were her only audience.

"Each dome had a Founder. The selection process was left to individual countries—or states, in your case—but qualifications for the position were universal and absolute; Founders would be role models for the domes they established. Their philosophies would set the tone for generations. It was critical, then, that each Founder not only be charismatic and true, but share Grand Chancellor Chang's vision of the new world.

"The Federated State of Wyoming, having democratic roots, let the domes' future inhabitants choose their own leaders from a pre-filtered list of candidates. The elections brought out the best and worst of each community, and this dome's was no exception."

The crowd edged closer. While the outcome was common knowledge, details of the election itself had been lost to the centuries.

"The strongest candidates were Revon Chase and Thorn Holton, rivals as different from each other as the desert and the sea. Thorn was a builder by trade whose reputation for treating his workers and customers with equal civility had won the people's hearts.

"Revon Chase was a successful businessman who'd acquired his wealth in the ways before The Fall, when trading with currency was legal. He bought all available goods of mid- to low-demand to create artificial scarcity, then sold them for ridiculous prices when demand increased. Many considered the practice shady, but more saw his wealth as a sign of superiority, as Revon himself did. And so these opposite men found themselves in a neck-and-neck race.

"Each candidate tried to tip the scales in their favor. Bribery was illegal, but lowering the price of their wares wasn't. Revon offered generous discounts throughout his campaign. Thorn did, too, but his business didn't have the day-to-day reach of Revon's, allowing Revon to quickly pulled ahead. Thorn needed a different edge.

"His solution came by accident during a campaign dinner. The chef was sick, leaving Thorn with a banquet hall full of hungry constituents who he might not be able to feed."

Fi stuck her fork in the pie, made a slow, precise cut, and put the perfect-sized bite into her mouth. Nin practically vibrated with anticipation, but Fi's exotic features betrayed nothing of what she thought of Nin's creation. She chewed slowly, thoroughly, as if the entire tavern wasn't waiting for her to continue. When she finally finished her first bite, Fi set her utensils down, wiped her mouth with her napkin, and resumed telling her story to her water glass.

"Thorn's sister, Holly, was a shy woman who supported her brother's bid for Founder. Afraid this social blunder may end his chances, she rallied the staff to see if any of them could use the ingredients on hand to produce a meal worthy of her brother's campaign.

"Holly's handmaiden, of all people, stepped forward with a recipe. It was a commoner's dish—a simple pork pot pie—that had been in her family for countless generations. Holly was doubtful, but the handmaiden swore with an age-old kiss to her knuckles that Thorn's constituents wouldn't be disappointed.

"And the handmaiden was right. Delicious smells from the kitchen stopped all conversation in the banquet hall. Holly herself delivered the first pie to Thorn's most influential guest. The older woman laughed, thinking the simple meal a joke, but her first mouthful led to another, then another, until nothing remained on her porcelain plate."

Fi took another languid bite. The entire tavern watched her meticulously chew, then wash it down with a sip of water. Nin remained tense, while Tad shuffled from foot to foot.

"'I must compliment you, my dear, on one of the finest dishes I've ever tasted,' the older woman said, backed by a chorus of agreement from the rest of the distinguished constituents, who had practically licked their plates clean.

"Shy by nature, Holly started to explain that the recipe wasn't hers, but the handmaiden subtly shook her head. Such high praise had more value to a Holton than a servant. So, with the handmaiden's silent blessing, Holly thanked the older woman, who showered her with praise and promised to bring a larger contingent of support if Holly would make her scrumptious pot pies again.

"The older woman made good on her promise. Not only did Holly and her amazing pot pies become the talk of the community, Thorn's popularity soared, leaving Revon a distant second in the polls."

Another deliberate mouthful. The tavern held its collective breath, but Fi's face may as well have been carved from marble, for it betrayed nothing. When she took a second bite, a murmur ran through the crowd. People began to disperse, probably assuming, as Seg had, that her story was done.

Is this the lesson Fi threatened to teach me? Could I be that lucky?

They hadn't made it far when Fi's voice rose over the growing din.

"Now, Revon Chase had built his fortune around a single idea: Never assume an offer is final. There was always one more lever to pull, one more arm to twist that could turn a good deal into a better one, or a hopeless venture profitable. The only question was how far one was willing to go.

"Founding a dome, which would secure his legacy for generations to come, was important enough for Revon to go all the way."

This time when Fi paused for a bite, no one moved, nor dared to whisper. Seg had never heard this story before, and he'd heard them all a dozen times over. Neither did any stories of Holtondome's beginnings—or of any time before The Fall—contain such detail. Most were either vague or conjurations of the teller's imagination, as they would readily admit, but Fi's ring of authenticity held him captivated.

"By this time, the election was just one day away," Fi said. "Revon didn't have enough time to counter with a smear campaign, nor did he have the political influence within the Federated Nations to have Thorn removed from the running. So, to solve his problem, Revon sought the third-oldest profession known to humankind: the assassin."

Gasps echoed through the room, including Seg's. That definitely wasn't in the stories.

"The night before the big election, Thorn and Holly held a last campaign dinner to secure him beyond a doubt as the dome's future Founder. Everyone who was anyone came, so many that Holly had to recruit outside help to prepare the meal.

"One of those helpers was Revon's hired assassin.

"The assassin waited and watched until, just before dinner was served, he identified the pot pie destined for Thorn Holton. A sprinkle of poison turned the delicious meal into a deadly trap, one that would swell his airway and suffocate him as if he'd simply choked. Thorn's death would be dismissed as unfortunate, but nothing more."

Eyes around the room glistened, including Nin and Tad's.

Fi's doing it, Seg thought with a touch of wonder. Holtondome itself was living proof that Thorn had not only survived but won the election. Still, Fi had managed to choke Seg and everyone else up at the thought of Revon winning in such an underhanded manner.

"Dinner was served as planned," Fi said. "On this special occasion, and to thank her, Thorn invited his sister to sit next to him. The pot pies were placed exactly where the assassin intended. Thorn cut a hunk from his poisoned pie..." Fi did likewise. "Raised his fork to his mouth..." She poised it just above her waiting tongue.

"...and was interrupted by Holly.

"'Brother,'" Fi said, her voice and accent assuming a lighter note, "'on this special night, let us all eat as newlyweds do.' Holly cut her own pie and held it out for Thorn. 'Let us feed each other in the age-old symbolism of trust and commitment, marking a new era of peace and cooperation for all who join our dome!'

"Thorn smiled, unaware of the death sentence his sister had unwittingly turned on herself, and they happily fed each other, dreaming of the wonderful future they would create together."

Fi turned and practically jammed the fork down Seg's throat. He gagged and coughed, so caught up in her tale that, for a moment, he thought he'd been poisoned. Several snickered at the show, which made Seg blush. He finished chewing and tentatively swallowed, not entirely convinced it wasn't.

"Thankfully, Holly's death was as swift and painless as suffocation can be. Thorn mourned her passing after the election, which he won by a landslide, and erected a statue in her memory, with a plaque attributing his position as Founder to her."

Statue?

Seg saw the same question reflected on every face. Nowhere in the stories was a statue mentioned, either.

If a statue of Holly existed in Holtondome, we'd all know about it.

"Begging your pardon, Miss Fi," Tad said, wringing his hands, "but what became of Revon Chase and the assassin?"

Troy scoffed. "They got away, obviously. Justice isn't always served, no matter what the fairytales say."

"Not always," Fi said. "But in this case, fate wanted revenge. The assassin was found two days later, dead in his home, having apparently choked on his steak dinner." Fi put another bite in her mouth and chewed slowly. "The following day, Revon Chase's wife found him swinging by his neck from the rafters with a note in his pocket, confessing his crime and naming the assassin."

"That's... convenient," Seg said.

"Mm. Many suspect a vigilante's involvement, but if so, they were never found. Nor were the authorities eager to find them."

Nin stared at her with wide eyes, tears running down her plump cheeks. "H-how do you know all this?"

The question was a dangerous one, which Nin should have known, but her haunted eyes told Seg she was beyond caring. Something had spooked her, and badly.

Fi kept her eyes on her plate. "The handmaiden stayed in Thorn's service long enough to settle him into his new position as Holtondome's Founder, where the residents' written materials were required by law to be surrendered to the Feds—including the handmaiden's diary, which documented the entire affair."

"You've… read her diary?"

"Mm."

Nin sagged against the counter. "Holly Holton was my great, great— well, many greats, to be sure—grandmother." She wiped her nose on her apron with a sniffle. "That pork pot pie recipe, it… it must be the same you're eating now."

Fi banged her utensils on the counter, making everyone jump, but her voice was soft when she spoke.

"*Not* the same. You've changed the recipe that put Thorn Holton himself in charge—the recipe that, without it, would have made Revon Chase Founder, and turned everyone's life in this dome into a living hell." Her black-ringed eyes finally met Nin's. "And how do I know that? Because the handmaiden's diary describes every intricate flavor of Holly's famous pot pies. Shall I recite them for you?"

Without waiting for a response, Fi assumed a different voice, lighter yet more confident than she'd used for Holly. "'Mrs. Holton did our family's recipe immense justice, though from this day forward, it belongs to her family in earnest, at least until Thorn is established enough that our little white lie will pass as acid runoff under the dome should it come to light.'"

Nin bit back a sob, and Seg could understand why. Fi's words were as close to the handmaiden's as anyone in Holtondome was likely to hear, the nearest to a living legend they would ever come. Others, too, sniffled at the power of the moment.

"'I haven't made these pork pot pies in years, but they taste just as I remember,'" Fi said in the handmaiden's voice. "'Notes of oregano and thyme were perfectly balanced, with a healthy amount of garlic and onion to liven up the carrots, celery, and peas. White wine was a heavenly addition to the sauce, especially from the fine stock Mr. Holton keeps in his cellar.

"'I hope the Holtons will hold this recipe as close to their hearts as I have. It was a difficult secret to surrender, even to someone as nice as Mrs. Holton, but the sacrifice was worth ensuring the new dome falls into the care of an upstanding person such as Mr. Holton.'"

Fi resumed her normal voice. "Thyme, oregano, and garlic. The handmaiden mentioned nothing about rosemary, basil, or curry powder. Not. One. Word."

"N-no, Miss Fi, she probably didn't. My family has made some adjustments over the centuries, to be—"

"Your *family?*"

Nin wilted. "Well… I may have made a few myself. But h-had I known —"

"Had you known, then you wouldn't have stomped all over your family's history. Is that what you were going to say?"

"In not so m-many words, M-M-Miss Fi." Tears flowed freely down Nin's reddened face. "I'm so sorry, I didn't know…"

"Yes, because if you had, you wouldn't have created this… this…" Fi closed her eyes and took a deep breath. "Masterpiece."

Nin's blubbering stuttered to a halt. "Miss?"

"I know the handmaiden's diary inside and out," Fi said. "Your creation blows the handmaiden's secret family recipe up to the high heavens. She'd be proud of Holly's many-great granddaughter's achievement."

Nin's waterworks resumed in earnest. She stammered a "thank you," then fled to the kitchen, followed by a beaming Tad, and a flood of pot pie orders from the rest of the tavern.

Fi sipped her water as if nothing had happened.

"You didn't have to do that," Seg said to her.

"Obviously."

"No, I mean… you didn't have to do it that way. You intentionally upset her."

"You get one more 'obviously' before I start ignoring you."

Seg bit back a terse reply. Fi was a guest, he the host, and the rules of hospitality were clear.

"Apologies, Miss Fi. If it's not too forward, I would appreciate if you'd help me understand the reasoning behind your approach with Nin."

"Ah. Finally, a real question." Fi slid her half-eaten pot pie to him. "Eat up."

"Thanks, but I'll order my own."

"I won't finish it, and I hate wasting food. Besides, we're sharing a room, so why not lunch?"

"And the utensils?"

Fi shrugged. She reached to take the plate back, but Seg pulled it in front of him and picked up the fork.

"I didn't mean I wouldn't, just that it's weird. Like we're married or something."

"Thirty minutes together and you're already proposing marriage. Fine, I accept."

"You… *What?* No! I-I didn't… I mean, that's not what I—"

Fi yanked the fork from his fingers and shoved another bite into his mouth.

"That was a joke," Fi said. "You're not ready for marriage, or even for sleeping in the same bed."

He opened his mouth to speak, but she immediately filled it with more pie.

"Before you make an ass of yourself, let me answer the first and only worthy question you've asked so far. The most obvious reason why I upset her would be to prove you wrong when you hadn't believed I'd actually make someone cry, right?"

Seg nodded.

"But that would be petty, and I'm not a petty person, so there must be a different reason."

"Leshun," Seg said around a mouthful.

"This is your third 'obviously,' but I'll pardon you if your explanation of what you took away from that lesson doesn't suck."

Seg considered that while he chewed. Several things from Fi's story jumped out at him: moral codes, bravery, sacrifice for the greater good, justice wins in the end... those were a few of the prominent themes— which meant they probably weren't what she was looking for, and would earn another "obviously" cane whip across his ego.

Or maybe the lesson doesn't lie in her story at all...

"Assumption without due consideration," Seg said.

Fi's fork stopped half-way to his mouth. "Keep going."

"When you mentioned crying, I immediately believed you meant to hurt Tad, which, by association, assumed you were a bad person. But that assumption didn't take into account all the evidence."

"Like?"

"Rescuing me from the storm, for one. Most City folk would have raced by without a second glance, but you risked yourself and the driver's ire to save a farmer, and have asked for nothing in return."

Fi arched an eyebrow. "Nothing?"

"No. You *invited* me to stay with you, but have made it clear that neither staying with you nor your, ahem... *other* offer were compulsory in any way."

Her lips twitched into a smile. "It isn't often someone surprises me. What's your name again?"

Seriously?

"Seg, Miss Fi."

"Is that a nickname?"

"No, my parents just liked the sound of it."

"It's rare, but I've known a few." Fi tapped his plate with a trimmed, unpainted fingernail. "When you're done, I'd like to visit an ag dome. One with trees."

"Sure, we have a whole dome with nothing but apple trees. I'll be just a minute."

Seg cut a large piece of pot pie with his fork, but Fi touched his arm, her enchanting eyes focused on a nearby table, where a couple sat with a pile of small rocks in front of each of them, and three small stone bowls in between.

"Don't rush," Fi said. "What are they playing?"

"Swaggle."

"Mm." She patted his arm, still watching the players. "Order another pot pie if you want. I'll be over there."

Without a backward glance, Fi walked over and knelt at the couple's table. They were understandably wary, but relaxed after a quick exchange with Fi, too quiet for Seg to hear over the tavern din.

Seg shrugged; another pot pie sounded good. Tad and Nin had yet to return from the kitchen, so he flagged Til on her way by, who was holding an armful of dirty dishes. Til's smile evaporated with a glance at his glassy white left eye, as it usually did. She acknowledged his order with a stiff nod and hurried away.

It wasn't until Seg's pot pie arrived that he realized Fi was perhaps the only person he'd ever met, including his family, who'd never flinched from his gaze.

Not even once.

Seg tucked into his pie with vigor. Fi wanted to see trees, and he intended to deliver.

4

Trees

ON THEIR WAY TO THE fancy car, Seg spied Troy dressed in his storm gear, carrying a box of tools. That he might be going outside during a lightning storm was cause for alarm.

"What gives?"

"Weather's let up some," Troy said. "The north water collector is jammed shut."

"It can wait. Fixing it isn't worth your life."

Troy scowled. "*Our* lives. Hap just discovered that the eastern reservoir is acid-tainted. The southern reservoir's still being cleaned from last month when it was acid tainted. That leaves the western reservoir, which is only a quarter full thanks to easterly winds."

"So?"

"So it isn't enough freshwater, Seg! Lightning storms often hit in twos. If this one does, we've got to have at least two collectors open or we might not make it to the next storm."

Fi listened with detached interest, as usual, her eyes roaming elsewhere. The driver, however, pulled a rectangular device with a glowing screen from his jacket, similar to those the Feds carried on their seasonal visits. He tapped it a few times with a drunken finger and nodded.

"Another storm's on its way. You've got about two hours."

Seg and Troy stared with envious eyes until the driver pocketed the device.

Troy shook himself. "That'll be cutting it close. I've got to get out there."

"After the lightning stops," Seg said.

"No sh..." Troy cleared his throat with a glance at Fi. "I'm not stupid, Seg, but I'm not going to let us die of thirst, either. You take care of your

31

business, and I'll take care of the rest of us."

Before Seg could say another word, Troy marched toward the north dome entrance, tools rattling in his large toolbox.

"Brave man," the driver said, then headed for the car. His drunken stagger was worrying.

"Are you sure you're okay to drive?"

"I'll be fine, kid," the driver said with a slur. "The car practically drives itself. But either way…" He took a case from his jacket and popped a small white pill into his mouth. "I'll be depressingly sober in a minute."

"There's a pill for that?"

The driver leveled him with a flat stare.

"Right, sorry I asked."

Seg started to open the front passenger door, but paused when Fi opened the rear driver-side door.

"Miss Fi, would you like me to sit in front or back?"

Fi shrugged and climbed into the rear.

Fine, if she wants to be that way…

Seg reached for the front door, but balled his fist just shy of the handle. This was another lesson.

No, it's a test to see if I learned anything from the last lesson.

Fi had shrugged as if she didn't care, but she'd also said in no uncertain terms that she hated being alone.

And she'd chosen Seg as her companion.

Seg shifted to the rear door and sat in the back seat. Beside him, Fi stared out the window as if she hadn't noticed, but a smile twitched the corner of her mouth.

The driver turned around. "Which way, kid?"

"North."

The driver consulted a glowing circle with strange markings beside the dashboard, then nodded.

Soon, the car was weaving around crates and pedestrians, drawing some looks of veiled admiration, and others of outright distaste for the technology it represented.

Seg didn't care. Right or wrong, riding in a car like this was something few in Holtondome would ever experience. This was Seg's *second* trip, and the way things were going, he suspected it wouldn't be his last. At least, he hoped not.

They passed Troy, who spared them not a glance, then drove out through the northern entrance. Rain and wind spattered the windshield, but with nowhere near the intensity of when they'd arrived. Ahead, the sky was a lighter gray, giving weight to the driver's claim of a break in the storm. A glance behind showed Troy and a few others making their way along the side of the dome to the stuck rain collector. Seg hoped for their sakes the driver's information device was right.

Seg leaned forward, resting his elbows on the seat in front of him. "Are you staying in Holtondome for the full three weeks Miss Fi is with us?"

"Hell no," the driver said. "My contract is through tomorrow morning, so I'm going to hit the road after lunch."

"Oh."

The driver grinned. "Don't worry, I'll be back a day in advance of Fi's pickup date, so you'll have plenty of time to ogle the car before we leave. Just don't drool on the leather."

"Thanks, mister...?"

"Cook. And you can nix the 'mister.' I feel old enough as it is."

"How old are you?" Seg clamped his mouth shut and silently swore. The manners required for playing host clearly weren't in his breeding.

Cook sighed. "Believe it or not, I'm not allowed to tell you. Let's just say I'm older than I look."

Seg whistled low. He looked ancient by Holtondome standards. Was he sixty? *Seventy?* The idea of living that long was hard to imagine.

And it made Seg burn with curiosity. If the advances of the City could afford a *driver* extended life, what other marvels did Cities hold?

He sat back with a resigned sigh.

There were three certainties in Holtondome. Number One: everyone died, be it by natural causes or the Feds. Number Two: everyone had to pull their weight, even if it was just serving at the tavern like Til.

And Number Three: the only way anyone left Holtondome was via Number One.

Five kilometers of flat, sharpgrass-covered terrain later, the sleek vehicle glided up to the southern edge of Appledome. Although not nearly as high or visible as Holtondome, Appledome's low, transparent roof spanned a full kilometer in diameter. Rows and rows of trees grew within the protective barrier, marred only by occasional lightning rods which, from a distance, looked like needles protruding from a giant pillow.

Appledome's southern doors were just sliding open when the car approached.

Val gawked like everyone else when Seg and Fi emerged from the vehicle, but she quickly pulled herself together.

"Afternoon," Val said. A twig stuck out of her red bun that surely didn't belong there. She removed her leather gloves, sticky with apple juice, and tossed them on a bench.

A glint of shiny gray metal between the cleft of her generous breasts made Seg's breath catch. The small, circular pendant's intricate red markings practically glowed against her flushed skin. He hadn't seen his old necklace in years, and he'd never again expected to see it around Val's neck.

Val seemed to notice his attention. She twitched a smile, but it disappeared with a glance at Fi. "What brings you here?"

I'm not sure myself, Seg thought, though he was suddenly glad he'd come. "Miss Fi is visiting Holtondome for a few weeks and wanted to see the trees."

"Ah." Val's frown made her confusion clear about why anyone would venture out on the tail-end of a storm just to see apple trees, but she smiled all the same. "Well, make yourself at home. You know your way around, Seg."

"Yep." He'd worked this dome for three years. Although he hadn't visited in a while, the smell of apples and fertilizer made him feel as if he'd never left. "This way, Miss Fi. There's a patch on the east side I think you'll enjoy." Seg poked his head inside the car. "Are you coming, Cook?"

Cook was staring intently at his rectangular device, completely absorbed. He started to shake his head, but a glance at the greenery brought him out of it. "I'll look around for a minute, sure."

Val met him on the other side of the car. "Right this way, Mr. Cook. I'll be happy to show you around." She flashed him a sultry smile.

Okay then…

Perhaps Val wearing Seg's pendant again after all these years meant less to her than he'd thought. Wishing Cook luck with Val, who evidently had other plans for the driver, Seg led Fi into the dome.

Familiar scents of apple blossoms and wildflowers washed over him. Seg breathed it in. He never tired of the wonderful smells, so full of life compared to the dusty and sometimes acrid odors outside.

"It's not far," he said.

Behind him, Fi ran a lazy finger across an apple tree's rough bark while she walked, then reached up to run her hands through its leaves. "Mm."

"The trees are pretty, I'll give them that. Even though my hands were perpetually sticky from apple juice, this was one of my favorite jobs."

"Mm."

On a whim, Seg snatched a shiny red apple from a low-hanging branch and bit deep. They always tasted better fresh from the tree. He plucked another and tossed it behind him.

Then he spun with a curse. Tossing an apple to Val would be one thing, but tossing one to a guest was out of the question. If he accidentally hit her...

Fi caught it with ease and bit down in one smooth motion, as if she'd expected him to throw it, then returned her attention to the trees.

"S-sorry," Seg said anyway.

She shrugged.

The next few minutes passed in silence. The apple trees became taller, fuller. Wild carnations, which had been sparse and small near the entrance, covered the ground like pink-and-purple carpet. Bees buzzed by with increasing regularity, meandering from flower to flower, and throughout the treetops.

"Here we are," Seg said. "Don't mind the bees. They'll leave you alone as long as you don't swat them."

"Mm."

Fi laid next to a tree, heedless of the weeds and dirt against her pristine leather jacket, folded her hands behind her head, and stared up into the branches.

Seg watched her for a few seconds. Fi didn't move.

He cleared his throat. "Is... is this what you wanted?"

"What I want doesn't exist, but it's better than I expected. Thank you."

Seg sat cross-legged beside her. "What do you want, then?"

"Another good question. You're on a roll."

"Don't sound so surprised."

"I'm not." Fi took a deep breath and exhaled slowly. "Do you know any stories of Earth before The Fall? Of how this planet looked eons before people destroyed their own home?"

"Of course."

"Tell me one." She patted the ground beside her. "Make yourself comfortable."

"Who says I'm not?"

Fi shrugged, but the hint of a smile said she knew the truth.

As always, it seems.

Seg arched his back, which had already begun to stiffen. Instead of laying alongside her, however, he laid in the opposite direction with his head next to hers. He was close enough to turn and kiss her, if he wished, but his goal wasn't romance. Fi had made a game of putting him on edge since she'd arrived. It was his turn.

If his close proximity bothered her, she gave no outward sign, and laid in patient silence. The sound of her breathing fell in perfect rhythm with his own, until Seg couldn't tell where his ended and hers began.

"Why do you do that?" Seg said softly.

"Mm?"

"Try to unsettle me. It's like you're doing it for sport."

"I don't know what you mean."

Seg explained about her breathing.

"I told you," Fi said. "We're compatible. Certain things just fall in step between us."

"You mean… you didn't do it on purpose?"

Fi shook her head.

"And I just made another assumption without due consideration, didn't I?"

She nodded.

"Sorry."

"Apology accepted. Can I have my story now?"

"Would a poem be okay instead?"

"Mm."

Seg nestled into the grass. He was close enough to feel her heat on his cheek, a distraction for which he had only himself to blame, but he eventually gathered his thoughts enough to begin.

"This poem is old, even by pre-Fall standards. Hap claims it's from the thirteenth century, but even he can't say for sure.

> *"O sinister twilight*
> *Where even' battles morn'*
> *I await the promised sun*
> *Brilliant orb of life*
> *Make crimson clouds*
> *Then rise, rise to the heavens*
> *That blanket of purest blue*
> *Your streaming light*
> *Golden fingers through aspen leaves*
> *To meadows of emerald, ruby, and amber*
> *Your warmth, your gift*
> *A kiss of welcome fire*
> *Until to dusk you fall*
> *Where the Valkyrie's aid you seek*

To fight for another morn'"

Seg lapsed into silence, trying as usual to imagine the vivid colors described in the poem. Crimson clouds, blanket of purest blue, entire meadows of colorful flowers, golden sunlight through the trees, and…

"A kiss of welcome fire," he said softly. "What must sunlight feel like?"

Fi stretched for the trees. Her long fingers fanned as if to touch the sun's fabled rays. "You asked what I want. I want what's in your poem." She wriggled her fingers, then dropped her hands to her chest. "I'd give everything to see the world as it was."

"That's a hefty price."

She turned until her nose gently brushed his forehead. "Wouldn't you?"

"I guess it depends on what 'everything' means."

This close, her eyes were beyond mesmerizing. Pools of perfect blue floating in a sea of white. Seg wasn't sure how long he'd gazed into their depths before remembering he was in the middle of an answer.

"If 'everything' means 'all my worldly possessions,' then sure, I'd have almost nothing to lose," Seg said. "But if you mean an arm or a leg or…"

"Or your good eye."

"Right."

What must my blind eye look like to her at this distance?

He'd only seen his white eye in the mirror, and had never felt the urge to examine the useless thing closely. Whatever the view, Fi seemed perfectly fine with it, so he swallowed his embarrassment and plowed on.

"If the laws ever changed, I'd…" Seg bit his lip.

"It's okay, I won't turn you in for speculating what you might do if and only if the world were different."

"Fine. I'd… I'd love to travel. Holtondome's great, but there must be something left out there of the Earth described in that poem. Not to mention the Cities."

"Cities aren't what you imagine."

"That's the problem. We have poems and stories of the world before The Fall, but nothing—nothing!—of the world around us *today*. I-I know it's for our own good that we stay isolated…" Seg gulped, fearing he'd gone too far with someone who could turn him in tomorrow, when the Feds arrived. "Anyway, how do you know what I imagine Cities are like?"

"A hunch," Fi said. "There used to be a saying, 'The grass is always greener on the other side,' which means our imaginations play up things that are beyond our reach as better than what we have."

"Do they have grass in Cities?"

"You know I can't answer that."

"My point exactly," Seg said. "The Feds tell us we've established a colony on Mars, but not how we got there, or even why. For all I know, Cities are spaceports with giant fleet ships, and aliens with three eyes walk the streets."

"Mm. Not knowing sucks."

Seg laughed. "You get one more 'obviously' before I start ignoring you."

"I wasn't mocking you. I was sympathizing."

"Oh. Sorry, Miss Fi."

"I won't accept your apology unless you tell me exactly why you apologized."

Why does everything with her have to be a lesson?

Seg swallowed a litany of sharp replies and considered. "I guess... the exact reason I apologized was out of fear that if I offended you, you wouldn't want me around anymore. What I *should* have apologized for, however, is yet again assuming you had malintent, when the evidence so far supports the opposite."

"And?"

"And what? That's the truth."

"On the surface."

Seg stared at her, clueless what she was digging for.

"This is the third time you've assumed I had malintent *and* apologized for it," Fi said. "That's a pattern, which means a deeper reason exists. Until you understand that reason, it'll just keep happening."

A deeper reason...

Was there?

As much as Seg wanted to deny it, Fi was right. She was quirky and detached, but neither of those explained the unease he felt around her. The deep sense of...

"Threat," Seg said. "I... I find you threatening."

Her enchanting eyes blinked, but she remained silent.

"In my defense, you *did* threaten me in the tavern, even if in the end it was simply a lesson, but that doesn't explain the deep... *fear* I feel around you, like I have to watch everything I do and say, or..."

"Go on."

Seg sighed. "Or you'll turn me into the Feds. Even if I was innocent, they'd never believe my word over yours."

Fi blinked again, the black rings around her eyes briefly forming perfect ovals. Apparently, she expected more.

"The Feds say their job is to protect us—to protect all of us—by ensuring we uphold the Pact to prevent us from straying down self-destructive paths," Seg said. "But if that's true, then why are we all so afraid of them? What makes them so different from us?

"We assume the same rules apply to everyone, but the rules themselves prevent us from knowing for sure. How do I know they enforce the same laws between Cities, or any other domes for that matter? Hel, how do I know there even *are* other domes? It's a complete imbalance of power and information."

Blink.

"All of that makes me... angry. And frustrated, because there isn't a damn thing I can do. I'm bound here by an oath my ancestors' ancestors made, like everyone else." Seg tried to keep the malice from his glare, and probably failed. "Everyone except you. You get to go where you please, when you please. You hold the secrets of the Cities *and* get to visit the domes, and probably a thousand other places I'll never know exist because I'm stuck *here* with no window to the outside world. I wouldn't be surprised if you've even been to Mars."

"I have. You aren't missing much."

"I'd like to believe you that I'm not," Seg said, clenching his teeth against a bitter well in his gut. "I should! But I can't because I'm... I'm..."

Fi's poker face betrayed nothing. She was going to make him say it.

"Because I'm jealous," Seg said. "Insanely, ridiculously, helplessly jealous."

"Too right."

"Pardon?" He'd expected a rebuke, or a lesson on why the Pact was necessary for the planet's survival, not vindication.

"Life isn't fair, or balanced," Fi said. "But that doesn't mean you should accept it. Change—real, meaningful change—never happens when people are content."

Seg opened his eyes wide. "Are... are you suggesting what I think you are?"

"Revolt? No. The Feds would put you down in days, if not hours. And with the communication ban, no other domes would even know you tried, so the effort would be wasted. My point is that you shouldn't be happy with your situation, because it *isn't* fair. Voicing that unfairness would be dangerous. But, if you're looking for a chance to make the world better, there's at least one unfairness you can correct right now."

"Not taking my anger out on you."

Fi nodded. "In a perfect world, I wouldn't have to say this, but I do: Unless I believe you're a danger to those around you—which I don't—I won't turn you or anyone else in Holtondome over to the Feds. I can't make you believe me, but I can say that our three weeks together in Holtondome will go much smoother if you do."

"Does the same go for Cook?"

"Who?"

Seg struggled to keep from rolling his eyes. "Your driver. Cook."

"How should I know? He's just my driver."

Seg frowned. "Why choose me as a companion when you could have chosen him? There would be no barriers between you."

"There are plenty. He and I aren't compatible."

"But you barely know him. How can you tell?"

"A hunch."

"You seem to get those a lot, Miss Fi."

"Mm."

The rest of their stay under the apple tree passed in silence. Seg worried he was being a poor host by not engaging her in conversation, but Fi seemed content both with the dialogue vacuum and his close proximity. Wary of the second storm predicted by Cook's pocket device, they returned to the vehicle just an hour after they'd arrived at Appledome.

Neither Cook nor Val were anywhere to be seen.

Seg was reticent to interrupt the driver—his guest—by actively searching for them, partly because he was afraid of what he'd find, and partly because he didn't want to incur Val's wrath if she'd succeeded in seducing her prey. He told Fi as much.

Fi shrugged, took out her own rectangular device, tapped the glowing screen a few times, then stuffed it back into her pocket.

Soon after, Cook emerged from a maze of stacked wooden ladders not fifty meters from the entrance. His normally clean-swept hair hung in less-orderly strands over his eyes. Val followed closely. A smile covered her flushed face.

It disappeared when she saw Seg.

Cook opened the rear driver-side door for Fi, who climbed in, then he looked at Val. "Will you be returning with us?"

Her smile flickered back into existence. "Is that an invitation, Mr. Cook?"

"Just Cook, please. And yes, if your work schedule permits, I'd enjoy your company for as long as you're comfortable indulging me."

"My work schedule doesn't permit, but neither does my sense of hospitality allow me to neglect my duties as host. As for indulgence…" Val curtsied, her smile spreading from ear to ear. "Consider me at your disposal for the duration of your stay, Mr.—er, Cook."

"Well, in that case, you can ride shotgun."

Val's blush deepened. "Ride your w-what?"

Cook chuckled. "It's an old expression. It means you can ride up front with me. Here…"

He rounded the car and opened the front passenger door. Val nodded in appreciation, though her wide eyes were on the plush interior. She shot Seg an excited grin, which he returned, then she scooped her skirt up and climbed inside. Seg scooted into the back seat behind her, and soon the car was away.

"Such a nice vehicle," Val said, lightly brushing a finger over the smooth leather dash. "Much nicer than anything in Holtondome. Is it yours?"

"Every inch," Cook said with a proud smile.

"You must be a very important person in the City."

Cook drew a breath, then closed his mouth and sighed. "I get by."

"And you, Miss Fi, to have someone like Cook to drive you around."

"Mm." Fi, as usual, was looking out the window without apparent interest in the conversation.

Val stayed silent, understandably hesitant to ask more for fear of breaking the law, but hoping as Seg did that they might let some small piece of information slip.

Neither did.

Nice try, Seg thought, touching her shoulder. Val patted his hand. They'd shared the same sense of adventure as children. Where adulthood had robbed most in their age group of their fearless curiosity, Seg's had stubbornly refused to leave—as, apparently, had Val's.

Their touch wasn't lost on Cook. "So, are you two, uh… siblings?"

"Third cousins." Val gave him a sly grin. "Why, are you jealous?"

"Depends on how close third cousins are allowed to be in Holtondome."

"The only forbidden relationships here are immediate family," Val said. "With only four thousand of us, we can't be too choosy. That said, Seg and I were just friends growing up. Right, Seg?"

"Right."

That had been their story since the one day as teenagers they had decidedly crossed the friendship line—a day they both remembered fondly, which was probably why Val gave his hand an affectionate squeeze —and Seg was sticking to it.

The mostly true declaration seemed to mollify Cook, who nodded. "I'm surprised you're not in a relationship, though, a pretty woman like you."

"My husband died of infection eight years ago. It started as a scrape on his arm, but spread to his blood."

"Very sorry to hear that." Cook frowned. "A course of antibiotics should have cleared that up, shouldn't it?"

"It was a drought year," Val said lightly, although her voice caught. "We had barely enough water for ourselves, let alone our crops. But the Traders didn't want to hear our sob story, so we ended up short on medicine. Just bad timing, really. It was the first infection he'd ever had." She fell silent for a minute, then shook herself. "But that's how it goes. People die all the time, be it from weather, disease, cancer, or old age. No one lives forever, right?"

Curiously, Cook and Fi remained silent.

Val's smile faded. "Well, not out here, anyway. Maybe you City folk have ways of keeping the Grim Reaper at bay, but in Holtondome, she plays Swaggle with us during mealtime, and tucks us in at night. Everyone knows her, and no one's afraid."

Fi pried her eyes from the window. "'She'?"

"That's right. Death is usually represented by a man, just like birth and life are represented by women, but that doesn't account for legends of Valkyries."

Cook frowned. "What's a Valkyrie?"

Seg and Val stared in shock. City folk knew everything. How could Cook be ignorant of something every Holtondome child knew?

"Valkyries are fabled women from Norse mythology," Seg said. "'Choosers of the slain,' they're called. Valkyries decide who live or die during battle, then choose which of the dead go to Freyja, and which go to dine with Odin in Valhalla, the hall of heroes."

"That's right," Val said. "Death is fabled to wear great black robes and ride a pale horse. Valkyries were also seen on great horses. When my husband died, I like to think the person under those robes who guided him to his ancestors was a kind Valkyrie. And when it's my time, if I'm lucky, that the same Valkyrie will come for me." She shook herself. "It's just fancy, of course. Religion is illegal, and we abide by the laws. For some reason, though, our ancestors took an interest in Norse mythology, and it's just become part of our stories and language."

"Northern states have strong Scandinavian roots," Fi said, "so it isn't surprising. Christianity was firmly expunged soon after the Federated Nations were established, along with other religions, but mythological references are tolerated as long as they don't lead to idolic worship."

"As you say, Miss Fi." Val sighed. "I would so love to see a horse, though. They sound like such majestic creatures."

"They are. Powerful, sleek, and beautiful. Children of the wilderness who run with the wind."

"You've seen one?" To Seg's surprise, it was Cook who asked.

"Mm."

Val's eyes widened. "Have you ridden one, too?"

"Mm."

"What was it like? Oh, please, if it isn't against the law, I'd love to know!"

Fi's stare unfocused, as if she were gazing into a different time. "Dangerous. Exhilarating. A wordless partnership of trust. Musk and sweat. Warm thunder between your thighs. Every hoofbeat makes the world dance." She shook herself. "What the stories don't say is how sore they make your butt when you aren't accustomed to riding."

Val giggled, a delightful sound Seg hadn't heard from her in a very long time.

"Thank you, Miss Fi! Perhaps one day the Traders will offer one. I can't imagine how many swine it would cost us, but in my opinion, it would be worth it."

"Which is probably why you aren't in charge of negotiations," Seg said with a grin.

"Hush, you!" She swatted his hand on her shoulder, then resumed her gentle grip. "Oh, it seems the second storm Cook warned of isn't far off."

Seg followed her gaze west. Dark clouds lined the horizon, growing bigger with each passing second. It would arrive in about thirty minutes, if he had to guess, which was more than enough time to return to Holtondome.

Not that it matters.

He'd seen this vehicle plow unscathed through the middle of a full lightning storm. They were as safe in here as any dome.

Seg held onto that thought until Holtondome's north entrance came into view, where he and Val breathed sighs of relief.

5

Sight

THE WESTERN SKY HAD DARKENED considerably in the short time it took them to near the northern entrance. To the west, Troy and several others were still working outside on the rain collector. Troy had wedged a crowbar in the top of the enormous, retracted drawer-like duct, and was trying without success to pry it open.

Fi gasped. Seg turned in time to see her look away from the work crew.

"Are you okay, Miss Fi?"

"Mm."

He waited for her to say more, but whatever had disturbed her, she kept to herself, and stared fixedly out the passenger window until the car pulled into its parking space.

Cook stepped out of the vehicle with a long stretch. "Well, that was interesting, but I'm ready for another drink. If you need me, you know where to find me."

Val politely cleared her throat and looked at him expectedly over the car. When Cook turned to face her, she simply smiled.

"Oh, right," Cook said. "If you'd care to join me, Val, I'd appreciate your company."

"It would be my pleasure, esteemed guest." Val hustled around the car, just short of skipping with girlish delight, and fell in step beside him.

"And you, Miss Fi?" Seg said. "Is there anything else you'd like to see this afternoon?"

Fi cast a furtive glance at the inside dome wall, where Troy and crew were on the other side working on the rain collector. "Drinks sound like a good idea."

"Um, it's a little early for me, frankly."

45

"I won't force you, of course, but I don't like drinking alone. If you feel you could make an exception this once, I'd like the company." Without waiting for an answer, Fi headed for the stairs.

Well okay, then.

Cities apparently had different drinking etiquette than Provider domes —or Holtondome, at least. Tad wouldn't serve alcohol to anyone at this hour, under normal circumstances, but for guests, he might make an exception. He already had for Cook.

And for Fi, he most certainly would.

The woman had a way of bending people to her will. Seg had a mind to refuse her invitation just to prove she couldn't always get her way.

The problem was, she would. If Seg didn't attend their guest, Hap would have his hide, and he'd get as much again from his mother.

Worst of all, however, although his conscious mind objected, Seg wanted to please her.

And, for the life of him, he couldn't figure out why.

With a sigh, he hurried to catch up.

It was smack in the middle of the workday, which left the tavern practically empty. In a few hours, people would return from the outlying agricultural domes, change into their evening attire, then Tad's and the other six taverns on this floor would fill to bursting. Seg could already smell the beginnings of dinner wafting from the kitchen.

Tad quickly masked his surprise with a warm smile on seeing them. "Miss Fi, Mr. Cook, welcome back. You're a touch early for evening meal, but I can wrestle up some snacks if you're peckish."

"No need," Cook said. "I'll have more of that wonderful gin, if you please, and some for the lady here."

Tad cocked an eyebrow at Val. "The lady's drinking this early now, is she?"

Val heaved a mock sigh. "I'm afraid our guest insists. Make mine a double, please."

"And mine," Cook said.

"Mine, too." Fi tapped the polished applewood bar where Seg sat. "And his."

"Master Seg, I daresay Val doesn't surprise me half as much as you," Tad said earnestly.

"This is the day for surprises, it seems." An idea came to him. "Change mine to a Sinkhole Twister."

Tad's eyebrows just about rose off his head.

"I'll have one, too," Fi said without missing a beat.

Tad laughed. "I'll serve it to you, Miss Fi, but you won't finish it, I promise."

"Care to bet on that, barkeep?"

"No, because I won't steal from an honored guest. Most are carried to their quarters after half a glass—people with greater mass than yourself, I'm afraid."

"What I lack in weight, I make up for with practice," Fi said.

"As you wish, Miss Fi. You're the guest." Tad shook his head with a chuckle and began pulling bottles from the shelves.

Fi glanced at the wall, although what she saw beyond shelves of tableware was anyone's guess. She tapped the bar with her fingernail. "I'll tell another story tonight if you have both drinks ready in the next thirty seconds."

"In a hurry to fall off your stool? No matter, I accept. After your last story, Nin would kill me for passing on such an offer."

With an alacrity Seg had never seen from the big man, Tad quickly filled four tankards and eight shot glasses in two equal sets with a variety of alcohols. He placed two tankards in front of Fi, lined two shot glasses to either side, then did the same for Seg.

Tad settled on his elbows in front of her. "We've no clocks to measure by, Miss Fi, but I'd say I beat thirty seconds by a fair margin."

"You certainly did. You've earned your story, and I'll throw in a song if I like your concoction."

"A song! By goodness, Nin will think Freyja herself has descended to grace our fine tavern." He tapped the side of one of her tankards. "Now, the Sinkhole Twister is a Holton favorite that old Thorn himself used to enjoy. There's a precise order to drinking it, which Seg can..."

Tad lapsed into silence when Fi appeared to not be listening. She instead gave each vessel a quick sniff, then grabbed the rightmost shot glass and downed it in a single gulp. Fi dropped the next shot glass straight into the adjacent tankard, then chug-chug-chugged it down until the shot glass rattled in its hollow interior. She set the tankard on the bar with a *clunk*. Her enchanting eyes honed on Seg, swaying unsteadily in her seat.

"Your turn."

"Well, that was, um... impressive, Miss Fi. How did you know what to do?"

"Flavors have natural complements. If you know what those are, then figuring out the correct order isn't hard." She cast a furtive glance at the stairway, then tipped her head toward his drinks. "Come on, bottoms up."

Seg looked at his own array of alcohol. Only once before had he dared a Sinkhole Twister. The only thing he remembered from that night was how much his head hurt the next morning, and that he'd vowed he would never order one again.

He grabbed the first shot glass. Strong notes of malt filled his nose. His stomach churned at the memory, but it didn't matter. Fi had conquered his challenge with aplomb. Although surprising, it didn't excuse him from finishing what he'd started.

Seg tossed it back.

Fire scorched his throat, stung his nostrils, and made his eyes water. Heat spread across his chest and into his cheeks.

Determined to see it through, Seg picked up the next shot glass with tingling fingers and dropped it into the tankard, splashing sweet frothy liquid onto the counter.

"Go on," Fi said, glancing again at the stairway.

Seg paused the tankard at his lips and turned to see what had captured her attention. The collector repair crew were just ascending the stairs. Three men and two women hung their rain-soaked storm gear on hooks and gathered around a table. One woman looked at their bar gathering with interest. She winced when she met Seg's glassy white eye and turned away.

"Told you," Cook said. "An eyepatch is the way to go, kid. She'd be over here right now, nursing you that tankard from your lap."

"Right."

"I mean it. Give me an hour and I'll make you a nice one."

Seg shook his head. "First, a Holtondome girl wouldn't degrade herself like that in public, even with her husband, because she'd never live it down. Second, I've tried a patch before. It didn't feel right."

"Probably because you used the wrong material. With a little padding —"

"No, I mean..." Seg sighed. "This may sound crazy, but when I put it on, I felt... blind."

"I've always had two eyes, so I can't say if it's crazy or not, but I'd happily accept a feeling of blindness if it lined up the girls."

"His blind eye isn't what puts Holtondome women off," Val said, giving Seg a sympathetic look. "It's that he's had it since birth. Holtondome can only support so many people. Each couple is restricted to two children, three if there are many deaths that year, which makes every child precious. Because of our small population and the high workload required to keep ourselves alive, it's important that those children be healthy and capable of producing more healthy children. Those with birth defects, like Seg, are considered poor breeding stock."

Cook winced. His eyes fell to his gin. "Sorry, kid. I wasn't trying to tease you."

"No apologies necessary," Seg said, although Val's speech knotted his gut like rotten fruit. "City folk probably don't need to worry about such things, and I gather you haven't spent much time in Provider domes, so how would you know?"

"Someone my age is supposed to be wiser than that. Guess I suck at being old." Cook clinked his shot glass against Val's, then raised it to Seg. "Cheers."

"Good health," Val said, correcting him with the traditional Holtondome toast.

Fi caught Seg's eyes, lifted her shot glass, and gave a slight nod. "*Skål.*"

"Skull," Seg said, mimicking the strange word as best he could.

Fi raised her shot to her lips and watched him closely, as if waiting for him to do the same.

The woman likes her alcohol.

Seg did likewise with his tankard. His sip turned into a larger gulp, spurred on when Fi tipped her shot back, dunked the next into her second tankard, and began chugging that one down as well with an encouraging stare.

All right, here goes…

He was four swallows in when his throat closed in protest. Seg spewed the remainder on the counter with a loud cough.

Tad was there in a heartbeat. He swiped a rag across the bar and handed another to Seg, who accepted it with a grateful nod and wiped the sticky sweet liquid from his chin.

"You win," Seg said to Fi.

"Hardly. I still have half a tankard left. Back on that horse, young man."

Seg barked a laugh, made freer by the warmth spreading through his body. If anything, he was older than Fi by two years at least. Cook had warned he was older than he looked, however. Was the same true of Fi? Seg burned to ask, but even the alcohol couldn't bring him to breach protocol like that again, especially not with her. Women seemed more sensitive to the subject, for some reason.

"Why are you so intent on getting me drunk?" His tongue felt thick.

"I told you, I don't like being alone. That includes while drinking." Fi glanced again at the stairway. "Finish up. There's time for us to go upstairs before dinner, even if we take our sweet time."

"Up… upstairs?"

"Mm. Sitting in laps is a no-no in public, from what you said, so I thought you'd be more comfortable if I did it in our room."

Seg took a swig to hide his embarrassment. It stayed down, but barely.

Tad openly gawked, while Cook just raised his eyebrows. Val, curiously, turned three shades of crimson, then stared at her shot glass as if she could break it with sheer will. The metallic pendant necklace he'd given her swung over her drink like a pendulum.

"Do I have to finish the whole thing?" Seg said.

"Depends. It won't be much fun if you make yourself sick. As for me…" Fi took two long gulps from her tankard. She swayed precariously for a moment but, to her credit, didn't fall off her stool, and managed to set her tankard down without spilling it. "Your turn, if you can."

Seg's throat constricted just looking at it. Fi surely had a lesson buried in there somewhere, but he couldn't for the life of him fathom what it was.

Unless she's just lonely, and needs a little liquid courage to get her through.

The thought gave him pause. Everything Fi said seemed to have layers of deeper meaning, so he'd become accustomed to taking nothing at face value. Was this another test? Or were her motivations this time really as simple as she claimed?

Another test…

Seg looked at the stairway leading down, where Fi kept glancing. What had he missed?

Gentle fingers drew his face back to hers until their lips were centimeters apart.

"Forget the drinks," Fi said breathily. "Come upstairs with me. Now."

Seg frowned. "Say my name."

"What?"

"My name, Miss Fi. What is it?"

"What does it matter? We're—"

"Compatible. Yes, you've mentioned that, without giving any details *why* beyond the vague assurance I'll eventually discover you're right, just like I do with everything else you've claimed."

Tad leaned on the bar. "Seg, my boy, I think that Sinkhole Twister has you sunk, else I wouldn't have to remind you that's no way to talk to a guest."

He was right, so Seg washed his next inappropriate reply down with another sip. The tavern was already spinning. Any more alcohol and Fi would be able to do whatever she wanted with him.

He shook his head. The tavern rocked and swayed, but he grabbed the bar to steady him.

This had to be a test. Seg had passed them all so far, to his knowledge. He refused to give up now.

Fi's breath was warm and sweet on his lips. A simple "yes" was all he needed to give, then they would go upstairs, and he could lose himself in those enchanting eyes over hours of uninterrupted intimacy.

Intimacy with someone who can't be bothered to remember my name.

No, this was definitely a test.

Seg stayed facing her, like she obviously wanted, but his mind strayed back to the stairway. What had she seen? The only thing of note was the rain collector repair crew. He glanced to the northwest side of the dome where the repair crew had—

A lightning flash blinded him. Seg was so startled that he nearly fell from his stool. Where the flash had come from was a mystery; there were no outside windows or doors in the tavern.

A glance around revealed two other disturbing facts. First, judging by the lack of reaction by the other patrons, no one else had seen the lightning flash. Second, unlike most afterimages, this one faded in and out, coloring his vision one instant and gone the next—like it was there, and yet it wasn't. Almost as if…

Seg shook his head.

No, it can't be…

But the experience was too close to how Val had described the sensation of covering one eye—of that sense of dual realities, where one image imposes upon the other for dominance.

The lightning flash, it seemed, had come from his blind left eye.

Fi looked puzzled for the first time he could recall. "Are you all right?"

"I… yeah, sorry. I-I'm fine."

The intense afterimage gradually faded, revealing a lone figure at the base of the lightning strike.

Seg rubbed his eyes. The afterimage was incredibly detailed. He could make out the hair, the storm gear, the masculine build…

Seg gasped.

He knew that figure. He'd seen it on the way back from Appledome.

It was his brother, Troy.

Seg looked at the returned collector repair crew.

Troy wasn't among them.

"E-excuse me, Miss Fi." Seg slid off the stool. The world lurched, but a nearby chair saved him the embarrassment of falling flat on his face. "I'll be right back."

Fi didn't try to stop him this time. She instead stared at her drink with an air of sad resignation.

If she's upset, I'll apologize later.

"Pardon the interruption," Seg said when he reached the repair crew's table.

Ten eyes met his one. All but a single pair looked away.

"What is it?" Len said, relaxing against his chair with a haughty smile. "*Looking* for something?"

The others sniggered.

"Just counting myself lucky I have half my sight instead of half a brain."

Len stood with a scowl.

Yep, the alcohol isn't helping.

Seg waved him down with an apologetic shake of his head. "Where's Troy?"

"He followed us in," one of the girls said, reluctantly meeting his good eye. "Why?"

"Are you sure?"

"Sure as his word. I didn't see him walk in myself, but he said he'd be right behind us."

"Troy isn't you, one-eye," Len said. "He's got sense enough to come in out of a storm."

Then you don't know him like I do, Seg thought.

Troy was inflexible at best, pig-headed at worst, and a martyr for whatever passing cause happened to raise his dander.

"Thanks," Seg said absently. Len tossed another barbed remark at his retreating back, but Seg had already tuned him out. He hurried down the stairs.

When Seg emerged onto the first level, his sister Jen and several others were just unhitching a charred wreck of a vehicle from the back of a truck. With a start, he recognized it as the hauler he'd been driving earlier.

Jen grinned at him. "You have Hel's own luck, little brother. If Miss Fi hadn't rescued you before the first storm hit, we'd be scraping your ashes out with a shovel."

Seg inspected the damage in a daze. A charred hole in the hood as big around as his chest exposed a mess of molten components underneath. Another hole in the roof explained why only half the driver's seat remained.

That could have been me...

"W-what about the harvest?" Seg said, although in truth he was too stunned to care.

"The lightning only hit the cab, it seems, so our biggest problem will be drying the wheat out before the Traders come tomorrow, which is unlikely, since the second storm is going to make it humid for a while."

The second storm!

Seg grabbed her by the shoulders. "Jen! Have you seen Troy?"

Jen grimaced at his hands, but didn't shake him off. "Not yet. We only arrived a few minutes ago. Good thing, too, because the storm hit as soon as we pulled in. Why?"

Seg ignored her and looked at the others. "Anyone else seen Troy?"

They shook their heads.

Damnit.

He risked a glance at the northwest dome wall, where the collector repair crew had been working on the other side.

Another phantom lightning flash blinded him. Seg staggered back with a cry, covering his left eye.

Jen was at his side in an instant. "Seg! What is it?"

"Flashes, like lightning inside the dome, and..." He waited for the afterimage to clear, hoping against hope he wouldn't see it again.

Troy's outline gradually filled in, clearer and more detailed than last time, leaving no doubt that it was him. His arm was bent down at a right angle, as if reaching into a cookie jar.

Seg gripped her arm. "We have to find Troy!"

"Um... okay. We've just started unloading the hauler, but as soon as we're—"

"Now, Jen! The grain can wait."

"Why, because of some... *glitch* in that white eye of yours?"

Seg's hurt must have shown. Jen winced and patted his hand, her voice softer than before.

"I'm sorry, Seg, but the hauler... *breaking down* has put Holtondome in an even tighter spot than we were. If we don't tend the grain now, we've no chance at all of having it ready for the Traders tomorrow, and I don't need to tell you how much we need that medicine. Fen won't make it to the end of the week, at this rate. Now we also need parts to fix the hauler."

"I... I know."

Holtondome had been in a bind even before he'd broken the hauler. He should be on the back of the truck with the rest of them, unloading wheat, but his visions had shaken him to the core. Jen might be absolutely right; his defective eye may just be glitching, and his subconscious filling in the details.

But if it isn't...

"Sorry to have disturbed you," Seg said. "Miss Fi's all right without me for a while, so as soon as I find Troy, I'll be back to help unload."

Jen opened her mouth to say something, then seemed to think better of it and nodded.

The northern entrance was closed tight when Seg arrived, as expected. The gatekeepers were just shedding their storm gear.

"Either of you see Troy come in?"

"Well hello to you, too, Seg." The woman to the right of the entrance, whose name Seg embarrassingly couldn't remember, shook her mane of light brown hair out to its full, impressive body.

A man to the left of the entrance, who must have been her brother, hung his soaked storm jacket on a hook, then shook out an identical mane of hair. Both of them met Seg's eyes only briefly before looking away.

"Didn't see him," the man said. "But can't say I was looking for him, either. Lots of people came in just before the storm. It's a rager."

Thunder from beyond the closed dome door punctuated his words, followed by another, then another, each louder than the last.

Seg grabbed the still-dripping storm gear from its hook.

The man laughed. "And where do you think you're going?"

"Outside. Troy was working on the north rain collector, and he may still be out there."

Both of them winced.

"Don't know why he would be," the woman said. "But if he is, he won't last long."

"Exactly." Seg went to the winch and began cranking the handle. The large entrance door slowly rolled upward.

"Whoa! I can't let you do that," the man said. "Opening the door during a storm is against the rules. And going outside in one is just plain stupid."

Seg continued to crank. "That rule exists to protect us from acid storms, which this isn't. A little wind and water inside the dome won't hurt anyone. And 'stupid' is my choice. I'm not asking either of you to join me."

The siblings looked at each other. The woman started to speak, but ended with a sigh. Neither of them, Seg noted with a despondent pang, dashed off for help, or tried to talk further sense into him.

Nor did they need to. The garage door had barely risen to his waist and already the wind and rain tore at his pantlegs like a feral dog. Lightning flashed faster than his pounding heart. Thunder and gale snarled incessant fury, threatening to devour any who dared enter their domain.

It was hopeless. Seg wouldn't last three minutes outside.

Unless...

"Keep opening the door," Seg said to the twins.

Without waiting to see if they complied, he ran back up to Tad's Tavern.

"Cook, I need a favor."

The gray-haired driver looked Seg up and down, taking in his storm gear. "No way, kid. Whatever your cockamamy idea, I want no part of it. I'm comfortably sloshed and intend to stay that way." He pulled Val by her hips until she was practically sitting on his lap, and latched on tight. "If you're smart, you'll do the same."

"Listen to him," Fi said softly.

Seg spun on her with fire on his tongue, but the woman who had been ready to sleep with him a few minutes ago wouldn't even look at him now. Fi hunched over the bar, staring at her drink as if it were her last friend in the world.

With a growl, Seg turned away in disgust and focused on someone who, he hoped, cared more than he let on. "Cook, I can't explain it without sounding crazy, but I *know* Troy is out there. Our storm gear is no match for a full lightning storm; I won't last long, and neither will he.

"But your car will. It's the only thing I've ever seen make it through a storm unscathed." Seg stepped closer, resisting the urge to fall to his knees. "Please... I'm not asking you to get out of the car or put yourself in danger. Just take me to him, and I'll do the rest."

Cook's grip tightened around Val's thigh. His jaw clenched, and although he remained silent, his gaze stayed on Seg.

Val, who had looked unsure until now, must have finally noted Seg's desperation. She ran a sensual finger down Cook's cheek and leaned close to his ear.

"I have a soft spot for heroes," Val said. "Hurry back and I'll show you just how soft."

Cook looked at her, then at Seg. "You're crazy. Both of you."

"Guilty," Val said with a laugh.

He sighed and extricated himself from her. "If you get yourself fried, kid, I'm not risking my neck to haul you inside."

"Understood. Thank you!"

Cook chuckled mirthlessly and followed Seg downstairs to the car.

6

Two Storms

WHEN THEY DROVE UP TO the north entrance in Cook's sleek vehicle, Seg was pleasantly surprised to see the brother-and-sister gatekeepers had done as he'd asked. The northern door stood open like the maw of a dark, howling beast, ready to swallow the car whole.

If Cook was worried, it didn't show. He shot Seg a sideways glance. "I hope you know what you're doing. Which way?"

"Left. The terrain's a little bumpy, so be careful."

"My car can handle it."

The vehicle veered off-road and along the outside of the dome. It glided over the rough terrain as if riding a cushion of air, terrain that would have shaken the hauler to pieces and pulverized its passengers.

Rain hammered the windows like a thousand tiny rocks. Lightning snaked across dark clouds in brilliant, jagged lines, rattling the vehicle with constant thunder.

A blinding flash to their left made them both jump. Several meters up, one of the dome's lightning rods glowed orange, a sight Seg had never wanted to see.

"Relax, kid. You're going to divot the leather."

Seg eased his grip on the seat cushion, but the icy knot in his chest remained.

Another lightning bolt startled him—this one from his blind eye. The phantom flash had come from just around the curve ahead.

"Oh shit," Cook said.

Seg would have voiced agreement, but his throat was frozen in panic. Runners on the dome guided rainwater toward the northern collector. Starting from a trickle higher up, the flow gained volume and intensity on its journey down. By the time it reached the bottom, it was a veritable raging waterfall.

The collector it was supposed to be flowing into, like a giant mouth toward the sky, was closed, or mostly so. The repair crew had managed to open it a few inches. Most of the precious freshwater, however, gushed over the lip and onto the gravel riverbed below, maintained by the water crew to prevent soil erosion.

What shot ice through Seg's veins, however, was the figure in storm gear inside the waterfall.

"What the fuck is he doing out here?"

"He must be trapped," Seg said, his throat loosening just enough to speak.

"He must be dead. How long has the water been raging over him like that?"

Long enough for him to drown, Seg thought, unable to voice the terrible words. "Get as close as you can."

"Kid, there's nothing—"

"Please! As soon as I'm out, you can drive back if you want, but I have to help him! I have to…"

Seg shook his head. He and Troy had never seen eye-to-eye, which was nothing new because Seg rarely got along with anyone. Even so, the thought of his brother drowning alone in a storm…

"You're crazy," Cook said, but he continued driving over rocks and splashing through runoff until they were at the base of the waterfall.

Seg was out of the car before it stopped. Gale-force winds tried to rip the door from his grip. He threw his weight against it and pushed until a brief ebb finally allowed him to close it.

Troy—it *had* to be him—was on the far side of the collector, across the raging runoff river. Seg ran as fast as the howling winds would allow. His first step into the runoff nearly swept him off his feet. Water up to his knees tore him in one direction, while wind pushed him in another. Seg widened his stance and concentrated on putting one foot in front of the other.

Lightning flashed from two directions at once: one in the near distance…

…and the second on Troy.

Seg cried in terror until he realized the second flash had come from his blind eye, and had reported no thunder. In a strange dual-reality, his brother jerked and jolted from the lightning strike, and at the same time remained eerily still. If visions they were, Seg fervently hoped they weren't of the past.

Once clear of the river, he bolted the last few yards to the collector, and saw with frightening clarity why Troy was still outside. His arm was bent at a right angle, just like Seg's visions had shown, stuck down inside the collector.

The collector panel opened outward on hinges along the ground, like a door facing up, allowing it to channel the raging runoff coming down from the dome into the reservoir below. The door was weighted to close inward by default to ensure it was only opened during freshwater pours, like this one, and not during acid storms where the reservoirs would become tainted.

Right now, that entire weight was clamping closed on Troy's arm, which was probably the only thing holding it open. Troy's head—there was no mistaking Seg's brother now—bowed over, facedown. Runoff from the dome pounded his back with steady, merciless brutality.

"Troy!"

Seg held his breath and strode into the waterfall, using his hands and body as a shield. Water crashed down on him, trying to smash him into the ground. It filled his ears and ran into his nose. He opened his mouth as a test, and was happy to find the pocket of air that he'd hoped his wedge-shape would create.

From within the raging waterfall, Seg heard another gasp.

"Troy!"

A coughing sputter. "Seg? You idiot! Get back inside the dome!"

Seg ground his teeth. Once his brother was safe, Seg was going to strangle him. "We've got to get your arm free."

"Forget it, the crew took the tools inside. I had a crowbar, but it washed away. Besides, my arm's the only thing keeping this collector open, and we need the water."

"Ever thought of using a rock, genius?"

"Fuck. You."

Seg grinned in spite of himself. "I have an idea. You'll be all right here for a second?"

"I'd be better if you'd get out of this storm before you get electrocuted."

Taking that for a yes, Seg backed out of the waterfall. Despite the storm gear, he was soaked inside and out. Water ran down his chest and legs in a steady stream into his already-full boots. He sloshed around the surrounding area, searching the ground, and quickly found what he was looking for: a wedge-shaped rock twice the thickness of his arm. He stooped to pick it up, and nearly jumped out of his skin when a lightning bolt struck a hundred meters away, followed by ear-splitting thunder.

With a groan, Seg heaved the rock up and cradled it in his arms. His back protested the weight with every step to the collector. Lifting it over his shoulders would have been difficult enough without the waterfall trying to tear it from his hands. He somehow managed to heave it up and wedge the thin end into the collector opening next to Troy's arm.

"Nice job, little brother," Troy shouted through the raging runoff. "What now, 'genius'?"

What now, indeed...

The collector panel was massive. Almost as tall as Seg and ten meters wide, it was solid metal, and ran all the way down to the ground. If the repair crew and raging waterfall hadn't managed to pry it open, Seg himself had no chance.

A loud thunderclap made them both jump. Two lightning rods not fifty meters away glowed white-hot.

"Get out of here, Seg!"

Ignoring his thick-headed brother, Seg dashed to the end of the collector panel, planted a foot on the dome, and pulled with primal desperation. His muscles burned, back strained, legs shook...

The stubborn panel refused to budge even a centimeter.

"Out of the way!"

Seg hadn't heard Cook approach through the howling storm and thunder. The driver's normally kempt gray hair streamed down his face and over his eyes. Bereft of even a jacket, his thin, fancy white shirt clung to his chest and arms, giving him the appearance of a well-dressed but thoroughly drowned rabbit.

Cook shouldered him aside and attached two large, metal hooks over the lip of the collector, each with a rope attached leading back to the car.

"There's nothing to latch onto inside the collector panel," Cook said. "Since you're already willing to be electrocuted, holding these down shouldn't affect your life expectancy much."

Before Seg could thank him, Cook sprinted back to his vehicle—which had somehow crossed the runoff river—and climbed into the driver's seat.

Seg pressed a hand down on each hook. He then thought better of it, hooked an elbow over each line, and lifted his feet so he was hanging from them.

The car reversed, pulling the lines taut. Seg felt more than heard the collector groan. The vehicle's wheels began to spin, throwing rocks and mud against the collector panel. Debris bounced from Seg's storm gear with light stings, but he barely noticed.

Cook's plan wasn't working.

Then the vehicle's wheels... changed. One moment, they were typical all-weather tires. The next, they'd sprouted ridges several centimeters tall, running across the outer surface like dozens of small paddles.

Rock and earth began to fly in earnest, pelting the collector with steady *clangs*. If one hit Seg, he'd have a broken bone at best, a dented skull at worst. He closed his eyes and prayed to Loki for luck.

The collector gave a loud *crack*. The lines under his arms jerked forward ever so slightly. The panel had moved, but not enough.

The vehicle's tires widened to almost double their original size. Long spikes appeared on top of the paddle-ridges, scoring the earth without mercy. Seg had never heard of such technology, nor even thought it possible.

The collector groaned, loud and long. A *crack* yielded another centimeter, then another. Troy shifted and attempted to pull his arm out, but he screamed and collapsed against the panel, dangling from it like a ragdoll. Seg wanted to run to him, but letting pressure up from the lines could free the hooks. The panel closing so suddenly may well shear his brother's arm off.

The line under Seg's left arm vanished with an earsplitting *twang* of breaking wire. Fire lanced his arm where the wire had sliced his storm gear open, showing an angry red gash beneath. Seg ground his teeth against the pain and hooked all four limbs over the remaining line.

Another *crack*. Another centimeter gained.

The tires spun faster.

A rock struck Seg's left thigh hard enough to make him see stars. If his leg wasn't broken, it would leave one heck of a bruise, but at least it hadn't been his head.

Crack-crack-crack!

The panel slipped several more centimeters. That had to be enough.

"Troy! Can you—"

Lightning blinded Seg, followed by deafening thunder that thumped the air from his lungs. For a moment, he thought his brother was gone, but when his vision cleared, a glowing lightning rod a dozen yards away said it had missed them, if barely.

The close call seemed to spur his brother into action. With an agonized cry, Troy pulled his arm free of the collector, where it fell limp to his side with an unnatural bend just below his elbow.

The hail of rocks ceased. The line slackened.

Seg lowered himself down. Pain shot up his left thigh when he put weight on it. He stood anyway. Bruised or broken didn't matter, as long as he could help Troy to the car before they both fried.

Cook opened the rear door when they limped over, slammed it shut as soon as they were inside, then jumped into the driver's side and sealed himself in. Troy listed against the door, eyes glassy beneath his storm hood, gasping in short, shallow breaths.

"You all right?" Cook said to Troy.

"Y-yeah, I'll be—"

Lightning struck the collector in front of them with a thunderous *boom*, leaving an enormous, blackened hole where Troy had been trapped not a minute before.

A grin spread across his brother's face, followed by manic laughter. "I'm fantastic," Troy said eventually, tears streaming down his cheeks. "If it's all the same, Mr. Cook, I'd like to go home now."

Cook nodded without expression or comment, and the car was soon on its way back to the northern entrance.

Word of their return spread quickly. Only the brother-and-sister gatekeepers greeted them initially, but when they saw Troy listing in the back seat, the sister ran off in a streak of thick brown hair. By the time Seg limped around the car to help his brother out, a large crowd had formed.

Getting Troy's attention was difficult. Seg's usually surly brother was pale and vacant, his hands like ice.

"Seg," Dr. Ven's friendly voice said behind him. "It's all right, I'll take it from here."

"His arm's broken," Seg said, not wanting to leave his brother even for the doctor. "He was in the cold water for a while. I... I think he's in shock."

Ven gently pulled Seg away, then leaned in to examine Troy. "You're probably right. He also looks hypothermic." He looked past Seg. "Jen, be a dear and fetch some blankets."

Their sister stared at Troy with wide eyes and quivering lips for a second longer before nodding. She pushed through the crowd and took off at a run.

Ven glanced at someone else behind Seg. "Len, get two short planks and three rolls of bandages from medical storage. Looks like a compound fracture. We'll need to bind his arm before we move him."

Len, who was staring at Troy with all the horror someone should be who'd carelessly abandoned his team member to a storm, stammered an unintelligible assent.

"Bring painkillers, too," Ven said. "We're in short supply, but when the shock wears off, Troy's going to need them."

Len nodded, then knocked two people over in his haste to reach medical storage, followed by the rest of the repair crew.

A touch on Seg's arm made him turn to find Val next to him.

"How is he?"

"Not good," Seg said, softly enough that only she could hear.

She hooked her arm around his, pulling him off balance. Pressure on his injured leg shot daggers right up to the base of his skull. Seg tried to suppress a whimper and failed.

"Seems like he's not the only one," Val said with a concerned frown.

"I'll be fine."

"That's what you said after you fell from the top of an apple tree when we were seven, and it turned out you had a broken ankle."

"Yeah, I remember. I also remember you telling me to buck up and take it like a man."

"Because I was afraid they would ban us from climbing, and I really, really wanted to climb with you again."

Seg arched an eyebrow. "Wow, *two* reallies?"

"Two reallies," Val said with a smile. "Of course, I was seven. What the Hel did I know?"

"Enough to not follow me to the top of the tree."

Val's face fell. "No, I should have followed you, Seg. We were in it together. Partners. But I let you take the risk because I was afraid, just like..." Her eyes misted. "Just like today. I should have been out in that storm with you, but I... I..."

"You didn't believe me."

Val shook her head. "I'm sorry," she said, then lifted her chin. "It won't happen again, though. Ever."

Seg patted her arm. Her betrayal weighed heavy on his heart, but so, too, did Val's words give him hope that maybe their relationship would return to the way it was when they were younger—before her tragic marriage had changed his childhood friend, and Seg's relationship with her, forever.

He was so lost in the moment that he almost didn't notice Cook staring at them. Seg cleared his throat and leaned away from Val, who still clung to his arm.

"Val," Seg said quietly. "There's someone else who risked his life to save Troy. Without him, I don't think either of us would be standing here."

Val reluctantly released his arm. When she turned to Cook, her exuberant smile was back—a smile Seg hadn't understood until that moment was just a façade to hide her misery.

She didn't want to be with Cook, he suddenly realized.

And Seg had just obligated her to him.

Before he could correct his error and snatch her back, Val was already sashaying away, showering Cook with the praise and sultry promises deserving of a City hero who had risked life and property to save a rural farmer. Finally able to see her stage performance for what it was, Seg felt guiltier than ever that he had not only failed to recognize it, but enabled and encouraged her substitute behavior.

He started toward her, but a shooting pain in his leg staggered him back against the car.

Seg *would* fix his mistake, hopefully before it was too late. Until then, he'd have to pray that Cook was half the gentleman Seg hoped he was.

Enchanting black-ringed eyes peered through the crowd, softening when they landed on Seg. Fi glanced in the car at Troy's catatonic form, then turned back to Seg with forlorn sadness.

"I'm so sorry." Fi put a comforting hand on his shoulder. "Let me know if there's anything you need."

Seg stared in confusion. "Um... thanks, but apart from a bandage for my arm, and probably some crutches, I should be fine."

"That's what most people believe in the moment. Then they wake in the middle of the night with no crowd, no one to talk to. Just them and their thoughts. That's when grief strikes. If it does, remember... I'm in the bed next to yours. Just wake me and—"

"Miss Fi... I appreciate the sentiment, but I have no idea what you're talking about. What am I supposed to be grieving?"

"The loss of your brother." She patted his arm. "You don't have to be brave with me. Holding it inside will only make it worse."

Seg glanced in the car to make sure he hadn't missed something crucial. Dr. Ven was gently probing Troy's broken arm. Troy stared at the seat in front of him, unmoving, until Ven took his elbow and tried to bend it.

Troy jerked upright with a wince. "Watch it, Doc! That hurts like Hel."

Seg's heart skipped a beat when he turned back to Fi and saw her look of wide-eyed terror.

"No..."

"Yeah, he's—"

Fi shoved him out of the way, then grabbed Ven by the shoulders and practically threw him out of the car.

Ven landed on his back and blinked in a daze. "What in Odin's name are you doing, young lady?"

Fi ignored him, wholly focused on Troy. She grabbed his jaw and turned his head from one side to the other, put two fingers against the throbbing vein in his neck, and gasped. She practically tore his storm shirt in half in her haste to put her ear to his chest.

"NoooooooooOOOOO!!!" The word ended in a shrieking growl. Fi shot to her feet, fingers curled like talons. Her black-ringed eyes looked at Seg, and then at Cook, with something between rage and terror. "Who did this?"

Seg stared at Cook, who was clearly as lost as him.

Fi leveled a shaking finger at Troy.

"Which of you did it? *Who saved him? WHO?!?*"

Her furious cries echoed over the crowd, who had fallen silent at her unexpected outburst.

Seg was the first of them to regain his tongue. "Well... we both did, I guess."

"Impossible! No, it had to be one of you—only one!" She grabbed Seg by the arms in a surprisingly firm grip and shook. "It was you, wasn't it? Tell me! How did you do it? *How?*"

Fi shook him so violently this time that he slammed against the car, sending shooting pains through his leg and his gashed arm. Stars colored his vision. Seg groaned and slid to the dirt-covered floor, protecting his injured limbs as best he could from the enchanting-eyed maniac.

The brother-and-sister gatekeepers, with hair like the lions Seg imagined from storytime, grabbed Fi by the arms and yanked her away.

Fi flowed like water in their grasp. A fluid twist freed her from the lion-brother's grip, then she spun, grabbed the lion-sister by her torso, and threw her over her hip into the brother, where they collapsed in a heap.

Nobody else tried to stop her.

Fi's wild eyes landed on Seg. For a moment, he thought she would lunge at him again, but a mark of sanity returned to her feral features. Fi took a long, shuddering breath, and visibly relaxed.

"I... I'm very sorry for my behavior. It was unbecoming of a guest who's been treated as well as Holtondome has treated me."

Her voice was controlled once again. As with Val, though, Seg suddenly wondered how much of her calm veneer was simply show—a mask to hide wounds running deeper than he'd ever suspected.

Fi helped the lion twins to their feet, who accepted her aid with wary concern, then she backed away without so much as a glance at Seg.

"If you'll excuse me, I need time to reflect on my actions." Fi turned to

Seg without meeting his eyes. "I'll be in our room, if you want to talk."

Before Seg could answer, she hurried away and ran up the stairs.

Troy leaned out of the car with a wince. "You sure know how to pick them, little brother. I bet she has baggage enough for all of us, with a few to spare."

That, Seg mused, was one of the few things he and his brother had ever agreed on.

7

Anomaly

SEG ADJUSTED THE WOODEN CRUTCHES under his arms, took the weight off his bad leg, and climbed another step. He looked up the imposing stairway leading to the second floor.

One down, a mountain to go.

He planted his crutches, grunted against a shooting pain in his left thigh, and climbed again.

Although he'd planned on going straight to his room, it was several floors higher than the tavern. Stopping at Tad's didn't sound nearly as unappetizing now as it had at the base of the stairs.

Sweat dappled his brow by the time he reached the second floor. His leg ached and throbbed, even without pressure, a sure sign that he should have taken the doctor's advice and stayed the night in the infirmary with Troy instead of returning to his room.

Or Fi's room. Or our room. Or whatever I'm supposed to call it.

In truth, Seg had no desire to see her, but he worried over her behavior. Fi was the epitome of carefully curated nonchalance. Boredom, even. She'd barely cracked a smile since arriving, let alone shown any hint of excitement or engagement.

From where, then, had her violent outburst come?

Seg gritted his teeth against a stabbing pain and climbed another step.

If it had just been a temper tantrum, he would have happily let her stew, but it had been more than that. Beneath her outrage, Fi had been truly terrified.

But why?

Assuming Seg made it to the fourth floor without fainting and putting himself back in the infirmary, he'd soon find out.

"Seg!"

Val ran to him the moment he entered the tavern. Without missing a beat, she took one of his crutches away, looped his arm over her shoulders, and helped him to a nearby table.

Even sitting down was a challenge. Bending his leg hurt, so he ended up sitting half-on the chair. His butt-cheek and injured leg hung over the side to keep it straight.

"Thanks, Val."

"Don't mention it." She sat across from him and leveled a worried gaze. "Broken?"

"Doc thinks so. He says it isn't bad, but..." Seg winced at another pain. "If that's the case, I'd hate to know what 'bad' feels like."

"Wimp."

Seg shot her a look, but her cheeky grin soon had him smiling, too.

"How's Troy?"

"Almost back to his ornery self," Seg said. "He's part of the reason I'm here instead of in medical. I couldn't stand his grousing about being stuck in the infirmary for a few days."

"Yikes! Can't blame him, I'd go stir crazy. Maybe we can convince a storyteller to pay him a visit."

"Fat chance. I don't think they like him much, either."

"Definitely a trait you two have in common."

Seg winced, although not from his leg this time. Coming from Val, that hurt.

Her eyes softened. She reached for his hand, but snatched it back when Cook arrived. The driver sat between them, set three shot glasses on the table, and slid one each to Val and Seg.

"You beat the odds, kid. No sane gambler would have bet on you if their life depended on it." Cook raised his shot glass. "To the Lightning Hero."

"Hero*es*," Seg said. "I couldn't have done it without you."

"But you would have tried anyway, and don't deny it. That's what separates us, kid. I don't have that kind of mettle."

"Hog-shit you don't. You got out of your car *without* storm gear to help me, carrying two metal lines, which made you a bigger lightning magnet than Troy or me."

Val gaped at Cook. "You *what?*"

"It was nothing," Cook said softly to his shot glass. His face, already red from storm exposure, turned another shade of crimson.

Val clutched his hand to her breast. "It wasn't nothing, Cook. It was brave, and it saved my best friend's brother's life."

Seg grabbed the table to keep from falling out of his chair. Since when had he become Val's best friend? When they were kids, sure, but he thought that ship had long sailed.

Val raised her shot glass, beaming at both of them. "Good health to *both* of Holtondome's newest heroes."

"Good health," Seg said reflexively.

They downed their drinks as one. Seg and Val placed theirs rim-down, as traditional. Cook noticed a second later and, to their delight, inverted his as well.

"You're becoming quite the local," Val said with a smile. "Careful, or we may not let you leave."

Cook grunted and stood. "I'll... get another round. I'm sure the kid could use it."

Val had a pensive look when he returned with three more shot glasses. "You keep calling him 'kid.' Not to spoil this good thing we have, but you do realize Seg and I are the same age?"

"On the outside, maybe, but... Don't take this the wrong way, Val, but my father would have said you have an old soul. Those eyes of yours speak of experience beyond your years. I won't ask why, not unless you're willing to share, but I know I'm right."

Val's smile buckled. For a second, Seg thought she might actually open up to him, but her pleasant façade quickly returned. He couldn't help being disappointed. Val needed to talk to someone about her past, someone other than himself.

"As long as it isn't a turnoff, I'll accept 'old soul' as a compliment, and a nod to your father's wisdom."

"It was meant as such." Cook raised his shot glass. "Good health."

Val's mirth finally reached her eyes. "You catch on quickly. Good health."

Seg echoed them and tipped his back. The fiery liquid didn't burn nearly as much as it should have, nor did its warmth spread through his chest with the intensity he'd hoped. The Sinkhole Twister from earlier still coursed through his veins, dulling the shot's effects, although he was happy to find his leg hurting somewhat less. He glanced at the empty stairway.

"Has... Miss Fi come out of her room?"

"You mean since putting those lion twins down like cubs?" Cook shook his head. "That scuffle must have taken the bite out of her."

"Mm," Seg said, then grimaced. First, Fi had him questioning himself at every turn. Now he was starting to sound like her, too. "Cook, I hope this isn't too forward, but… what do you know about her? That you can share, of course."

"Not much in either case. First time I'd met or even heard about her was when I picked her up to bring her here."

Val plopped her chin on her hand. "That's it? You didn't even know her before agreeing to cart her from Thor-knows-where, and to be at her beck-and-call?"

"I'm not at her beck-and-call. And it might seem strange to you, growing up in such a tight-knit community, but where I'm from, that's how it works."

"Sounds awful," Val said with a shiver. "Maybe Cities aren't that great after all."

"Anonymity has its perks, but yeah, you might be right."

"Anonymity? How…"

Val stopped her inquiry at his flat stare.

"Right, forget I asked."

"Look, it's nothing personal," Cook said. "If I had nothing to lose, I might think about bending the rules and sharing some of what I know, but I do. You have no idea what that car cost me. The Feds could take it in a heartbeat if they found I'd broken the law."

Seg nodded. After what he'd seen that vehicle do, he could only imagine its worth.

Val stared at Seg. Her eyes narrowed.

Crap.

She knew Seg was holding out. Val would corner him later, like she always used to, and pester him until he told all.

Just like I'd do to her if I knew she was holding something interesting from me.

Cook caught the interaction and gave Seg a slight shake of his head, cementing what he'd begun to suspect. Cook wasn't supposed to have revealed the vehicle's true capabilities to a Provider dome. In saving Troy, Cook had broken the law, and put his livelihood at risk.

The thought weighed heavy. The Feds were due tomorrow, along with the Traders. If Seg was unlucky, he'd be chosen for questioning. He'd inevitably have to tell of Troy's rescue to ensure consistency with the other's stories. That would lead to an investigation, which would mean more questions. Eventually, Seg knew, they'd discover the truth. They always did.

Hopefully not always.

He would protect Cook's secret, if humanly possible. Cook had saved his brother's life. The least Seg could do for the man was keep one, tiny secret, which meant not telling a soul what he'd seen. He caught Val's eyes and slowly shook his head.

Not even my best friend.

"Um... thanks for the drinks," Seg said. "Between that and the breather, I think I'm ready for the rest of the climb. Lying in my own... er, lying in a bed sounds good."

Val frowned, her lips tight. "All right," she said eventually. "I'll help you up the stairs."

Cook rose. "*We'll* help. Climbing those stairs of yours is definitely a two-person job."

Several pain-filled minutes later, Cook and Val bid Seg an early goodnight and left him in front of his new bedroom door. He started to knock but caught himself. This was his room, too, so he simply entered.

Fi appeared to have been waiting for him, and was standing at the foot of the nearest bed. She sized him up with a glance. "Lie down. Let's look at those injuries."

"Doc already did."

"Mm. Here, let me help..."

She took his crutches, then guided him to the bed. Seg braced for the inevitable shooting pain when he started to lay down, but her skillful hands seemed to know just where to support him. He released his unnecessary breath with a *whoosh.*

"Thank you."

"Mm."

Fi started with his arm. He worried when she casually unwound the wrappings Dr. Ven had so painstakingly placed, but she hushed him with a look and examined his open wound with a critical eye.

"Partially severed tendons. If we don't repair the damage, you could lose the use of your first and second digits, or at the very least, suffer reduced range of motion and strength."

"W-what? Doc never said anything about that. Are you sure?"

"Mm. Lucky for you, I have a medical kit."

"Are you a... a doctor?"

"I was. My license expired a while ago, but I still remember the craft."

Expired? At her age?

Apparent age, Seg reminded himself. Odin only knew how old she actually was.

Fi retrieved a big black bag from a drawer and unfolded a large paper mat on the bed. Seg gulped when she laid an arsenal of sharp instruments down, including knives, syringes, and a few devices he didn't recognize.

"Are you *positive* you know what you're doing?"

Fi flicked a particularly huge needle with a fingernail and leveled him with a stare.

"It's just… I mean, it *might* heal on its own, right?"

"Sure. Aliens might also come by after dinner and take us to their mothership for a ride around the solar system."

"Very funny."

"Mm. Now, if you're done stalling, this will only hurt for a second, then you won't feel a thing."

Seg looked away. He had only received two shots in his life that he remembered, both when he was young. They weren't pleasant memories.

"There, done," Fi said. "Let's give it a minute to take effect."

"That's it? I didn't feel anything."

"Which means you may have also severed a nerve or three. Can you feel this?" She poked his wrist just below the gash.

"No."

Fi poked higher. "This?"

"No."

"This? This?"

Seg shook his head at each prod. It wasn't until she probed the back of his hand that the sensation he *should* have felt finally registered with his brain.

"Mm." Fi picked up a pair of jagged-looking scissors. "Hold very still. Reattaching nerves is a delicate operation, and I'd hate to cause permanent damage."

"Whoa, whoa! You aren't going to knock me out first?"

"I packed for a three-week trip to the country, not major surgery. Be thankful I have any supplies at all."

"But I…" Seg let his head fall back onto the pillow. "All right, I'll do my best."

Fi nodded and set to work. Seg was curious about what she was doing, but not enough to risk flinching at the wrong moment and cause her to slip, so he looked away.

Sounds of clipping and snipping of his own flesh floated up to him. Seg closed his eyes, trying to drown them out, willing himself to hold still. He felt tugging, something wet, then more tugging.

"Done."

"What… seriously? You only just started."

"I'm quick," Fi said. "Avoid using that arm for the next two days. You should have normal use after then."

"In only two days? H-how is that possible?" Holtondome had seen its share of injuries. Recovery was usually measured in months, not days.

"I can't answer that, and you know it. Now, let's look at your leg."

When her fingers slipped inside his waistband, Seg nearly jumped off the bed.

"W-hat are you doing?"

Fi put a hand on her hip. "Why? What are you *afraid* I'm doing?"

"Sorry, it's just… in the bar, you were, well… you kind of suggested…"

More than suggested, Seg thought, flushing at the memory.

"Do you really think I'd molest a patient with a possibly broken leg and fresh stitches in his arm?"

"Um, no…"

"And would it be that horrible if I did?"

"Well… n-no, I suppose not."

"Then what's the problem?"

What *was* the problem? "Sorry, I'll get them."

Seg reached for his trousers, but she lightly slapped the back of his wrist.

"Don't use your left hand, remember? I'll bandage it up later as a reminder. Now, just relax."

Far from relaxed, Seg managed to not throw himself off the table this time when her fingers snaked inside his waistband and shimmied his pants down. To his great relief, she left his underwear in place.

Fi retrieved a flat, glowing screen from her bag, along with a palm-sized silver cylinder with glowing lights on one end. She pressed the cylinder gently down on his left thigh.

Even the light pressure made him wince.

"Sorry," Fi said. "If a slight touch hurts, it may need immediate attention."

"Yeah, especially since the rock whacked me on the back of the leg, not the front."

"So the enormous bruise below tells me. Even if nothing's broken, you'll be sore for a while." Fi glanced at the screen, which lit her face with colorful hues, then moved the cylinder down his leg a few centimeters.

Seg had a thousand questions about the device, the procedure, and her seemingly magical healing medicine. But, as with Cook's morphing tires, the knowledge was forbidden—if not by federal law, then by the Pact, which Holtondome's Founders and thousands like it around the world had sworn to uphold, shunning technology in any form except those necessary for survival. And even that technology was mostly left to the Cities.

Seg shouldn't want anything to do with the infernal stuff humanity had nearly destroyed itself with.

If only his burning curiosity were as wise.

"That was quite a rescue you and Cook pulled," Fi said, her eyes fixed on the screen. "Your brother's a lucky man."

"You didn't seem too thrilled about it earlier. Almost like you would have preferred if he died."

"That's a heartless thing to say."

"I…" Seg bit his apology off with a snap of his jaw. "Don't turn this around on me. You went ballistic when you saw Troy had survived. Why?"

Fi continued to stare at the screen, but her eyes unfocused. "I told you before: it's not often I'm surprised."

"You didn't react that way in the bar earlier when I 'surprised' you with my insightful responses."

"There are different levels of surprise. Your responses were like discovering one last chocolate in a box you thought was empty."

"And Troy?"

Fi considered for a second, then turned her attention back to the screen. "Imagine you were driving your hauler to one of the agricultural domes, just like you always do, and the vehicle suddenly plummeted into a pit next to a giant, ferocious tyrannosaurus rex. How surprised would you be?"

"Surprised enough to need a change of underwear."

"Yeah, I did that as soon as I returned to our room."

"But… *why?* Troy can be a jerk, but he's no dinosaur."

"It doesn't take a dinosaur to destroy a village."

Seg pinched the bridge of his nose. "I… I'm really not following."

"That's because I'm being intentionally abstract."

"I noticed."

"Good, otherwise I'd suspect you have a brain injury as well." Fi put the screen and cylinder back in her bag. "You have a middle, oblique, non-displaced fracture in your left femur."

"Oh, thank goodness. For a minute there I thought I had a broken leg."

Fi started to reply, then closed her mouth. "Congrats, you almost caught me. You *do* have a broken leg. Not completely, which is why you can still walk, but one wrong step could change that in an agonizing instant."

"Ah." Seg gulped. "I, um... don't suppose you have a splint in that medical bag of yours?"

"I have better." Fi pulled out a syringe with a needle bigger than any Seg had ever seen. "I've already administered all the anesthetics I safely can, so you're going to have to bear the pain this time."

"Pain" turned out to be an understatement. Neither the anesthetics in his arm, nor the remaining alcohol in his system, dulled the jaw-clenching torture of the enormous hypodermic piercing his skin and muscle, nor the stomach-turning vibrations of it clanking against his leg bone.

Seg gripped the blanket with all his might, until he remembered he wasn't supposed to use his left hand, and made a conscious effort to keep it splayed on his stomach. His right hand, however, tore holes in the fabric.

After what felt like an hour, Fi finally withdrew the needle. Seg released his death grip and collapsed.

"Keep that leg as still as you can for at least an hour. You can test it on the stairs when we go down for dinner."

An hour?

Seg shook his head. Doc would have had him on bed rest for two weeks, minimum. Whatever medicine she carried wasn't standard Trader fare. The disparity made him suddenly bitter.

"Think I'll skip dinner, for once," Seg said. "I'm exhausted."

"I'll bring some back for you. We can eat here."

"Don't feel obligated. You'll miss storytime. Worse, Tad will miss out on the story you promised."

"I'll make it up to him. The only story I'm interested in tonight is yours."

"Huh?"

Fi laid next to him and propped herself up on an elbow. "Tell me what happened in the lightning storm. I want to hear every detail, no matter how small."

"Everything? That could take a while."

"I have time."

Seg shrugged. Despite her request for detail, he skipped over the lightning flashes in his blind left eye, which would have made him sound crazy, and started from the point when he realized Troy wasn't with the rest of the repair crew in the tavern. By the time he reached the part where they returned through the northern entrance, he was shaking with adrenaline, just as he had then.

"Quite an adventure. You'll be the hit of storytime for the next few years at least." Fi surprised him by brushing a lock of hair from his forehead with a delicate finger. "Tell me again how you knew Troy was in danger."

"Oh. Well, when neither of the gatekeepers remembered seeing him—"

"I mean before that. In the tavern."

"I-I didn't."

Fi studied him. "One of my gifts is reading people. I sometimes miss things in the moment but, given a little time, I can usually fit the pieces together.

"Except for this afternoon. I didn't catch it then, but even when his own crew believed he was fine, you *knew* your brother was outside in the lightning storm. How?"

"That's ridiculous. How could I..."

Seg wilted under her stare.

"You... you wouldn't believe me."

Fi was the one person who had never treated him differently. If he told her what he'd seen—what he *believed* he'd seen, anyway—she'd think he was a freak. An aberration.

Just like everyone else did.

He couldn't stand the idea of losing that sense of normalcy. Not one bit.

Please, just drop it...

Fi leaned closer until their noses touched. Her warm breath tickled his lips. For a second, Seg thought she was going to kiss him. It wasn't a terrible feeling.

"No matter what you say," Fi said instead, "I won't judge. I promise."

Seg stared at her, his lips tight. He wanted to tell her—tell *anyone*, just so the strange experience wasn't bottled up, eating his insides with doubts of his own sanity.

But doing so would make him vulnerable. Fi could use that information against him, hurt him as so many had before. It was a trust not easily given, even if he believed she was different from the rest.

"My other gift is keeping secrets," Fi said, as if reading his mind. "I swear, whatever you tell me, I won't breathe a word of it to anyone." She ran her fingers down his cheek and cupped his face. "Please, this is very, very important to me. How did you know your brother was in danger?"

"You won't believe me," Seg said again.

"You don't know that. How?"

"I..." Seg ground his teeth.

Fuck it.

"I saw him get hit by lightning. I couldn't let it happ—"

Fi lurched up, suddenly over him on all fours.

"Saw? *Saw?* What did you see? Tell me!" Her black-ringed eyes were wild with excitement, a stark contrast to her usually uninterested demeanor.

"A l-lightning flash," Seg said, pressing himself back into the bed against her intensity. "And Troy's outline. Through the dome."

Some of her excitement wilted. "Through?"

"Yeah. When you and I were sitting at the bar. I looked in the direction where Troy was stuck and saw a lightning flash with…"

"With what?"

"With… my blind eye."

"*Through* the walls?"

"Yes, and not just once. Every time I looked, it became clearer, more defined."

"More certain," Fi said softly, as if to herself. Her attention snapped back to him. "How did you save him?"

"I told you. Cook brought hooks over and—"

"No! I mean how did you change his f…" Fi closed her eyes and took a deep, shuddering breath. "I've harassed you enough for one evening. Get some rest. We can talk more in the morning."

"Not until you answer me one thing, Miss Fi."

"Mm?"

Seg leveled her with his good eye. "How did *you* know Troy was in danger?"

Fi's mouth tightened. Seg thought she was going to deny it, or claim it was yet one more thing she couldn't tell him by law, but she simply sighed, then sagged until her head rested on his chest.

"I saw his death, too," she said quietly.

The pieces came crashing together. "That whole scene in the bar… you trying to get me drunk, then seducing me. You… you tried to stop me!"

That she would prevent Seg from saving his own brother—that Fi knew he was in peril and hadn't said anything!—scorched his insides like molten metal, but his fury came out in a thin whisper.

"I thought you were different from other City folk. I really believed…"

Her enchanting eyes met his, filled with sorrow and excitement. "There's so much you don't know."

"Then *enlighten* me."

"Tomorrow. I was serious when I said you need rest." She frowned at him. "What's your name again?"

"Seg!"

Fi nodded. "I won't forget it again, believe me." She shook herself, then began collecting her medical supplies. "I'm going to clean up, then I need to do some research. In the meantime…" She pulled a small container from her bag and shook a pill into her palm. "Take this. It will help you sleep, and prevent you from tossing and turning so you don't injure yourself."

"I don't want to sleep! I want answers."

"I do, too, so if you don't mind…" Fi pulled another syringe from her black bag, thankfully much smaller than the one she'd attacked his leg with. "Can I take a blood sample?"

"Didn't you get enough already?"

"Not clean samples, no. Besides, collecting genetic material without your consent would be unethical."

Seg narrowed his eyes. "What do you need it for?"

"Answers. For both of us."

Although Seg dreaded another needle stick, he nodded. He couldn't imagine how a blood draw would explain his prophetic visions, and he was still fuming over her active interference with his attempts to save his brother.

But the problem was… Fi was right. There was so much he didn't know, so much the Feds ensured he couldn't… If cooperating meant Fi might be more forthcoming with information, then it would be worth a little discomfort.

Once the clear vial shimmered red with the contents of his veins, Fi carefully packed it in a container, then fetched a glass of water for his sleeping pill. The small white tablet was flavorless and went down easily.

Soon, his body relaxed, and his eyelids weighed heavy. The last thing Seg remembered before sleep claimed him was Fi sitting cross-legged on her own bed, hunched over a screen, with his blood sample plugged into an attached device, more engaged in her work than he'd ever imagined the normally indifferent woman could be.

8

Downer

To Seg's surprise, Fi was still hunched over her screen when he awoke. His tongue felt unusually thick with sleep. When he tried to rise, his body was so comfortable that it practically refused to obey. Seg gave up after a few attempts and relaxed into his pillow.

"Did you find any answers?"

"Several," Fi said, "though not the ones I'd hoped for."

After a few attempts, Seg managed to convince his body to prop itself on an elbow. "Care to explain?"

Fi continued typing on the small keyboard, eyes fixed on her screen. Just when Seg was about to give up, she punched a key with finality and slid her devices aside.

"For one, we aren't related. Not at all."

"You hoped we were?"

Fi nodded. "But the genetic analysis did show something surprising. You've had that blind eye since you were born, right?"

"So my parents tell me."

"That means it's a birth defect, and a defect of this type could only be genetic. The problem is, your genes are fine. In fact, I couldn't find anything in medical history matching your condition."

"W-what are you saying?"

"That you *shouldn't* have a blind left eye. What's more, the smooth, glassy texture may not even be a possible result of standard DNA combinations."

That woke him up. Seg threw the covers back and shot to his feet. A twinge in his leg reminded him of Fi's warning that one wrong move could snap it in two. He hastily sat back down. Fortunately, the twinge remained only that.

"I scanned your leg earlier," Fi said. "The compound set nicely. You should be okay to walk on it."

"Oh, thanks."

Seg carefully flexed his left fingers. A dull pain throbbed just beneath the long scar running diagonally across the fleshy part of his middle forearm, but, thankfully, his digits responded. He then poked the area that had been numb last night.

"Feeling?"

"Yeah. Not quite the same as it was, but close enough." *And certainly better than nothing.*

"Give it a day or so. Your nerves are still re-attaching themselves."

Seg nodded. "In case I forget to say it later… thank you, Miss Fi. I was a little short with you last night. I'm sorry."

"Don't apologize for speaking your mind, as long as you think it through before you do."

"Glad to hear you say that, I *have* thought about last night and some of what I said still stands."

Fi arched an eyebrow, although her neutral expression hinted she knew exactly what he was going to say.

"I've run through it again and again, and I keep coming to the same conclusion. You tried to stop me from saving Troy."

Fi nodded. "I know how it seems, but that wasn't my intention. Not precisely."

Seg sighed. "Miss Fi—"

"It's not a great answer, I know. Hang on, I'm working up to it." Her enchanting blue eyes unfocused for a moment. "When someone's time is up, it's up. I had a vision similar to yours on the drive back to Holtondome yesterday, though not exactly the same. It was your brother's time to die, and nothing you did could have changed that. Or so I thought."

Seg considered that.

It still didn't make sense. How did she know Seg couldn't save Troy when he most definitely had? He was about to bark a nasty reply, but her other lessons cut him short. Fi had urged him at every turn to consider all the facts before blurting accusations, and the facts indicated she approached situations with good intentions. He would be a fool to think otherwise now.

Troy's death had been inevitable in her mind. Preventing Seg from saving him would have been pointless, because she hadn't believed he could, which ruled that out as a motivation.

Leaving one other possibility.

"You were trying to console me," Seg said softly. "Ease the pain of losing my brother before I actually had. You… you were willing to sleep with me just so I'd have something to cling to when I received the news."

"I wouldn't say that was the only reason, but a compelling one, certainly."

Seg hung his head. "Once again, I misjudged you, Miss Fi. I'm sorry."

"Forgiven. You had no way of knowing, though I'm glad you reached the right conclusion."

Seg closed his eyes, his mind reeling. "It must be hard going through life knowing how and when people are going to die, and that you can't do a damn thing about it. How do you live with it?"

Fi sucked a breath and considered him for a moment. "I didn't say I couldn't do anything about it. What I meant"—Fi raised a hand to forestall Seg's heated reply—"is that interfering with someone's predetermined death—their destiny, really—can have consequences. Serious, devastating consequences that outweigh the benefits of letting them live."

"Devastating how?"

"Devastating on a scale I hope your conscience never has to bear."

Seg frowned. "What aren't you telling me?"

"Enough to fill an entire mountain with books. But I know what you're asking, and, for personal reasons, it will have to wait. The Traders arrive today."

"Along with the Feds!"

Anything Fi told him would be subject to inquiry, which scared him witless. How far would they dig into the incident with Troy? Would they discover Seg's secret?

"Does… anyone else know what we can do?"

"No one," Fi said. "And we should keep it that way."

Seg couldn't have agreed more. "W-what do I tell them?"

"The same story you told me: You noticed Troy hadn't returned with the repair crew, asked around, and, when you discovered the gatekeepers hadn't seen him either, you enlisted the only person who had a reasonable chance of helping you rescue him."

"Cook."

"Mm. They'll have no reason to suspect anything unusual."

Although Cook might have some explaining to do.

There was no help for it, though. As much as he hated to, if the Feds asked, Seg would have to inform them of Cook's aid. There were too many witnesses to convincingly corroborate otherwise.

"And what about the medical treatments you administered? Are those sanctioned?"

"Don't worry about me," Fi said. "This isn't my first inquiry. Just tell them what you know, and I'll handle the rest. Now…" Fi jumped from the bed with teenage exuberance and clapped her hands. "Let's wash up. We could both use a shower before meeting your parents."

"My… parents?"

"Yes. I'm hoping they can answer some questions about your history that your medical records didn't. Come on, it'll be faster if we shower together."

Before Seg could argue, she grabbed his good hand and towed him into the bathroom.

True to her word, Fi wasted no time in the shower. Although Seg was shy shedding his clothes in front of her, Fi had no such reservations, which had given him ample opportunity to admire and clean her body. Her curves were gentle. Perfect. Everything from her smooth skin, to her silky hair, to the intricate, flowing black marks circling her pert breasts and flowing down to the heavenly spot between her legs made him want to linger in the shower for the rest of the morning, water shortage be damned.

Cleaning was, unfortunately, all Fi left time for in her hurry to get them downstairs for breakfast, where she wanted to speak with his parents, Hap and Peg, before the Traders arrived. So Seg set his disappointment aside and changed into his second-finest outfit: a collared shirt, slightly worn at the elbows, and slacks with only a single stain. Fi donned a dress even more to Holtondome's fashion than yesterday's: beige with a firm bodice, exposing just enough of her chest to be tantalizing, and a long skirt down to her ankles.

No sooner had Fi pulled it on than she was tugging Seg into the stairway. He was pleasantly surprised when she took his good hand, as if they were already a couple, and led him downstairs, which she took two at a time in her excitement. Miraculously, his left leg endured the rugged trip without complaint.

Seg found himself smiling after her. Regardless of the reason, he liked seeing this side of her—this energized woman burning with curiosity and purpose. This was a different person from the Fi who'd only stared out the window and avoided conversation just yesterday.

The morning was later than Seg thought. Tad and Nin were cleaning up when they arrived, the tables and bar practically empty.

Either that, or…

"Have the Traders already arrived?"

"Not yet, Master Seg." Tad grinned at their joined hands. "I must say, you're in much finer shape than the man who could barely get off his chair yesterday evening."

"Thanks, Tad. A good night's rest was apparently all I needed." Seg followed Fi's suit and sat at the bar, where, even then, she didn't release his hand.

"Good morning, master barkeep," Fi said cheerily. "Is there any breakfast left, or do we have to beg for scraps?"

Tad laughed. When Seg looked over at Fi, he could see why.

Fi was smiling so broadly she had dimples. Dimples!

"I'm beginning to see what put the spring in Master Seg's step." Tad winked with a chuckle.

She looked at Seg, a sparkle in her enchanting eyes as if Tad's insinuation were actually true.

"It was a night I won't forget," Fi said. "So magical, in fact, that he's agreed to introduce me to his parents."

Tad's smile faltered. He stared at them as if waiting to be let in on the joke. "W-well, that's… that's fine, I suppose. Begging your pardon, miss, but how long did you say you'll be staying with us?"

"Three weeks, assuming I'm still welcome after my outburst yesterday."

"I wouldn't worry about that. I was certainly shocked when I heard you'd put the twins down like babes, but there was no serious injury. I've even heard there may be a resident or two interested in hand-to-hand combat lessons, if you're willing."

"I might be persuaded, though the law restricts me from teaching the more advanced techniques."

"I'm sure they'll be happy with whatever knowledge you can spare. There's also the matter of the story you promised, but seeing as you've taken such good care of the brave master here, I think we can consider that debt paid."

"Nonsense, a promise is a promise. Assuming our brave master can keep himself out of trouble, I'll deliver the story tonight."

Nin swept in beside her husband, beaming. "That would be delightful, Miss Fi! We had quite a crowd here last night in anticipation, and I daresay it won't take much to get them back. Now, what can I get you for breakfast?"

Fi squeezed Seg's hand. "What would you like?"

"Me? Oh, um… how about ham and tomato with toast?"

"Sounds delicious! I'll have the same."

Nin took in the adorable couple schtick with a giggle and shuffled into the kitchen.

Tad didn't seem as pleased. He leaned on the counter with both elbows in front of Fi. "Understand, I'm only asking out of concern for Master Seg, but what could you be wanting with the likes of Hap and Peg?"

"Permission to marry their son. What else?"

Tad and Seg gawked at her.

"That was a joke, gentlemen. Master barkeep, I can appreciate your concern. Here I am, a City girl here for who-knows-what, staying for only three weeks, and acting like I'm courting one of your residents, when we all know it would never work out."

There were so many things to dissect in that statement that Seg didn't even know where to begin. Fi plowed on before he could interject.

"The short answer is that I find Seg interesting, and, at the risk of torturing myself, would like to learn as much about him as I can. His parents seemed like a good place to start, though I'm sure his brother and sister also have a story or two to share."

"They do at that, along with Miss Val," Tad said. "She and Master Seg were quite a pair back in the day. Under different circumstances, I could have imagined..." Tad cleared his throat and looked down at the bar. "Well, things are what they are, and you can't change the past."

Fi's smile faltered. "No, you can't. The only thing we can do is to learn from our mistakes to make a better future. Wouldn't you say?"

"Aye, Miss Fi. Holtondome stands as a testament to that very philosophy. We believe to a one of us that technology belongs in the hands of the responsible few, so the rest of us don't make the same tragic mistakes as our ancestors. Freyja knows this planet can't take any more punishment than we've already given her."

Fi's smile slipped again. "Grand Chancellor Chang the First couldn't have said it better himself, master barkeep."

"Be sure to tell him so if you see him," Tad said with a chuckle.

"Mm." Fi withdrew her hand from Seg's, the last of her good humor evaporated, and stared at the bar. Seg found himself suddenly missing her dimples.

"Are you all right?"

"Mm, just hungry. I skipped dinner last night."

"As did you, Master Seg, if I'm not mistaken," Tad said. "I'll go help Nin so we can have your food out here on the double."

Once they were relatively alone, Seg leaned close to her. "What is it?"

"Nothing I want to talk about."

He wilted at her harsh dismissal. Fi seemed to catch her mistake and flashed him a half-smile, although it held none of the vibrance of her earlier mood.

"It's nothing to do with you, I promise. I really am looking forward to speaking with your parents to learn more about you."

Me, or my genetics?

It was an important distinction. Unfortunately, Seg was pretty sure he knew which she meant. He turned away.

Tad was right. One day with this City girl, and Seg was already acting as if they were in a relationship. Fi had made it clear from the start that any intimacy they shared would be casual, and even that would end when she left in three weeks. Any attachments he formed would only lead to heartache. He'd be a fool to believe otherwise, even if…

Even if we share something no one else does.

Seg grabbed a fork with his good hand and squeezed until the metal edges hurt his palm.

It was so damned unfair.

He was still stewing in silence a few minutes later when Val descended, followed closely by Cook. The glow on her face and his chipper whistling told Seg they had actually done what Tad believed he and Fi had, which did nothing to improve his mood.

Val faltered when she spied Seg and Fi, who were still sitting close together. Her face went ashen, as if she'd just caught her lover having an affair, but she quickly rallied.

"Good morning, Hero Number Two," she said to Seg with a smile.

"I'm number two, now, am I?"

"I… w-well, it was Cook's car that saved the day." She twisted her dress's waist tie tightly around her finger, just like she used to as a child when the tutor asked a question she didn't know the answer to.

"Just teasing, Val. You're right." Seg looked at Cook. "How are you feeling this morning, Hero Number One?"

Cook grimaced when he sat down. "Old. Serves me right for trying to keep up with young people."

Val blushed and cleared her throat. "A-and you, Seg?"

"Fine. It, ah… seems my leg wasn't as bad as Doc thought. I should be fit for work again in a few days."

"That's wonderful. Did you, um… sleep well?"

It took Seg a second to recognize their old code for, "Did you sleep together?"

"Not as well as I'd hoped," he said, confirming they hadn't. Of course, Val was the only person Seg had ever slept with, so he'd never answered otherwise. "You?"

"V-very well, thank you."

So they did sleep together.

"That's... ah, that's great," Seg said, feeling his gorge rise. "Sleep is important."

Fi coughed a laugh and looked away.

Of course Fi picked up on it. I can't seem to hide anything from her.

Fi turned back to him with a smirk and patted his hand. "Don't worry, you'll sleep better tonight. Better than you've ever slept before."

"How can you be so sure?" Val said tightly. "Maybe Seg doesn't *want* to sleep better."

Cook frowned. "What in the blazes are you two on about?"

"Oh, I think he does," Fi said, ignoring him. "I don't believe he's slept well in years, and it's amazing what a difference the right bed can make."

"And how would *you* know what sort of bed Seg needs? You've only just met!"

Fi arched an eyebrow. "Do you?"

"Yes! He needs one that's soft and warm, but not so soft that he can stay in it all day and wallow. Wide enough to catch him when he falls, but not so wide that it takes up the entire room to the exclusion of all else. But most of all, he needs something sturdy that won't fall out from under him in less than a month!"

"Mm, that's pretty specific. Sounds like you already have the perfect bed in mind for him."

"I..." Val squeezed Seg's injured hand so hard that a shooting pain made him cry out. She gasped when she realized what she'd done and backed away. "Sorry, I... I'm going to skip breakfast this morning. I need to freshen up before the Traders arrive. Excuse me." She turned and fled up the stairs.

Seg sighed. "Why did you have to go and rile her up?"

"I couldn't help it," Fi said with a giggle—the first sound he'd heard from her befitting her apparent age. "She was too tempting a target. Are you two really the same age?"

"Near enough."

"Mm. I don't have to translate any of that exchange for you, do I?"

"Nope."

Fi glanced across him to Cook. "Or you?"

"Nah. I've known she was sweet on the kid since our ride back from

Appledome."

Seg sighed again. "That makes one of us."

"Even with one eye, you should have spotted that a kilometer away."

"Wouldn't matter if I had."

"You'd better not mean because of me," Cook said. "Tomorrow, I'll be just a memory. A pleasant one, I hope, but that won't keep her bed warm. Not like you would."

"Don't..." Seg shook his head. "You don't understand. You don't live here. It's... complicated."

"Is this about her dead husband? Because he won't warm her bed, either."

Seg grimaced at the thought. "Look, it's not my story to tell." *Not really, anyway.* "If you want to know more, you'll have to ask her."

"No thanks. Too much drama for the short time I plan on sticking around. You might want to ask her, though, Fi."

"I plan to." Fi considered Seg carefully. "But I have a feeling hers is only part of the story."

Oh brother. "Just... be gentler with her than you are with me, okay? She's been through a lot."

"And you haven't?"

"Not compared to Val."

"Mm. Just what a close friend would say, even if it wasn't true."

"Or a lovesick pup," Cook muttered.

Fi shrugged.

"I'm not pining for her," Seg said through clenched teeth. "We were good friends once, but that ended a long time ago. She went her way, and I went mine. End of story."

"Went your way?" Cook gave a bitter laugh. "Where the fuck did you go, kid? To the other side of the tavern? If you're going to lie, at least make it convincing."

"Just *drop it,* all right!"

Seg was on his feet and heading for the stairs before his sense of propriety could stop him from making yet another blunder.

He didn't care. He needed to be away from them, away from any thoughts of how his life—and Val's—may have been better had he made different choices.

Things are what they are, and you can't change the past.

Seg clung to that half-truth all the way to the medical ward.

9

Val

VAL LET THE HOT WATER run down her hair and sooth her knotted shoulders.

Why had she said those things? How could that blasted woman have goaded Val into confessing her feelings for Seg?

And in front of him, no less!

She turned off the shower, toweled dry, and pulled her nicest outfit from the closet.

The answer was simple, of course. Val had been jealous of Fi since the minute she and Seg stepped out of the car together at Appledome. Latching onto Cook had been an impulse decision, a poor attempt to quell her heartache at seeing her teenage crush with another woman.

No, she isn't just another woman.

Fi was beautiful. Exotic. An educated City girl.

Val, on the other hand, perpetually had twigs stuck in her hair from harvesting fruit. She'd picked so many apples in her life that applesauce must surely run through her veins. How could she possibly compete?

She threw her towel on the bed with a growl.

She shouldn't *need* to compete! Seg was, well... Seg. His glassy white eye was a put-off to most women, but Val had known him since they were kids. To her, it was simply part of him, a part she liked just as much as the rest. That didn't stop her from staring on occasion—it *was* odd—but she'd never made fun of him for it, nor made him feel like less of a person. Not once.

How many others, including his own family, could claim the same?

Not a soul, Val was willing to bet.

She pulled the dress over her head and let it fall around her.

That had always been Val's claim to fame—her ace in the hole she believed would forever secure her place in Seg's heart.

But it wasn't true anymore. Fi treated him with the same respect—or lack thereof—that she treated everyone. City girl or not, Seg was intrigued by her, and becoming more so every hour they spent together.

Few understood that sympathy and conflict weren't what made Seg tick. He was curious, adventurous, and clever—just like Val. He needed new information, new things to explore, and new challenges to be happy. Fi fed those needs in the same ways Val always had by pushing his intellect to its limits, making him thrive under pressure, and glory in his victory.

Except Fi did it better. Much better.

Val attacked her long brown hair with a brush, yanking knots free that the shower and soap had inevitably failed to dislodge, and reveled in the pain.

The infernal woman was wise beyond her years. Val would need another lifetime at least to even compete.

It isn't fair.

The two things she prayed for was that Fi would leave earlier than planned, and that the exotic beauty hadn't made Val seem too ordinary to be interesting anymore to Seg.

With the last stubborn knot gone, Val tied her hair with a leather strap into a ponytail that ran down to the middle of her back.

The situation wasn't all Fi's fault, of course. Val attaching herself to Cook, if anything, had backfired. She'd originally hoped the ploy would make Seg jealous enough to pay more attention to her. Although she'd seen hints of territoriality, he'd been characteristically Seg and had instead seemed happy for her happiness.

What Val wanted was to be fought for—to be so important to Seg that he'd even risk insulting a guest to claim her as his. Just as she'd always thought of Seg as hers.

Val sat on the bed and hung her head.

She'd ruined any chance of that dream when she bedded Cook last night.

Worse, it wasn't until Seg had started paying attention to someone else that Val realized just how much she had taken their relationship—or *potential* relationship—for granted. The eight years since Nat had passed now seemed like a blur of excuses. It was never the right time to tell Seg how she'd felt about him since before he mysteriously distanced himself after their one, magical night as innocent teens, causing Val to instead marry someone else.

She'd recently begun wearing the medallion Seg had given her when they were younger, against his family's wishes. Val had hoped that wearing that precious symbol for everyone to see would be a strong enough signal to make clear her intentions to resume their relationship and take it to the next level.

Except I waited too long. Now his heart may soon belong to someone else.

A knock on the door made her sit bolt-upright.

"Yes?"

"May I come in?"

Val ground her teeth at Fi's voice, but she could hardly refuse a guest. She looked around to make sure the room she used to share with her husband wasn't an undue mess, checked the mirror to ensure her eyes weren't puffy from the few tears that had escaped during her wallowing, and nodded to herself.

"Of course, Miss Fi. Please enter."

Fi's sky-blue eyes quickly took in the room before settling on Val. "Sorry for goading you in the tavern. It was deliberate, inappropriate, and uncalled for. Especially from a guest."

"No, Miss Fi, my reaction surprised me as much as you," Val lied. "I don't know where it came from, so please don't read anything into it. Seg and I are just old acquaintances."

"Mm." Fi stepped over to a painting on the wall. "Your husband?"

"Yes, gone eight years ago now."

"I'm sorry."

"Thank you. I've done my grieving, however, and have moved on."

Fi studied her. "You didn't get along, did you?"

"I'm sure I don't know what you mean." Guest or not, Val's former married life was none of Fi's business.

Fi nodded as if she'd seen right through the deception. "I had a rocky marriage, too. It lasted years longer than it should have."

"Sorry to hear that, Miss Fi." Val bit her lip to keep from asking the question she burned to know.

Fi gave a mirthless laugh. "It's okay, you can ask me."

"Begging your pardon, then, how... why did your marriage end?"

"Those are two different questions. I'll answer both, starting with the ugliest. We ended bitterly. He cheated on me with someone I thought was a friend. I divorced him soon after, and we never spoke again."

"Aye, Miss," Val said, feeling hollow. "That would be reason enough to leave him."

Fi shrugged. "His cheating was just a symptom of a bigger problem. He shacked up with my friend because... because I couldn't give him the children he wanted."

"That's ludicrous! Absolutely absurd! He had no right to do that to you. None! It's not your fault, after all."

"No, but in this case, I share some of the blame. I knew I was infertile before we married, and I never told him. It was years before I mustered the courage to explain why our attempts to conceive had been in vain."

"Still... the right man would have understood, and loved you anyway."

"Maybe, but the right man would also have been someone who didn't want children above everything else. By not telling him, I denied the opportunity to discuss having children before we committed to spending the rest of our lives together. He could have chosen then, or maybe it would have been early enough for him to adjust to the idea of life without kids. Unfortunately, I'll never know."

Val wrung her hands, her insides churning in sympathy and relived pain. "Miss Fi... how did you deal with the news when you first discovered you couldn't conceive?"

"Not well. I wanted kids as badly as anyone in my vil—" Fi coughed and patted her chest. "As badly as any of my friends. Learning that I couldn't give birth to my own flesh and blood was... devastating."

"I know what you mean," Val said softly. She swiped her tears away with an angry growl. "How did you know I'm infertile? Did Seg tell you?"

"I didn't, and no, he never said a thing."

Val closed her eyes, cursing herself a fool. "So you laid a wide net with a variety of baits, sure that at least one would lure me in. Was any of your sob story even true?"

"Every word."

"Oh... Oh, I'm so sorry, Miss Fi! Sorry for your condition, and sorry for accusing you of lying."

"I'm used to both. Infertility is something you and I share, and assuming I have malicious intent is something you and Seg have in common. One of many things, it seems."

Val chuckled despite the heaviness in her chest. "Probably why we got along so well when we were younger. We were inseparable, especially when it came to mischief."

"Oh? Do tell."

"Where to even begin? There's so much to cover."

Fi flashed a rare, genuine smile that crinkled her eyes.

"Tell me everything."

* * *

Seg emerged from the medical ward clenching his fists, feeling no better than when he'd entered two hours earlier. A near-death experience had apparently not been enough to change Troy's sour demeanor. It had taken every gram of Seg's self-control to keep from punching his brother's broken arm.

"How is he?"

Cook's question startled him. The driver uncrossed his arms and pushed from the wall, where he had apparently been waiting.

"Making me question our decision to save him," Seg said.

"You two don't get along, eh?"

"Never have. He's always seen me as the runt of the family, incapable of even trivial responsibilities."

"He right?"

Seg glared at him, then sighed. "Maybe."

"So you act out and do something stupid, proving him right, which makes him trust you less, makes you act out more, blah, blah, blah. No wonder you're so fucked up."

"You... you think so?"

"Yeah, but it's nothing that can't be fixed. I've seen guys older than you, more messed up than you, who pulled their lives out of the gutter and made something of themselves. And let me tell you, if those jerkos could do it, you've got no excuse."

"Thanks, Cook. That's encouraging, and at the same time... not."

"Wasn't meant to be on either account. I'm a driver, not a life coach."

"So why are you here?"

"Fi is still holed up in Val's room. I got tired of drinking alone, so I came to pester you."

"Wait, Fi is... where?"

"Don't tell me those thunderclaps messed with your hearing," Cook said. "Val's. Room. Probably talking about you."

"Or you."

"Wouldn't that be something? I could go for a threesome." He stretched with a wince and rubbed his hip. "Tomorrow."

"I'm sure they'll be disappointed."

"Yeah, especially since you aren't running on all cylinders, either."

"All what?"

"Pre-Fall expression. Means your one working hand probably wouldn't be enough to—"

"I caught the meaning, thanks."

"Good. Never sure what I have to explain to who these days."

"To *whom*."

"Whatever, grammar Nazi. And don't ask me what a Nazi is, either."

Seg crossed his arms. "I have to say, you're doing a great job so far."

"Huh?"

"*Pestering* me."

"Now is that any way to talk to a guest?"

Seg blushed. He started to stammer an apology, but Cook waved him off with a chuckle.

"Just joking. Truth be told, I get tired of all the niceties. You're fun because I can make you slip. Feels more genuine."

"Do me a favor and don't tell Hap."

"Your dad?"

Seg nodded.

"'Hap'? You two don't get along or something?"

Yep, we're definitely past host-guest propriety. "No, it's a… a status thing. My family has the cleanest lineage tracing back to Thorn Holton in all Holtondome. Hap's the oldest in our household, which kind of puts him in charge."

"Your dad's the head honcho around here?" Cook shook his head.

"What?"

"Even *with* a blind eye, I don't see how in the blazes you don't have girls clamoring all over you. Must be doing something seriously wrong, kid."

"My biggest mistake was not being first-born," Seg said.

"Let me guess. Troy?"

"Yeah, though it's too bad, because I think Jen is a better leader. She's tough as nails, but fair. Troy is too temperamental to…"

Seg's mouth fell open at a sudden thought.

Is that why Troy was supposed to die? So Jen could lead instead?

Did I accidentally screw Holtondome's future?

"What is it, kid? Leg bothering you?"

"No, it's… it's nothing." Seg took a deep breath, but the knot in his stomach remained. "Let me ask you something. Say you had a choice of saving someone's life, someone you were pretty sure would only make everyone else's life more miserable if they survived. Would that be reason enough to… to *not* save them?"

Cook whistled low. "I may need another drink if you're going to go all deep on me. Guess it depends on how sure you were, and if we're talking annoying-miserable or hot-poker-in-the-eye miserable. Is your brother really that bad?"

"I-I'm not talking about Troy!"

"Kid, you can't follow a concrete statement up with a nearly identical hypothetical and expect me to not connect the dots. I thought you were a hell of a lot smarter than that. And it was a legitimate question. Is he the kind of person who needs killing?"

"That's a horrible way to put it."

"I'm not saying you have to, or that if you say 'yes' I'm going to walk in there and snuff him out. But now that thought's in your head, and it's going to stay there until you resolve it. Best to set yourself straight before the situation presents itself again and you make a rash, *wrong* decision."

Seg put his face in his hands. "Is this conversation really happening?"

"You started it, kid. Better to bounce it off the guy who won't be here tomorrow than one of your rural rumor mongers."

"You're really leaving today?"

"As soon as I say a proper goodbye to Val," Cook said. "Have to pay the bills somehow."

"I wish we could pay to retain your services. You're... refreshing."

"After a lifetime in a dome with the same families, I imagine anyone who isn't a resident would be. Now, stop changing the subject."

"Well..."

Seg flushed at his own hesitation. The answer should have been an instant "no," but his conversation with Fi last night made him wonder. That deaths could be predicted at all hinted at a pattern to existence—or a plan. The problem was, seeing *only* someone's death coming wasn't enough to make a decision. He couldn't see the long-term effects their survival might have beyond his own, usually wrong intuition.

Or is that enough?

Had some power-that-be deemed him worthy to judge whether people lived or died? It was a weighty responsibility that Seg frankly didn't want.

It also wasn't relevant to Cook's question.

"No," Seg said after more consideration. "He's a jerk, but he's also capable of good things. If I had to choose, I'd give him the benefit of the doubt."

"Great, now let's hope you never have to decide again."

I'll say.

Cook pulled the small rectangular screen from his pocket and frowned at the indecipherable symbols. "Damn."

"What? Another storm?"

"No. Traders will be here in about two minutes, which means I probably won't get to say goodbye to Val until they leave. Guess I'd better settle in for the afternoon."

Seg was pleasantly surprised the idea of leaving without saying goodbye hadn't even entered the conversation. One-night-stand or not, Val would have been hurt, and she'd already suffered enough for one lifetime.

"If Fi's still occupied, I'd better see if Jen needs any help setting up the grain stall," Seg said. "Coming?"

"Might as well."

Seg nodded, feeling relieved. Val being with Fi meant the host responsibility for Cook's comfort now fell on Seg. Still, his guilt over roping Cook into helping at the stall didn't outweigh the uselessness he'd felt since Cook and Fi's arrival. Tending guests didn't yield harvests or put food on the table.

Jen, unsurprisingly, had everything well in hand when they arrived.

"Good day to you, Mr. Cook," she said with a tip of her head.

Like everyone, Jen was dressed in her finest for the Traders' arrival: a deep-blue blouse with a fine, white-laced collar, puffed at the shoulders, and a long skirt that billowed at her hips, creating an hourglass figure around her otherwise trim body.

"I trust my brother's hospitality is not so decrepit that he's convinced our distinguished guest to assist with today's trades?"

"Not so, my lady." Cook surprised Seg with a formal bow to his sister. "His hospitality skills have been top-notch. I'm just here to kill some time until my departure this afternoon."

"Ah." Her brown eyes lingered on Seg with unspoken concern: *Where's Val, and is she all right?*

"Val is—"

"Right here," Val said.

Her long skirt stirred a dust trail in her haste to reach them. Unlike Jen, Val's voluptuous figure needed no embellishments. A tight, low-cut bodice showed enough cleavage to make Seg blush and look away...

...where he spied Fi a dozen paces behind. Her long dress shimmered of fine silk and clung to her modest figure, somewhere between Jen and Val's in curviness, but magnified by her height. The bright-yellow material and her enchanting eyes reminded Seg of the brilliant sun and clear blue skies they'd talked about under the tree in Appledome.

With a gasp, Seg remembered to breathe.

"Do you like it?"

Val's question snapped his gaze to her. She twirled in a circle like a teenager at her first dance.

"Well?"

Seg scratched his head. "Oh, you're, um…"

"A vision, my dear," Cook said. He caught her hand and planted a kiss on her knuckles. "The Traders couldn't possibly bring enough to match the worth of your beauty."

Val tore her eyes from Seg and blinked at Cook in stunned silence. "W-why thank you, Mr. Cook, even if I daresay your assessment is a touch exaggerated."

"Not if I were the Trader."

She blinked again. A smile spread across her face, one of genuine delight that Seg had long forgotten her capable of. One that brought him joy to see.

"I… I suppose it's good I'm not for sale, then. It would be an uncomfortable ride back to the City in your trunk."

"Don't be so sure. You haven't seen my trunk."

Val laughed, a beautiful, melodious sound that filled Seg's heart. She proffered an arm. Seg had to wrestle a bout of jealousy when he realized she hadn't proffered it to him.

"Care to accompany me on a stroll through the stalls, Mr. Cook?"

"With pleasure."

Seg watched them saunter away with a bitter taste in his mouth. They seemed so happy together.

A light touch on his injured hand snapped his attention to Fi.

"How does it feel this morning?"

Seg gave his fingers an experimental flex. "Stiff, but no pain. Thank you again, Miss Fi."

"Mm. Just remember to take it easy today. You're officially off Trader duty." She arched an eyebrow at Jen. "Right?"

"Of course, Miss Fi. Seg isn't so indispensable that Holtondome can't survive without him for a day or two. We might even see a boost in productivity without him constantly breaking our vehicles."

"I'd like to think I fix more than I break," Seg said.

"I've never measured, so I'll have to take your word." Jen turned a bemused smile on Fi. "In addition to a hauler racer, Seg fancies himself a mechanic in-as-much as we're allowed to tinker."

"So I've just learned, among other things."

Seg raised his eyebrows. "Other things? What else did Val tell you about me?"

"Everything, I think." Fi turned her enchanting eyes on Jen. "After the Traders leave, I'd love to steal a few hours of your valuable time to learn more about you, too."

"Me? Sad to say an undramatic marriage and almost-teenaged twin boys make my history more hectic, but less interesting, than my rogue brother's."

"Less interesting to some people. Molding two energetic boys into gentlemen sounds like quite an adventure to me."

"An adventure I may not live to regret, unfortunately."

"You and every other mother with boys their age." Fi nodded. "That settles it, then. You need a night off. What do you say to an evening of after-dinner dessert and adult conversation?"

"Oh, I don't know. My husband—"

"Will survive. And if he's really that terrified of taking the kids for even a single evening, then the experience will do him good."

"Don't forget your promise to Tad," Seg said.

Fi raised her eyebrows.

Seg sighed. "The barkeep. Tad."

"Oh. No, I haven't forgotten. There's time for both."

But you forgot his name easily enough. Seg was tempted to test her promise of not forgetting his, but it would be petty, so he dismissed the idea. *Besides, there will be opportunities later.*

"Well, when you put it that way," Jen said. "Consider it a date."

"I do." Fi gently patted Seg's injured hand. "You'll survive this evening without me?"

That answers the question of whether I was invited. "Yes, Miss Fi. I'll be fine." *Besides, with Cook leaving this afternoon, Val might need company.*

Fi winked as if she'd read his mind, then turned with everyone else at a rumble of vehicles from the nearby western dome entrance.

The Traders had arrived.

10

Traders

THE ENTIRE DOME GATHERED TO watch the dusty caravan vehicles drive in through the western entrance. One by one, the long, brushed-steel busses parked in organized rows, angled so their wares could be easily unpacked into vendor stalls that would be set up alongside the vehicle itself.

A middle-aged woman in loose, colorful fabric stepped out of the lead bus. Golden tassels shimmied all along her arms and legs in a gaudy display typical of Traders.

Hap approached her with open arms, his formal long coat trailing like a grand cape. While not as ostentatious as the Trader's outfit, it was certainly more regal and commanding.

"Holtondome welcomes and protects you, brave travelers." Like his attire, Hap's usually gentle voice carried a weight of authority over the murmuring crowd. "I'm Hap Holton, at your service, and shall ensure your needs are attended to during your stay."

"We accept your shelter with gratitude, Hap Holton, and formally acknowledge that the requirements laid down by the Laws of Hospitality have been fulfilled. I'm Gina Teladar of Teladar Traders, here to exchange goods, if you're willing and in need." Gina's voice was deeper than Seg expected, almost sensual, but held just as much authority as Hap's.

"We are. Which Keepers accompany you this season?"

A man with neat red hair and freckles stepped forward. He was dressed in neither Fed armor nor the gaudy colors of the Traders, but simple tan overalls with the telltale high thread count of City-manufactured clothing.

"I'm Jonah Whittaker, Mr. Holton. My crew and I are here on behalf of our City, which in compliance with the Pact shall not be named, to fulfill the technical services negotiated in exchange for Holtondome's fine goods."

"Welcome, Jonah and company," Hap said. "Holtondome extends its protection to you, and thanks you for sacrificing the simple life to bear the burden of technology. Our harvest this season is... not what we'd hoped, but I'm sure we'll find an equitable arrangement, especially for our ailing hauler."

Hap shot a half-smile at Seg before returning his attention to the guests.

"And who from the Federated Nations have you brought to ensure fair and equal trade, and to verify Holtondome holds to the Pact, sworn to by our ancestors to free us of the corrupted thinking and technology that so nearly destroyed our species and crippled our beloved planet?"

Gina gestured to a man in polished white body armor. "Captain Bharta and his company have braved the journey to oversee the proceedings, serve as inquisitors of the Pact, and, if necessary, administer justice."

Bharta stepped into the center of the three-person circle, as per tradition. He removed his matching white helmet and visor, releasing a cascade of silver hair that hung neatly to his neck, and smiled at each in turn.

"On behalf of the State of Wyoming and the Federated Nations, I wish to thank you for your parts in ensuring humanity's continued survival. I stand as an instrument in these proceedings to maintain the delicate balance envisioned by Grand Chancellor Chang the First, necessary not only for our recovery from the brink of oblivion, but to continue this era of peace unprecedented in humanity's long history of violence and war."

Hap nodded reverently. "Welcome also, Captain Bharta. Holtondome extends its protection to you and the noble men and women in your company. We swear to abide by your decisions in accordance with the law."

"So noted."

"Teladar Traders also swear to abide by your decisions in accordance with the law," Gina said.

"So noted."

"We also swear to abide by your decisions in accordance with the law," Jonah said.

"So noted." Bharta spread his arms and gestured to everyone around. "It is my pleasure, then, to declare that trading may officially commence!"

The floor erupted into action. Residents surged toward the caravan, where Traders were setting up their stalls with practiced efficiency. Shirts, dresses, shoes, tools, exotic spices, fragrant soaps, colorful fruits and vegetables, cured meats, oils, liquors pungent and sweet, fine wines...

Traders haggled their wares against experienced Holtondome negotiators for bushels of apples, pork products, sacks of wheat, grain alcohol, and, of course, baked goods of every variety.

The only things not traded openly were mechanical parts, repair services, and medicine, all of which Holtondome desperately needed.

Knowing Holtondome's prosperity was in Hap's capable hands, Seg started to ask what Fi wanted to see first, only to find her weaving after Hap and their guests. He hurried to catch up.

"Captain Bharta, Gina, Jonah," Hap said with his characteristically warm smile. "May I introduce my daughter, Jen. She'll be assisting with negotiations this season."

Gina raised her eyebrows. "Is Troy well?"

"Well enough. An accident yesterday landed him in the medical ward, but Doc Ven says he'll be fine."

"Glad to hear on both counts. The boy was ruthless last year. You've taught him a little too well."

"Don't think you'll have it any easier with me," Jen said.

Gina flashed a charming smile, bordering on flirtatious. "I look forward to it, my dear."

"As do I," Bharta said. He took Jen's hand and began to raise it to his lips, but she stopped him short with a strength wrought from a lifetime of field labor, and wrestled him into a firm handshake.

"Likewise, Captain."

Bharta's chuckle held little amusement. "Of course." He pulled out of her grip and cleared his throat. "The long drive has left me as parched as the barren countryside. I don't suppose we could continue over drinks?"

"Our taverns are always open to you," Hap said, and led them upstairs.

Fi moved to follow, but Seg caught her arm.

"Negotiations are usually conducted only between the faction heads."

"Yes, I know."

"Then why are you following?"

"Because they didn't say I couldn't. Have you ever participated in negotiations before?"

"No, that's usually Troy's area. This will be Jen's first time at the table."

"Then you should come, too. You might find it educational."

Her tone left no doubt in Seg's mind that another lesson awaited him, and that there would be no talking her out of it. With a sigh, he followed her upstairs.

Hap, Jen, Bharta, and Jonah were just settling at a table. Hap shot Seg a quizzical look when he and Fi approached, but didn't shoo them away when they slid a table and chairs over to join the conversation.

Hap gestured to Fi. "Lady and gentlemen, it's my honor to introduce our est—"

"Call me Fi," she said over him. She extended a hand to each, ending with Bharta. "A pleasure, Captain."

"The pleasure is mine," he said, not taking his gaze from hers. "If I may be so forward, your eyes are quite striking."

"They aren't my only fine quality, to be sure."

Bharta glanced at her green-tinged hair and nodded with a weak smile.

Hap recovered quickly from Fi's redirection, as confused as Seg why she had prevented him from introducing her as a guest. "And this is my other son, Seg. He's... an unexpected but welcome addition to the negotiation circle."

"Pleased to meet you," Seg said, shaking hands with everyone. As with most people, their effort to avoid staring at Seg's blind white eye was almost comical.

Bharta eventually dropped his gaze, which landed on Seg's left arm. "That's quite a long suture you have there, son."

Seg bristled at the "son" comment, but decided to let it slide. "Same accident as Troy. We were both lucky."

"Ah." Bharta glanced at Seg's white eye and nodded, as if his impaired vision explained it. Gina cut in before Seg could set him straight.

"So, you've had a smaller harvest than usual this season?"

"To put it mildly," Jen said. "And to compound things, a mechanical failure in one of our haulers exposed a portion of our wheat harvest to yesterday's lightning storm. It's one of the many reasons we're glad for Mr. Whittaker's presence."

"Indeed," Hap said. "One of our rain collectors is also in dire shape, along with six solar panels, two storage batteries, and a host of other system failures across the dome that we'll be happy to point you to."

"Of course, Mr. Holton," Jonah said. "My team is here to ensure that the Keepers of Prosperity, such as Holtondome, can thrive in our devastated land without worry of technological corruption."

"We of Holtondome thank you for carrying that burden in sacrifice of prosperity, and promise to keep food on your tables."

Gina was still staring at Jen. "How much of your wheat crop was affected by the lightning storm?"

"One-fifth."

"Oh. Regrettable, but not crippling. If memory serves, that should still leave you with, what... a hundred tons?"

Jen straightened. "Sixty-two."

"Sixty..." Gina paled. "What about apples?"

"Seven hundred and ninety."

"But... that's less than *half* of your normal yield! I hope your pork fared better."

Jen's eye twitched, but she otherwise maintained her cool. "We're down from two hundred tons last season to... to fifty-three."

"One-*quarter?* How is that even possible?"

"Pigs eat apples and wheat—and lots of it. We slaughtered more than usual to compensate for the reduced harvest. Lower numbers mean slower breeding. It will take two quarters at least to regain our normal yield, assuming our crops recover sufficiently to support them."

Gina just stared, her mouth open, then looked at Bharta. "That's two-fifths of the expected goods, Captain. I... I'm not sure how to proceed."

Hap leaned forward. "What's the problem? It's low, but not unprecedented."

"No," Bharta said, plucking at a gloved finger, "but it's ill-timed."

"Trade value of medicines are at an all-time high," Gina said. "Repair services, as well as the necessary parts and materials, are even higher."

Jen smacked the table, her cool façade broken. "Higher? *Higher?* We didn't have enough food last time to acquire the medicines we needed, which left us with shortages and a ten percent higher mortality rate than the quarter before. Now you're saying we'll get even *less?*"

Gina held up her hands. "I don't set market values, my little desert flower. I only facilitate fair and equitable trade between parties. *All* parties. You're in a tough spot, but so are others. We must all make do, my dear."

Jen went as stiff at the "my dear" comment as Seg had at "son," but continued in a professional tone. "Mrs. Teladar—"

"*Miss,*" Gina said with a wink.

"Apologies." To her credit, Jen didn't blush at the obvious advance. "Miss Teladar, market values be as they may, I think you'll find the quality of our goods a cut above the rest. Certainly enough to offset the difference in demand."

"Quality can only compensate so far."

"But we have nothing else to trade! I..." Jen took a deep breath and lowered her voice, something Seg wished she'd done when they were growing up instead of losing her temper at him. "Miss Teladar, we need that medicine. Surely we can come to an arrangement."

Gina folded her hands on the table. "You're pretty, Miss Holton—"

"*Mrs.* Holton."

"A shame. In any case, demand is what it is. The only flex point you have is with Mr. Whittaker's services, I'm afraid."

"Oh."

Jen turned to Jonah, but Gina recaptured her attention with a throaty laugh.

"You still have to go through the Traders, dear girl, to ensure fair market values are observed."

Jonah nodded. "Perhaps if you list the parts and repairs you need, Mrs. Holton, we'll see which can wait until next season."

"Thank you, Mr. Whittaker."

By the time Jen and Jonah had finished discussing the long list, the grim picture was clear for everyone. Even excluding non-critical repairs, Holtondome's technical needs this season were as dire as Seg had feared.

"All told," Jen said, "how many medical supplies would that buy us?"

Gina closed her eyes for a second. "Twenty."

"We're four thousand strong, Miss Teladar, all performing strenuous labor. That will hardly last us a fortnight. We need eighty at least."

"Eighty!" Gina shook her head with a chuckle. "Captain Bharta would put me in irons for unfair trading, and Mr. Whittaker's City would never deal with me again. I can't give them away for so little. I need more."

Jen's face reddened, but her voice remained cool. "I'm afraid you have us at an unfair disadvantage. The remaining repairs are necessary for our survival. Delaying any would cost even more lives, hamper production, and put us even further behind next quarter, where we will undoubtedly need as much medicine again."

"Yes, it does seem a downward spiral." Gina stared at her, but remained silent.

Jen growled—a low sound that raised the hairs on Seg's neck with memories of it being a precursor to a thorough tongue-lashing. "What do you suggest, then, Miss Teladar?"

"Well, there are… other forms of compensation." Gina cast a brief but suggestive glance at Fi before returning to Jen with a smile. "But apart from that, I suggest you get creative."

Seg stared at Gina, open mouthed, and then at Bharta. Surely this was against some ethical regulation. The Feds always seemed to have thousands of them at the ready, but the captain simply watched the ludicrous exchange unfold. When Seg could stand no more, he leaned forward to object.

Fi cut him off. "How about this…" She rose from her chair like a stalking panther, sashayed to Gina under her appreciative eye, and leaned over the table until she was so close they were practically kissing.

"You. Get. *Nothing.*"

Gina's leer vanished. "What?"

"Nothing—as in the opposite of the something you're Pact-bound to procure from Providers like Holtondome so everyone else can eat."

The Trader's surprise melted into a soft, purring laugh. "You can't do that, my pretty. Holtondome wouldn't last the season."

"We can and we could. Never underestimate the will to survive."

Gina reddened. "Be careful what you wish for, my exotic beauty. With a single order I could—"

"Have everyone pack up and leave, yes, we know. No medicine, repairs, or other trade goods for Holtondome. And zero—zip, zilch, nada!—apples, pork, or wheat for you."

"This is where I must intercede," Captain Bharta said. A tick of his cheek was the only betrayal that anything was amiss. "Refusal of a Provider settlement to engage in trade negotiations is an explicit violation of the law—Section 822.5.323.a, to be precise—subject to punishment up to and including—"

"How considerate of you to quote the law to those who have no ability to verify them," Fi said, "nor access to the mountain of text they would need to refute your allegation."

"It is not an allegation, for this is not a court. Here I have full authority to interpret the law *and* execute justice."

"In the field, yes. But if called into question, your decisions are subject to review by a council of Adjudicators, where sentencing may be passed not only for the accused transgression, but retroactively for any misconduct unearthed in the inevitable investigations that follow."

Seg glanced at Jen, who raised her eyebrows. Apparently, this was new information for her, too.

Hap jumped to his feet. "Miss Fi! I think you've taken this far en—"

Fi waved him down without taking her gaze from Bharta. Her height put them at eye-level. "As for 822.5.323.a, the intent of that section is to prevent hoarding and market gouging of necessities, such as food, clothing, and, yes, medicine."

Bharta glared at her. "You do realize you've all but admitted to a violation of the Provider Information Protection Act, and possibly the Literacy Laws as well? We needn't debate that here, for the truth will be revealed during the inquiries, but you've also conveniently made my point. Refusal to trade, in this instance, is hoarding."

"Let's explore that, shall we? Section 822.4.51 defines hoarding as 'the withholding of goods necessary for the prosperity of others in excess of that required for the withholding party's survival.'"

Bharta shook his head. "Miss Fi, I'll give you one last chance to stop this heresy, and I'll pretend I didn't just hear you quoting that which you should not have access to."

"Literacy is forbidden to the Providers, Captain, as is outside information not directly pertinent to the Provider's welfare. This exchange clearly demonstrates the relevancy of these sections to Holtondome."

"In condemning you, yes, I agree." Bharta looked at Hap. "You may wish to rein in your delegate before she buries herself and the rest of Holtondome deeper than my ability to excavate."

To Seg's disappointment, Hap nodded. Jen started to object, but a stern look from Hap quieted her.

"Miss Fi, I sincerely appreciate your passionate defense of Holtondome," Hap said. "But I've successfully negotiated on our behalf for twenty-three years running, just like my mother before me, my grandfather before her, and four generations of Holtons before him, leading back to Thorn himself. Now, if you would be so kind, I would hate to keep you from the excitement of the trading floor any longer than I already have."

Seg expected another skillful twist of words from her, but Fi merely shrugged.

"As you will. I spotted an exquisite Damascus paring knife on the way up that would make a nice addition to my collection."

Gina had the audacity to take Fi's hand and kiss her knuckles which, unlike Jen, Fi allowed without resistance.

"It's been a pleasure, my beauty," Gina said. "I hope you have more luck negotiating for your coveted knife, assuming it's still available, than you've had in your endeavors for Holtondome."

"The pleasure was all yours, I'm sure." Fi wiped her knuckles dramatically across her blouse. "As for the knife... if it's no longer available, I'll just track down the buyer and negotiate another trade."

"If they're willing to part with it, of course."

"They will. I rarely lose, miss Trader."

"This seems to be an off-day for you, then."

"Mm."

Seg rose to follow when she started away. Fi pressed him back down into his chair with a friendly but firm pat on the shoulder, then went downstairs without a backward glance.

"Forgive my lack of hospitality," Hap said to their guests. "You must be parched. I'll be right back with refreshments, then perhaps we can re-examine this situation from a fresh perspective."

"Of course, Mr. Holton," Bharta said. "Thank you."

Jen wrestled a smile with visible effort. "So, Miss Teladar... how was your journey? Not too harrowing, I hope?"

"Not at all. Two minor breakdowns on the way, but with so many vehicles over such distance, a few mechanical problems are to be expected. And you? Do you have children?"

"Yes, two wonderful sons who..."

Seg let their small talk fade to the background. His mind raced with the sudden responsibility placed squarely on his shoulders.

This was another lesson. Fi had laid the puzzle pieces on the table, and it was now up to Seg to assemble them.

He reflected on what he'd learned so far. This was his first participation in harvest negotiations, which made him a poor judge, but it seemed to be going badly.

The Pact, he'd always been led to believe, was crafted to prevent exactly this scenario, yet here Holtondome was with its proverbial back to the wall. Despite Fi's claim, Seg had his doubts about Holtondome surviving to the next season without medicine or repairs. He was equally sure that Holtondome refusing to give its excess goods would be catastrophic to the surrounding domes and Cities, although he had no evidence, which made the situation bad for everyone.

What was he missing?

Fi quoted those specific laws for a reason.

Why she hadn't revealed her status as a non-resident of Holtondome was another mystery. The truth would come out during the census, when every resident was accounted for, and if not there, then in an inquiry session with almost any resident, which made it even harder to understand why she'd try to hide it.

Seg shook his head. He could ask her about that later, but he wouldn't be able to re-negotiate with Gina once the deal was made. He had to focus.

Fi had done several things: Offered nothing to trade, which, to Seg's knowledge, had never been done in Holtondome's history; clarified the *intent* of the anti-hoarding section quoted by Bharta; and laid out the definition of hoarding itself, Seg assumed, exactly as written.

She had also revealed something he still wasn't sure she was allowed to.

An Adjudicator council...

The inner workings of the Federated Nations were intentionally obfuscated from Provider domes to prevent contamination of their sworn, simple lives. However, Bharta hadn't refuted her claim that his decisions could be called for review by an independent committee.

Could a Provider dome initiate that call? How would they even go about it?

Maybe the mechanics don't matter.

The threat alone might be enough to keep Bharta from making unjust rulings.

Seg's mind was still churning when Hap returned with a pitcher of apple juice and a tray of five wooden cups. He sat next to Jen and gave Gina a warm smile, though his eyes were still troubled.

"Now, Miss Teladar, I'm sure I don't need to highlight Holtondome's exemplary production record," Hap said. "Even in the face of two major disasters, we've never failed to provide for the Federated Nations."

"Your reputation is not in dispute," Gina said. "But I can't fabricate demand when the products you're bartering for are in even higher demand."

Jen swallowed hard. "What if... what if we offered twenty-five percent more trade goods next quarter, without compensation?"

"You're now talking credit, my dear, which was outlawed with currency over four hundred years ago."

"But o-our reputation... you know we'll deliver."

"I don't know that any more than you do," Gina said. "Just like I can't predict what the demand for medicines will be. Should I speculate wrong, I would be robbing someone else of their livelihood, which would destroy Teladar Traders' good reputation, and possibly sentence our own people to a slow death by starvation."

"The only other place we can flex would be agricultural vehicles," Jen said. "One of our haulers, the one with the wheat, took two direct lightning hits. I'm no expert, but it's probably beyond repair, and was old to begin with. We'll need a new one."

Gina blew a long sigh. "A new hauler..."

"In addition to new blades for two of our wheat harvesters, both of which need significant repairs, and another hauler that may not last until next quarter. Sacrificing any of those areas will significantly reduce our production."

"As would an unhealthy population," Seg said. "Without medicine, we'll have fewer able hands, and will need more people to care for them."

It was a perfect storm. The more Seg thought about it, the more he started to panic. Medicines were necessary not only for spot treatments, but for preventing the spread of illness. Without them, the chances of a debilitating disease sweeping through Holtondome increased dramatically, which could all but halt production, not to mention cost many, many lives.

"It's a tough situation, I agree, but..."

Gina spread her hands and looked at Bharta, who shrugged.

"Even if I wanted to bend the rules, which would be unfair," Bharta said, "as Miss Fi so rightly pointed out, my decisions are subject to review to prevent exactly that sort of corruption. I'm sorry, but my hands are tied."

Jen's expression darkened. She cast a thunderous glance at the stairs Fi had retreated down, then her eyes became sorrowful.

"I'm sorry, Father, I'm at a loss. Even foregoing equipment repairs and the hauler replacement may not cover all the medicine we need. Sacrificing either one will reduce our output next quarter. Offering any more tonnage would eat into our reserves. Unless the market takes a drastic turn in the next few months..."

Hap nodded slowly. "We can't see the future, so we must do what's right in the present—and that's saving our people." He put a gentle hand on her shoulder. "We'll just have to hope the vehicles hold, and we can always tighten our belts for a while."

Her mouth quivered, and Seg knew why. Vehicles were their only means of keeping up with the stringent production demands necessary to keep Holtondome afloat in the trade market. Without vehicle maintenance, the problems they had would grow worse, and that didn't account for breakdowns in vehicles with problems they *weren't* aware of. Worse, less food meant lower morale, lower energy, slower recovery from illness, and even lower productivity.

Holtondome's production next quarter might be its worst ever—possibly too low to sustain its populace.

Too low to sustain our populace...

"All right, Miss Teladar," Jen said in a shaky voice. "W-we're prepared to offer—"

"Nothing!" Seg said, the pieces slamming together in an outburst that made everyone jump. "Not an Odin-blessed thing."

Bharta sighed. "We've been through this, young man. Section 822.5.323.a states—"

"That refusal of a Provider settlement to engage in trade negotiations is illegal. We're not refusing, Captain Bharta. You've heard our offer."

"'Nothing' isn't an offer! It's a blatant act of hoarding, and punishable —"

"By what? Refusing to allow us to trade with the Federated Nations?"

"Yes, Seg," Jen said through grated teeth. "If we're found in violation of the Pact, that would be *exactly* within his rights, which would basically be a death sentence for us. Sit. *Down.* Let me handle—"

"It's a death sentence anyway you look at it," Seg said, keeping his eyes on Bharta. "If we don't get the medicine we need, people will die. If we can't repair our equipment, we won't have a prayer of meeting *next* quarter's needs, and people will die. If we trade our reserves, we'll run out of food, and people will die."

Seg stood and leaned on the table. "Captain Bharta, the definition of hoarding is 'the withholding of goods necessary for the prosperity of others *in excess* of that required for the withholding party's survival.'

"Without functioning equipment, we're going to be doing a lot more manual labor in order to even come close to the same productivity, which means much higher food consumption. By my reckoning, we're going to need to sock away *every scrap* of food to ensure the people who don't die from lack of medicines have enough food to stay healthy and productive to even give us a shot at breaking even next quarter. Wouldn't you agree, Jen?"

Jen's eyes had grown wider with every sentence. "Yes, I... I believe you're right."

"So you see, Captain Bharta, we are *not* in violation of the law because we're offering precisely what we can spare in excess of our survival needs, which is nothing."

Bharta reddened, but his expression remained neutral. "As I believe I made clear, interpretation of the law is delegated to me, and I do not agree with this... *technicality.* Holtondome must offer goods for trade, or be found guilty of violating the Pact."

"That's your prerogative. But I promise you, we *will* be calling your judgment for review by the Adjudicators."

Bharta slowly stood until they were eye level. A smile crept on his lips. "Tell me, *boy*, how will you call for this review when you have no means of communication? Do you even know where the nearest City is? How would you get there if you did?" His triumphant smile widened. "Even if you somehow made it, leaving a Provider dome is illegal. You'd be arrested on sight. Or worse."

"We have a means, Captain. A legal one." He glanced at Gina. "One that might also help us validate this so-called medicine and repair service shortage."

Gina's eyes narrowed. "You're lying."

Hap, who had gone pale, shook his head. "As you'll soon discover, we have guests from the City who, even with the restrictions placed upon them by the Pact, have already earned a place of honor among us. Asking a few questions about current affairs *directly relating* to trade with Holtondome would compromise neither of our oaths, and I'm certain those people would help us call for a review."

"Certain, are you?" Bharta's smile turned frightening. "You know, I do this same routine with all the domes. Why not change the schedule up a bit?" He straightened. "Mr. Holton, please assemble your residents. We'll begin with inquiries this season instead of trading, followed by the census. If after that you've decided you *can* spare something to trade, negotiations will resume.

"But until such time, the caravans are now officially *closed* to the residents of Holtondome."

11

Insight

FI WAS WALKING AROUND A nearby caravan when Seg finally came downstairs, her attention on the patrons rather than the Traders themselves.

"How did it go?" she said without looking at him.

Seg watched an excited resident haggle his small collection of hand-carved applewood boxes for a skein of silk, apparently without success, and sighed.

"Bharta declared the caravans closed when I reiterated that we couldn't spare our harvest even for medicine."

"Mm."

Seg arched an eyebrow at her. "You're not surprised by either?"

"Should I be? You have ears, a head on your shoulders, and you used both."

"And I managed to take away Holtondome's biggest joy."

The haggling resident had added a fresh apple pie in a straw basket to his bid, which the merchant appeared to be considering.

"You think it was the wrong decision?" Fi said.

"I… No, I don't."

She nodded. "It must be hard for the rest of these Traders, too, having come all this way for nothing. How do you think they'll react?"

"Well… in their shoes, I'd be furious. Perishable wares they'd counted on unloading here may spoil by the time they reach the next dome. They also won't have the goods the next dome was counting on, putting them in a position where they might need to take a loss. The next dome, too, will be unhappy. If Bharta had kept the trading caravans open to the populace, they'd have something, at least, for the next stop."

"Mm. Seems as if the captain's decision made a bad situation worse." Fi touched his arm. "Walk with me?"

"Sure. Should we find Cook and go visit an ag dome? When word gets around, it's going to be downright depressing here, possibly ugly."

"You're not interested in seeing the results of your expert negotiations?"

"I am, but I assumed you wouldn't be."

Fi stared at him.

"...and there I go assuming again. Sorry, Miss Fi. One of these days I'll learn."

"Forgiven, because you made a hard decision and didn't back down. Now let's see what happens." Her bored tone made Seg suspect she already knew.

Just like everything, it seems, except...

"Miss Fi, please don't think me morbid for asking, but have you had any more... visions?"

Her enchanting eyes snapped to him. "No, have you?"

"Thankfully not." Seg looked around at the thousands of people gathered and sighed. "Seems strange. With everyone here, you'd think at least one of them would... you know."

"It's not as strange as you think. This is a trading floor, not a critical care ward. Only healthy people travel with the trade caravans, the Feds regularly screen their members for health defects, the Cities take good care of their citizens with advanced medical treatments, and Holtondome's elderly and infirmed would send family to trade on their behalf."

"Mm." Seg winced. He seemed to be imitating her more and more.

A smile twitched one side of her mouth. "Don't sound so disappointed. There will probably be opportunity to verify your visions before I leave. If you have one, tell me immediately."

"You too."

"That could invalidate the experiment. My visions are the scientific control, because they're real, and their boundaries are known. Yours are the variable. Telling you of my visions beforehand might accidentally contaminate the results."

"Oh. I... I suppose that makes sense," Seg said, even though he didn't like the idea of being kept in the dark.

"Mm."

To Seg's surprise, Fi hooked his arm, then led him through the trading floor throng. The thrill he normally felt was tainted because he knew it would shortly be called to an end. Combined with his mission of spotting for people who might soon die, Seg felt downright melancholy.

What would he do if he found someone? Confront them?

Excuse me, sir, but did you know you're about to die in a tragic harvester accident? Sorry to tell you, miss, but your next meal will be your last, because you're going to choke on a pork bone.

The more Seg thought about it, the less he wanted anything to do with these new visions.

People died. Period. If what Fi said was true, then their deaths might all be according to some larger plan, the tampering with which could produce dire results.

What, then, was the point of knowing, except to torture the knower?

Fortunately, he didn't spot any impending dooms during their stroll through the crowd. Seg even tried closing his good eye periodically to make sure he didn't miss anything, and relied on Fi to guide him. The spectacle startled several into giving him a wide berth and abhorrent looks. He ignored them, figuring his reputation could hardly fall lower than it already was, but Seg soon became the least of their concerns.

One by one, the trade caravans began packing up their wares. Fi stopped in front of a caravan who hadn't yet closed, although her attention seemed more on Seg than the Trader or patrons.

"…give you ten pork sausages for those jars of orange marmalade," a Holtondome man was saying.

The Trader started to reply, but a Fed in shiny white armor whispered something to him. With a nod, the Trader collected his marmalade jars from the table and began stacking them in a wooden box.

"Sorry, friend," the Trader said evenly. "Stall's closed."

The man blinked a few times before finding his tongue. "C-closed? Why?"

"Your leader has refused to trade goods this season."

"You must be mistaken," the man said with a laugh. "Holtondome has never missed a season. Never!"

"I only know what I'm told. Take it up with Captain Bharta, if you like, but for now, I've been ordered to close the stall." The Trader hoisted the box into his caravan, then began collecting a set of raspberry jams.

The man watched him with forlorn eyes. "Refused to trade? B-but… that would put us in violation of the Pact."

"So it seems."

"Hap would never be that stupid! There must be a mistake."

"Like I said, friend, not my call, but if it's true… Losing trade rights within the Federated Nations sounds like a quick way to die. You might want to talk some sense into your leader."

"He wouldn't put us in that position..." The man shook a finger at the box of marmalades. "Hold onto those. I'll be back once I've had a word with Hap. This is just a misunderstanding. You'll see."

"For the good of you and your children, I hope you're right. Best of luck, friend."

The man cast a last, longing look at his denied orange treasures, then stormed off toward the stairs. The Trader continued packing as if the exchange had never happened.

Seg shook his head. A sudden weight dragged his shoulders down. "This isn't good."

Fi captured his gaze and held it with eyes of purest blue. "Why?"

"What do you mean, 'Why'? You heard him. At this rate, there will be a full uprising in a matter of hours!"

She continued staring at him with seemingly infinite patience. He'd missed something. Something important.

Seg played the scene back in his mind, then again, but couldn't see anything but the Holtondome man's anger, and trouble coming for Hap.

What was Fi saying earlier about the Traders' reactions...?

It suddenly clicked.

"The Trader wasn't upset," Seg said. "The trade ban disrupts their livelihood, too. In his place, I would have at least tried to finish the bargain before packing up, but he didn't even blink. In fact..." He shook his head. "Never mind. I'm just being paranoid."

"Paranoia doesn't necessarily make you wrong. Tell me."

"Well, it was like the Trader was deliberately trying to pit his customer against Hap."

"Mm. A desperate merchant might use any leverage at his disposal to resume business."

"But he didn't seem desperate. If anything, he was... complicit."

"That's a strong word," Fi said. "Complicity implies criminal intent."

"I know. I-I can't explain it..."

"Try."

Seg took a deep breath to gather his thoughts. "If the Trader had been upset, his action could be excused, just like you said. He doesn't want to get in trouble by going against Bharta's orders, so he primes the customer to talk to Hap. Hap capitulates, Bharta allows negotiations to resume, and the Trader gets what he needs for his next stop, or his family, or whatever."

"The Trader wasn't angry, though. He didn't *need* those goods."

"Maybe it's been a good year for them," Fi said.

"There hasn't been a good year for humanity since The Fall. Excess food is carefully preserved for next year, in case the harvest isn't as kind. It's *never* squandered." Seg paled, the stark reality finally hitting home. "Gina and Bharta are colluding against us."

"Another serious accusation."

"But the only one that makes sense. The Trader wasn't angry about the trade embargo. He wasn't even surprised—which means he knew it was coming."

"Or this is a common occurrence at other domes. He might be desensitized." Fi said it without conviction, as if she were just playing devil's advocate to his thoughts.

"Even then, I'd expect *some* reaction, but he just nodded as if he'd been expecting the news."

"That doesn't mean they were colluding. The Trader would already know your primary commodities were valued low, and might have been expecting Holtondome to refuse to trade."

"Holtondome has never in four hundred years missed a trade season. There's no precedent, as any Trader worth their name would know."

"So the captain might have warned them ahead of time," Fi said. "He knew the trade value of items critical to Holtondome was high, and that this was a possibility. How is that collusion?"

"Because I think Gina's lying about the high trade values." Seg shook his head. "How can they possibly trade higher than food? The only arable land on Earth is under the domes, and there are only so many of those to feed a rising population. And every season, they tout how industry is growing for critical supplies, like medicine, to meet the people's needs."

"Maybe mass deaths elsewhere have reduced food consumption? Or a medical goods production facility is out of order?"

"Either of which they would have mentioned as an excuse. Population statistics and critical supply issues are some of the few things we're allowed to know, so they'd have no reason to hold back. They couldn't lie about it because it wouldn't be in the news broadcast they'll play before they leave, so they had to lie about something we couldn't verify." Seg raised his eyebrows. "Did I miss anything?"

"Nothing major," Fi said. "The defense rests."

"What?"

"It's a saying in the legal system. It means I have no more questions. Let's watch a few more shops close to make sure this wasn't an anomaly."

Sure enough, it wasn't. They observed three more traders receiving the news. One seemed mildly annoyed, but the other two had the same non-reaction as the first.

And all three used fear tactics to urge their customers to talk Hap into capitulating.

"It's the same message," Seg said. "Like they rehearsed it. First they lowball us into not trading, then try to incite a rebellion against our own leaders. What's going on?"

Fi stared at him.

Right, I have to figure it out. Freyja forbid she ever just tell me the damned answer.

"First, it doesn't seem they intentionally goaded us out of trading," Seg said. "They had no idea you were from the City, and therefore couldn't have predicted you'd pull those laws from your bag of tricks—without which we wouldn't have thought we had the grounds to refuse. That means they wouldn't have prepared for this scenario ahead of time, yet the merchants still weren't upset or surprised. The only possible explanation is..." Seg lowered his gaze. The thought was too absurd to even utter.

Fi stepped closer until their lips were just centimeters apart. "Say it."

"Like... the traders are *working* for the Feds." Seg glanced around. No men in white armor rushed forward to drag him away. He sighed in relief.

Fi cupped his cheeks and rested her forehead against his. "Your heaviest accusation yet. If true, it would shake the foundations upon which Holtondome was founded."

Not just Holtondome, Seg thought.

It would be a fundamental violation of the Pact—of everything civilization had depended upon for hundreds of years to scrape itself from the brink of annihilation.

Provider domes grew the essentials, but isolated themselves and refused harmful technology.

Cities kept the secrets of technology safe, kept the domes in good repair, and worked on reversing the damage humanity had done to its own planet, but didn't produce their own essentials—except ones that required technology to produce, like complex medicines.

Between them stood the Traders—nomadic parties who risked Earth's wrath to travel from dome to City to dome, ensuring balance between the Providers and the Cities, and that each settlement was doing its part in the great supply chain sustaining the planet's few remaining residents.

Above everyone stood the Feds. They governed the entire process: auditing Traders, Providers, and Cities to ensure each honored the Pact, and that unfair alliances weren't formed that would compromise the delicate balance. They were also the only party allowed a military force.

For four hundred years, the system had worked. If Cities didn't uphold their end of the bargain, they received no provisions and starved. If the Providers kept everything for themselves, Mother Earth would destroy their dome in just a few seasons, sentencing its denizens to death. If the Traders didn't trade—and fairly—not only would they starve, but their vehicles would cease to work. The disruption to other domes would compromise everyone's safety.

All of this depended upon the Pact. Adherence to the Pact was enforced by the Feds, which required them to be absolutely neutral. Siding with any one faction created an imbalance with the other two. Because Provider domes had forsworn communication with the outside world, they were especially vulnerable. Taking advantage of one would be easy since they had no means of discovering otherwise.

Except, with Fi's help, I just have.

"This is bad," Seg said softly. "Even if it's true, what recourse do we have?"

"More than you think, and at the same time, not nearly enough."

"It's hopeless, then."

"Just as the Feds designed it. Despite what they'd like you to think, however, they don't know everything."

"Something they don't have in common with you, it seems."

"Lucky for Holtondome."

Seg pressed his head against hers, enjoying her proximity, her warmth, and her scent that reminded him of beautiful meadows from poems before The Fall, even though he'd never smelled one, and probably never would.

"Why are you here, Miss Fi?"

"I could give you the same excuse I gave the Feds when I obtained authorization to travel here, but the truth is…" Fi ran her fingers down his cheek and let them rest on his chest. "I was looking for you."

"Me?"

"You." She looked up. Their noses touched, and Fi smiled. "Seg."

His heart skipped three beats and did a double backflip.

Did she really just say my name?

He tried to hide his own smile and failed miserably. "You're… you're not going to start with that 'we're compatible' crap again, are you?"

Fi laughed, a symphony of chimes and mystic flutes he wished would play forever.

"You just proved my point," Fi said. She rested her head against his again. "I have to get you away from here."

"C-come again?"

"Back to the City. I don't have the equipment here to run the tests I need, and the Feds would never allow me to bring it."

"Tests?"

"Mm. Your blind eye is a mystery, which is a word I don't use lightly. Don't you want to learn more about it? Why you have an organ that's nowhere in your genetic code?"

"Frankly? Not really."

"But—"

"Miss Fi, this eye has caused me nothing but misery and isolation. The only thing I'm interested in is curing my condition, which means getting rid of the godsforsaken thing and replacing it with an eye that works."

"Works like everyone else's, you mean."

Seg nodded.

Fi traced a finger over his left eyebrow and circled down his cheek. "You may have something extraordinary, Seg. A gift. Don't be so quick to throw it away."

"I don't want it. What good is seeing people's deaths if I can't change their fate?"

"I said 'shouldn't,' not 'can't.' There's an important difference."

"If the consequences are as dire as you suggest, then you may as well have. Who with a sliver of a conscience would save someone knowing so many others might suffer?"

"And what if you could be sure of the consequences? Then would you consider it a gift?"

Seg frowned. "Can you?"

"No. But maybe you can." Fi grabbed his shirt and shook him playfully, her curious excitement from last night back in her eyes. "That's the thing, Seg! We know almost nothing about what happened yesterday, and even less about that eye of yours. Let's find out." She smiled and brushed his cheek. "Together."

He returned a weaker smile he certainly didn't feel. "Why do I feel like I'm just a lab experiment to you?"

"'And,' not 'just.' I know you don't like hearing this, but we *are* compatible. It's a rare thing, and I take it seriously." She released him and pressed her forehead against his. "Do you want to come to the City with me?"

"It doesn't matter, because it could never happen. Providers never leave. No one in Holtondome's history ever has."

"Wrong on all counts."

Seg jerked upright, searching her face for some hint that she was joking, but found none.

"We're standing on the edge of a cliff," Fi said softly. "It's not too late to step back, but once we jump, there will be no changing our minds. I won't take you to the City against your will, though, so I need to hear you say it. Do you want to come with me?"

He glanced around. Everyone was in such a roar over the stalls closing that no one would hear his heretical answer even if he spoke at normal volume, but Seg whispered anyway.

"Yes."

Fi nodded as if she'd known what his answer would be all along.

And she probably did.

"What happens now?" Seg should have asked that question before committing, but, short of Holtondome's complete destruction, it probably wouldn't have mattered.

He wanted to explore the world. See the Cities. Drive fast cars like Cook's. Travel to space, if they'd let him, and visit Mars Colony. Seg had only spared himself any sort of torturous hope because there hadn't been any.

Now that there was, he wanted to jump in with both feet and never look back.

Fi grinned. "Now, my brave Seg, things get interesting."

12

Choices

A WANDER THROUGH THE TRADING floor revealed more of the same: merchants closing their stalls without any thought of continuing trade, and stoking the populace into outrage against Hap. It did not, however, reveal any visions of pending death, nor did Fi hint that she'd seen visions of her own.

What if mine was just a fluke?

As realistic as the experience had been, it had never happened before in Seg's life. Had it been a one-time occurrence? A glitch in the cosmic continuum, never to repeat?

The possibility was both depressing and a relief. Control of someone's destiny wasn't a responsibility Seg wanted. He had only trouble to show for the decisions he'd made in his own life; putting destiny in his control felt like a tragic mistake.

On the other hand, his alleged ability had opened Fi up. Even now, the enchanting-eyed beauty hummed happily at his side. It was such a change from her usual melancholy that he had trouble believing this was the same person. If his ability proved false, would she become flat again? Lifeless?

Seg took her hand, which earned a smile that creased her black-ringed eyes.

I certainly hope not.

"Seg!"

He turned at Val's hail to find her pushing through the crowd, with Cook close behind. Her excitement faltered when she spotted their joined hands. Her cheeks flushed. Val locked eyes with him, pointedly ignoring Fi.

"The Feds have stopped trade! What was your father thinking?"

Not her, too.

"It wasn't his fault," Seg said. "It's sort of... mine."

She laughed, but quickly sobered at his serious expression. "Yours? What in Odin's name were you doing at the negotiating table? You've never haggled in your life!"

"I was, ah... inspired. Once we got talking, things just clicked. I might have spoken out of turn, but Hap didn't correct me, so I couldn't have been too wrong."

"Inspired, huh?" Val shot a withering glance at Fi. "That decidedly *outside* inspiration may be the death of us all."

"I don't think so," Seg said. "Just listen before you jump to conclusions."

Val crossed her arms, but nodded, so Seg filled her and Cook in on everything to date—minus their dead-person-walking hunt. When he finished, Val and Cook were both pale, although Seg suspected for different reasons. Cook had hardly taken his shocked eyes from Fi during the entire recounting.

"I don't have Jen's logistical insights, but it sounds right," Val said. "Dome life is a delicate balance. Taking one pebble from the stack can cause the whole thing to come crashing down."

"Fi... did *you* start this?" Cook said.

"I gave them the tools they needed to defend themselves, and they did."

"Yeah, but aren't you worried about the inquisitors?"

"I would be if I'd violated the law."

Cook gave a hollow chuckle. "That's subjective, and you know it. Especially out here. If the Feds think you had anything to do with this— and they know you do—you'll be selected for questioning, or I'll eat my steering wheel."

"I hope I *am* selected, otherwise I'm losing my touch."

The three of them stared at her with open mouths.

"Don't worry, I can handle myself. Don't risk yourselves by lying to the inquisitors on my account. All of us will inevitably be called for questioning. Be honest and tell them what you know."

Seg didn't need her gentle hand-squeeze hint to know that their visions were an exception to her instruction.

A worried look from Cook reminded him of his other promise.

The car. I wasn't supposed to have seen what it can do, but he risked exposure anyway to save Troy.

Seg returned a subtle nod to let the driver know his secret would be safe. Cook relaxed.

Val clapped her hands. "Well, on that cheery note, shall we see if we can sneak a drink in before the—"

A gong clanged over the clamor, silencing the crowd like a death knell. It was a sound they knew well.

"—census." Val sighed. "Guess we'd better line up."

Fi gave Seg's hand to Val as if he were a gift horse from the stories.

"Take care of him," Fi said.

Val turned three shades of red—which was one shade lighter than Seg. They both glanced at Cook. The driver shrugged and clapped them each on a shoulder.

"Take care of her," Cook said to Seg with a wink. "Fi and I need to catch up on a few things before the inquisitors start."

"Mm," Fi said.

With a nod, she led Cook away, leaving Seg and Val with their joined hands swinging.

Val cleared her throat. "I-is it my imagination, or did that sound sort of... final?"

"More likely Miss Fi's strange sense of humor," Seg said, acutely aware that neither of them had made any attempt to separate. "Shall we, ah... go line up?"

"Sure, yeah. Let's, um..." Val started to move, then glanced at their hands. "Do you..."

Seg held his breath, afraid she was going to ask if he wanted to let go.

"Do... do you want to lead, Seg?"

His relief was ridiculous on a reliving-his-teenage-years level. "No, that's fine. You always liked to go first."

"Things change," she said softly. "People change."

"Not too much, I hope. I've always admired your spirit."

"Oh." She surprised him with a giggle. "Funny, that's what I love about you, too."

She what?

Val's eyes widened, as if just realizing what she'd said. She turned away with a loud *ahem*. "W-well, follow me, then. I think I can get us through this crowd in one piece. Stay close."

"Val, I—"

She yanked him forward, causing him to bite his tongue, and plunged into the crowd. Seg took the hint and kept silent. Val would open up when she was ready, and not a moment sooner.

Some things don't change, he thought with a grin.

Even in the line, Val refused to relinquish her grip, which drew more than a few looks. White-armored Feds walked the rows with rectangular screens similar to the one Fi had used last night, talking to each resident in turn.

"Name?" a Fed said, not even looking at Seg.

"Seg Holton."

The Fed swiped his finger a few times, tapped, nodded, and walked in front of Val. "Name?"

"Valerie Gannon."

The Fed repeated his routine, then down the line he went. Seg fidgeted, wishing as he did every time that they would release people who had already been accounted for, but, like everyone, he was stuck there until the census finished. His palm was sweaty, though whether he or Val was the offender was hard to say.

Val studied the person in front of her as if he were the most important thing in the world. Seg tried to pull his hand away to politely dry his palm. Val tightened her grip, making it clear he wouldn't be getting it back anytime soon, but she still wouldn't meet his eyes. He didn't try again.

A half-hour or so later, the census completed.

"Before you go," a Fed said loudly to everyone, "we've already selected names for inquisition. Come forward when called. As for the rest of you, inspections will begin immediately. Please ensure all areas are available and accessible to the inspectors."

Seg sighed. He must have really rubbed Captain Bharta the wrong way for him to have put these activities back-to-back-to-back without any breaks for the residents.

One more reason for everyone to hate me.

The more he thought about it, the more he couldn't wait to get away, like Fi had said they would.

Seg caught himself mid-chuckle.

What if she hadn't been serious? Or couldn't deliver? Fi was clever, of that he had no doubt, but the Pact was the Pact. Providers never left. It was a fact as old as the domes themselves.

A hand-squeeze brought another worry.

How would Val handle him leaving? Worse, how would Seg handle losing his best and only friend, even if she was estranged?

He looked at their joined hands.

Maybe not so estranged after all.

"...Seg Holton..." he heard amid the Fed's list, but was spared separating from Val when her name came next. They exchanged uneasy looks. It wasn't the first time either of them had been called for questioning, but that didn't make it any less daunting, especially since he actually had things to hide this season.

They always discover the truth...

The saying had been indoctrinated into him since he was a child. Could he hide the truth from the inquisitors? If so, would it do more harm than admitting what he'd seen Cook's vehicle do?

Seg steeled himself, trailing Val only by the distance their arms would allow.

He'd made a decision. A promise. Right or wrong, he'd stand by his word.

They waited in silence for the Fed to finish reading his list. The results so far were no more or fewer people than usual.

The Fed squinted at his list. "F... Fee?"

"Fi," Seg said. "Like 'high.'"

The Fed nodded. "Fi, Troy Holton, and Cook Moreno."

"Troy is in medical," Seg said, not wanting his brother to get in trouble for non-attendance. "Fi and Cook aren't residents, but you can probably find them in the tavern upstairs."

The Fed whispered to his companion, who trotted off, then tucked his screen under his arm. "Those called forward, please remain on the first floor until summoned for inquisition. The rest are free to go. Have a pleasant day."

"Surprise, surprise," Seg said to Val once the Feds wandered off.

Val remained silent, her face pale.

"You okay?"

"Fine," she said softly, but wouldn't meet his eyes, and stayed quiet after that.

Fi and Cook appeared a few minutes later. Cook acknowledged their joined hands with a genuine chuckle and fell in beside Val. Fi filed in on Seg's other side without any attempt to retake possession of him, for which he was oddly disappointed.

All told, the Feds had gathered roughly a thousand people for inquisition, who broke into groups and began chatting amongst themselves.

Two hours of nervous waiting later, Seg heard his name called by a Fed with short, rusty hair. He reluctantly detached from Val and made his way over.

"Just be yourself," Fi said on his way by. If she was worried, she gave no indication. Seg nodded and followed the Fed away toward the caravan.

The rusty-haired Fed stopped in front of a Federated Nations-marked vehicle, smaller than the Traders', but still large enough for several adults to stand inside. Black bars over the windows gave it the feeling of a mobile jail.

"In here," the rusty-haired Fed said, gesturing to the open side door.

Seg entered. He was surprised when the Fed didn't follow but instead closed the door, sealing Seg in relative darkness.

"Seg Holton," a familiar voice said.

"Captain Bharta?"

"Yes. Sorry for the dank lighting. We like to conserve power wherever possible. Please, sit."

Once his eyes had adjusted to the darkness, Seg settled on the bench seat across from Bharta. To his knowledge, a Fed captain had never personally conducted an inquisition, which did nothing to steady his nerves.

"Forgive me, it's been a while since I've questioned a resident, so I may be a little rusty."

Bharta flipped a switch on a wall-mounted device next to him—truth machines, as they called them in Holtondome. A red light shone from a round apparatus no bigger than his thumb, attached to a stiff wire, which Bharta adjusted until the light shone squarely on Seg.

"Ah, there we are. Let's get the basics out of the way, shall we?"

"Sure."

Bharta glanced down at a portable display in his lap. "Seg Holton, have you been true to the Pact since your previous inquisition session in spring of last year?"

"I have."

Bharta examined the truth machine and nodded. "And do you swear to continue to uphold the Pact so sworn by your ancestors?"

"I do."

"So noted." Bharta tapped the screen a few times, then set it aside and relaxed against the seatback. "You've become close with your guest, I see."

"Miss Fi? Yes, she's very interesting."

"What has she told you of the City?"

"Nothing, Captain Bharta."

Another glance at the truth machine, followed by a nod. "I heard from some of the other residents that she told quite a story last night. Something about a diary and pot pies?"

"Yes, it was a piece of history we'd lost and were excited to recover."

"Did she show you this diary?"

"No."

"Oh, come now. You're sleeping in the same room together. You must surely have spied something."

"No, Captain Bharta. If she does have the diary, she's kept it hidden."

"I see." Whatever the truth machine told Bharta seemed to surprise him, but he kept the results to himself. He glanced at the suture on Seg's left arm. "That's fine work. Who did it?"

Seg hesitated only briefly before answering. "Miss Fi, sir. She's very skilled."

"I'm sure. Did she use technology or anything strange during the procedure?"

"There were a few instruments I didn't recognize, and a portable screen similar to yours, but I didn't ask questions."

Bharta held his eyes, as if searching for something, then smiled. "Good man. And please forgive my rudeness for not asking sooner: How is your arm feeling?"

Seg carefully flexed his fingers. They felt stiff and weak, but less so than earlier that morning. "Fine, sir. She says I should have full use in another day or so."

"Must have been a shallow wound."

"No, sir. Miss Fi said there was extensive nerve and ligament damage."

"Were that the case, I'd expect recovery to take weeks or more."

"Agreed. She must have used something to accelerate my recovery, though I couldn't tell you what."

"You're not in the least bit curious?"

"Asking would have violated the Pact, so I didn't."

"That wasn't my question."

Seg squirmed in his seat. "It... it's hard not to be curious, Captain. If what she says is true, she uncovered a problem our own doctor hadn't, and probably saved the use of my hand. Such medical technology might be considered essential for agricultural workers like Holtondome to stay productive."

"Those decisions are above my station, I'm afraid, but I'll be sure to file it in my report for due consideration."

Meaning it will probably go nowhere.

Of course, Seg had no way of finding out either way, so he took the polite route and simply thanked Bharta.

"You mentioned earlier that you acquired that injury while saving Troy, correct?"

"Yes. My left leg was also injured."

"Miss Fi treated that as well?"

Seg nodded. "It was fractured. I could barely walk on it yesterday, but as you can see, I'm doing fine today."

"More miracle medicines?"

"That's my guess. She used a big syringe and a strange cylinder that showed her the damages without having to open my leg. I don't know anything beyond that."

"And what did Miss Fi receive in exchange for her services?"

"Nothing, sir. She didn't ask for anything."

Bharta tapped his screen for a minute, his eyebrows drawn into a frown, then set it aside again. "Sounds like quite an adventure you had out in the lightning storm."

"One I'd prefer not to repeat."

"Yes, I heard your brother's account. Cook Moreno used his extraordinary vehicle to assist."

"He did. I felt guilty asking, but I couldn't think of another way to rescue Troy that wouldn't have killed us both. Cook's selfless heroism is the only reason we survived."

"To hear Troy tell it, the hero of the hour was you."

Troy said that?

Seg masked his surprise with a simple nod. "Most would view dashing into a lightning storm as suicidal rather than heroic, but I got lucky."

If one can consider strange visions from an otherwise blind eye to be lucky.

"Indeed." Bharta leaned forward. "I'd like to hear the story from your perspective. From the beginning, if you don't mind."

"Of course, Captain."

Seg recounted the events as he remembered them. It was easy enough to substitute his strange visions for realizing his brother was missing when the repair party returned to the tavern without him. When he reached the part where the car's tires had morphed for more traction, Seg simply pretended he hadn't seen anything because he was too focused on hanging onto the wires.

"I see," Bharta said when Seg had finished. "You're indeed lucky to be alive, and doubly so to have City medicine available. A pity your healthcare provider was unlicensed, but in this case, it appears you were fortunate that she did no harm."

Seg blinked in surprise. "Has Miss Fi harmed others, sir?"

"I'm not at liberty to say, as you should well know, but I would recommend having her work checked by your own physician, if you haven't already."

Seg was too shocked to apologize for his misstep. Bharta had all but admitted that Fi *had* hurt someone. She'd warned him that she wasn't licensed and hadn't practiced in a while. The woman radiated competence, however, so he'd dismissed it as self-deprecation.

But if Seg had been wrong about her medical expertise, how else might he be mistakenly placing his faith in her?

He ground his teeth against a growing knot in his chest.

That was the problem. He knew *nothing* about the exotic woman beyond her proclivity to not answer questions in favor of torturing Seg to reason them out.

How, in truth, did he even know her visions were real? He'd been so eager to find someone to connect with about his strange experience—to not feel like a complete freak—that he would have believed just about anything.

What if her strange behavior that night had been for an entirely different reason? What if she'd simply been telling Seg what he wanted to hear?

"Sorry to have upset you," Bharta said. "Doc Ven is one of the finest Provider physicians I know. I'm sure you'll be in good hands." Bharta flicked his screen a few times. "Almost done, my boy, just one more item."

Only one more?

If so, that would make this the shortest inquisition Seg had ever attended.

"I'd like to confirm you witnessed Cook Moreno's tires adenomorphizing."

"Sorry, sir?" Seg fought a bought of panic. He didn't recognize the term, but it wasn't hard to guess he was referring to the strange transformation Seg had seen. Had he accidentally slipped Cook's secret at some point? He didn't think so.

Bharta glanced at the truth machine. For the first time, he grimaced. "It's all right, son, you aren't the only witness. Several other residents saw the tires change form when Cook's vehicle returned to the dome. I just need an accounting of the damages. I will, of course, need to know everyone you talked to about it to see if it can be contained."

"No, sir, I didn't notice anything when we returned," Seg said truthfully. "I was too occupied with Troy. Is the knowledge forbidden?"

Bharta covered his eyes and sighed. "So forbidden that I've already told you too much. Teach me to make assumptions." He took a deep breath, then flipped the truth machine's switch. The red light went out. "I think we can forget that happened, hmm? Just promise to keep to your Pact oath and not repeat what you've seen or heard to other residents."

"Oh, of course." Seg fidgeted with his jacket. "Is that it, sir? We're done?"

"With the inquisition, yes, but I wonder if you'd indulge me a minute longer? Off the record, so to speak."

Seg nodded, though he didn't like where this was going.

Bharta leaned forward, elbows on his knees, and considered his hands for a second before speaking. "As you know, Feds are supposed to remain neutral in trade negotiations unless we see illegal practices at play. As you may also know, what's legal and what isn't is up to interpretation, which is my responsibility as well."

"Yes, sir. Those and other rules are repeated every season. Every Holtondome resident knows them by heart."

"I'm sure they do. There's an old saying you won't hear me repeat outside of this vehicle, though." He captured Seg's gaze and breathed a long sigh. "Rules are meant to be broken."

Seg blinked. Those were the last words he expected to hear from someone whose sole purpose was to enforce the law. "W-which rules did you have in mind, sir?"

"That is, unfortunately, something I need to leave to your imagination. And you do have quite an imagination, don't you, Seg?"

"So I've been accused."

"And so Holtondome might suffer." Bharta's eyes wandered the inside of the vehicle. "I spoke to Hap before meeting with you. Outside of the inquisition, of course. He's convinced that the doomsday yarn you spun is correct, and that Holtondome's best option is to abstain from trading this season."

"Abstaining would be illegal," Seg said quickly. "We're trading what we can spare, which happens to be nothing."

"That's a technicality, son, and you know it."

Call me "son" one more godsdamned time...

Seg reined in his annoyance and cleared his mind. Holtondome's welfare might hang on this conversation. If he handled it as if he were arguing with Troy, he'd lose, and might be punished in the process. Seg needed to approach it calmly and rationally.

Like Fi would.

Bharta stood and paced the small space. "Cities, domes, and Traders exist in a delicate balance. Our fragile ecosystem can endure few disruptions without creating famine, disease, or exposure to Mother Earth's wrath, which we've brought upon ourselves."

"Yes, sir. Those dangers are the reason the Pact exists."

"Which it does well. Usually."

"Usually?"

Bharta stopped in front of him. "Today, it failed. If Holtondome refuses to trade, it will disrupt the balance. Others, who I'm not even allowed to name, will suffer."

"I don't understand how that's possible. If they're in such dire need, then demand for our goods should be higher."

"If trade worked as it did before The Fall, where countries abused Earth's resources to shuttle meaningless commodities across the globe to benefit from artificial economies instead of producing locally, this would, ironically, not be an issue. Shipments can no longer cross the world in a single day. Caravans must plan their routes to avoid storm damage, and even then must move cautiously and with purpose. This means that a dome on the other side of the country with plenty to spare can't help domes in need here."

"So… their excess goods are too excess, even if others far away need them, because they can't be effectively transported. I understand the logic, Captain. That must have always been true, yet there's never been a reported medical supply shortage in post-Fall history. What changed?"

"Producing medicine requires raw materials. Those materials have been in short local supply from the mining domes, which means medicine manufacturers have had to trade other goods to miners at a loss to obtain their materials. Fewer goods means they need to trade their wares at higher value. Much higher, if they don't want to starve. The chain reaction is that other non-agricultural domes have had to tighten their belts to get the medicines they need, exacerbating the shortage for those down the trade chain."

"Fine," Seg said, "but that doesn't explain the high repair costs."

"It does if the mining shortage also includes raw materials needed for machinery and domes. Cities have to be very choosy about who they service and how, or there won't be enough to go around for the most critical repairs, including their own."

"You're reinforcing my case for us not trading, Captain. Cities are being stingy with medicines and services to protect their own. We're just doing the same."

"You're not seeing the big picture! Your refusal to trade will drive *up* the value of foodstuffs, making it even harder for non-agricultural domes to acquire food, medicine, *and* repairs. It might be enough to start a statewide famine."

Seg started to reply but caught himself. If he demanded the medicine

Holtondome needed to alleviate the famine, he would instead be inflicting a wave of medical shortages, which might cause as many deaths or more. The same went for repairs.

Whether Holtondome chose to trade or not, it would be a losing proposition for someone.

Maybe several someones.

Seg didn't have access to the trade ledgers—and couldn't read them if he did—so he had no means to compare Holtondome's food output with other domes'. Based on Bharta's desperate stance, however, he guessed it was high. Perhaps the highest output in Wyoming.

How much of the state depended on Holtondome for nourishment? How much of the country?

And how many will suffer if we abstain from trading?

Bharta watched him mull without twitching a muscle.

What to do?

Such a weighty decision was definitely above Seg's station. He turned from the Captain, uncomfortable with everything about the situation—

—and almost fell out of his seat.

There on the dark van wall—or through it, rather—stood a distant figure wearing a dress.

Visible only through his blind left eye.

He couldn't see her surroundings, and she was too far away to identify. Unlike his previous vision, this was more than a flash, and in full color. The figure turned as if surprised by someone. She held her hands up and backed away.

A phantom flash of light made him flinch.

The figure clutched her chest and collapsed. A red stain bloomed on her back. She didn't move again.

"...to take in, son."

Seg dragged his attention away from the now-blank vehicle wall and focused on Bharta. "Sorry?"

Bharta nodded with a sympathetic smile. "I realize that's a lot to think about. But you understand the stakes now?"

"I... Like you said, it's a lot. I need time to process," Seg said, though in truth, he couldn't have recited a word of their conversation.

Who was the woman in his vision? Had she been shot? Who shot her, and why? If he looked again, would the vision replay? He was sorely tempted to turn around and see, but Bharta was already speaking again.

"Good man. I've known your father for years, and have every faith you'll be able to talk sense into him."

"Right. Well, Captain, it's been a pleasure, but if there's nothing else...?"

Seg was pushing the bounds of propriety for sure. Inquisitors dismissed their subjects when they were finished, and not a moment sooner. Asking to leave usually earned a longer session, with more invasive questions than before. Why would a resident ask to end questioning early unless they had something to hide?

And so Seg's suspicion increased when Bharta simply nodded and opened the door.

13

Vision

STEPPING OUT OF THE PRISON vehicle to Holtondome's first floor was like waking from a bad dream into the comfort of his mother's arms. Seg breathed deep, relishing the rush of air as if his lungs had been wrapped in iron bands and were now free.

The bands constricted again when he remembered his new vision. Seg averted his eyes from the would-be crime scene until he'd cleared the caravan area and was hidden behind a rack of drying wheat. Half-hoping he wouldn't see the vision again, he covered his good right eye and looked in the direction he'd seen the phantom woman fall.

Her image appeared immediately—a splash of color in a sea of darkness. Once again, the woman in the dress turned as if startled by someone, then held her palms out to ward off whatever was threatening her. The flash seemed brighter this time. The woman clutched her chest and fell in a pool of her own blood. For a moment, Seg swore he could hear her whimpering, but the piteous sounds were coming from his own throat.

He peeked around the wheat rack.

The vision's source was deep within the caravan camp. Distance was difficult to judge with only one eye. Although the woman's image had disappeared, a rough guess placed the apparition between a Trader caravan and a Fed vehicle almost twice the size of the one he'd just exited.

Seg yearned for a closer look to see if he could identify the unfortunate woman, but wandering too far into Fed territory during the inquisitions would be begging for another round, and he doubted his new inquisitor would be as gentle with him as Bharta had.

But how long does that poor woman have before my vision comes true?

And what would he do about it, anyway? Seg had no idea how long it would be until the event took place. He could be waiting there for hours. And if the assailant was armed, as the flash suggested, Seg had nothing resembling Fed body armor to protect him. All he may succeed in doing is adding his own corpse to the crime scene.

No, what he needed was advice—preferably from someone who'd done this a time or ten.

Fi wasn't on the first floor when he searched for her, nor in the tavern, or their bedroom. Cook and Val were also absent.

Apparently their inquisitors are giving them the full treatment.

He shuddered, feeling both relieved to be free, and guilty for their suffering.

On his way down from the bedroom, his father's call from the tavern distracted him from his quest.

"Son! Join me, would you?"

Seg fumbled for an excuse to decline, but came up empty. He'd all but stolen the negotiations from Hap and Jen's laps. The least he could do was endure the tongue lashing he surely deserved.

He sat across the table from Hap and ran both hands through his hair. "Go ahead. Say it."

"If I must." Hap unfolded a leather cloth on the table, revealing different colored stones. A series of squares etched the leather. Within the squares, Hap arranged the stones in a complex pattern. "See this?"

"I'm not that blind."

Hap pressed his lips. Instead of rebuking Seg for his terse reply, he blew a long sigh. "I know why you do that."

"Do what?"

"Goad everyone into arguing. It's easier to delude yourself into believing you're a monster if everyone treats you like one. What better way to achieve that than by being abrasive?"

"You call that abrasive? Guess I've been going easy on you."

"And what better way to ease that same pain than by joking about it?"

Seg ground his teeth. He'd rather talk about the fate of Wyoming any day than this. "Why the sudden burst of wisdom? Did the stones speak to you or something? Doc might have medicine for that."

"The stones did speak to me, wise ass. And if you'd cut the sarcasm for a second, I'll tell you what they said. As for why... If you're going to decide Holtondome's fate all by yourself, you should at least be informed so you don't inadvertently kill us all."

Seg paled. Apparently, he'd blown it. Big time. "Hap, I'm sorry. I had no business—"

"You were right."

"I... what?"

Hap rotated the leather cloth around and slid it over to him. "You know what this is?"

"Something to do with dome logistics, right?"

"Right. Each column represents a different trade good. The first row is our production, the second our consumption, and the last is the tally. Different colored stones represent different amounts."

Seg stared at them. Many of the bottom rows were empty, which didn't jive with the amounts in the two rows above. There also seemed to be more columns than Holtondome had goods. He said as much.

"The reason the rows don't add up is because of these last three columns. Two represent birth vs death rate and population vs productivity. The last I just added based on our conversation." He tapped the column, which contained several black stones. "Healthy vs infirmed. This column has a cascading effect on the others that we hadn't accounted for in previous years, because we've never had to. Granted, it's mostly guesswork, but if my numbers are anywhere close to correct... Seg, Holtondome is about to face its worst year in history."

"Even with us not trading?"

"Even with. But the numbers confirmed that *not* trading is Holtondome's best shot. I don't know how you and Miss Fi figured it out in such short order, but I can't argue with your conclusion." Hap folded his hands and sat back, looking suddenly ten years older. "For the first time, Holtondome will abstain from trading. Or, excuse me..." He gave a weak smile. "Offer only what we can spare, which is nothing."

"I... I may have been wrong."

Hap rolled his eyes. "Did you hear a word I said? The matrix says you're right."

"The matrix only accounts for Holtondome."

"Of course, what else would..." Hap eyed him suddenly, his face ashen. He leaned forward and continued in the softest of whispers. "Son, don't tell me you let Miss Fi or Mr. Cook violate the Pact by giving you outside information."

"It wasn't them," Seg said just as quietly. "The information came straight from Captain Bharta."

Hap's jaw dropped.

"And it wasn't a violation of the Pact. He may have skirted it close enough to lick its panties, but I don't think he violated it."

"That's a disgusting metaphor."

"Which is how I felt when I walked out from that joke of an inquisition. I think Bharta was trying to butter me into agreeing to trade."

"What exactly did he say?"

"Sure you want to know?"

"That's the problem. I won't know if it's illegal until you tell me."

Seg couldn't argue with that, unfortunately, so he gave Hap a summary of the conversation. Hap asked question after question with a tenacity that would have made an inquisitor squirm, until Seg had pretty much recited the conversation word for word. When Hap was finally satisfied that he hadn't missed any details, he sat back and shook his head.

"Bharta violated the Pact, all right," Hap said. "The problem is that he's also judge, jury, and executioner when it comes to Pact rulings. If we call him on it, he could banish either of us on the spot, and the world would never be the wiser."

What little remained of Seg's meal suddenly lodged in his throat. The idea of being cast from the dome to suffer Earth's wrath was terrifying. He'd barely survived his last two encounters, which was more than most people could claim who'd faced similar. He didn't fancy his chances of living through a third.

"But... Miss Fi said we can challenge his decisions. Can we leverage that somehow?"

"It must have been a load of hog slop," Hap said. "Bharta is just as liable as us. If what she said was true, he would never have taken that risk."

"Unless the stakes are high enough that he felt he had to," Seg said.

"We may never know." Hap rubbed his face. "Sometimes I hate this system of ours."

"Just sometimes?"

"Yes, just sometimes. I believe wholeheartedly in the system Thorn Holton and the rest of the founders swore to uphold to save us from ourselves, and I'll stand by it with my dying breath. But the system only works when everyone plays by the rules—and Bharta isn't."

"So what do we do?"

"What we know to be right with the information we *should* have, not conjecture based on what might be falsely planted information. We offer nothing in trade, and see what happens."

"Aren't you worried Bharta will retaliate? He clearly wants this trade to happen."

"I am. But we can't play his game, not without breaking the Pact, and I won't do that." Hap's eyes softened. "I'm... proud of you, Seg. No matter how things turn out, you did the right thing by standing up for Holtondome."

Seg's churning stomach indicated otherwise. "W-would you excuse me? I have some questions for Miss Fi. Hopefully the Feds are done with her by now."

"Sure. I don't have to remind you of the Pact, though, do I?"

"No. I'll keep our conversation legal, as always."

"Good man." Hap pulled the leather cloth across the table, and, within three heartbeats, seemed to have forgotten he even had a son.

Val and Cook were nowhere to be seen when Seg returned to the first floor, but Fi was just emerging from a Fed vehicle. If she was upset about her inquisition session, her blasé expression certainly didn't show it.

"How did it go?" Seg said.

"As you'd expect. They accused me of unfairly tipping trade balance by giving Holtondome insider information. It was bogus, of course, so then they tried to pin me with betraying technological secrets when I gave you medical treatment. It was perfectly legal, which was easy enough to prove, so they resorted to accusing me of passing unauthorized historical information in the story I told. That, too, was dismissed when the barkeep —"

"Tad. His name is *Tad*."

"Yes, him." She ignored Seg's frustrated sigh and continued. "His accounting cleared my name easily enough."

"Sounds like they really dragged you through the mud."

"I'd have been more concerned if my inquisitor knew the law better, but they rarely do. How did your conversation with the captain go?"

"How did you know he was my inquisitor?"

"Hunch. The Feds tend to use people in higher authority when they want to influence, especially when their intentions are less than pure. Since you're not in handcuffs, I'd guess he placed the guilt of humanity's starvation squarely on your shoulders to try to change your mind."

"He did." Seg crossed his arms. "Your hunches are a little too on-the-nose, Miss Fi. Is death really all your visions show?"

"Yes. My hunches are just applied experience, which I'd hoped you understood by now."

"That's unfair. I've known you for all of twenty-four hours, and a lot has changed in the last twelve."

Fi studied him. "Maybe you're right. Well, we'll have plenty of opportunities to get to know each other in the coming years. For now, and until we can speak more freely, I have to ask that you take my word."

Years?

The idea made his head spin. Just hours ago, they'd spoken of their relationship in terms of weeks, with no thought of reacquaintance. Now she was talking as if they were already married.

What exactly had Seg committed himself to when he agreed to leave Holtondome?

No more than that, he told himself.

But her comments led to another question—one she'd stonewalled him on the last time he'd asked, but seemed more relevant with every conversation.

"How old are you, Miss Fi?"

She studied him again, and eventually sighed. "Later. Until the Feds leave, you're still a target for inquisition, and *that* they could pin me on."

"Oh. S-sorry."

"Don't apologize for being curious. It's a valid question, but for now, we have to play it safe."

"Right."

Seg was more curious now than ever. Was she his mother's age? Cook's age, whatever that was? Older? How could she look even younger than himself?

Fi took his good hand as if reclaiming a favorite lost toy. "Where's your mother?"

"Assuming she wasn't called for inquisition, probably in the salvage shop. Why?"

"I didn't get to speak to her this morning, and I'd like to before the next round of inquisitions."

"Next round? You really think they'll do that?"

"Of course. You're going to refuse to trade, despite Bharta's attempted play at your conscience, so he'll apply pressure the only other way he can. One of your family members will be found guilty of some—"

"But they aren't! My family lives by the Pact. You won't find anyone more devout."

"Then he'll make something up. Believe me, though, they *will* be charged, and the penalty will be severe enough that you'll do anything to save them."

Seg sighed. "You don't know Hap, then."

"Better than you do, it seems. Everyone has their pressure points, and your father—"

"Hap!"

"That's the guy. He'll be thrilled you remembered his name." Fi spoke over Seg's heated reply. "*Your father* is no exception. They'll find his weakness. They'll exploit it. And Holtondome *will* agree to trade at a loss."

"So you're saying there's nothing we can do?"

"Not unless we can find enough leverage to deter the captain from pressing the matter."

"Bharta."

"Mm. What exactly did he say?"

As he had with his father, Seg recited as much of his conversation with Bharta as he could remember.

"A mining shortage," Fi said once he'd finished. She tapped her lip, lost in thought.

"Was he lying?"

"I won't know until I do some research, but that can wait." She tugged him toward Holtondome's southern exit. "The salvage shop is this way?"

"Yes, but… isn't finding leverage against Bharta to *save Holtondome* a little more important?"

"There's time for both. Now, be a gentleman and introduce me to your mother."

14

Peg

By the time Seg remembered the other important topic he wanted to discuss with Fi—his vision of the soon-to-be-murdered woman—he was already inside the salvage shop, staring at his mother's modest backside. The rest of Peg was lost under the hood of the lightning-wrecked hauler.

"The motor's shot, but we might be able to salvage the cooling system," Peg said from its depths. Her hand snaked out. "Give me the nine-millimeter, would you?"

A salvager reached inside a wooden toolbox and started to hand over a socket wrench.

Fi intercepted with a gentle wave, earning a startled look from both Seg and the salvager. She retrieved a different wrench from the toolbox and placed it in Peg's hand, which promptly disappeared.

"Thanks, I…" Peg sighed. "Jim, this is a ten. I asked for a nine."

"Ten is factory standard for cooling system mounts," Fi said. "Even old ones like this."

Peg extricated herself from the vehicle with practiced agility and leveled Fi with cool brown eyes. Her eyebrows rose, then rose another notch when she noticed Fi holding hands with her son. Peg crossed her arms over her greasy leather work apron.

"Seems your request for shared accommodations with Seg wasn't as innocent as you led us to believe, Miss Fi."

"I haven't compromised your son's virtue yet, Mrs. Holton."

"*Yet.*" Peg's frown melted into a grin. "Please, call me Peg."

"Mm."

Seg shook his head at Fi's willful refusal to say his mother's name, but kept quiet. He'd needle her about it later.

"Sorry for disturbing your work," Fi said. "Should we return later?"

Peg patted the hauler with a sigh. "No need. This old girl isn't going anywhere, unfortunately. If we're not going to trade this season, like Hap says, then I want parts ready in case our other hauler breaks down. But I don't need them this instant." She removed her grease-blackened gloves and gestured to a side door. "Make yourselves comfortable. I'll be right in."

Seg led Fi into the small breakroom. Once she was comfortable, he poured three glasses of water and handed one to her.

"I forgot to mention, I had a vision," Seg said softly.

Fi fumbled her cup, sloshing water into her lap.

"Tell me," she said, ignoring her wet dress. "Tell me everything."

Seg fetched a clean rag from the cupboard next to her and dabbed her lap. "It happened during the interrogation. I saw—"

"Uh oh, what happened here?" Peg *tsk*ed from the doorway and marched inside. "Sorry, Miss Fi. I swear I raised him better than to spill drinks on guests."

"It was my fault," Fi said, "though Seg did surprise me."

Peg planted a fist on her hip. "Really, Seg? I thought you outgrew scaring people when Val rightly clocked you for it. It's a wonder either of them is still speaking to you." She ignored his indignant scowl, snatched the rag from him, and resumed dabbing Fi's skirt. "I have a spare dress that should fit, though it may not cover as much of your long legs as it does mine."

"It's no trouble. A little water doesn't bother me."

"Far be it from me to contradict a guest, but I think I'll fetch it anyway, just in case you change your mind." Peg gave a final dab, then went into the back room.

Fi grabbed Seg's shirt the moment they were alone and pulled him close. "What did you see?"

Seg quickly and quietly described the scene.

"And you have no idea who the woman is?" Fi said after he'd finished.

"No, do you?"

She stared at him.

"Right, you're the scientific control." Seg tried to keep his annoyance in check, but it was hard. Someone's life was in jeopardy. Semantics felt like a poor excuse for Fi to not help. "I need to get closer, but—"

"Here we are." Peg returned from the back room and laid a burgundy dress with white lace on an empty chair, then sat in the one next to it. "I'm not sure how it will match that green-tinged hair of yours, but it may be better than a wet lap. How do you make the color look so natural?"

"It's a secret, I'm sorry to say."

"Like everything about you City folk. No matter, I've always preferred the hair color I was born with."

"As you should. It's a wonderful color, just like Seg's."

Seg couldn't say he'd ever compared, but now that Fi had mentioned it, he and his mother's hair were the same shade: just shy of jet-black.

Peg smiled. "Flattering me and my son in one compliment. Very smooth. Now that I'm nice and buttered... To what do I owe the pleasure of your company, Miss Fi?"

"Your son. Specifically, his blind eye."

"What of it?"

"I'm somewhat of a medical researcher. While the Pact prevents me from discussing what brought me to Holtondome, I can tell you that I've never seen a condition like his before, nor can I find anything similar on record. I was hoping you would answer a few questions about your family history, pregnancy with him, and his birth."

"I will, though I don't see the point. Even if restoring his sight was possible, doing so would go against the Pact. The Feds would never allow it."

"They might. I have connections who could make it happen, assuming, as you say, we discover a treatment, and that Holtondome would be okay with the direct use of technology on one of its residents."

"Holtondome can go swim in pig slop," Peg said. "If you can swing both miracles, like you claim, then I'll happily deal with the fallout. What do you need to know?"

Over the next hour, Fi told her. She started by confirming if Seg had been born with his eye that way, then asked about Peg's condition leading up to her pregnancy, including diet, exercise, environmental exposure, previous medical conditions, and work duties. Once she'd exhausted that, Fi asked the same questions about Hap. The conversation then turned to family history, where Peg recited as much about their lineage as anyone could reasonably remember. Fi listened and nodded, but kept any opinions she may have had to herself.

"Thank you, Mrs. Holton," Fi said. "Please forgive me, since there's no delicate way to ask this, but you're absolutely sure your husband is Seg's father?"

Peg straightened. Anger flashed her eyes, but quickly passed. "Yes, Miss Fi. I'm as sure as sure can be."

"Did you have any outside sexual relations around the time of Seg's conception?"

"No," Peg said through clenched teeth.

"During your pregnancy?"

"No! Hap and I were happily married for eight years before having Seg, and have been ever since."

"That's great to hear, Mrs. Holton. Not all couples are as lucky."

Peg relaxed slightly and nodded. "Was any of that helpful for your research, Miss Fi?"

"Only in eliminating possible causes. Will you permit a few more questions?"

"Yes, but if they're similarly direct, I may have to tie my hands to maintain my reputation as a good host."

"These are less sensitive, I promise. Do you remember any... strange behaviors from Seg as a child?"

"Plenty. That willful son of mine is responsible for at least half of my gray hairs. Are you fishing for something in particular?"

"Just casting the net, Mrs. Holton. Any incidents you can recall that suggest visual anomalies would be a good place to start."

"Well, he had his share of imaginary friends, but that's hardly abnormal. Kids naturally shied away from him, or were cruel enough to make him want to stay away. Except for Val, of course."

Fi's eye twitched, but her face remained otherwise neutral. "Of course."

"That left plenty of time for solo play. He would often pretend to go on space missions, speeding to the Moon in a rocket ship. No amount of disciplining could ever tame his fascination with anything fast, as our poor hauler's numerous repairs can attest."

Seg blushed and cleared his throat. "Sorry, Mom."

Peg frowned at him, but her smile ruined the admonishment. "Apart from that..." She put her hand to her chest, rubbing a small bump under her shirt.

"What is it, Mrs. Holton?"

Peg pulled a familiar pendant out from her neckline. The gray metallic disc was twice as big as her thumbnail, and dangled from a worn leather strap that, as far as Seg knew, had never left her neck.

"It's beautiful," Fi said. Her eyebrows slowly knitted. "One could say *unique*."

"Not exactly. We obtained five of them from a Trader, one for each family member. But I admit, I've never seen a material like it."

"May I see?"

Peg hesitated only a moment before slipping it up over her hair bun and handing it over.

Fi ran a finger over its smooth surface. The pendant was too flat and perfectly round to be a natural stone. It reminded Seg of coins from the stories before The Fall, when currency was legal.

"I've never seen you wear a similar pendant," Fi said to him.

"Yeah, I, ah… gave mine to someone. A long time ago."

"Your busty childhood friend?"

Seg nodded.

"Troy still wears his," Peg said, "though Hap's has sat on his dresser for the last several years."

"It's lovely," Fi said absently.

"Thank you. The reason I bring it up is because I remember Seg commenting once on how much he liked the pretty red markings."

Fi turned it over, revealing a series of tightly packed marks that practically glowed with vibrance. She ran her finger over the surface. "Fascinating. How long did he claim to see these markings?"

"Only once. Troy and Jen made right fun of him, and he never mentioned it again."

Seg laughed and shook his head. "I'm a little old for this game now, don't you think, Mom?"

"It seems not. I suppose you're going to insist you still see them?"

Seg blinked at the marks—sharp, angular, intricate, and vibrant enough to spot from across the room.

On a whim, he closed his blind left eye.

The marks disappeared.

"N-no," Seg said, swallowing hard. "It must have been my overactive imagination." He gave Fi a subtle nod.

Fi gasped, but covered it with a cough and a smile. "At the risk of imposing on your good hospitality, Mrs. Holton, may I borrow your pendant? Since we're unsure of the material, I'd like to analyze it for harmful chemicals."

"If there are, the damage is long since done."

"What do you mean? These were recently acquired, right?"

"Hardly. We traded for those pendants just after Jen was born."

"Impossible! The—" Fi clamped her mouth shut and took a deep breath. "It just… looks so new. There are no scratches or any other signs of wear."

"I know. Believe me, I've banged it against everything in the salvage shop a hundred times over. Whatever it's made of, I wish they'd build our equipment out of it. We'd never need repair services again."

"I bet. Do you remember the merchant who traded it to you?"

"Only saw him the once, which is a shame. I'd hoped to obtain more."

"Any information you can provide about him would be very helpful."

"Of course." Peg told her what she remembered, which wasn't much, then laughed. "I have to say, Miss Fi, I've had inquisitions less thorough than our little chat."

"Sorry, Mrs. Holton. You have my word that this discussion will stay between us. Nothing we've talked about breaches the Pact in any way, so the Feds have no reason to ask, nor do I have any reason to tell them."

"I expect nothing less from an esteemed guest such as yourself."

Fi nudged Seg with her elbow. He racked his brain, trying to divine what he'd missed, but couldn't figure it out. Her second nudge included a poignant glance at Peg's pendant.

"Oh! Um, if Hap isn't wearing his pendant, Mom, do you think he'd mind if I borrowed it?"

"No. In fact, I think he'd like that, though I'd be happier if you got yours back from Val instead of taking his."

Believe me, I will.

"It was a gift," Seg said instead. "Asking her to return it feels wrong, even if giving it to her was inconsiderate on my part."

Peg cracked a smile. "Seems I did impart a tiny sense of propriety on you, after all. Very well, come with me to our room and I'll fetch Hap's for you."

Seg nodded, then followed her toward the stairs. Fi caught his hand again and gave an excited squeeze, her enchanting eyes positively gleaming. It was enough to make Seg smile, even through his growing unease that something was very, very wrong.

Fi laid down on her bed and let Hap's pendant—identical to Peg's—dangle from her fingers, staring up at it with such intensity that she might have been trying to levitate it with her mind.

"You sure you don't see anything?" Seg said.

Fi shook her head. "It looks like a plain, unmarked pendant to me."

"Want me to draw the markings for you?"

"More than anything. But if the Feds search our room and find even a tracing, it could be dangerous. We can't give them any reasons to hold either of us in contempt of the Pact until we're away from here."

"When will that be?"

"Soon. For now, the less you know, the better off we both are."

Story of my life.

"I suppose that includes asking for your theory on what these pendants really are?"

"Mm."

"Or if the markings are actually writing of some sort?"

"I won't know until I see them, but..." She turned her enchanting blue eyes to him. "This is new territory for me, too. I honestly can't even guess what the markings are. But if the material is what I think it is, it's *vitally* important that we avoid calling the Fed's attention to them."

"Vitally?"

"Yes, as in they might stop being so cuddly-pleasant and decide to raze Holtondome to the ground."

Seg jumped out of his bed. *"What?"*

"No need to worry just yet. Most of them probably couldn't guess what the pendants are. I'm not even sure myself, beyond a hunch, but we should definitely err on the side of caution."

"Like I said before, your hunches are frighteningly accurate, which means we should act."

"Mm. Can you sweet-talk your busty friend out of the one you gave her?"

Seg leaned over the bed until his face was right over hers. *"Val.* My 'busty friend' has a name, and it's Val."

"And a wonderful name it is. I'm sure she's quite attached."

"What is this aversion you have to using people's names? I don't get it."

"I know. Someday I'll explain, but it'll have to wait."

"Right, just like everything else!"

Seg launched himself away in a huff, but Fi caught his arm and pulled him back.

"I'm not withholding information to hurt you. Do you believe me?"

Seg took a moment to let his anger subside so he could think clearly. The answer was obvious. He cast his eyes down and nodded.

"Good. And, to be honest, I'm glad you're comfortable enough with me to express your frustration." She sighed. "It also means I need to try a little harder to remember how frustrating it must be to walk in your shoes."

Seg rubbed his face. "No, I'm sorry, Miss Fi. I'm just... mentally exhausted."

"All the more reason for me to be sensitive." Fi pulled him down until he was sitting next to her on the bed. "The reason I avoid names is because they're... painful to me."

"Saying someone's name hurts?"

"Saying is easy, it's the remembering." She put a hand on his cheek. "Even your name, Seg."

His anger fled, replaced by a warmth that seemed to lift him right off the covers.

It hurts, but she does it anyway.

For me.

He burned to ask her why remembering names hurt, but doing so would only prove he hadn't been listening. He'd made his point, although in a less-suave manner than he would have liked, and Fi had responded as best she could. Seg would have to be content with that for now. He patted her hand and smiled.

Yes, he could survive in darkness a little longer.

For her.

"I'll do my best to get the pendant back from Val," Seg said.

"Good. And unless I've misread your relationship with your brother, it will be easier for me to get his than you."

"You haven't misread. The next question is where we should keep them until the Feds leave."

"Someplace convenient. We may need to flee Holtondome on a moment's notice, and we absolutely can't leave those pendants behind."

"Hmm, I have an idea."

"I thought you might." Fi pocketed Hap's pendant, then sat up and headed for the door. "Things are going to move quickly, so don't delay. Find me as soon as you have the other pendant. I'll do the same."

"What about Jen's?"

"I have after-dinner plans with your older sister tonight. I was originally going to go alone, but it's probably better if you come with me."

"She won't part with hers easily. Jen was furious when she discovered I'd given mine away."

"So was your mother, even if she didn't say it, but we convinced her anyway. Together, I'm sure we can convince your sister."

"And if not, we can probably get one of her kids to talk her out of it."

"Close to their Uncle Seg, are they?"

"With similar mischievous streaks, unfortunately for Jen. How Mom put up with me, I'll never understand—probably because I'll never have kids."

Fi froze with her hand on the doorknob. "Do you... want kids of your own, Seg?"

"In truth, I haven't thought about it much. My marriage prospects have always been so low that it wasn't worth considering."

Fi took a shuddering breath. "Please do. I'd really like to know."

Before Seg could ask what had spooked her, Fi opened the door and headed downstairs without a backward glance.

15

Seeds

TROY HOLTON HID HIS UNEASE when Doc Ven approached his bed in the medical ward. Ven's constant poking and prodding had left Troy finger-shy. His arm was still broken, and hurt like a mother. Ven verifying that over and over felt less like medical treatment than revenge for all the times Troy and Seg had sent each other to see him after one of their infamous fist fights.

Ven flashed the same smile he gave all his patients, probably so reflexive by now that he didn't realize he was doing it, or how fake it appeared.

"Mind if I take a look?"

Yes, you sadistic son-of-a-bitch.

"Go ahead, Doc, though I don't know what you hope to find that you haven't the last six times you checked today."

"What I hope to *not* find are signs of infection. The collector left you with numerous lacerations, which were exposed for Freyja-knows-how-long to runoff water from the dome—a recipe for infection if ever I heard one."

"Wish I'd stuck around a minute longer, then. That lightning bolt would have sterilized it right up."

"It would have saved me some trouble, that's for sure."

Troy grimaced. "Sorry, Doc. I guess you'll be happy to not hear my complaining when you finally let me out of here."

"I think I'd mind less if I knew why you did it. You're lucky to be alive, Troy, but you've treated this like you treat everything else: as a curse instead of the gift it is."

"Excuse me," a woman's voice said from outside the door, cutting off

Troy's reply. "I'm here to speak with Seg's brother."

"Brave woman," Ven said softly to Troy. "Or a masochist. Are you up for another visitor?"

"Depends. Will it save me from the torture you were about to inflict?"

"No."

Troy cursed under his breath. "Come in! Doc was just finishing up."

Doc turned on him with an indignant scowl.

They were both surprised, however, when the tall blonde outsider appeared.

Ven recovered first. "Begging your pardon, honored guest, but I think you should leave." His voice was unsteady despite his bold words. "My patient has had enough trauma without your... *aggressive* examination techniques compounding his condition."

"I agree, which is part of the reason I'm here. I wanted to apologize for my behavior, and to see how Holtondome's hero is recovering."

Troy laughed. "That title goes to my brother and that driver of yours, Cook. I'm just the moron who got caught in the storm."

"People may be focused on those who rescued the man with his arm wedged in the collector, but that doesn't mean your actions are any less heroic. If they had an ounce of sense, they'd be singing your praise for risking your life to ease the coming water shortage."

Troy started to cross his arms, but a shooting pain stopped him short. "So I was right?"

"*Are* right. I overheard someone from the water crew on the way over. Your arm and Seg's rock wedged it open enough to collect a few hundred gallons Holtondome wouldn't have had otherwise."

"It wasn't enough."

"No," Fi said, "but you bought the entire settlement a few more days—days for which they'll be thanking you when they have clean drinking water instead of parched throats."

"Nobody will even remember this event by then. Not that I care."

"*I* care. Few are willing to sacrifice themselves for the greater community, otherwise you wouldn't have been stuck out there alone. Your selfless act should be touted as model behavior."

Troy studied her for a moment to see if she was making fun of him. He wouldn't put it past his brother to have sent her here to set him up, only so she could dash his hopes by mocking him for being careless. Fi, however, just lifted her chin, her blue eyes sparkling with admiration.

"I... Look, it was nothing," Troy said, feeling his cheeks flush.

"You're not listening." She sat next to him and ran a gentle finger over the bandage on his right arm.

Troy cleared his throat. "Doc, w-would you excuse us?"

Ven eyed him like he was crazy, but eventually nodded and left the room.

Troy grinned at her, his heart racing. "Here I thought you were hot for my brother."

"I'm just trying to get your attention—not that you aren't attractive."

"Nice save, lady. Consider my ego unbruised."

"I'm guessing there are enough layers of protection around your heart to keep an army at bay. Or, at the very least, a love interest."

"Says the woman who kung fu'd half the dome when she found out I was alive."

"That wasn't an accusation," Fi said. "As you rightly pointed out, you and I are similar in that way. I know what bottled frustration does to a person, when you can't understand why no one sees things the way you do—things that should be as obvious as the noses on their faces. Like the coming water shortage, and why that collector had to be opened at any cost." Her fingers trailed to his chest. "You would have sacrificed yourself so the rest of the colony could have survived for just a little longer. It's hard to have meaningful relationships with people who don't share your depth of understanding. Your caring. Your passion."

Troy cracked a smile, although the growing heaviness in his chest made it difficult. The conversation wasn't going where he'd expected, and the accuracy of Fi's observations made it clear she wasn't the spoiled, City-born, baggage-carrying mess he'd pegged her for.

Which makes her even more dangerous, not less.

"If you were trying to make me feel better, Miss Fi, you might have better luck letting the pigs in here to rub mud in my wounds, because you failed miserably."

Fi shook her head. "There isn't much I could do in this medical ward to lift your spirits, even hanky panky, and we both know it. No, the only time you feel engaged—when you feel *fulfilled*—is when you're putting yourself on the line to solve critical problems the others can't. Or, in some cases, won't."

Troy gasped, finally remembering to breathe. He'd never spoken of this to anyone. Heck, he wasn't sure he could have articulated it himself until he'd heard the truth from this stranger's lips. It was as if she were peering into his very soul.

"How… how can you possibly know that?"

"Because I recognize a kindred spirit when I see one," Fi said. "And I've known too many others like us to miss the signs."

Troy smiled in full. This time it was easy.

His brother was one lucky bastard.

Still...

"This kindred spirit can't help feeling there's a reason you're telling me all this, Miss Fi. What do you need?"

"For you to do exactly what you've been doing your entire life: Understand what others don't. Risk yourself to save those who are unable or unwilling to save themselves."

"And you're not doing it yourself because...?"

"I'm risking more than you can imagine." Fi slipped a hand in her pocket and presented two tiny skin-colored devices no bigger than her pinky nail. "These contain the information you need to save Holtondome."

"What are they?"

"Audio players."

She pinched one of the odd-shaped devices between her fingers, brushed the hair back from the side of his face, and placed it in his ear. Troy recoiled at the strange feeling, but it passed a moment later, as if it were no longer there. Fi repeated the process with his other ear.

"What the Hel are you doing? A Provider owning technological devices is a stark violation of the Pact!"

"These aren't gifts. I expect you to return them as soon as you've finished listening to their contents, so your oath and honor are still intact."

"That will depend on what the players say."

"Nothing against the law, as you'll soon learn," Fi said, "though it will annoy the Feds that you managed to legally obtain the information."

"Huh. How do I use them?"

"Click your tongue, like you're smacking your lips for a delicious meal, then tell the players what you want them to do. They're pretty versatile and will guide you through the options."

Although he felt ridiculous, Troy imagined one of Nin's mouthwatering pot pies and clicked his tongue. An electronic *beep* sounded as if the source were right in front of him. "Um... start talking."

"Introduction," Fi's voice said in his ears, so naturally that he checked her lips to make sure she wasn't pulling a ventriloquism act to fool him. *"This audiobook is a curated collection of Federal laws relevant to Provider welfare. The contents have been approved for Provider distribution by the Bureau of Provider Affairs, the Pact Secretary, and his excellency Grand Chancellor Chang the Fifth. Any modification to this text is strictly prohibited under Section —"*

Troy clicked his tongue. The voice in his ears stopped, followed by another *beep*. On a whim, he clicked his tongue again. A series of tones played from high to low, giving him the impression of someone going to sleep.

"Your voice claimed this was approved by Chang the Fifth," Troy said. "Unless I've been mishearing my entire life, aren't we on Chang the Sixth?"

"That's right."

"Then why is this the first time I'm hearing about this, what did you call it… audiobook? It sounds pretty damn important to Holtondome."

"It is. As for why, telling you would be a violation of the Pact. After you listen to its contents, though, it won't be hard to guess."

"How much is there?"

"Enough that you might want to listen at double speed. We don't have much time."

"We?"

"Seg and I in particular, but more generally, everyone here. Once the Feds leave, remediating Holtondome's situation may not be possible until next season, where much of the damage will already be done. Worse, new laws may be in place by then to make remediation impossible."

Troy shook his head. "I still don't get it. This is your voice in the audiobook, Miss Fi. You know these laws better than I ever will. If you care so much, why not pick up the torch yourself?"

"I'm not a Provider. Coming from me, it would be too easy for them to sweep my accusations aside with charges of Pact violation pertaining to unlawful information exchange. But if you discover the information on your own, carefully…"

"I get it." He studied her for a moment. Fi's face might have been carved from stone. "I still can't help feel you're piling all the risk onto me."

"You'll glimpse what I'm risking in the next twenty-four hours, but if you still need convincing…" Fi grabbed a medicine bottle and absently rolled it between her fingers. "There are a few other pieces of information that weren't safe to record. Things you need to know that will definitely get me arrested if the Feds discover I told you."

Troy leaned forward with an eager grin. "*Now* we're talking."

16

Kindling

VAL WASN'T ON THE FIRST floor when Seg checked, nor in her room. A few queries confirmed that she was still in her inquisition, which was worrisome. Inquiries over an hour long usually meant they'd uncovered something suspicious, and were taking their time to dissect the problem from several different angles, including calling additional witnesses for cross-verification.

When she finally did appear over half an hour later, Seg had to clamp his feet together to resist running to her. Such a display in front of the Feds would be a quick way to get on the witness list.

Val, too, maintained her composure until they were well away from the Fed encampment, where she blew a sigh and collapsed against him.

"That bad, huh?"

"The worst I've ever endured. I'll need three showers to wash away the stink they tried to rub on me."

"No charges?"

"Not on me," she said softly into his shirt. "Dear Mr. Cook might not be as lucky, though."

Seg paled. "So they asked you about him, too."

"To put it mildly. They... drilled into our relationship quite far." Her voice broke on the last, becoming quiet sobs that shook her body against his.

Seg wrapped her in an embrace and held her for a minute, until her sobbing subsided. She looked up at him with tear-filled eyes.

"Seg, I... I made a terrible mistake."

What little blood remaining in his face drained completely away. "What happened?"

161

"I asked questions I shouldn't have. Cook resisted at first, but you know how it is in bed. People say things they don't mean, or have no business sharing. I... I used that to my advantage, and he caved. He caved to please me. And now..."

Seg's mouth went dry, but he forced himself to speak. "What things?"

"Everything!" Val broke into tears again. "I couldn't help it! I had to know. Once he started talking, we just kept going on and on and on, as if the Pact didn't exist. It was fascinating and wonderful and terrifying, so I kept asking questions."

"Right before an inquisition... Val, how could you?"

She pushed away from him, her face twisted in anger. "He was leaving today! We never get visitors from the City who aren't strictly monitored by the Feds. Never! When would I get a chance like this again? A chance to *know!* Isn't that what we always fantasized about? How wonderful it must be to build a spacecraft capable of carrying human beings all the way to Mars? What must the Cities be like who crafted such marvels?" Her expression darkened further. "Well, I did more than wonder, Seg. I got answers!"

"At what cost? Cook's life? *Yours?*"

"Don't you *dare* stand there and judge me as if you wouldn't have done exactly the same in my position! I know you too well. Our insatiable curiosities drew us together as children, and have drawn us *both* to these outsiders today."

Her anger melted into another shuddering sob.

"Don't you dare leave me alone in this," Val whispered, tears cascading down her cheeks. "Not when I need you the most. Not again. P-please..."

Seg was holding her before he realized he'd moved, and crushed her to him while she cried.

Is that how she regarded his stepping away all those years ago, when her marriage prospects had come into question? He'd done it for her, removed himself from the equation so she'd be free of the stigma that attached itself to anyone Seg associated with, free to choose any man she wished, to have healthy, happy children, and a rich social life—none of which Seg could offer.

The result had been less than ideal, although neither of them could have predicted it at the time. After much trying, Val and her husband hadn't been able to conceive, and Nat hadn't been half the man about it that Val deserved. Then he'd died, leaving her in a cruel limbo of not knowing if she was fertile, of not being approachable by suitors out of respect for the deceased, and out of fear that she was somehow damaged goods.

Distancing himself had been a mistake Seg wouldn't repeat.

"I won't leave you," he said into her hair. "Not this time. We'll see this through together, I promise."

Her arms tightened around him. She nodded into his shirt and cried harder.

"Val," he said after she'd calmed a bit, "I need a big favor."

She sniffled. "What is it?"

Seg reluctantly withdrew from her arms and pulled the leather strip around her neck, lifting his old pendant out from its comfy home between her breasts.

Val snatched it away and shook her head. "Not. A. Chance. Not unless you plan to give me something even more sentimental in exchange."

"But I don't have anything else."

"Exactly. This is your most precious possession, and you gave it to me. Me! It means more to me than that thick head of yours will ever know. I won't let you give it to that…" Val bit her lip and turned away. "She won't appreciate it, Seg. Not like I do. Please don't take it away from me."

The lion twins appeared from around a stack of apple crates. Seg froze, worried what they may have overheard, but the brother-and-sister pair spared him only a disparaging frown before passing on.

Seg gently drew Val deep within the crate maze to give them some privacy. His tongue stuck to the roof of his mouth when she turned to him, her eyes large and cheeks flushed. It was a look he remembered fondly, one that shot liquid heat through his veins.

"The first time we kissed was behind a stack of apple crates," Val said breathily. "Do you remember?"

"I do," Seg said, although it was a massive understatement. That day, and especially the night following, had occupied his dreams for most of his adult life.

Val edged closer. Her heat warmed his already flushed face. "Is that why you brought me here?"

Yes…

"N-no," Seg said, shaking his head to clear the lust-fog clouding his thoughts. There was so much at stake. He had to focus…

She sagged. "Why do you torture me so? You know how I feel, thanks to that insidious woman's goading. You hold my hand, crush me to you as if we're lovers, and then cast me aside as if I'm n—"

Val gave a startled squeal, muted by Seg's mouth covering her own. After a moment, she returned his kiss with fervent passion. Val tasted just like he remembered—of cinnamon, sweetness, and elemental fire that kindled his loins into a roaring inferno. How many times he'd daydreamed of her tongue dancing with his. How many solitary nights he'd yearned just one more time for her body to press against him—hot, supple, and heavenly, as if she'd been hand-carved just for Seg.

Her fingers slipped down to his trousers and began fumbling with the drawstring. Seg caught her hands and reluctantly stepped away. How he wished Holtondome's fate could wait just a few more hours...

"Val," he said softly, trying to wrestle his breathing under control. "There's more going on than you know. I would give you everything I have—everything I ever will!—to make you happy, and it would never be enough to equal the joy I'd receive each and every morning to wake up with you beside me."

Her face split into a dazzling white smile that made his heart melt. She closed for another kiss, but Seg drew back.

"But there are things we need to discuss, and they can't wait. Not even for this moment I've been dreaming of since the day we gave ourselves to each other as teens."

Her face fell. "What is it? Are you in trouble?"

"We all are." Seg reached for her pendant, unable to keep his eyes from lingering on its heavenly resting place, and held it up. "Fi says these are important somehow, important enough that the Feds might wipe us all out if they knew we had them."

Val's expression darkened into a scowl. "So it's just 'Fi' now, is it?"

Was it? Seg rewound the sentence in his head, and was just as surprised as her when he realized it was true. He gently took her by the shoulders. "Val, please, *please* listen. We've already collected Peg and Hap's pendants. *Miss* Fi is talking to Troy right now to get his, and we'll hopefully have Jen's tonight after dinner. Once I have yours—"

"You'll go back to *her*," Val said, tears brimming again. "Is that all this was? Were those sweet words crafted just to make me pliable? Was that kiss—"

"From my heart! Damnit, Val... I've loved you for so long that if Doc Ven cut open my chest, he would see your face staring back at him. But this isn't about our relationship—or about me and Miss Fi, or you and Cook. You've just told me that you're about to come under a *lot* of scrutiny, which I'll do everything in my power to help you out of. But if what Miss Fi says is true, there's a chance one of them will recognize that pendant for what it is."

"And what exactly is it?"

"I have no idea. I honored the Pact and didn't ask."

Val blushed furiously, but remained quiet.

"I do know its discovery could be fatal for everyone in Holtondome. Please, Val, I need that pendant so we can hide it away with the others."

Val narrowed her eyes—another look Seg knew well, and it wasn't good.

"I still need something in return," she said eventually.

"I told you, I don't have anything else."

"All right, then, a promise."

"What promise?"

She grabbed his collar and drew him close. "That everything you just told me is true."

"Well, I can't promise my heart is *actually* in the shape of your face, but apart from that…" He kissed her briefly, tenderly. "Yes, it's all true."

"And that Miss Fi means nothing to you?"

"I…" Seg ducked his head, unable to meet her eyes. "There's something else we need to talk about. Val, I… I'm leaving Holtondome."

Val gave a dismissive laugh, but it died when she saw his serious expression. Her eyes glistened. "With her?"

"Yes."

"Because you love her?"

Seg met her gaze, the heat of conviction in his voice. "No. I love *you*."

"Then you're going to find a way to take me with you."

"I… but I don't even know how she's going to get me out of Holtondome, let alone both of us."

"She's clever. I'm sure she'll think of something." When Seg lapsed into troubled silence, Val cupped his cheek and forced him to meet her eyes. "I'm serious. If you're going off, then you're damn well not leaving me here to rot. We had the same dream once of seeing the wonders of the City *together*. Mine hasn't changed. Has yours?"

"No," he said softly.

Val nodded, then slipped her pendant up over her head and stuffed it into Seg's pocket. "If I see this around her pretty little neck, I'll feed you to the pigs."

"You won't. Thanks, Val."

"If Miss Fi can do as she claims—for *both* of us—it will be worth losing the most precious gift I've ever received. I just hope she does it quickly, before the Feds discover my breach of the Pact."

"What? I thought they already had."

Val shook her head. "But it's only a matter of time. They'll find the truth."

"They always do," Seg finished for her. "Any idea where they're questioning Cook?"

"Yes. Shall we go wait for him?"

Seg fingered the pendant in his pocket, eager to get it in Fi's hands and safely away, but one look into Val's beautiful eyes destroyed his resolve. With a nod, he hooked her arm and led them out of the apple crates to the main thoroughfare and back to the Fed encampment.

Where an officer was just bringing Cook out of a vehicle, bound in handcuffs.

17

The Greater Good

FI WAS JUST EXITING THE medical ward when Seg and Val arrived, walking as fast as they could without drawing attention.

"We have a problem," Seg said quietly.

Fi glanced at their hooked arms. Her eye twitched. "A big-boobed one, I'd say. Did she give you the item in question?"

"Yes, though she didn't make it easy."

Seg had meant it as a joke to break the tension, but neither of them laughed. Val stiffened at his side.

Fi took two long steps to close the distance between them. She stared at his mouth, sniffed long and poignantly, then ran a finger down his lips.

"Yes, I can tell you suffered greatly."

"It was just a kiss," Val said, her cheeks as red as Seg's felt. "You of all people should understand, Miss Fi."

"Absolutely. In fact..." Fi pulled Troy's pendant from her pocket and dangled it in front of Seg. "Should I ask for similar payment, Seg? Actually, I scored your mother's pendant as well. What steamy favors could I earn for two?"

"Stop it!" Val said through clenched teeth. "You're the one who badgered me into admitting I love him in front of everyone just for sport. Now you're being petty because I acted on it before you could, and succeeded in getting Seg to..." Her angry expression melted into concern. "Are you all right, Miss Fi?"

Seg had been so focused on Val that he hadn't noticed Fi turn completely white, staring as if a ghost stood between them.

"Miss Fi?" He waved a hand in front of her.

Fi blinked. Her eyes focused once again. "Yes. Yes, I'm fine." She absently handed Troy's pendant to Seg with a trembling hand, then leaned against the wall.

"I'm sorry if this is upsetting," Val said gently. "I really do love him."

"Yes, I know." Her enchanting eyes turned back to Val with a compassion Seg had never seen from her. "You're wonderful together. He's lucky to have you."

"Oh. Um… th-thank you, Miss Fi."

"Mm." She took Val's hand. "Sorry to even ask, but can I borrow him for a short while?"

"I… y-yes, of course. I'm sure you two have a bit to catch up on. I'll just… I'll be in Tad's tavern." Val caught Seg's eye and tossed her head at Fi, a not-so-subtle reminder of his promise to convince her to bring Val when they departed Holtondome, then she headed for the stairs.

"Miss Fi, I need to ask a favor," Seg said when they were alone.

"Mm?" Fi's voice was dreamy, as if she'd slipped back into a trance.

"Val made a mistake, one that might cost her life. I'd like to bring her with us."

"Mm."

Seg blinked. "What, just like that? No cryptic lessons or anything?"

Fi shook herself. "That… might be difficult, Seg."

"I have no doubt. And really, I wouldn't even ask if it wasn't life or death. I can only imagine how hard it will be to get one person out of here, let alone two."

"That isn't the problem. I can take even more people with us, if needed."

"Then what's the issue?"

Fi stepped close and fiddled with a button on his shirt, then dropped her hands. "I saw her death. Just now."

The words rattled in Seg's hollow chest. "No, it… it couldn't be. You must be mistaken."

"I'm many things, but rarely that. Your friend's time has come."

Seg tried to look at her, but his vision was too blurry to see. He wiped his tears away. "How? When?"

"Same as your vision. She has hours, at most. It will probably happen just after sundown."

"But… we can save her, right?" After all, what good was this godsforsaken precognition if he couldn't use it to save the people he loved?

Her eyes roved his forehead, nose, cheeks, and pointed chin. She brushed a tear from his face and nodded. "I'll try to save her. I'll also bring her with us. I ask for only one, simple thing in return."

"Name it."

Fi wrapped her arms around his neck and drew him close, but this time, she didn't stop there. Her lips brushed his like a breeze through a sunny meadow—soft, warm, caressing. When her mouth opened to drink him in, Seg swore he could taste flowers and a refreshing river. Her heat was like he imagined the sun, basking him in its loving glory. Her tongue moved with a dancer's grace, stealing his breath, his senses, his will to do anything but beg for more of her primal perfection.

He almost cried when she pulled away.

"Don't count me out," Fi said breathily.

Seg could only nod. He couldn't have refused her even if the Feds had held him at gunpoint.

She rested her forehead against his and sighed. "It was the same vision you described. I saw her get shot through the chest."

"Did you see who did it, or where?"

Fi shook her head. "It's a reasonable assumption that it happens by the Fed encampment, though. Has your vision played recently?"

Seg stared in the direction of the encampment for several minutes. "No, which is strange. The vision usually triggers as soon as I look at it, but I'm getting nothing now."

Fi held a pendant up. "You still see the markings, though?"

"As clearly as your beautiful eyes."

Her eyes widened, then she giggled.

Giggled!

"I never expected a line like that from you," Fi said with a smile. "And I *really* didn't expect to fall for it. You're a refreshing bag of surprises, Mr. Seg."

"'Mister,' now, is it?"

"Seems only fair. Unless you'd like to change the rules…?"

He wrapped his arms around her waist and pulled her close. "Yes, I think I would. Fi."

"Much better. Now…" She twirled out of his embrace with a grand flourish and bowed. "We have much to do, and precious little time. We should start with the pendants, then rendezvous with your busty lady love and form a strategy. You can fill me in on the details of her little *faux pas* along the way. We should also locate my driver, since we'll need his services very soon."

"Ah… that's the other problem we need to talk about."

Seg led her down the main thoroughfare and toward the east entrance, and quietly filled her in on the details of Val and Cook's situations along the way.

"You like to make things challenging for me, don't you?" Fi said once he'd finished.

"I'm sorry, Miss Fi, really."

She stopped in her tracks and leveled him with a stare.

"*Fi*, I meant. Sorry, that's going to take some getting used to."

"Forgiven. And, despite what you might think, I wasn't complaining."

"Seriously? With all the trouble we've caused, in your place, I'd be furious."

"They're puzzles to be solved, that's all, and I like a good puzzle. The more pieces there are, the more satisfying it is when they all snap together." Fi graced him with another smile. "And you, Seg, might be the most challenging puzzle I've ever faced. I won't give that up without a fight."

"Um… thanks?"

"You're welcome, but don't take it as permission to push the limits of my problem-solving skills." Fi glanced at a nearby garage, then did a double-take. Her grin widened. "I might have just found a better hiding place for the pendants."

"What, there?" Crates and other agricultural supplies filled the large storage warehouse. "I suppose, as long as no one needs to fetch a wheelbarrow. Besides, you don't know the hiding spot I had in mind. It might be better than yours."

"Let's see if you still feel that way in a minute."

Fi glanced around. The thoroughfare was empty except for a couple with their backs to them. She nodded and slipped inside the warehouse. Seg followed.

They weaved through a maze of baskets, crates, and empty fertilizer boxes into the growing darkness, until Seg had to navigate by feel. Fi continued undaunted, as if she knew exactly where she was going.

Small surprise.

She stopped at a blank section of wall. "See this?"

"Not very well."

"Me neither." Fi ran her fingers over the smooth surface, side-to-side, down to the floor, then as far up as she could reach in the high-ceiling room. "I know it's here somewhere… ah!"

In the near-total darkness, Seg could barely make out Fi's finger depress into the wall, followed by a *click*. She slid her fingers up the wall and pressed another hidden button, then down to her knees and pressed a third. With a nod, she put her shoulder to the wall next to the circular depressions. After a few grunting tries, a section of wall the size of a door grudgingly swung inward. Fi dusted her hands, then gestured him to follow her into the pitch blackness.

"Close the door behind you," Fi said.

Seg hesitated, loathe to cut off their only light source, as weak as it was, but eventually complied and slid the stubborn thing shut. It settled in place with three audible clicks.

Her warm hand took his. "Good. Follow me."

Seg walked a pace behind in total darkness, keeping one hand on the wall if only for his own sanity.

"Where are we going?" His imagination conjured a sleeping dragon ahead. Although his rational mind knew it was absurd, he couldn't bring himself to speak above a whisper.

"You'll see, right about..."

Overhead lights bloomed with painful brilliance, revealing a tall, octagonal space not much bigger than their bedroom.

What their bedroom didn't have, however, was a life-sized statue of a woman standing on a pedestal right in the center of it.

Realization took his breath away. "This... this is the statue of Thorn's sister, Holly, from your story."

Fi seemed not to hear. She circled the statue, her eyes drinking in every detail. She reached up and trailed her fingers along the statue's metal ones, which were turned outward in an eternal gesture of giving.

"Holly..." Fi shook herself, as if just remembering Seg were there. "The pendants should be safe here. Neither this statue, nor this room or its secret door, are anywhere on Holtondome's blueprints. The Feds have no reason to believe it exists."

"But how is that possible? How could something like this exist without its builders—or even its residents—knowing about it?"

"Erecting icons that might rally people around the old ways is illegal. It was even then, as Thorn Holton knew, but he was resourceful, and very determined that his sister's memory live on—as was Holly's handmaiden. They conspired with private contractors to sneak into the construction site after hours. What they built here, they did quietly, and in a single night."

"Including the statue?"

"The pedestal, yes, but not the statue itself. The statue was made in secret and smuggled inside along with that day's construction material delivery."

"Who made it?"

"The handmaiden. Her name is here on the plaque, along with a personal message to her dear friend, whose life she failed to save."

Seg stared at the golden squiggles on the dusty black plaque, nestled just below Holly's bare feet peeking out from below her dress. "Would you read it to me?"

"Mm." Fi cleared her throat, then again, but her voice was still raspy when she spoke. "'Dance in sunlight, my sweet Holly, and bring peace to the angry heavens as you have to me. Your eternal friend and servant, Ofilia.'"

"Ofilia... what a beautiful name. I still can't believe she and Thorn went through the trouble of erecting a statue that no one might ever see."

"As you can tell by the inscription, the handmaiden was very close to Holly. She and Thorn were both guilt-ridden that she had died instead of them on that tragic night. More than that, they hoped the statue would survive to see an age where domes were unnecessary, and people could once again be free to read, write, and erect monuments of those they admire."

"You really don't agree with the Pact, do you?"

"I'll answer that question at length if and when we get away from Holtondome. Speaking of..." Fi circled to the rear of the statue and curled a finger beneath the hem of Holly's metallic dress.

A large drawer popped open just below the lip of the pedestal.

Fi withdrew the two gray pendants from her pocket and placed them inside, next to a weathered, leather-bound notebook with loose sheets of paper on top.

Seg placed Val's pendant inside as well. He ran a finger along the book's cracked surface, and the paper's brown, frayed edges.

"What are these?"

"The papers are a few of Holly's favorite recipes, including the original copy of her famous pot pie. The book is her diary."

"As in... the diary you've already read? But how is that possible if it's been here the entire time?"

"Who do you think put it here? The handmaiden's journal is filled with rebellious ideas on government and society in general, a reflection of her strongly opinionated personality. Having contraband like that in my possession would be dangerous, especially with the Feds present."

"Okay, but you've been glued to my side almost every moment since you arrived. I think I'd remember if we'd visited this statue before."

"That's because I left it here on my last visit. And before you ask, no, it isn't safe to tell you when that was, so that conversation will have to wait."

Seg ground his teeth. He wasn't mad at Fi, per se, for he understood her reasoning. What he couldn't get around was the frustrating chasm between them that only answers could bridge. He couldn't feel close to someone he knew almost nothing about.

That was the difference between them. To Fi, Seg was an open book, but Fi was closed down tighter than a dome in an acid storm. It was no wonder why a relationship with Val was so much easier to imagine, why he'd said the things he'd said—things he still couldn't believe had come out of his mouth.

He turned away, the thrill of the hidden statue and its treasure trove lost in feelings of helplessness.

Fi caught his arm and gently turned him back around. "I will fix this, Seg. If we get you out of here, then, for better or worse, you'll have all the answers you ever wanted, and you can decide then if I'm worth your affection. Until that time, I can only ask for your patience, an open mind, and your faith that I'm doing my best to protect *both* of our interests."

"But you barely know me," Seg said softly. "Why are you risking so much?"

"I probably know you better than you know yourself. If you don't believe me, then ask yourself how many times I've been wrong about your feelings, or about what you're thinking, or about your needs. How many others—even people you've known your whole life—have ever come as close?"

Seg sighed. "Val has."

"Has she?" Fi put a hand on his chest. "I know better than to compare the two of us; you have little reason to trust me, and every reason to trust her. So I ask you to carefully consider: if you and I had grown up together, even with what little you know about me, how differently things might have turned out than they did with her. And, most importantly, why."

Seg wanted to object, but it would have been empty and baseless, and Fi knew it. Even without trying, he knew the answer—saw their happy lives together as clearly as his vision of that poor woman's death.

Of Val's death.

He shook himself to shed the unpleasant thought and crossed his arms. "And what if you're wrong?"

Fi arched an eyebrow.

"What if big boobs are the only thing I'm looking for in a woman?"

"You aren't that superficial. Now, let's go before you say anything else to damage my high opinion of you."

Fi pushed the drawer closed with a *click*, surreptitiously shifted her modest bust within her bodice, and brushed past him to the secret door.

Seg chuckled. "You know I was only joking, right?"

Fi froze with her hand on the door. Her arm dropped. "I know. That isn't the reason I'm upset."

She's upset?

From her calm demeanor, Seg would never have guessed. "I'm sorry."

Fi turned to him. Seg was shocked to find tears in her eyes. "Have you given any more thought to my earlier question about wanting children?"

It suddenly clicked. Seg's heart dropped to his feet. "You... you're infertile. Like Val."

"Not like her," Fi said, sniffling. "I ran a few tests, with her consent. I haven't told her the results yet, but she's perfectly capable of conceiving. Her husband must have been the infertile party. I shouldn't be telling you this without her permission, but..." She took his hand with trembling fingers, her usual confidence replaced with teenaged insecurity. "Seg, children are the one thing I can never give you. You're at a crucial decision point between us, so it's only fair that you know. I'll apologize to her later for the breach of patient confidentiality."

The look of pure misery on her exotic face—of complete, unabashed vulnerability—was heart-wrenching. Fi had confessed her condition to him knowing it was an area where she couldn't compete.

A confession, he knew with sudden certainty, that she had been forced to make before, and at great personal cost. It was written all over her devastated face.

"I think... there's still time for me to make a decision," Seg said. "As you've mentioned, I know Val well, but, through no fault of your own, I haven't had the opportunity to get to know you yet."

Fi studied him. For the first time since he'd known her, she seemed completely at a loss about what he was thinking. "Neither time nor the best medical treatments can ever fix my infertility. I won't blame you for walking away."

"And here I thought you knew me," Seg said with a warm smile.

She placed a gentle hand on his cheek. "I'd hoped you wouldn't, but it's good to hear the words."

Fi leaned in for a lingering kiss, tasting again of fresh breezes and long-extinct forests. He pulled her body against his, longing for more of that world he would never know—a world that somehow lived inside her.

Fi responded in kind. Skilled fingers caressed his back like waves on a tropical shore, washing away his anxiety, his inhibitions, slowly drawing him into a deep sea of desire.

Gently she tugged his shirt over his head and paused to appreciate his toned chest with probing fingers. It might have been Seg's imagination, or perhaps his lust-addled mind, but the dark circles around her eyes appeared larger, pulsing with a strange life of their own. She started to hike her dress up, but Seg caught her arm and chuckled.

"Are we really going to do this? Here?"

In answer, Fi pulled her dress up over her head and tossed it aside. Not taking her eyes from his, she unfastened her bra and let it fall, revealing her athletic figure. Like the marks around her eyes, the black markings on her body seemed larger than before. They throbbed around her pert breasts, forming smooth waves that carried his eyes down to the gentle swell of her womb, and then into her white-laced panties.

Fi was, in a word, breathtaking.

"I've learned the hard way when to be patient, and when to seize opportunities I may never get again." Fi's voice was throatier than usual, which stoked his desire. "You've already had your busty lady love. It wouldn't be fair to choose her without giving me the same chance to sway you."

Fi slid her panties off in one smooth motion, giving him a full view of her in all her glory. His heart was beating so fast he feared it might break. She pulled at his waistband. Seg needed no encouragement to strip out of his pants and underwear. The air was cold on his skin, but he hardly noticed, his attention wholly, helplessly on the creature of beauty before him.

Fi took a sultry step forward, closing the gap between them. Her body's heat radiated like a welcome hearth, beckoning him closer.

"My womb may be barren, but everything else works perfectly. Let me show you what I can offer that she never could."

Her gentle fingers washed down his chest, slowly, torturously, caressing his stomach. Seg shuddered from her sensual touch and let out a small moan, his desire at a height he had long forgotten possible.

He wanted her. Needed her. And he wanted Fi to feel the same.

Fi flashed a smile. The black markings around her eyes and all down her front throbbed with increasing speed.

On a whim, Seg put an index finger on the top of each of her breasts, where the flowing black marks began.

The marks responded to his touch with a shudder that rippled through Fi's entire body. Her mouth opened with a long gasp. Pleased by her response, Seg followed the strange, undulating waves, his fingertips skimming her smooth skin with strained patience. He wanted to touch her. Everywhere. Now. But the markings called to him, so he heeded their languid pace.

Fi's breathing became ragged pants. Her enchanting eyes fixed on his, hungry, but helpless to his touch. By the time his fingers completed their circles around her lovely mounds, she was shuddering with small, grunting whimpers. The lines pulsed rapidly with her urgent breaths, encouraging his fingers to move down.

Seg was more than happy to oblige. He followed the waves down her ribs. Each bump made her cry out, pant heavier. Her pupils dilated until her eyes themselves appeared almost completely black. Seg traced his fingers along the marks down around her navel, then over the gentle swell of her belly. Fi's breathing became frantic, her whimpers more insistent, her limbs shaking.

Slowly, gently, his fingers reached the warm heaven between her legs.

Fi arched her back with a sensual roar that shook her entire body. When she looked back at him, it wasn't as a woman or lover, but as a primal beast intent on devouring her prey. Her normally enchanting eyes were wild with desire.

Fi knocked him hard on his back, cold against the metal floor, then pounced on him like a ravenous animal in heat.

After what must have been a solid hour of nonstop bucking, Fi finally collapsed on top of him, completely spent. Their lovemaking, if that was what he could call her frenzied attack, had been a frantic marathon, ending with a cry of release so loud he was sure they'd heard Fi from the very top of Holtondome.

Seg rubbed her back and held her, afraid that if he let go, she might return to whatever altered state had possessed her. Although his heavenly night with Val had been many years ago, he didn't remember her getting worked into anything near Fi's rabid frenzy.

Fi rolled her head from side to side. Her voice was hoarse and raw in his ear. "I couldn't stop. And the pleasure... I've never felt anything like it."

"You mean, that wasn't normal?"

"Mm-mm. What did you do to me?"

"All I did was trace your markings."

Fi struggled up and rested on her elbow. Her haggard face regarded him with a frown.

"The black markings on your chest," Seg said. "Like the ones around your eyes."

Fi held his gaze, then took a shuddering breath and collapsed against him.

"Seg," she said softly, her voice haunted, "I don't have any markings."

18

Fi

SEG GATHERED FI CLOSE. HER body was as limp as wet noodles, as he'd expect after such an intense, feral burst of passion—which gave him time to wrap his head around what had just happened, and her startling words. The Fi who'd attacked him just now was so different from the calm, measured Fi he knew that Seg had trouble believing they were the same person, and it had started when he'd traced her markings.

The markings she apparently didn't have.

He brushed her hair back to get a good look at her eyes, which were red and puffy, but, more importantly, at the thick black marks circling them. Her marks had stopped pulsing. As he suspected they would, they also disappeared when he closed his left eye, just like the strange symbols on the pendants.

"What do the marks look like?"

Fi sounded so exhausted that Seg tightened his arms around her to make sure she wouldn't slide off him to the cold metal floor.

"I thought they were black tattoos," Seg said, "so that's probably the easiest way to describe them. Want me to trace them for you?"

"Very much, but if the same thing happens as last time, I'll need rest and a full meal to survive another round."

Seg chuckled. "That's not at all what I was suggesting, but... You'd really go through that again?"

"In a heartbeat. The experience was... *unworldly,* and deserves thorough exploration. However, we've dallied long enough already. Blissful as it might be, further experiments will have to wait."

Fi rose on shaky limbs. Their unjoining left Seg feeling empty, as if part of him were suddenly missing. Fi, too, gave him a last, appreciative look before heaving a sigh and gathering her clothes.

Seg stood with a wince. The frenetic ordeal had left his hips sore, so he could only imagine how Fi felt.

"One thing I will ask," Fi said once their outfits were in proper order. "Are the markings on my body similar to those on the pendants?"

"Not at all. Yours are long and flowing, almost like they're alive. The marks on the pendants are smaller, angular, and consistent, like I'd imagine writing to be."

Fi frowned. "Have you ever seen markings like mine on anyone else?"

"Never. I mean, I've seen tattoos before, but they were real ones."

"You're sure?"

"Definitely. I know the tattoo artist."

"Mm." Fi's expression softened. She cupped his cheeks and gave him a tender kiss. "You are without a doubt the most exhilarating puzzle I've ever faced."

"Is… is that all I am to you?"

"If you have to ask, then you aren't nearly as perceptive as I thought. This incredible sight of yours is just icing on an already scrumptious cake."

Seg smiled. "I'd hoped, but it's nice to hear the words."

"*Touché*. And, at the risk of sounding pushy, I'm more convinced now than ever that you and I are somehow bound. This is too much for coincidence."

"You believe in fate, Miss—er, Fi?"

She grimaced at his slip, but patted his arm warmly. "We foresee people's deaths. How couldn't I?"

"And despite Val's fate, and that she and I are, ah… compatible, too, you're still willing to help her?"

Fi considered him with a neutral expression. "I am," she said eventually. "Although I hate to admit it, I don't dislike your busty lady love. She has spirit, even if it's misdirected. With time, guidance, and a little temperance, she'd be formidable."

"That's a brave admission. I thought you were trying to sway me to your side, not sell me on Val."

Fi took his hands and gave a gentle squeeze. "I know people, Seg, better than you can imagine. I can see your relationship with her play out as clearly as a vision. You would have a wonderful, energetic life together, filled with ups and downs and shared adventure, born of your mutual curiosity and willingness to try new things. Your children would be beautiful. She would be a caring mother, involved in all the right aspects of her children's lives, which would both drive them crazy and be the best thing that ever happened to them.

"And you would be an amazing husband and father. Your family would never lack, because you would accept nothing less than the best for all of them that was within your means to give. You would die old together, happy with each other for company, and that you had wonderful children to carry your legacy."

Seg was so enraptured he'd forgotten to breathe. How she had so exquisitely captured the fantasy he had never himself dared to dream was beyond reckoning.

Fi laughed—a sad, hollow sound—and brushed a tear from his cheek. "I know, too, how desperately you want those things you never thought you'd have. And how heartless I would be to even think of denying them to you. I won't, Seg. If you choose her, I'll wish you every happiness, and do everything I can to keep you together, hoping only that you'll both think of me not as a rival, but a friend, so we can stay in touch."

Seg brushed the wetness from his eyes, his voice thick. "W-why are you telling me all this?"

"Because I don't want you to hate me when you eventually discover I could see these outcomes when you couldn't. For that same reason, I need to also tell you how our relationship would be."

Fi stepped closer, her breath warm on his lips. Her enchanting eyes sparkled with hope. "You would get your answers about me and many other things, though they may not be what you want to hear. After the shock and…" She gulped, but took a deep breath and continued in a steady voice. "And possible revulsion passed, you would appreciate everything I have to offer—the knowledge I can bestow, the doors I can open.

"We'd travel the Earth, everywhere you want to go—even to Mars Colony. I'd answer questions you can't imagine asking at present, paint a picture of the world for you as no other person can. You would bask in the knowledge, soak it in like the clever person you are. Together, we'd expand that knowledge, explore our unique talents, and unravel this new mystery of your blind eye that isn't really blind, the implications of which are beyond even my imagining."

She edged closer until their lips brushed.

"It would be a very different life from your and hers, but wonderful, nonetheless. If you choose me, Seg, I *will* make you happy."

Seg stared at her as if seeing her for the first time. He took her by the shoulders if only to keep from falling over. His heart pounded with a different kind of excitement, one filled with promise and hope that he'd denied himself until now.

And at the center of it all was this beautiful, mysterious creature, who teased him at every turn, tantalizing him just enough to drive his curiosity wild. It twisted his gut and suffused his mind until he could think of nothing else. It burned, eating him from the inside. His fingers tightened, divoting her arms.

"Who are you?" he said in a strained voice.

Fi opened her mouth, then snapped it shut and shook her head. "You wouldn't believe me. Not yet."

"Try me."

"No. I told you, Seg, I know people. Your curiosity burns, but there aren't enough puzzle pieces in place for you to guess the full picture. If I tell you now, your mind will fill in what it wants to believe. What it *fears*. It will drive you away, even more than not knowing would, and I won't do that to myself. I won't lose you so carelessly."

Seg ground his teeth. Her answer was unacceptable. Not that she was wrong—he'd seen too much in the day-and-change he'd spent with Fi to doubt the truth of her insights—but the familiar glint in her eye told him this was a lesson. She wanted him to know who she was, perhaps badly, but her approach was consistent with how she'd handled most of his questions.

He realized with startling clarity why.

The process of discovery—the intimate journey of discerning the truth without being told—was the most powerful form of learning he'd ever experienced.

And Fi was a master at it. She would give no unnecessary hints; if Seg couldn't reason it out, then he wasn't ready—or worthy—to know. She'd never bent on that philosophy, and he was positive she wouldn't do so now.

Fi watched him with such hope that his heart nearly burst with affection. She'd placed her faith in him—believed in him as no one in his life ever had. Now she was counting on him to assemble the pieces she had undoubtedly laid throughout their conversations so he could finally see her—the *real* her.

And he wanted to. Desperately.

I'll be damned if I let her down!

He raced through the facts in his mind, aware that Cook, Val, and all of Holtondome's clocks may well be ticking.

"You're... old." Seg knew how lame his declaration sounded even as he said it, but once it was out there, puzzle pieces started to snap into place. "Older than Cook."

Fi crossed her arms, but remained silent.

Of course, she'll want evidence to back my claim.

"We don't have many elders here, so it's hard for me to compare, but Cook's insights speak of years beyond anyone in Holtondome. If I had to guess, I'd say he's over a hundred at least. Maybe one-twenty."

Fi nodded. "Cook celebrated his one hundred and twenty-second birthday seventeen days ago."

Seg paled. He hadn't expected to be right, but that wasn't what made his head spin.

"And you're older than him. A lot older. Cook has insights, but he's irresponsible, and, more importantly, often wrong. It's hard for me to imagine what it must be like to be alive for that long, so I can only speculate what he's seen, and how that must contribute to his experiences and judgment. But even so, comparing his errors to some of the elders in Holtondome, like Hap and Peg, give me a measuring stick.

"You're rarely wrong, Fi. In fact, the only time you've erred since you arrived was when you tried to talk me out of rescuing Troy by trying to get me drunk and into bed." Seg grinned. "Which would have eventually worked, by the way, except you had no way of knowing my freaky eye could see the future through walls."

"Don't disparage yourself like that! Neither you nor any of your body parts are freaky," Fi said. "Not to me."

"Which is another point. Young or old, male or female, everyone either stares at my eye, or avoids me like the plague. Even Val, my closest friend. The first time you gave it any attention, however, was when you learned it was more than just a blind eye, and you've never even blanched during our conversations."

"So?"

"*So,* by my reckoning, the only way a person becomes that desensitized is if they've been around the dome a time or twenty. More than that, they've seen horrors that make a white eye seem positively bland by comparison."

Fi drummed her fingers on her arm. "I hope this disjointed speculation is leading somewhere concrete."

Me too.

Seg was gathering his thoughts while he spoke, hoping against hope they would fit well-enough together to form a convincing argument.

"Cook is a hundred and twenty-two, and pardon my saying... when he saw my eye, he gawked like a schoolboy seeing a girl naked for the first time."

"Forgiven for the amusing, if colorful, visual. Continue."

"Not only did he gawk, he had no idea how to behave around someone with a birth defect. I know nothing about the City, but that tells me he—and probably everyone else there—live healthy lives compared to the domes. You, on the other hand, haven't misstepped around me even once."

Fi shrugged. "One could chalk that up to good upbringing."

"Hardly. You also blend well with the locals, almost like you're one of us, where Cook stands out like a hog in heat. If I didn't know better, Fi, I'd say you've lived in a dome before. *This* dome, by your own admission." He captured her enchanting eyes with a level stare. "In fact… I can't read, but if I could, I'd be willing to bet the handmaiden's diary mentions nothing about this room, nor how to access it."

"More speculation."

Seg bit back a growl. "The Pact's restrictions make speculating the only thing I can do in this instance, but there's more. The look on your face when you saw Holly's statue was that of old friends reunited, of regret and loss, things you simply can't get from reading someone's diary.

"You called me out last night in the bar, citing that I *knew* Troy was in peril. Well I'm calling you out, Fi. I don't know how it's possible, but you *knew* Holly. What's more, I'd be willing to bet the handmaiden who exacted her revenge on Holly's killers—and don't deny she didn't—is standing right here in this room."

"And how is that possible? As you've said, the Pact restricts your knowledge, so let me fill you in on a little fact that our fine captain could have me arrested for telling you. Longevity treatments weren't introduced until 2368—over a hundred years *after* Holly died."

Seg blinked in surprise. It was one thing to speculate about medical treatments that extended lifespan; it was quite another to have stark confirmation—and angering in the extreme to know they had been denied to Provider domes for over a hundred and fifty years.

"I… I can't pretend to know how you did it, only that you *were* the handmaiden—O-*fi*-lia, wasn't it? And that you must have been alive for centuries before then, well before The Fall."

"Oh, this keeps getting better. Do tell how you came to *that* conclusion."

"From you, and a little math."

Fi arched an eyebrow.

"You mentioned you were a field medic. Tell me, since the Feds won't:

When was the last war? I'd be willing to bet we haven't had anything of scale since The Fall."

"You'd be correct, but I could have been referring to non-combat practices."

He gently rubbed her arms. "The only horrors I can imagine suffering that would desensitize anyone to this"—Seg pointed to his blind eye—"is living through The Fall."

Her smooth veneer faltered. For a moment, Seg could almost see the worst travesty in human history playing out across her face. It was gone in an instant.

"Still speculation," she said, although her voice broke.

Oh, Freyja's Green Fields...

If he was right, then he truly couldn't imagine what she'd been through. Unfortunately, Seg wasn't done.

"'I know people.' You've said it many times. Several in Holtondome claim the same, but none have your unerring, repeatable accuracy. You sized me up in my first three sentences when you picked me up on the road, and have done so with everyone you've encountered so far, including Tad, Nin, Hap, Captain Bharta, and even the Trader, Gina. The only way someone can so rapidly assess anything—especially complex things like human beings—with such precision is if they've been around a lot of them for a very, very long time. And by 'a lot,' I mean hundreds of thousands—millions, perhaps—on an intimate level. Such an accomplishment would take fifty lifetimes."

Fi remained quiet. Seg gently brushed the hair from her face.

"Tell me I'm wrong, Fi. I'm listening."

Her lips quivered. A single tear rolled over the black marks that weren't there and down her high cheekbone.

"You're wrong," she said in a hoarse whisper. "It doesn't take fifty lifetimes to gain that level of insight. It takes two hundred and seventy."

Seg's mouth fell open. "T-two *hundred?*"

"And seventy."

Fi ran a trembling finger along his slackened jaw.

"To the best of my knowledge, Seg, I'm over twenty thousand years old."

19

Dancing and Digging

SEG WASN'T SURE HOW LONG he stood in the hidden statue room, staring at Fi. Her last words echoed in his mind.

Twenty thousand years...

It was difficult to comprehend, let alone imagine.

What wonders had she seen? What triumphs and tragedies had passed before her enchanting blue eyes? What incredible knowledge? What skills? What lore that humanity believed lost to the ages lived on in her mind alone? What...

Seg's heart dropped into his gut.

What loneliness? What terrible sadness to have generation after generation pass before her eyes, gone just when she was getting to know them? Just when she was settling with a family?

So many of the strange things she'd said now made perfect sense.

Remembering names was painful for her. Would Seg want to learn anyone's name if he knew that next week they'd be gone? Not remembering names created a sense of detachment from those around her, a defense mechanism to protect her from the pain of becoming too close to someone who, from her perspective, would soon die.

But there was one name she'd made the effort to remember, even if it would ultimately cause her to suffer.

His.

Fi also hated being alone. Seg would, too, if ninety-five percent of the world's population had died in an instant around him. Those who'd survived such terrible times were dead, and their misery along with it.

All but one.

But neither of those, he suspected, were the source of the torture playing across her face right now. She watched him closely, searching for signs of how Seg had taken her enormous news. Fi had the same fear that Seg had lived with since he was a child.

She was afraid he would treat her differently. Like a freak.

Seg ground his teeth.

Not on your life.

The greatest gift Fi had ever given him was a sense of normalcy, inclusion, and acceptance.

He'd make damn sure she felt the same.

Seg took her hand, just as she'd taken his, and casually nodded, as if Fi had just informed him dinner was ready. "Thanks for telling me. Anything else I should know?"

Fi blinked. Her mouth hung open for a few seconds, then she frowned and shook her head.

"Good. And just so you know, I'm going to hold you to your word."

"W-which one?"

He grinned. "I'm looking forward to testing your marks again."

"Oh." Fi blushed, acting in a rare show as young as she appeared.

She stepped toward the hidden door, but stumbled on weak legs. Seg caught her by the arm, which she acknowledged with a grateful nod.

"Assuming my legs are working again by then, it'll be my exquisite, torturous pleasure. Until then, I may need your help to walk."

"Of course." Seg slipped an arm through hers and carefully supported her on their way to the door. "Shall we bring Val with us?"

"As long as you're not asking because you want a threesome, sure."

"And if I did?" Seg said teasingly.

"Then you'd be as disappointed as my poor thighs are sore." Fi rubbed her leg and winced. "It's a wonder I didn't pound you through the floor."

"It wasn't for lack of trying."

"Mm. Well, hopefully I'll have better luck next time."

Seg chuckled and examined the door. The mechanism wasn't complex, and he soon had it open. A quick glance showed the warehouse was still dark. He slipped out, helped her through, and closed the door behind him. Fi followed on wobbly legs, using the surrounding crates for balance, then leaned on him for support over their long walk to the stairs.

Val had eyed Fi's wobbly gait for the entire, slow trip up the stairs, but didn't speak until they entered Fi and Seg's room.

"Miss Fi! What happened? Do you need a medic?"

"Something unexpected. And no, thanks, I'm fine. A little bedrest should do the trick."

Val frowned at the obvious dodge, but held her tongue and helped Seg lay her down. She took a pillow from Seg's bed, propped Fi's knees up…

…and froze. She sniffed, just over Fi's crotch, then sniffed again. The color drained from her cheeks. Val backed away as if Fi were a viper, then looked at Seg with the incredulous shock of someone who'd just been stabbed in the chest by their closest friend.

"You… you said you loved me," Val whispered.

"He does," Fi said before Seg could respond, her gaze fixed on the ceiling. "You have this young man wrapped around your little finger, and have since you were children."

Seg winced at the "young man" comment, less from the insinuation that he was immature than calling attention to their extreme age difference. Fi's gasp hinted that she'd realized her slip, too. She flashed him an apologetic look before turning her gaze to Val.

"He's been pining for you his entire life, so of course he fell over himself when you professed your undying love. How many nights do you think he dreamed of hearing those words from the only woman he's ever tasted? All I did was broaden his palette so he could make a more informed decision."

"That's a thin rationalization, and you know it!" Val's eyes narrowed at her. "I confided in you. I trusted you! Is this what your integrity is worth?"

"My integrity is fine."

"You said he and I were wonderful together, that he was lucky to have me! Then why did you steal—"

"Unless there was a marriage proposal I'm not aware of, I didn't steal anything." Fi arched an eyebrow. "Was there?"

Val started to reply, then sagged and shook her head.

"As for the other things, I meant every word. You're wonderful together, and he's fortunate to have a partner-in-crime like you in his life. You're like siblings with benefits. If Seg chooses you, you'll be a wonderful couple. He and I will also be wonderful, just in different ways."

Val sat on Seg's bed, her eyes haunted. "You're twisting the situation, like you always do, justifying your actions on technicalities. You know how I feel about him. And I know Seg's hunger for knowledge. It's… it's an area in which I can't compete. Not with you."

Sudden understanding sapped the strength from Seg's knees. He sat beside Val on the bed. "Is that why you broke the Pact? To compete?"

For me?

Val glanced at him, then looked at the floor and nodded. "I was trying to level the playing field before she stole you away."

"So was I." Fi heaved a resigned sigh. "Whether you know it or not, the odds are still in your favor. You have a lifetime of shared experiences with Seg that I lack, and you don't have the same… reproductive impediment as me."

"What?" Val looked at Fi, then at Seg. A smile spread across her face. "You mean… you have the test results?"

"Mm. Congratulations, you're as reproductively healthy as a rabbit."

In an unexpected turn, Val threw herself at Fi and wrapped her in a hug. "Thank you, thank you, thank you!"

Fi chuckled and patted her back. "You're welcome. I play to win, but I do it fairly."

"I see that now. I'm sorry, Miss Fi."

"Speaking of the game," Fi said, "there's another player we haven't talked about yet."

Val sat up and blinked. "Cook?"

The realization hit Seg as well. "Yes, Cook. If you think about it, he made the same sacrifice for you as you made for me."

"What? N-no, that… that was just pillow talk." Val paled. "Wasn't it?"

"One slip could be excused as pillow talk," Fi said, "but he went all-in. A man of his advanced years knows better, trust me."

"And I wasn't exaggerating about his heroics out in the storm," Seg said. "He may be crude at times, but he's a good man."

Val studied him. "Seg, are you trying to sell me on Mr. Cook?"

Seg clamped his mouth shut.

Was he?

Fi's knowing grin said it was true.

"W—ah… W-well, maybe 'sell' is a strong word," Seg said. "I'd be lying if I claimed I didn't feel guilty about my, um… testing the waters with Fi, and about my indecision between you two. Or that I don't feel jealous when I think of you and Cook together."

Val smiled at that.

"But I could claim the same about Cook as you complained about Fi," Seg said. "How many times have you said we share the same insatiable curiosity? Cook has knowledge I never will. He and Fi can fill those voids like we never could for each other. It… it's worth considering, isn't it?"

"Seg, I'm not allowed to give specifics, but Cook is… old. Much older than he looks."

"So are you. He said as much."

"That's not what I mean! He's *really* older. Physically."

Seg shrugged. "He seems perfectly fit and healthy to me. Did it present any problems last night?"

"Well... no." Val blushed. "If anything, his experience was a welcome surprise."

"Then I don't see how his age is a barrier. So he knows more than you. Learn from him, enjoy his company, and look for ways you might fill some of the holes in his life as well. Even at..." Seg caught himself before he blurted Cook's age, which he wasn't supposed to know. "Even as old as he must be, Cook has needs like everyone—needs a wonderful person like you can fill." Seg grinned. "If nothing else, he'll have a right challenge with you keeping him constantly on his toes."

Val batted his arm with a smile, but it was Fi's grateful, tear-filled eyes that caught Seg's attention.

"Thank you," Fi silently mouthed, then hastily wiped her eyes and said aloud, "All right, if we want a prayer of beating the captain, I need to do some research."

"Sorry, Miss Fi," Val said. "How can I help?"

"Find out the current charges against our driver. No sense showing a hand they haven't called us on yet."

"Right, I'll see what I can dig up." Val paused at the door and looked back at Seg. "Are... are you coming?"

Seg debated for a second. There was so much he wanted to ask Fi, but at the same time, he didn't want to bother her.

Then he remembered his visions of the dying woman.

Val.

"Definitely," Seg said. He turned to Fi. "Do you mind?"

Fi waved him away. "Go, there isn't much you can do here. If the Feds call either of you in for questioning, don't resist, but send for me immediately. And for heaven's sake, stay out of trouble."

Val batted her eyelashes and flashed an innocent smile. "Whatever do you mean, Miss Fi? We're perfect angels."

Fi shook her head, then withdrew the screen and attached keyboard from a bag at her bedside, and was soon busily typing away. Seg and Val left her to it.

Fi was in the shower when Seg and Val returned to their room. Having learned his lesson, Seg called into the bathroom, saying that he and Val would wait outside until she finished, to which Fi replied her typical, "Mm."

A few minutes later, the bedroom door opened. Fi had eschewed the

Provider and City looks for something altogether different. A high, white-laced collar brushed her jaw, attached to a regal dark-blue felt dress with gold trim that made her enchanting blue eyes practically glow. Her skirt puffed at the hips, accentuating her figure. A sparkly jeweled pin decorated her neatly bunned hair.

"Come in," she said, gesturing with a white-silk gloved hand.

"M-Miss Fi, you look lovely," Val said once they were inside. "What's the occasion?"

"I'm speaking at storytime tonight, and it sounds like there will be quite a crowd. I'm also meeting Seg's sister later. Wouldn't want my potential sister-in-law to think I'm a scruff."

While Seg was still staring in disbelief at the "sister-in-law" comment, Val laughed.

"She's riling you up, Seg. Even I saw through that."

Fi chuckled. "I must be losing my touch. So what did you discover?"

"Our boy wonder here came up dry," Val said. "But I managed to convince a Fed that helping a poor, lonely Provider like me by sharing a little information might persuade me to return later tonight for a personal thank-you."

"You little hussy," Fi said with a wink. "I knew there was a reason I liked you."

"It may have worked a little too well. But, apart from getting a touch grabby, he confirmed Cook has only been charged with unlawful revelation of advanced technology to a Provider. Apparently, half the dome witnessed his tires transform when he returned with Troy, which bumps the severity up a few notches. He could be banished."

"When is his trial?"

"Tomorrow at first light."

"Mm."

Val crossed her arms. "You don't sound surprised, Miss Fi. Or upset."

"I know Federal procedure, so no, I'm not surprised, and it's too soon to get upset. I'd rather focus on getting him and Holtondome out of their respective messes."

Val lowered her eyes. "Sorry, Miss Fi. It's just that I'm... worried."

"I understand, but until he—or you—are actually convicted, worrying will attract the wrong kind of attention, which we definitely don't need."

"Yes, Miss Fi. I-I'll try."

"What did you learn?" Seg said to Fi.

"A lot, though none of it good, and nothing I can share without breaking the law."

"That's not helpful, or encouraging."

"I didn't mean it wasn't helpful, just that it confirmed my suspicions in an I-wish-it-hadn't sort of way. The stakes are high, which means the Feds are going to be playing to win. We have to be ready."

Val growled. "But how can we be ready if we don't even know what the game is!"

"Because you have me. I know the game better than anyone, and I don't intend to lose. Speaking of which, it's time to play our next move." Fi swept past them to the door, fine dress trailing her like a regal princess. "Ready for storytime?"

20

Alliances

DINNER WAS JUST BEING SERVED in Tad's Tavern when Seg, Val, and Fi arrived. Patrons normally strange to this establishment filled the large seating area to capacity. Word of Fi's pending story had undoubtedly attracted them, and would attract more. Combined with their Trader and Fed guests, it promised to be a busy night.

Three teenagers lumbered up the stairs, each carrying two chairs, followed by two more teens with a stack of crates. Til paused her frantic server bustle long enough to direct the teens, then hurried to the kitchen. The teens set their cargo in an open space near the middle of the large room, arranged the chairs around the crate stack, then threw a burlap cloth on top.

"I do believe our table is ready," Val said with a smile. "Let's grab it before anyone else does."

No sooner had they sat than one of the last people Seg expected to see walked over. Troy didn't mince words, as usual. He simply pulled out a chair and joined them as if he had a standing invitation.

"Please, have a seat," Val said, rolling her eyes. "Are you here because you need Seg to cut your food for you?"

"I'll be fine. Freyja gave me teeth for a reason."

Val deflated, clearly disappointed he hadn't risen to the bait, but she quickly rallied. "I saw you talking to Gina Teladar earlier."

"Yeah," Seg said, remembering the same. "What was that about?"

"Just some friendly conversation. And maybe a little reconnaissance."

"Oh." Val's eyes sparkled. "Trying to get some dirt on her?"

"Something like that." Troy scanned the tavern, then sat back with a huff. "Haven't seen her yet, have you?"

"No, but she shouldn't be long," Seg said. "Hap will be here soon, and he always dines with the head Trader."

"Let's hope this season is an exception."

Val grinned. "Why Troy Holton, whatever are you planning?"

"Keep your nose where it belongs. I swear, you're as bad as Seg."

"And there's that infamous Troy charm." Val shook her head. "It's a wonder anyone wants to talk to you, let alone someone like Gina, who could have her pick of the entire dome for company."

"She'll want to talk, believe me."

Til hustled over. Wisps of brown hair had escaped her bun and fell over her face, which she absently brushed away. "Sorry, it's busy already. What can I get you?"

"A nice warm soup would help my vocal cords," Fi said.

"I've got just the thing, Miss Fi." Til flashed a knowing smile. "And I must say, I'm looking forward to your story as much as anyone."

"With this much buildup, I hope it lives up to the hype."

"I'm sure it will." Til held her breath and gripped her apron, shuffling from foot to foot. "Will it... contain more of our history, Miss Fi?"

"No, but I think you'll find it interesting all the same."

"Oh, maybe it's just as well." Til's mouth twisted into a grin. "You created quite a stir with that story of Holly's statue. Half the dome has been searching for it since yesterday."

"Best of luck to them."

Til studied her, then put a hand on her ample hip. "You've sent everyone on a wild goose chase, haven't you?"

Fi remained silent. Seg put on his best poker face, while Val looked at both of them in turn, eyes narrowed. Troy seemed to be ignoring the entire exchange and was watching the stairs.

"Oh, they'll be so disappointed," Til said. "Shame on you for leading them on."

"I understand your disappointment, but let's pretend for a second that the statue did exist. Telling you about it would only get me—and maybe Holtondome—in trouble. Is that what you want?"

"Well, no..."

"And what would happen when someone found it? How long until the Feds learned? Do you really think they'd let you keep it?"

Each question deflated Til until her shoulders were as rounded as the dome. "No, Miss Fi. They'd tear it down and banish those who tried to hide it."

"That's right." Fi took her hand and pulled her closer, holding her gaze with rapt intent. "Remember that. Remind your would-be treasure hunters what the Feds would do to them, and to the statue—even a harmless one of Holtondome's savior, Holly."

"But, miss, why even tell us that story if..." Til's eyes grew wide. "Sweet Freyja," she whispered. "I have to tell them right now!" She planted a quick kiss on the back of Fi's hand. "Thank you, Miss Fi. Thank you!"

And then she was off down the stairs, leaving a sea of turning heads in her wake.

Val sat back with a frown. "What in Odin's name are you doing, Miss Fi? I thought Til's head was going to spin clean off her pretty shoulders. Is there a statue or not?"

"The waitress' head is firmly attached, though I wonder about yours."

"No need to be snippy! I'm just a bit... confused."

Troy leaned forward with a rare smile. "Oh, there's a statue, all right. And within the hour, every soul in Holtondome will know it."

"Know it without being able to prove it," Seg said, matching his brother's smile.

Val gasped. "Since Miss Fi never actually admitted the statue exists, it's just hearsay! Which keeps us all safe from the Feds."

"And with the additional reminder of the consequences," Seg said, "it will hopefully keep people from poking around. At least for a little while."

"It can't be easy to find if it's been hidden in our own dome for three hundred years."

Seg sagely shook his head. A sharp squeak from Val told him it was a mistake.

"You've seen it!" she hissed. Her eyes widened. "That's where you hid the pendants, isn't it? Is that also where you two..." Val cleared her throat and looked away.

Seg expected a sharp rebuke from Fi, but it was Troy who spoke.

"If you had a gram of sense in that straw head of yours, you'd stop asking questions *right now*."

Val crossed her arms. "Don't act so high and mighty! You're just as curious as I am."

"But unlike you and my fool brother, I know when to keep my curiosity in check, and when to focus on more important things." Troy glanced at the stairs, then did a double-take. "Like now."

Seg turned to see Gina Teladar enter the tavern, followed closely by Captain Bharta.

"Damn," Troy said.

"Go enjoy an intimate dinner with the beautiful Trader," Fi said. "We'll take care of the captain."

"Something tells me dinner with you would be just as interesting." Troy didn't wait for a response, though, and went straight for Gina.

Val sighed. "Is there anything you don't have your hands into, Miss Fi?"

"Not much, though I sometimes wish it were otherwise."

Fi watched Troy and Gina talk for a few seconds, then slid her chair back and joined them. Seg couldn't hear their conversation over the growing crowd, but Bharta's sudden smile and gesture to their table told him she'd succeeded. While Fi walked Bharta back, Troy guided Gina to a table for two in the rear of the tavern.

Seg stood to greet Bharta, but Fi walked right past him and sat with the captain several tables away.

"What do you suppose she's up to?"

"I don't care," Val said, "as long as she keeps him away from me. I'm wound so tight that I might spill my guts on accident. Of course, Miss Smarty-Pants probably knows that."

"Maybe." The explanation seemed too simple for Fi's complex way of thinking. Everything she did had layers of meaning and purpose. Seg suspected this was no different.

Hap soon emerged from the stairwell and made a bee line for Gina and Troy.

"Hap! Over here." Seg hurried over and intercepted his father. Whatever Troy's plans with Gina, he suspected they would be easier to accomplish without their father present. "Will you join us for dinner?"

"You know the drill, Seg, or, at least, you should by now. Tradition puts me with Miss Teladar tonight, so if you'll excuse me..."

He tried to move around, but Seg blocked his path.

"Troy said he wants the honor tonight," Seg said. "He and Miss Teladar seem to have hit it off."

He and Hap peered at them over the crowd. They made less of an odd couple than Seg had first imagined. Each of them was hunched over the table in heated conversation. Gina's intense expression matched his brother's, as if they were perfect conspiracy partners.

Maybe he's finally found his martyr-match.

Hap's eyebrows rose. "Well, maybe you're right. Still, I should probably find Captain Bharta. He'll..." His sentence died when he spied Bharta at a private table with Fi. Hap chuckled. "Seems I'm unnecessary this season."

"Hardly. Come tell us how everyone's handling the trade shutdown."

Val nodded to Hap once the three of them were seated.

"Val, you're looking well," Hap said.

"And you, considering the pressure you must be facing to re-open trade."

"From all sides." Hap rolled his eyes and sighed. "Truth be told, I wasn't looking forward to dinner with Gina. She's nice enough, but I've faced a steady stream of disgruntled locals since the shutdown was announced. If I have to repeat my reasonings one more time, they're going to etch it on my tomb. Not that anyone believes me."

"What?" Seg and Val said at the same time.

"Oh, some do, I'm sure, but I get the feeling most of them think I'm just being obstinate." He looked at them each in turn. "I'm not, am I?"

"No," Seg said. "To the best of our knowledge, this is what's right for Holtondome. We have to stick to it."

Hap eyed him, then smiled.

"What is it?"

"Something I'm not used to seeing in my youngest child: responsibility." He chuckled at Seg's indignant look. "Don't get me wrong, it's a welcome relief. Troy's had an overdeveloped sense since he could talk, and Jen not far after. Until now, I thought they'd hoarded it all for themselves, but it seems these outsiders are having a positive influence on you."

"I... I think they are, too."

"Well, you could certainly do worse." Hap glanced at Fi, then waggled his eyebrows at Seg. His grin disappeared, however, when he noticed Val's stricken look. "Wait, are you and Val...?"

"No," Seg said. At the same time, Val said, "Yes."

Uh oh.

"What we mean is that it's... complicated, and we're still figuring it out," Seg said.

Val's scowl indicated that she strongly disagreed. She crossed her arms and glared at him, but kept her tongue.

Hap gripped Seg's shoulder. "You know Miss Fi won't be around forever, right?"

You couldn't be more wrong.

"Oh, I know," Seg said instead. "W-what I meant was, with Nat's death and all, Val is still—"

He grunted when she took his hand and surreptitiously impaled him with her fingernails.

"Hap, let's say Seg and I were together," Val said. "Would you object?"

"No. In fact, I'd always hoped some twist of fate would bring you two closer. I never imagined it would take a City girl sleeping in the same room with him to break the final wall, assuming it's been broken, but I thank Freyja for small miracles that it did." He smiled at Val's hand, which still covered Seg's. "Not that I ever wished any harm to Nat."

"Of course not," Val said. Some of the tension left her. She squeezed Seg's hand with a contented smile. "But, like you say, sometimes we can only chalk it up to fate. Right, Seg?"

Memory of his vision of Val falling in a pool of her own blood made his mouth go dry. "F-fate, right."

What was Val's fate? Would he or Fi be able to save her? His vision would come to pass very soon, if Fi was correct. And she usually was.

He couldn't let that happen. Not to Val.

Seg turned to her and swallowed his emotions to keep his voice steady. "Will... will you stay with me tonight?"

Val blushed behind a grin that spread to the tips of her ears. "Seg, that's hardly an appropriate question to ask me in front of your father."

"I agree," Hap said with a laugh. "That's an exit cue if I ever heard one." He started to rise.

"No!" they both shouted, drawing looks from the surrounding tables.

"Please stay, Mr. Holton," Val said, sparing a glance for Troy and Gina, who were both hunched over their table, speaking with sharp gestures and intensity in their eyes. "We'll keep the conversation socially acceptable, I promise." She looked at Seg, her eyes wide with hope. "You'd better not be teasing me." Fortunately, she left the "like you did earlier today" accusation out.

Which I would have deserved.

Worse, Seg couldn't promise that he wasn't teasing her now. His heart was genuinely torn between her and Fi. The romantic landscape seemed to be changing by the minute, making any sort of choice difficult.

One thing he knew for certain, however, was that he couldn't let Val die. The best way to achieve that was to ensure she didn't leave his side, and to keep her away from the trade caravans. If that meant promising a night with her that may not live up to her expectations, then so be it.

Seg clasped his hand on top of hers. "I know things are strange right now; the last twenty-four hours haven't gone according to any sort of plan I could have dreamed up. It's been terrible, but also wonderful, and mostly because of you. Just holding your hand today in public was like living a fantasy."

Val's lips quivered. "But?"

"But nothing. I want more. Stay by my side, Val. Please."

"'Please,' now, is it?" Val sighed. "First you pledge your undying love, then you sleep with that..." She glanced at Hap and cleared her throat. "Next thing I know, you're trying to convince me that Cook is my perfect match, and now we're back to pledging your undying love. What will it be tomorrow, once you've had your wicked way with me? Will you leave me beh—" Val bit her lip before she finished "behind." "Leave me for *her?*"

"You know he can't," Hap said, his voice full of sympathy.

They both shot him a look.

Hap held up his hands. "You're the ones who insisted I stay, so don't get upset with me for participating in the conversation. Val, I can't say I approve of my son's behavior, but I *can* tell you that his housing arrangements and his relationship with his current roommate are temporary. In three weeks, Miss Fi will be back in the City where she belongs, and will have forgotten all about Holtondome. I can also tell you with authority that no other woman has held Seg's fancy for as long as you have."

Seg closed his open mouth. "Since when did you know about that?"

"Since you were eight, when you would gush every day about something Val did, something she said, how she looked, smelled, dressed, or giggled. And how the gushing ended in stoic melancholy just before she started dating Nat." Hap looked at Val. "He hasn't spoken like that of anyone since."

Seg stared at him, then laughed. "Dad, you're playing all my cards here."

"Someone has to, because if you keep holding them, you'll only lose. But you're right; they're your cards to play, and I should leave you to the game." Hap stood and stretched. "I haven't seen Til around, so I'm going to find a space at the bar until Gina or Captain Bharta are free. I've earned a drink."

"You certainly have," Val said, although her sparkling eyes were fixed on Seg.

Hap gave her a smile, then headed for the bar.

"You weren't just trying to get me to hand over my pendant when you kissed me earlier, were you?" Val said.

Seg shook his head.

"I think I knew that, but... it's nice to have confirmation." Val leaned close. "Kiss me again, like you did behind the apple crates."

"In the middle of the tavern? Aren't you worried who will see?"

"To Hel with what they think. I could be dead tomorrow, if the Feds find out what I've done, so I want to enjoy every minute I have left." She edged closer until her breath tickled his lips. "I want you."

Heart pounding, Seg closed the final distance.

Their mouths had barely touched when a woman's nearby "Eww" made them both jerk away.

Three women who he recognized as Val's friends skirted the table with disgusted looks, focused on Seg. The last swept her skirt away, as if contact with either of them would soil her dress, then followed the others to a table a few meters away.

Their treatment didn't hurt Seg nearly as much as Val's mortified expression.

He felt as if a sword had pierced his chest and pinned him to the chair. Seg couldn't move. Couldn't breathe. He sat there, waiting for her to say something—to at least look at him—but her eyes stayed fixed on her hands clasped between her knees, brow creased in worry.

"I see." Seg choked out the words, but could say no more. The elation he'd felt at finally being wanted by the object of his lifelong affection had suddenly turned to poison, leaving his tongue bitter, his gut twisted, and his heart a cold, rotting husk.

Val looked up, as if just remembering he was there.

And then Seg was walking away. He scanned the tavern for an escape, someplace he wouldn't feel like the abomination Val had just confirmed he was—an unlikable, unwanted plague, sure to inflict his socially fatal disease on anyone who made the mistake of getting too close to him.

He instinctively sought Fi. She and Bharta were engaged in what seemed to be light conversation. He dashed toward her—the only person who had never once made him feel out of place.

A burst of laughter from their table stopped him in his tracks.

They were having a good time. *Fi* was having a good time.

Without him.

Another sword lanced his chest. Seg spun away, frantically searching for another target.

Hap had already engaged a small group at the bar and was smiling broadly. Seg would only ruin the conversation if he joined them. Tad was busy serving, and Nin was probably in the kitchen. At some point, Troy and Gina had moved their chairs next to each other, their shoulders touching in intense, intimate conversation.

Seg had the sudden urge to barge in. Fighting with Troy always took the pain away, for a time, and his brother was usually eager to oblige. But, even through his desperation, Seg knew they were discussing something important. He couldn't interrupt.

And then he spotted Len—the piece of hog shit who'd left his brother outside in the lightning storm to die.

Seg marched across the tavern, not caring whose chair he bumped. Len wasn't Troy, but he'd do.

He made it halfway there before a pair of shrieks froze him to the spot. One of them was Val's.

His childhood friend, who had moments ago crushed his hope and his heart, was screaming bloody murder with the woman who had *eww*'d them.

Heartache forgotten, Seg hurried to their table.

"Apologize to him!" Val screamed at the woman.

"I did nothing wrong!" the woman screamed back.

Val stamped her foot, fists trembling. *"Apologize!"*

"You apologize!"

"I will *not* apologize for loving a good man!"

"You had a good man," the woman said, tears running down her cheeks. "But you destroyed my brother's life, took his happiness, and then you killed him! Apologize to *me* for—"

Val's hand lashed across the woman's cheek like a whip crack. The woman yelped and staggered back into her chair.

"You. Know. *Nothing* of our married life," Val growled through clenched teeth. *"Nothing!* You saw only what Nat wanted you to see: a young couple in love, trying in vain to start a family with our chins held high. What you didn't see—what *none* of you saw!—were the arguments that went well into the night. The accusations that somehow the entire situation was *my* fault, because he couldn't possibly be infertile. The rumors he spread, smearing my name in backhanded ways to make him seem innocent."

"And how wrong was he? You who so freely speak ill of the dead!"

"I held my tongue for years out of respect for a man who had even *me* convinced that I had somehow wronged him. That I wasn't worthy to be his wife. That I owed him a debt for my presumed deficiency that I could never repay, no matter how much I begged forgiveness, or how hard I worked to prove my value."

"Lies! How convenient for all of this to come out now when Nat isn't here to defend himself—and right in front of the man you're trying to lure into your web."

Val turned stiffly, and jumped when she saw Seg standing right behind her. Her furious expression vanished, replaced with sorrow and anguish. "S-Seg, I—"

"Don't have anything more to prove." He rubbed her shoulders. "Not to me, and certainly not to her."

Nat's sister sneered at Val. "You weren't worthy to tie my brother's shoes. But it seems you finally found your perfect, broken match. I hope you both rot!"

With a roar, Val swung at the woman, but Seg caught her around the waist and pulled her away before her fist connected. The woman's friends restrained Nat's sister from pursuit, leaving her and Val growling and clawing at the growing distance between them.

By the time they reached their own table, Val had stopped trying to wrestle out of his grip. She plonked into a chair and hung her head, shoulders heaving in quiet misery. Seg rubbed her back, ignoring the stares from all around.

"They don't matter," he said gently. "They don't understand, and they never will, because they don't want to."

"But you do," Val said around a hiccupping sob. Red-rimmed eyes peered up at him through a veil of tangled brown hair. "You're the only person who's ever truly understood me. Who ever wanted to. And I..." She shook her head and began sobbing in earnest.

"You did nothing. I'm the one who distanced myself because I thought I was doing the right thing to make you happy. It's my fault."

"No, you're right. I did nothing, Seg, *nothing* to try to win you back. I've always taken your friendship for granted—something I didn't have to work for, because it had been so unwavering, so absolute, that I couldn't imagine not having it. So when you stopped seeking me out, I simply waited, sure that you would eventually come back to me, but you never did. Your absence created a gaping hole in my chest that made me restless and irritable, though I couldn't see it for what it was at the time. And then Nat asked me out."

"I remember," Seg said. "That was the first day I'd ever picked up a scythe. I think I harvested an entire acre with broad, angry swings."

Val laughed and unceremoniously wiped her nose. "Yes, the whole dome was talking about the furious one-eyed reaper. Nobody dared to stop you, even when they closed Wheatdome for the night."

"Not one of my prouder achievements. Sleeping in a wheat field without so much as a blanket is an experience I could have lived without."

Val's smile faded. "If I hadn't been so dense, I might have put the two events together. It may have been enough to make me reconsider dating Nat."

"And if I hadn't been so dense, I would have talked to you about my decision to part ways instead of leaving you in the cold to wonder why I left."

Just like Fi was brave enough to talk to me about her infertility, even though it hurt. I suppose that's the wisdom of age.

"Part of it was cowardice," Seg said. "Not telling you meant I didn't have to face rejection from the only girl I'd ever connected with, which kept my hope alive."

"I... I can't promise I wouldn't have rejected you."

A sword pierced his chest for the third time that night, driving the air from his lungs. Val disarmed her mortal blow with a weak smile.

"Like I said, I was dense. I didn't realize what I'd lost, so maybe it was fate after all. Who knows if you'd have had any interest in me after that?"

Fate...

The blood drained from his face.

Was it possible? Was Val fated to die tonight so that...

He glanced at Fi, who was still engaged in jovial conversation with Bharta a few tables away.

So that he could be with Fi?

Or is that the fate I'm supposed to prevent?

What if Val dying was some cosmic glitch that only Seg—or Fi—could fix?

That was the problem: it was impossible to even guess.

Val touched his hand, snapping him out of his paradoxical thoughts.

"I'm sorry if that hurts you, but I don't want to lie to you, Seg. I don't want to give you any reason to not trust me. Not anymore than I already have."

Seg racked his brain to remember what they'd even been talking about before his thoughts had wandered into fate-of-the-universe territory. Was this one of the reasons Fi seemed so disinterested in everything? Because she had such grand, unsolvable puzzles like this to worry over?

Puzzles that, until now, she's had no one to discuss with who could possibly understand.

A gentle touch on his cheek made him realize his gaze had once again strayed to Fi.

"I-I know you're interested in her," Val said, the hurt evident in her unsteady voice. "She's already proven that she's willing to play fair, so I won't stoop to trying to make you dislike her. All I can offer is who I am, and hope you can see I'm a wiser person today than when we were younger."

Seg grinned. "And feistier. I don't remember young Val having such a devastating right hook. Nat's sister was lucky it didn't connect."

Val matched his grin. "Like you said, not one of my prouder moments, but there's a part of me that wishes you hadn't pulled me away. She disapproved of me dating Nat from the very start, and has had that coming for a while. If I didn't know better, I'd say she had a thing for her brother."

"Yuck!"

"Yeah, and *you* didn't have to sleep with him."

They looked at each other and laughed. These random, candid conversations were what Seg missed most about her. Val's regretful smile suggested she felt the same.

They were lost in a deep conversation about what attracted pigs to one another when Fi climbed onto her table and stood tall, clapping her hands to gather attention.

"Good news, ladies and gentlemen," Fi said loud enough to project over the chatter. "In a gesture of good faith, the captain has permitted me to tell a story that would usually be restricted. It includes previously undisclosed technology, so I'll need Holtondome's permission as well, but I promise I'll keep the details light, and only include those relevant to the tale."

A deafening cheer filled the room, which was now packed wall-to-wall, with many patrons having to stand. Everyone turned to Hap.

Hap finished a long pull from his tankard and set it on the bar. "Well, as long as you promise to at least try to respect the Pact, I don't see the harm in it."

Another round of cheers drowned anything else he might have said.

"That's no longer your decision!" a man bellowed from the stairway. Seg recognized him as the resident who'd been denied his orange marmalade when the stalls had closed.

The tavern lapsed into stunned murmurs. The man and a large contingent of unhappy-looking residents pushed their way through the crowd and surrounded Hap. Seg moved up to the edge of the crowd to get a better look, followed closely by Val.

Hap's eyes narrowed on the man. "What's this about?"

A grim smile crossed his lips. "Holtondome's safety—and your removal."

Hap searched his face as if gauging whether he was really serious about staging the first coup in Holtondome's long history. Sweat dappled the man's mostly bald head, but he stood resolute.

"Den, let's talk this through," Hap said. "Sit. Have a drink with me."

Den put his fists on his round hips. "We tried talking, but you still refuse to trade."

"And I've told you why, at length, but I can't seem to make you understand that trading this season will only hurt Holtondome."

"Is that really *your* opinion, Hap? Because I heard the idea came from someone else, who may not have our best interests at heart."

Seg ground his teeth. After everything he'd seen, he was furious that *anyone* would question Fi's motives.

His fury evaporated when he noticed everyone wasn't staring at her, but at Seg.

"M-me?" He rubbed his eyes, sure this was just a nightmare he would soon wake from, but when he looked again, the accusing glares remained. "You're willing to throw logic to the pigs and overthrow Hap because you question *my* loyalty?"

"Loyalty, integrity, and plain old common sense," Den said, scowling. "Your list of irresponsible, mischievous deeds rival Loki's own, up to and including the wanton destruction of our precious hauler, and your... *immoral* living arrangements. Not to mention the woman on your arm who, if she had a shred of decency, would still be mourning the loss of her good husband instead of bedding any desperate soul who comes along, no matter how damaged they might—"

Seg had closed the distance and buried his fist in Den's round gut before he realized he'd even moved. Seg was used to being disparaged—often sought it, in fact—if not for his birth defect, then for his reckless actions.

But no one insulted Val.

The large man collapsed with an explosive breath and curled against a bar stool, gasping for air. Rough hands grabbed Seg from all sides, but the restraint was unnecessary. He'd already stopped the sewage from spilling out of Den's mouth.

Hap darted between them. His pride from earlier was gone, replaced with knitted eyebrows and tight lips that were somewhere between anger and disappointment—the expression Seg was used to from his father. Hap held his gaze for a moment, then shook his head and knelt to check on Den.

What he hadn't expected was Captain Bharta's furious look, and it was aimed squarely at Seg.

Bharta stormed over, veins throbbing on his crimson face. "Idiot! The upstart was about to resume trade negotiations—food the Federated Nations *needs*—and you interfered! Do you have any idea what you may have done?"

Seg ground his teeth, ready to lay a sarcastic reply that would probably land him in even more trouble, but, from the corner of his eye, he spotted Fi back at her table, slowly shaking her head. Whether she was upset with his rash display was difficult to tell from her neutral expression, but her message was clear. Seg kept his mouth shut and held the captain's gaze.

Bharta grunted in disgust. "It seems my confidence in you was misplaced. Worse, you assaulted the man who might have taken Hap's place and agreed to trade—a clear act of sabotage!" He straightened and lifted his chin. "Seg Holton, you are hereby charged with willful and destructive interference in Pact negotiations. Furthermore, despite being warned of the dire consequences to other members of the Federated Nations, your violent actions contradict the core Provider tenants of sacrifice for the greater good, putting you in violation of the Pact itself.

"You will be held in Federal custody until tomorrow morning, where you will then be sentenced with formal and permanent banishment from Holtondome."

21

Jen

VAL HEARD THE WORD, BUT her brain refused to accept it.

Banishment.

Seg—*her* Seg—had just been given the worst form of death sentence.

She clung to his arm, even while Captain Bharta hauled him through the tavern toward the stairs. Someone was crying, screaming, begging for his release. Someone desperate who couldn't stand the thought of losing him to nature's wrath.

Someone who sounded exactly like Val.

"No, please!" she heard that person scream in her voice. "He was defending me! It was my fault. Mine! Don't take him away! *Please,* Captain Bharta! I'll do anything, just don't take him away from me! *Don't take him away!"*

Firm hands tried to separate her from Seg. Val dug her fingers into Seg's arm as if he were her only tether to the planet, screaming incoherently. Seg shook his head and looked around, as if he'd just realized what had happened. His one good eye locked onto her, silencing her screams.

"Stay with Fi!" he said in a frantic voice. "Promise me you won't leave her side for any reason!"

Val stared at him, unable to understand why he would make such a ridiculous request at a time like this.

"Promise me, Val!"

Someone pried her fingers from his arm. Seg struggled to return to her, but two men joined Bharta to overpower him. They dragged him toward the stairs.

"Swear to me! *Swear it!"*

"I-I swear!" Val would have promised him anything in that moment, but the hysteria in his voice would have made him impossible to refuse under any circumstance.

And like that, he relaxed. Seg's gaze slid to someone just behind Val. He nodded with a mirthless smile, then disappeared down the stairs.

The hands restraining her withdrew. Val spun to find her captor was none other than the person she had just sworn to stay with.

"W-why?" Val said, her throat raw. "Why didn't you help him?"

"I only fight battles I can win," Fi said. "Neither he nor the captain were in a particularly receptive mood, if you hadn't noticed. Besides, his sentence had already been passed. For Bharta to go back on that would be showing weakness to the enemy."

"We're… the enemy?"

"Mm." Fi lowered her voice so only Val could hear. "Make no mistake: the Feds would banish a hundred Segs to maintain their authority. That's how police states in authoritarian governments work. I thought your enlightening pillow chat with my driver would have made that clear."

"Seems he skipped some important details." *Like what a police state or an authoritarian government is.* Val didn't have to know their definitions, however, to guess they weren't good.

"Details we don't have time to cover here," Fi said.

Val took a shuddering breath to calm herself. Seg was gone, but his sentence wasn't until tomorrow morning, which meant they still had a chance. At least, she hoped they did. "What's the plan, Miss Fi?"

"I'm working on it." Fi cracked a half smile. "You two really do keep me on my toes."

"So… there's hope?"

"Of course. But for goodness sake, do me a favor."

"Anything! What is it?"

"Keep your promise to Seg and don't leave my side until tomorrow, when we'll hopefully have this whole thing sorted out."

"Oh, sure."

"I've heard two-year-olds tell more convincing lies. Now, promise me, and say it like you mean it this time."

"I…" Val hid her indignity behind a scowl. "I won't promise. Not until you tell me why you both seem to think I need adult supervision."

"Your escapade with my driver last night should be all the reason you need. If it isn't, then you've simply made my point."

Val crossed her arms, refusing to rise to the bait, and remained silent.

"Fine," Fi said. "Seg cares about you, if you hadn't noticed, and is worried something might happen to you tonight."

"Well, he cares about you, too, but I don't see him leashing *you* to anyone's side."

"I—" Fi blinked. "You really think he cares about me?"

"Yes," Val practically spat through clenched teeth. She bit back the "idiot" poised on the tip of her tongue.

A dreamy look crossed Fi's face, then vanished just as quickly. "Ah. Well, be that as it may, Seg knows I can handle myself around the Feds. You they would tear to pieces."

Val started to object, but Fi held up her hand.

"We can argue the point all night, but our time would be much better spent trying to dig Seg and Holtondome out of their respective holes. Now, either promise me you'll honor your word to Seg, or get out of my way so I can concentrate on saving at least *one* of you."

"Pardon me, Miss Fi?"

Val could have kissed Hap for his timing. Fi's pressed lips said she hadn't missed Val's lack of promise. When Fi turned to Hap, her threatening look was gone, replaced by her usual, even demeanor.

"Yes, Mr. Holton?"

"I couldn't help but eavesdrop, and I hope to Odin I heard right. Can you save Seg?"

"That depends on what your other son has discovered," Fi said, "and whether we can get the captain back up here for a proper storytime."

"Then, even if I have to drag Bharta up here by his ankles, he will. As for Troy…"

They all looked at Troy and Gina at the far end of the tavern. The couple were still shoulder to shoulder, as if they had missed the entire ordeal. They held hands—not like lovers, but with the white-knuckled grip of two people afraid for their very lives to let go. Whatever they were discussing, Val was certain they shouldn't be interrupted.

"I'll go with you, Hap," Val said. "Maybe I can…"

A warning glare from Fi made her clear her throat.

"Or not. I'm sure you'll do fine on your own."

"I appreciate the offer anyway," Hap said. "If you really want to help, though, see if you can talk sense into Den and the others where I failed."

"The upstarts aren't your problem," Fi said. "Whether you trade or not won't solve the larger issue."

"Which is?"

"You should know better by now, Mr. Holton. I can't answer that without breaking the law six ways from Sunday. But I *can* tell you this might be the most enlightening storytime in Holtondome's history—*if* the right people attend."

"I'll make sure they do." Hap hesitated, then took her hand. "Thank you, Miss Fi."

"Thank me when Seg is safe. Saving Holtondome will be a bonus."

Hap nodded and headed downstairs.

Val blew a sigh. "What now?"

"Now we see if we can move my later appointment up a few hours."

Val stood next to Fi in the sixth-floor hallway and knocked on Jen's door.

Two young male voices inside shouted "I'll get it!" followed by a stampede of racing footsteps. After a short scuffle, the door whipped open, revealing Jen's eleven-year-old twins, who were elbowing each other out of the way.

They froze when they saw Fi staring down at them.

"Miss Fi," they said in one voice. Tom quickly straightened his wiry light-brown hair, while Jak pulled his shirt straight. They didn't move from the doorway, enraptured by Fi's mystical blue eyes.

The same eyes that captured my Seg, Val thought bitterly.

"Good evening, boys," Fi said. "Is your mother here?"

"Coming," Jen called from somewhere inside. "Tom, Jak, back to your studies at once."

"Aw, Mom!" They couldn't have been more in unison if they'd choreographed it.

"Lighting fires in Wheatdome does *not* earn storytime. You'll instead learn from your father precisely how your little stunt could have been catastrophic for Holtondome and the Federated Nations."

Val arched an eyebrow at the boys. "Fires? Really?"

They had the grace to look embarrassed, faces red under sprays of freckles.

Val leaned closer and lowered her voice, although not so low that Jen couldn't overhear. "How big?"

"Three meters high," Jak said, trying and failing to mimic her quiet tone.

"And at least two meters wide," Tom said, matching his brother's grin. "We piled it up into a tee-pee, just like you and Uncle Seg taught us."

"Evidently not, since you were caught."

"Barely," Jak said. "The only reason we were is—"

"*Not* the point!" Jen yanked the door open and planted her fists on her hips. "Studies. Now. I'll be back later this evening. And there *will* be a quiz."

The boys groaned. With a last, wistful look at Fi, they moped back inside.

Jen stepped into the hallway and closed the door behind her. "Where's Seg?"

Val's heart sank. *Straight to the point, as always.*

"That's one of several things we need to discuss," Fi said calmly, as if Jen's youngest brother had been sentenced to a night in the tavern instead of death. Her enchanting eyes took the shorter woman in. "You look lovely."

"Oh, thank you." Jen swept her hand over her silken blue dress and matching gloves. "I traded pigskin boots and a jacket for it last year. The merchant seemed quite pleased with himself, but I'm sure I got the better deal."

"The person he up-traded your garments to in a dome with no pigs undoubtedly thought the same." Fi gestured to her neckline, where a dark gray pendant rested, identical to the one Val had surrendered to Seg. "I especially love your necklace. Was that part of the trade?"

"In fact, it was."

Val and Fi blinked in surprise.

"But I... I thought Peg obtained the pendants just before Seg was born," Val said.

Jen leveled her with a cool stare. "*That* pendant is tucked safely in my drawer. As for this one... I'd rather not discuss it, unless you feel like telling me why the precious family heirloom my brother *mistakenly* gave you isn't around your shapely neck."

"It wasn't a mistake," Val said, her cheeks flushing with heat. "Seg—"

"Is generous to a fault," Fi said.

She hooked Jen's arm and walked her down the hall, as if Val didn't exist. Val muttered a curse and stomped after them.

"A lovestruck fool is what he was," Jen said. "I practically begged him to get it back from her. I begged them both, but neither would hear it, as if Val were going to marry into the family or something." She sniffed. "Well, we all know how *that* turned out."

"Mm. And what would you say if he married an outsider? Say, someone from the City?"

Jen turned to her so quickly that she stumbled on the stairs. "Miss Fi, if that was a joke, it was in poor taste." She turned to go downstairs, but Fi swiveled her around so they were heading up.

"I thought we'd see if the observation deck is free," Fi said. "And let's pretend for a second that such a thing was possible. Would you welcome me into your family?"

"Well, I... th-that isn't a fair question, miss. I hardly know you."

"Perhaps we can fix that tonight, hmm? And if I pass the muster, I hope you'll tell me from which merchant I can acquire a remarkable pendant like that to make my Holton membership official."

Jen yanked her arm free and glared. "This charade has gone far enough! I do *not* appreciate these games you play, nor how you string my brother along when you *know* it will only end in heartache—for *him*, at least. Now, if you'll excuse me, I think I've changed my mind about this evening. I have no wish to see you again, unless you're in the back of Mr. Cook's car driving far away from my brother. Goodnight, Miss Fi."

Although Val was fifteen centimeters taller and heavier by far, she jumped out of the way when it seemed the smaller woman would march right through her if she didn't move.

"Seg has been banished."

Fi's words stopped Jen in mid-stride. Her dark brown eyes were wide when she turned.

"Banished? W-when? *Why?*"

Jen's mouth tightened in fury. She stormed back to Fi until they were standing on the same step. Despite being a full thirty centimeters shorter, Jen managed to look intimidating.

"What did you do, Miss Fi? Tell me!"

Where Val would have been a stammering mess, Fi didn't even blink at the miniature storm.

"I opened his eyes to the truth," Fi said. "The rest was an unfortunate combination of his ineffable integrity and a miserably timed coup."

"A... a what?"

"Den Lawson," Val said. "He's sore about not getting to trade this season, and riled some others into speaking out against Hap's decision. They laid the blame squarely at Seg's feet, saying the idea came from him, and that he wasn't a model citizen with Holtondome's best interest at heart. Then, when Den turned his accusations on me, Seg..." Val swallowed, unable to continue.

"He did us both proud and stopped the brazen slander," Fi said. "With his fist."

Both of us?

As Val recalled, Fi had seemed none too pleased with him, but she wasn't about to argue.

"Then Bharta accused him of trying to sabotage negotiations," Val said. "And of violating the Pact. His banishment will be carried out tomorrow morning."

Jen's jaw hardened. "I see. So it's *both* of your faults!" She jabbed a finger at Fi. "You for putting that idea in his head, then leaving him to face the fallout, and *you*"—she aimed her accusatory finger at Val—"for stringing him along for his entire life! Only now—when Seg is finally finding his footing!—do you deign to associate with him, after sleeping with an outsider who's just been arrested for breaching the Pact, dragging him down to the depths of your own depravity!"

Val reached inside herself for the fiery retort that should have been awaiting Jen's accusation, but found only spent charcoals. She was tired of defending herself—to Seg, to Fi, to Nat's family, to her former friends, to Holtondome at large, and now to the person she hoped would be her future family. The constant fight had left her drained of the conviction needed to vindicate herself, and devoid of the will to try.

For better or worse, Val didn't need to. Jen's rage turned to trembling, then a hiccupping sob. She wasn't angry at Fi or Val; she was trying to cope with the idea of losing her brother, and failing.

Risking Jen's infamous temper, Val took the smaller woman by the arms. Jen fought at first, but eventually let herself be drawn into an embrace, where she quietly cried into Val's shoulder.

"Just like Seg didn't give up on Troy, even though it seemed hopeless, we're not going to give up on Seg," Val said softly. "Miss Fi has a plan to save him, but we're going to need your help."

Fi raised her eyebrows in a gesture that clearly indicated she *didn't* have a plan, but her uncertainty vanished before Jen turned to her with hopeful, tear-filled eyes.

"Anything. *Anything!* What can I do?"

"You can start by answering my question," Fi said. "From whom did you acquire that pendant?"

"His name was Carlos de Sangavoy. I remember because it was such an exotic name."

"And I don't suppose he was a member of the current trading group?"

"I... yes, I believe he was. Teladar Traders were visiting that season."

Fi lit up with a rare smile. "Would you recognize this gentleman by sight?"

"Absolutely. He was..." Jen blushed. "Easy on the eyes." She held her circular gray pendant up and frowned. "What is this, Miss Fi? Why is it so important?"

"Depending on whether we can find your Trader, and what his answer is about where he acquired it, it will either be very good for Seg and my driver, or devastating for Holtondome."

"That isn't very encouraging," Jen said.

"It wasn't supposed to be. You need to understand how critical it is that we find this person, and that we get complete, truthful answers from him."

Jen gulped, but nodded.

"Good." Fi swept past them down the stairs. "We should hurry to the trade caravan, otherwise we might miss storytime, and I have a feeling this will add some very flavorful context."

"Coming, Miss Fi," Val said.

Fi jerked to a halt and spun to face her. She regarded Val with critical eyes, then sighed. "I guess it's unavoidable. Just remember your promise: stay close to me, as if your life depends on it."

"I *haven't* forgotten, Miss Fi."

Fi gave a slight shake of her head. She'd seen through Val's lie, as she seemed to with everything, but didn't argue the point. She resumed her flight downstairs, followed closely by Jen and Val, who had trouble keeping up with the long-legged Amazon who ran as if charging into battle.

22

Turns

JEN HOLTON HAD BEEN BORN and raised in Holtondome. She'd been up and down these stairs more times than she could count, knew them like the back of her work-calloused hands, but she still had trouble keeping up with the long-legged outsider. Fi cascaded down the steps like a waterfall, moving with a speed and grace that would have taken Jen another lifetime to perfect, if not longer.

Next to her, Val bounced as hard as Jen to keep up, her large chest threatening to spill out of her dress with every step. For once, Jen didn't envy the woman's generous endowment.

Fi didn't slow when she hit the first floor until they reached the trade caravan, where she turned back to the two women.

"Let me do the talking," Fi said. Although they had just run down six flights of stairs, she was barely winded, unlike Jen and Val, who were puffing as if they'd wrestled an entire pen of hogs. "Agreed?"

They bobbed acknowledgment, too winded to reply.

Finding the Trader, Carlos, among the many caravans took a few minutes of asking around, but when Jen finally laid eyes on him, there was no mistaking his wavy black hair and creamy brown skin.

Carlos set aside what looked like a fire-roasted chicken and sized them up with a regretful smile. "Sorry, ladies," he said in that dreamy voice Jen remembered so well. "Stall's closed. Captain Bharta's orders."

Despite what they had just promised Fi, Val stepped forward with a swing of her hips and the same sultry smile that had no doubt snared Jen's brother.

"Surely the captain hasn't also forbidden dinner and good conversation?"

Carlos' warm smile and greedy eyes said he would welcome more than just conversation with the busty apple picker—a look he'd never once given Jen, no matter how many times she'd shamelessly sashayed past his stall. Gods, she hated the woman.

"He hasn't at that." Carlos gestured to some fluffy silk pillows on the ground around his steel fire pit. "Make yourselves comfortable. I'll put some more chicken on the spit."

Jen attempted without success to avert her eyes from his perfect backside when he retreated into the vehicle.

I'm too old and too married to be lusting after younger men, she thought with a sigh. That didn't stop her from glancing wistfully at the doorway he'd disappeared into.

What she didn't expect was a grubby little face to peek back at her.

"Well hello," Jen said, smiling. "What's your name?"

The boy, who couldn't have been older than three, put a finger in his mouth. "Jared."

"Please to meet you, Jared. I'm Jen, and this is Val, and Miss Fi."

Jared looked at each of them in turn. Whatever thoughts were going through his young mind were hidden behind his hazel eyes and chubby cheeks. Without a word, he ducked back inside.

Jen sighed. It was hard to remember when her own boys had been that small, and she was sure they'd never, ever been that quiet.

Just when she thought she'd lost him, Jared reappeared, carefully climbed down the last, large step, and toddled over to them.

Jen patted her lap with a warm smile. "Would you like to sit?"

Jared nodded. He ambled around the fire pit with a wide enough berth that Jen didn't feel the need to shout a motherly warning. She opened her arms, eager to once again feel a warm little body snuggled against her, but Jared stopped just short of falling into her snare. His fascinated gaze landed on Fi and her enchanting eyes. Like a hypnotic slave, he shuffled over and curled into Fi's lap. Fi cuddled him close as if she had done it a thousand times, to which his suddenly droopy eyes attested.

Jen wanted to hate her for robbing her of that simple pleasure, but Jared's content smile made it impossible to fault the woman, so she instead focused on the fire of dried sharpgrass, crackling and warm. Dark smoke drifted up to the passive ventilation where, like all fire smoke, it would be vented outside.

"Jared?"

Carlos stepped out of the caravan and frantically looked around. He sighed in relief when he spotted the child safely in Fi's lap. Suspicion clouded his features. He kept half an eye on them while he affixed more chicken parts to the spit, then knelt on a pillow and began slowly cranking the spit handle.

"He likes you," Carlos said to Fi. The smile Jen expected on him never appeared.

"Mm, and he fits nicely. Thanks for letting me hold him."

Carlos' cautious veneer cracked. He relaxed onto his haunches and tipped his head. "No, I should thank you. You're the first woman he's approached since his mother passed last year."

"I'm sorry."

Carlos shrugged, but a sorrow crept into his brown eyes, now fixed on the fire. "We're all subject to nature's wrath. Traders more so. My wife was one of the unlucky ones."

"Fortunately, she lives on in this beautiful child." Fi examined Jared's face. "His mother had green eyes. A soft chin. Delicate mouth, with a prominent lower lip. Full black lashes that seemed too big for her narrow face. And her hair..." Fi studied Carlos for a moment before returning her gaze to Jared. "Black, like yours, but full bodied and unruly, which means she probably kept it short."

The squeak of the turning spit stopped. Carlos stared at Fi, transfixed, then blinked and shook his head.

"I'm sorry, Miss... Fi, was it? Have we met before?"

"I don't think so."

"I wouldn't have guessed. You described her perfectly."

"Children are puzzles with only two pieces. When you have one piece before you, it's easy to imagine what the other looks like."

"I'm not sure I agree," Jen said. "How do you explain my twins, then? Born within minutes of each other, but different as can be."

"Different to you, but I can easily see you in both of them, just like I can see their father. In a crowd, there would be no mistaking they belong to either of you."

"I may put your bold claim to the test later," Jen said with a smile. She knew a few children who bore no resemblance to their parents, and relished the idea of Fi being wrong for a change.

Carlos squinted at Jen's chest. For a moment, she was both thrilled and indignant that he would openly ogle her wares: thrilled because she couldn't shake her teenage fantasy of being the object of his desire, especially with more pronounced specimens sitting on full display to her left, and indignant because... well, she'd think of a reason later, but it wasn't proper.

Then, of course, she remembered the pendant around her neck, which he had sold to her.

Jen cleared her throat to hide her embarrassment and held it up. "Remember this?"

"Absolutely, and even more clearly how thrilled you were when you learned I still had one left."

Fi's eyes became as big as Jared's. "How many did you have to begin with?"

"Twenty-two, if I remember."

"T-twenty-two?" Fi's voice squeaked.

Jen wasn't sure if she should be happy that the taller woman seemed genuinely disturbed, or scared out of her wits.

"Good sir," Fi said, "may I ask where you acquired them?"

"You can ask, but you know I can't answer without breaching the Pact. Bharta has already proven he's in a banishing mood, and I have no desire to provoke him."

"This is one instance where my authority outranks his."

Carlos' mouth fell open. "You're a Fed?"

"Not exactly. Can we speak in private?"

He looked like he might protest, but his eyes fell to Jared, nestled protectively in Fi's lap.

Fi glanced down at the boy and shook her head. "I would never use the child as leverage against you, and would sooner cut off my own hand than harm a hair on his beautiful head. Say the word, and I'll give him back to you." Her striking blue eyes fixed on Carlos. "But my request stands. I need to know where you obtained those pendants."

"I... Even if you are who you say, I'd need proof, and I don't have any idea how I would verify it even if you showed me. If you want the information, you'll have to go through Bharta. I'm sorry."

"Don't apologize to me," Fi said. She pointed at Jen. "Apologize to her. She and her twin boys are the people who will suffer when sickness ravages Holtondome because they couldn't obtain the medicine they needed to survive."

"This has to do with the trade stalemate?"

"It may, but I won't know for sure until you tell me exactly where those pendants came from."

"Why? What are they?"

"Depending on your story, it could be fatal for you to know."

Carlos jumped to his feet. "I want no part of this! Please, leave me and my son alone."

"I can't do that. And if you think these two ladies want to be here, either, risking their necks for something they thought was an innocent trade, then you're wrong. Intentionally or not, you've put this entire dome at risk, and perhaps other domes as well. Now it's time to take responsibility."

Carlos swayed, looking pale. He sagged against the vehicle. "I'll still need proof of your identity."

"Will a recorded Statement of Authority from Grand Chancellor Chang do?"

"From… the Grand Chancellor himself?"

Fi nodded.

Jen felt the blood drain from her face.

She has explicit authority from Grand Chancellor Chang, ruler of the entire world.

All three of them stared at Fi, not daring to breathe, and undoubtedly wondering the same thing: Who in Freyja's Green Fields was this woman?

"Um, yes, I suppose it will." Carlos trudged to the caravan door like a prisoner on death march. "The caravan should give us enough privacy. If it's all right with you, that is, ma'am. I might need a minute to straighten up."

"Don't bother. I'm used to worse conditions than anything you and your son can conjure, I promise."

Fi stood fluidly with Jared still in her arms. Jen instinctively stood, too, feeling like she should salute. Val did likewise.

Fi carefully handed the boy to Jen. "Keep him out here, please. Even at his age, there may be things he shouldn't hear."

"Of course, Miss Fi." Jared nestled into her bosom without fuss, bringing Jen a much-needed smile. She felt an absurd pride that Fi had bypassed Val and entrusted this treasure with her instead. "We'll be just fine. Won't we, little man?"

Jared blinked his long lashes and heaved a contented sigh, which was all the confirmation she needed.

No sooner had they disappeared into the vehicle than Fi popped her head back out. "Stay. Here," she said to Val. "I'll be out as soon as I can."

"Yes, Miss Fi."

Fi stared at her a second longer before retreating inside.

Jen rocked her bundle like she used to with her own boys on the rare occasions they would stay still. Jared's eyes drooped more with every sway.

Is this what it's like to have a girl? Or was I just unlucky with my two dynamos?

As nice as it might be to find out, Jen had no desire to raise another child, so she contented herself with the one in her arms that she would happily, if reluctantly, soon return.

"So what was that all about?" Jen said to Val.

"Which part?"

"Miss Fi seems adamant that you stay close, like she doesn't trust you to be out of her sight."

"The feeling's mutual, then. But in truth, I don't know. Seg was just as adamant before they took him. He even made me swear."

Jen eyed her. "And you're absolutely sure you don't know why? Not even a hint?"

"Well, there might be something…"

Of course there is.

Jen ground her teeth. Trouble had stuck to her brother and Val like mud on pigs since the day they'd let the hogs loose together as children. They'd been a bad influence on each other then, and she suspected little had changed.

Up until now, however, their mischief had been annoying but not harmful. That Val had caught the attention of someone as evidently important as Fi was alarming to say the least.

Jen started to ask her about it, but a male voice from around the neighboring caravan froze her tongue.

"…seen Valerie Gannon? One of the local residents, about this tall, brown hair, green eyes."

"It was dark," another man said, "but I think someone like that passed by just a few minutes ago, along with two other women. She couldn't have gone far. Is she dangerous, sir?"

"Dangerous enough to warrant a shoot-on-sight order."

A gasp. "Is she armed? Do we need to secure ourselves?"

"That shouldn't be necessary. But if you see her, be sure to shout the alarm."

Jared grunted, and Jen realized she had crushed him to her chest. Val's eyes were so wide that Jen wondered what was holding them in her head.

"I have to hide!" Val said in a sharp whisper. "They can't find me!"

She glanced around, and Jen did the same. The only exits from Carlos' campsite were out to the main thoroughfare, where the voices had come from, or around the front of the caravans to either side, which were parked angular to the dome wall. Overhead lights had been dimmed for nighttime energy conservation, offering more shadows than usual, but most of the Traders had bright fires similar to this one.

Approaching footsteps jolted them both to attention. The Feds would be here any second.

A sharp pain on the back of Jen's neck made her gasp. Val had snapped her pendant free and was dashing around the front of Carlos' vehicle before Jen could even think to question why she would flee *toward* the Fed encampment instead of away from it, but Val was gone before she could utter a word.

Not one heartbeat later, two Feds sporting shiny white armor and frighteningly large black rifles rounded the back of the neighboring vehicle.

"Hail, Trader," one said.

Jen almost blurted that they were mistaken, then realized that not only was it a bad idea, but her exotic silk dress made her look the part. She clutched Jared to her chest, praying his good behavior continued.

"H-hail, gentle officers. Can I offer you a meal? The chicken will be ready soon, and there's more here than my son and I can eat."

What in Odin's name am I saying? Me, a purebred Holton, lying to a Fed without provocation! I'm just as straw-headed as Val.

But the truth was, she knew exactly what she was doing. Jen was protecting one of her own, and would do it again.

Once the Fed finished the same spiel she'd overheard from the last Trader, Jen shook her head and claimed she'd been busy trying to soothe her "son" and hadn't seen anyone of that description walk by.

"Really?" The Fed on the left backed up and counted the caravans with his finger. "Isn't this Carlos de Sangavoy's spot?"

Freyja help me…

As a rule, Jen didn't lie, so she had no practice fabricating them, let alone making them sound convincing. This did nothing to steady her voice while she told the wildest fib of her life to two people who, if they caught her and had a mind to, could shoot her for aiding and abetting a wanted criminal.

"No, sir. One of the new Traders—Tricksy, I think her name was—has a strange fear of curved walls. Something to do with being attacked near one as a child.

"Anyway, once trading halted, Tricksy swapped places with someone against the straight wall across the way. That triggered another swap with Yandis, who didn't like being so far from the dome entrance, and someone else who wanted to be farther away from the nauseating grain smell. Before you knew it, the whole caravan was topsy-turvy from where we started.

"Truth be told, I have no idea where Carlos ended up, but I don't plan on packing again until it's time to leave, unless someone holds me at gunpoint. Forgive the expression, of course, if that's what those monster cannons are for, in which case I'll be out of here before you can say, 'Long live Chancellor Chang!'" Jen topped off her pile of steaming lies with a weak smile.

Now where did that come from? No place respectable, that's for sure.

Jen kept her mouth shut, however, and prayed to the merciful gods that they bought it.

The Feds blinked a few times, evidently processing her verbal onslaught, then one pointed to the caravan door. "Anyone inside?"

"At one time, it would have been my husband, rest his soul, but it's just the two of us now."

She bounced Jerald for effect, who woke briefly before settling back to sleep. Jen shuddered to think what a nightmare this would have been with her own boys at his age—or any age, for that matter.

"Mind if we take a look anyway?"

"Only if you don't mind the smell," Jen said. "I haven't cleaned the diaper pail in days."

They winced. One Fed jerked his head up the road, and the other nodded.

"Thanks, we'll pass. If the fugitive is in there, you might have saved us a bullet."

"True at that," Jen said with a hollow chuckle.

She waited until they were well away before allowing herself to breathe again, then knocked softly on the caravan door.

No one answered.

She knocked softly again, afraid that doing so any louder would attract the Feds, who would call out her lie that the vehicle was empty.

Fi opened the door, scowling. "What is it?"

Jen filled her in as fast as her quivering lips would allow.

That was the first time she had the privilege of hearing Fi swear.

23

Visitor

VAL CREPT LOW ALONG THE curved dome wall as quietly as her cursed fancy dress would allow, darting from the front of one parked vehicle to the next. Every step rustled her skirt against her leg, or the ground, or the wall, or against different layers within the godsforsaken thing itself.

What she wouldn't have given for a good pair of leather work breeches. Gods, even plain underwear would have been an improvement. The next rustle set her teeth on edge. After glancing around the corner of the caravan to make sure no one had heard, she was tempted to strip right then and there. How much more could her reputation suffer? Running around half-naked was expected behavior from the hussy everyone thought Val was, so she might as well live up to her ill-gotten reputation.

And now, to top it off, the Feds want me dead.

What she'd done to earn that delightful sentence was anyone's guess. Feds shooting on sight was a penalty that parents scared their children with so they'd obey the Pact. It was an extreme measure reserved for the vilest crimes, like murder. To Val's knowledge, it had never in Holtondome's history been enacted.

Until now.

The next caravan over revealed an unexpected surprise. A dark gray blanket lay near the front tire, abandoned—and perfect to hide her colorful dress in the shadows.

Val draped it around her shoulders and over her head like a medieval cloak. Feeling much stealthier, she darted to the front of the next caravan. Each sprint brought her closer to the western entrance. What she'd do when she reached it was a problem for later. For now, she wanted to stay as far ahead of the execution squad as possible.

Nearby voices made her hunker down against the dirt-caked bumper. If she somehow made it out of this alive, she'd wash the blanket before returning it to its owner. The voices whispered, low but not urgent, as if they, too, didn't want to get caught.

Her heart leaped when she recognized the voices' owners.

Seg! Cook!

A cautious peek around the corner confirmed her suspicion. Across the stall, looking through a small, barred window, was Cook. The driver didn't seem to have noticed her, and continued his whispered conversation.

"...are you going to do? Assuming Miss Fi comes through, like you believe."

Oh, believe it, Val thought.

Fi was single-mindedly determined to have Seg. Somehow, Val didn't believe a pesky little thing like banishment would keep her from him. It was fantasy to think she'd do the same for Val. Then again, all Val seemed to have left were dreams, so she let that one ride. It was either that or cry, and she wasn't quite there. Yet.

"I don't know," Seg said. Although Val couldn't see his face, she could clearly picture him speaking from inside the caravan she hid behind, down to the large brown freckle on his cheek that wrinkled when he talked. "I mean, she's the closest thing I have to a soulmate, you know?"

"Oh, I know," Cook said. "That girl's one in a billion. You're a lucky S-O-B."

"A what?"

"Son-of-a-bitch. Sometimes I forget you're from a Provider dome."

"Is that a compliment?"

"Sure, why not?" Cook scratched his chin, which, even in the dim light, Val could see had grown stubbly. How often did the man have to shave to keep it as smooth as he had for Val? "And I mean the 'forgetting you're a Provider' part, not the S-O-B."

"Yeah, I got that."

"Just checking. I don't want to accidentally insult the only company I've had all day. I—"

Cook snapped his mouth shut and disappeared from the window, and Val soon saw why. A Fed meandered into view between the two vehicles, with an intimidating, Val-killing rifle in hand.

Val flattened onto her stomach, hoping for all the world that she looked like a lumpy, discarded blanket.

The ruse proved unnecessary. The guard peered into Cook's cell, went over to Seg's side, then wandered back the way he'd come.

"He's gone," Seg said softly.

"Don't know why they have this stupid 'no talking' rule anyway. They're going to kill us both tomorrow, so what does it matter?"

Cook has been sentenced to death, too?

Last she'd heard, he was still awaiting trial. Had Bharta skipped that small but important process with Cook as well?

Seems to be an annoying trend, she thought bitterly.

"Kill *me*, you mean," Seg said.

Cook waved his hand through the bars. "It's just a formality at this point. Bharta's going to banish me to make an example. If we're really lucky, they'll drop us off together, so we can at least have some company before the next storm hits."

"Any idea when that's supposed to be?"

"Tomorrow afternoon, and it's going to be an acid storm."

"Of course it is. Thor forbid we get a couple of sprinkles and a light wind for a change."

Cook laughed. "That's what I like about you, kid. You have just the right amount of pessimism." He sighed. "Soulmate, huh?"

"Yeah. Like you said, she's special. I've never connected with anyone so suddenly, and so completely."

Val sagged, feeling like she wanted to sink into the floor. It was one thing to know she was competing with Fi, but another to hear the love of her life speak about his interest in another woman so plainly.

"I hear you, kid. She has this... *joi de vivre* that makes you want to get out there and actually do all the shit you only talk about doing."

Val had no idea what *joi de vivre* meant, but she hoped it was an incurable disease that made Fi perform poorly in bed.

"That means 'joy of life,'" Cook said to Seg's silence.

Oh.

"Ah, yeah, she certainly has that." A fingernail tapped against a metal bar. "Let's say you make it back to the City with her, but I don't. What will you do?"

Cook's face melted into a smile. "Treat her like a queen."

Val sank lower. Cook was taken with Fi, too? It was so damned unfair...

"I've made my share of mistakes in relationships, but I've done some things right, too. I'd like to think I've learned my lessons, and that she'll benefit from them."

"Like what?"

"Breakfast in bed every damn morning. With champagne. And a fresh-picked rose from our garden, which I'd make sure was well-tended, just so we could sit together under the transparent dome and watch Earth's wrath while surrounded by beauty. Not that having her by my side wouldn't be beauty enough."

"Telling her that would go straight to her head, believe me."

"I don't care. She's beautiful, inside and out, and I wouldn't ever let her think otherwise."

Val felt a small splash on her hand, then wiped her eyes. What she wouldn't give for someone to think of her like that. Nat had been pleasant enough, but he'd always treated Val as if she was the lucky person, not him. Then, when the infertility subject reared its ugly head, he'd turned downright hostile.

But to be loved… No, truly adored by someone! Not for the revealing outfits she wore, but for the carefree, adventurous person she was, and for all her flaws.

Someone who loved the *whole* Val.

More tears pattered her arm. She angrily wiped them away.

What does it matter? I have hours to live, if I'm lucky.

And those hours would be spent hiding from the Feds, not in the arms of a lover.

Fi, on the other hand, would have her choice of two.

"You think she'd marry someone like me?" Cook said.

"You mean someone as old as you?"

"Yeah, I suppose that's what I'm asking."

"Absolutely. She's an old soul herself, and sees past superficial things like age. And physical deformities, lucky for me."

"Would *you* marry her?"

Seg blew a wistful sigh. "In a heartbeat."

Val's own heartbeat slowed to a crawl. Tears flowed freely down her cheeks.

She'd never stood a chance against Fi. Not one. The woman had bewitched both of the men in her life, like she did everyone else, leaving Val with nobody.

"Can't blame you, kid. But hey! Assuming we make it out of here in one piece, no hard feelings whoever Val chooses, yeah?"

ME?

Like flipping a switch, her heart went from catatonic to jumping around in her chest.

They'd been talking about her. Val!

Seg wanted to marry her. *Cook* wanted to marry her! No, Cook wanted to spoil her in every way possible. Treat her like a queen. Adore her like she was the only woman in the world.

And both of them have only had a taste of what I can offer.

Her cheeks ached from the ridiculous grin that surely reached her ears.

This couldn't be the end for them. Not now! Not with those scrumptious revelations. Val suddenly felt as if her life wasn't over, but was only just beginning.

And she wouldn't bloody well give it up without a fight.

She rose from her hiding place.

A solid *thunk* on the back of her head, followed by a dull ache, reminded her that she was still under Seg's prison van. The vehicle's metal bumper rang in testament to her stupidity.

When she looked up, Cook was squinting into the shadows where she lay. Val obliged him and shed her blanket. His shock quickly became a soft chuckle.

"Should have known you'd show up. It's the one place in Holtondome you're not allowed to be."

"Har har. And here I thought you'd be happy to have the chance to actually propose to the object of your affection instead of just musing about it. Assuming Seg doesn't propose to me first."

"Val! W-what are you doing here?"

Seg's sharp whisper set her heart racing even faster. She composed herself before replying. "Don't sound so surprised. You didn't think a little thing like Feds with guns could keep me away, did you?"

"Yes, I absolutely *did* think you'd have more sense! Get out of here before they find you!"

"But—"

"Now! I... I don't want to see you," Seg said. "Not now, not ever again. Go away!"

"Nice try, but you've already told me your true feelings, even if you didn't mean to. So how about you drop the bravado and be glad for a friendly visitor?" How she wished she could see his face...

"You don't understand! Val, you have to leave *right now!*"

Val grinned. "Happily. And you're *both* coming with me."

24

Valkyrie

Seg's mind raced. The person he most wanted to see was the same person he hoped would be as far away from here as possible. But, even without fate's intervention, he should have known that nothing would keep Val away. Things like rules and mortal danger had never been deterrents to either of them. If anything, taking risks spurred their sense of adventure, fueled enjoyment of their shared capers, and inspired them to push their boundaries.

Nothing Seg could say would drive her away, especially if she'd just overheard what she claimed.

Still, I have to try.

He hadn't seen the vision of her dying since earlier that day, before he'd visited the statue of Holly with Fi.

But Fi had.

He had to keep trying, or—

For an instant, Seg thought he was seeing double. To his right, through the small, barred window, Val stood and brushed the dirt from her dress. Despite his panic for her safety, her triumphant smile melted him.

What put ice in his veins, however, was the apparition of Val that appeared to his left. Not ten feet away, near the rear of the vehicle, a ghostly image of her in the exact same dress sneaked toward the real Val.

As the apparition had a dozen times earlier that day, she froze, as if caught, and slowly turned around with her hands up. A flash made him blink. Val's ghost staggered and clutched her chest. A red stain spread down the back of her dress.

Then she collapsed, unmoving.

The apparition blurred with his tears and faded.

He couldn't let this happen!

But what could he do? At least when Troy had been in trouble, Seg had had the option of braving the storm to get to him. Here in this mobile prison, he felt absolutely helpless. He looked around the small vehicle, hoping he'd spot something he'd missed the last ten times he'd searched, but there was nothing. The only features in his cell were a locked, reinforced rear door, which he'd already tested, and two hard metal benches with no moving parts to dismantle. Whatever his plan, he would need to execute it from within his prison.

What could possibly chase her away from here?

"Val," he said, hoping his desperation wasn't too evident, "I have an idea that might just get us off the hook, but we'll need Miss Fi's help. Find her, and hurry!"

It was a lie, but if it got her safely away from the site of her pending death, he'd happily apologize later. Assuming he had the opportunity before the Feds banished him.

Her smile wilted. "I… I can't do that."

"Of course you can! Go back along the—"

"If the Feds see me, I'll be shot on sight."

Seg's blood went from cold to sub-zero. "W-why?"

"I don't rightly know, but I overheard their orders straight from the horse's rear, and I wasn't curious enough to risk being shot and ask."

"Then get out of sight," Cook said. "When the guard comes by, maybe we can find out."

Val spun on him. "What does it matter? The Feds want all three of us dead! Our only chance is to get you guys out of these cages and take that car of yours far away from here."

"Take it *where?* As soon as they found out we'd escaped, they'd call for reinforcements to hunt us down. Hardy as my car is, it wouldn't last ten seconds against even one of their armored units, and they'd send a lot more than one. Even if we did manage to evade them, we'd be registered criminals with the Federated Nations. Cities would arrest us at the gate, and no sane Provider dome would harbor fugitives for fear of retribution."

"Cities and Provider domes can't be the only human settlements left on Earth," Val said. "There must be some who are tired of living under constant oppression."

"If there are, I've never heard of them," Cook said. "Though the Feds don't exactly tell me everything."

"Which means they *could* exist. I'd rather take the slim chance of braving the wilds and living than staying here to die." Val tapped her lip.

"What we need is a way to distract the—"

"Guard!" Seg hissed. One shiny boot had appeared under the corner of the vehicle and was about three steps away from coming into view.

Val ducked out of sight. Her hiding spot must have been effective, because when the Fed turned toward them, his face held the same boredom it had the last twenty times he'd walked by. The Fed stopped in front of Seg's window and tapped the bars with the barrel of his gun.

"No talking among prisoners. If I have to warn you again, I'm going to carry out your death sentence personally."

"Sorry, sir."

The Fed banged the window with his fist, making Seg jump, then walked away.

Val reappeared seconds later. The front of her fine dress was covered in dirt. Pieces of straw poked from her hair, giving her a wild air that somehow suited her.

The apparition appeared behind her and began her fatal routine.

"All right, we're going to need to get these prisons open, and to do that, I'll need to distract the guards." Val held out one of the dark-gray pendants, dangling from a broken leather strap. "My dress has no pockets. Hold this so I have two free hands to work with."

Seg took it from her.

The apparition disappeared in mid-motion.

Oh no…

But it was too much to be coincidence.

"Wait," he said when she started to leave. He pushed the pendant through the bars. "Hold onto this for just a few more seconds."

"Seg, I really don't have time to—"

"Please! It's important."

Val looked like she was about to argue, then shrugged and took it from him.

The apparition reappeared immediately and started its tragic routine from the beginning.

That cinched it. The only other vision Seg had ever had was of Troy—who had *also* been wearing his pendant at the time. The pendants and Seg's visions were directly linked.

Val sighed. "Happy?"

She handed it back to him. Seg took it, but quickly caught her wrist and tied the leather strap around like a bracelet. Painful as they were to watch, he needed the visions as a guide to have a prayer of saving Val, in case they changed or contained some clue he missed.

As he predicted, the apparition remained.

"There," Seg said softly. "This way your hand is free, and I won't get caught with it if they come in here to rough me up."

Her expression darkened. "Have they hurt you?"

"Not yet, but it's only a matter of time. Must be my charming personality."

"It certainly is." She smiled and pinched his cheek through the bars. "Don't worry. Val to the rescue! Those thugs will touch you over my dead body."

I really wish she hadn't said that, Seg thought, just as the apparition clutched her own chest and collapsed.

But what could he do to stop it? He'd tried chasing Val away with apathy, and then luring her away with the tease of a plan. With a shoot-on-sight order hanging over her head, calling the Feds would turn his visions into stark reality. Seg watched the real Val move out of view, toward the shadows along the dome wall, feeling utterly helpless.

Think, Seg. Think!

He needed options. Levers. As a prisoner, unfortunately, he had few of either.

Could he fake a heart attack? The excitement might keep Val away from her terminus spot, but if they decided to cart him away for treatment, he wouldn't be present to thwart her death.

Seg whacked the bars with a frustrated growl. He had to do something!

If only he knew what. Any action he chose might very well set off the chain of events leading to her death. Troy's situation had been straight forward: get him away from the collector before lightning fried him. But Seg was the one trapped this time, and his victim had free rein.

No matter how he looked at it, he couldn't figure out how to save her.

"Halt!"

Oh no!

Sure Val had been caught, Seg waited for the guard to march her around the corner and execute her. He was ridiculously relieved when he heard Fi's voice instead.

"I'm unarmed. I'm just here to see the prisoner."

The guard walked into view between the prison vehicles, rifle leveled with deadly intent presumably at Fi. "No visitors. Leave the area immediately."

"Or what?"

"Don't be smart, lady."

"If I wasn't, then I wouldn't be a very effective adjudicator for the accused, now, would I?"

"Providers don't have rights to adjudicators."

"Yes, they do."

The Fed snorted. "Never heard one ask for an adjudicator."

"That's because Providers are largely ignorant of their rights, thanks to non-literacy laws and strategic misinformation by the Federated Nations during their annual 'education' sessions. Lucky for my client, I happened to be in Holtondome when this unfortunate misunderstanding occurred."

"Misunderstanding?"

The Fed gave Seg an uneasy look before returning his attention to Fi. Seg sighed in relief when he lowered his rifle.

"Lady—er, ma'am… Captain Bharta was just here. He was pretty clear about the prisoner's crime—and a few other important things. I'm afraid I can't let you near him."

"What 'other important things'? I'm sure my client feels his life is quite important, too."

"You'll have to take that up with the captain."

"I'm not asking the captain, I'm asking you. What is so important that merits violating my client's rights, thereby sentencing him to an unjust death?"

The Fed pressed his lips together.

"Officer…?"

"Doohan," the Fed said, sighing.

"Yes." Fi stepped into view and leveled him with a serious gaze. "While you may believe that deferring to a higher authority absolves you of responsibility, Section 5.3.441.e cites that every citizen of the Federated Nations—including yourself—is personally responsible and required to uphold the law. Failure to do so makes you subject to Section 7.8.225. I'm not surprised by your blank expression that you're unfamiliar with the laws regarding trial by adjudicator council. Providers are routinely denied their rights simply because they don't know they exist. Likewise, Feds often escape justice because there is no one to call them on their actions.

"But not in this case. Let me be clear, Officer: if you don't cooperate with me *right now*, my very next action will be to request an adjudicator council to review your disregard for my client's rights—which, since I've just informed you what those are, would be a blatant and willful violation of the law."

"I…" Doohan stood tall and held is rifle across his chest. "The prisoner hasn't said anything about having legal representation."

Fi raised her voice without taking her eyes from Doohan. "Seg?"

"Yes, Fi is my adjudicator." *Or lawyer, or whatever.* "And I'm requesting her counsel."

Doohan looked like he wanted to faint. "This is a mistake," he said softly to Fi.

"Your argument might be more convincing if I knew why."

"Fine. But I can't tell you in front of the prisoner."

Doohan nodded away from the western entrance, which would take them out of the heart of the Fed encampment. If Fi was worried for her own safety, as Seg would be in her place, she gave no indication and followed him out of view.

"Wonder what has him so spooked?" Cook said. With their only guard out of earshot, he apparently didn't feel the need to whisper.

"I just assumed you knew."

"No. Do you?"

Seg shook his head. "And the deeper I get into this mess, the more I'm convinced that's exactly how the Feds want it."

"I thought that was the whole point of the Provider Pact: willful ignorance for the greater good."

"It's hard to believe in a greater good when all the smaller goods are constantly being stepped on."

Cook grinned. "There's that measured pessimism I admire. Think anyone else in Holtondome has seen the light?"

"At least one," Jen said.

They both startled at her voice. She crept from the shadows, eyes darting around as if the Feds would jump out at any moment and arrest her for her heretical statement.

"You've been hanging around Val too much," Cook said with a chuckle. "You here to spring us, too?"

Her mouth fell open, then she shook her head. "Foolish girl! I should have known she'd try a stupid stunt like that."

"Then why are you here?" Seg said. "Not that I'm unhappy to see you, but the guard made it pretty clear that being around us is against the rules."

They all jumped when Val emerged from the shadows, too, grinning like the fool Jen had just accused her of being. She wrapped Jen in a brief hug, who grunted in surprise.

"So glad you could join us," Val said. "Fi has lured the guard out of sight. Go stand watch while I unbolt the prison doors."

"Are you crazy? They'll shoot us *both* on sight!"

"Only if they catch me in the act, which they'll have much less chance of doing if I have advanced warning. Just clear your throat loudly if you see someone coming."

"I-I don't know…"

"I do! We haven't always seen eye to eye, so you have little reason to stick your neck out for me, but your brother and Cook are worth saving. I'm not asking you to spring them yourself, just to give us a fair chance of making it out of here alive." Val took the smaller woman by the shoulders. "Will you do that? Please?"

Jen started to speak, then closed her eyes, took a deep breath, and nodded. "Be quick!"

"Like the sexiest fox you can imagine." Val winked, then shooed her away.

The apparition appeared again and started her death routine, although her performance felt different this time. Crisper, more defined.

More certain.

Seg's instincts screamed that if he was going to change Val's fate, this was his last chance.

"Val," he said, putting as much urgency into his word as he could. "Fi said she'll act as my adjudicator. Maybe we don't have to do this."

"*Your* adjudicator," she said, her eyes softening. "Not mine, and not Cook's. Besides, I have no faith left in the Feds, or even in the Pact. It's escape, or death. If we're going to die, I'd rather die trying than roll over and let it happen."

"But… Val, wait!"

Seg blew a frustrated sigh. She had already turned away and was creeping to the end of Cook's prison vehicle. Val peered both ways, then disappeared around the corner—an easy target for any guard who happened by.

His stomach lurched at the thought. Seg didn't have to imagine what her death would be like; he'd seen it over and over, taunting him, torturing his heart and soul.

And there wasn't a damn thing he could do to stop it.

A faint squeal of metal on metal from the end of Cook's vehicle snapped their attention. Cook gave Seg a last, uneasy look, then disappeared from his small window.

Val appeared an instant later, creeping back between the vehicles.

Something about her stance was frighteningly familiar.

This is it, Seg realized.

Terror seized his chest in an icy grip. His vision was about to become reality.

Before he could scream for Val to duck, run, or do anything to *not* be where she was, a figure in white armor with long silver hair appeared where Val had been moments before.

It was Captain Bharta.

And he had a large pistol aimed at her back.

Jen's urgent "Ahem!" came far too late, drowned out by Bharta's commanding, "Don't move."

The sense of *déjà vu* made Seg's head spin. Val froze and put her hands up, as her apparition had so many times before, then slowly turned around.

Two things happened at the same time. Fi appeared on the left side of Seg's field-of-vision, her intense gaze fixed on Val, who was too far away to save even if Fi made a mad dash. To the right, the rear door of Cook's vehicle silently swung open, followed by the man himself, who quietly crept behind the unsuspecting captain.

Bharta raised his weapon. Seg knew from Val's stance that she was moments away from being shot.

What didn't make sense, however, was Bharta's posture. Although Val was in his crosshairs, his stance was relaxed—as if he had no intention of shooting her.

Cook either didn't pick up on it, or didn't care. He lunged at Bharta.

As mortifying as the spectacle was, what caught Seg's attention was Fi.

The thick marks around her eyes surged across her face in a mass of writhing lines that reminded Seg of tentacles, spreading until nothing remained of her fair skin. Black tendrils splayed from her scalp, mixing with her blonde-green hair as if night and day were fighting an epic battle for dominance. Even the whites of her eyes turned dark ebony.

Fi had, in the span of a heartbeat, become more alien than any creature Seg could imagine.

Cook grabbed Bharta's gun hand. His finger clamped over Bharta's, crushing it around the trigger, which Seg had all but expected. Val was almost in position, with her arms half-raised, and her posture stooped. She had one backward step remaining before the bullet took her life.

But then something changed: an unexpected gust of wind swept Val's dress under her heel, which it certainly hadn't in Seg's vision.

Val stumbled backward the instant before a deafening shot hammered Seg's ears. He screamed, unable to hear his own voice. Val tumbled onto her back and cradled her shoulder. Blood poured from between her fingers. Seg banged on his prison bars, frantic to reach her.

Then reality hit him, stunning him to silence.

Val hadn't been shot through her chest.

The bullet had instead pierced her shoulder. More to the point, she was still moving. Even seeing her gripping her shoulder in agony, Seg was overjoyed.

Val had beaten fate. She was alive.

Undoubtedly, in Seg's mind, thanks to Fi.

25

Choices

SEG PRIED HIS EYES FROM Val, who was still writhing in pain and holding her shoulder, to look at Fi. The strange black creature she'd turned into just a moment ago was gone. The dark marks around her eyes still writhed, but were much closer to their original size. Soon, they stilled entirely, leaving only the exotic, enchanting beauty Seg had always known.

Bharta and Cook had ceased their struggle, eyes locked on Val with open shock. They exchanged a mutual nod, then disengaged and rushed to her side.

"She needs a medic," Cook said more calmly than Seg would have managed.

Bharta nodded. He gently rolled her onto her back and touched her fingers, which were clamped tightly on her shoulder.

"Relax, my dear," he said in a soothing voice. "Let me see."

Val groaned, eyes roaming without seeing. When they finally landed on Bharta, she yelled and tried to back away, but Cook held her firmly in place.

"Val, you're going to be fine," Cook said. "Let the captain have a look."

She blinked, as if trying to make sense of his words, but eventually lowered her hand.

The wound looked terrible. A gaping hole above her collar bone the size of Seg's finger leaked a constant stream of red. Bharta winced, then rolled his finger in a circle at Cook. Cook obediently propped her up, allowing Bharta to see underneath.

"A clean exit. Fortunately for her, I didn't have hollow points loaded, or the damage would be much worse."

Val barked something between a laugh and a cry. "Gods, I can't imagine

241

what 'worse' would feel like! I hope childbirth isn't this painful." She scrunched her eyes with a moan and leaned into Cook, who cradled her head.

Bharta turned around. "Fetch a medic, Miss Fi, unless you'd like to watch this young woman bleed to death."

Fi blinked at him with glassy eyes. She'd gone completely pale, and swayed as if she might collapse.

"I…"

She shook her head, then wiped a shaky hand down her face.

"N-no need, I'll take care of her." She looked at Cook. "Strip your shirt, please. We need to bind her wound to staunch the blood flow. Captain, if you have a stretcher nearby, that would be better than walking her halfway across the dome to the medical ward. Otherwise we should send for one."

Seg tried to speak, but his voice caught. He had to clear his throat three times before it would work properly. "Is she going to be okay?"

"Yes." Fi's extra nod confirmed Seg's real question: Her visions of Val dying were gone. Whatever happened from here on out, Val would live. Which meant…

"Captain Bharta, does this mean you're commuting Val's sentence?"

"What sentence?"

Val coughed a laugh, then scrunched her eyes in pain. "The shoot-on-sight order," she said, panting. "I heard it myself… from a pair of Feds… a few minutes ago."

Bharta frowned. "I gave no such order."

"Then why did you shoot her?" Seg said.

"I didn't. I was going to escort her out of the encampment with a warning." Bharta glared at Cook. "But *someone* jumped me from behind and squeezed the trigger while trying to wrestle my gun away."

Cook turned his eyes to the floor, looking as if he wanted to sink right into it.

"Now," Bharta said, turning back to Val, "what's this about a shoot-on-sight order?"

The Fed who Fi had been talking to, Doohan, pulled out a pocket computer screen similar to Cook's. "The order's right here, sir." He sighed. "It's a Code 36."

"Code 36…" Bharta closed his eyes and pinched the bridge of his nose. "Young lady, you don't make my job easy. Doohan, who reported it?"

"Michaels. He finished questioning the prisoner next to you about thirty minutes ago."

Bharta gave Cook a long look, who had stripped his shirt and was wrapping it around Val's shoulder, and shook his head. "Even assaulting a Federal Officer I could have forgiven with a few lashings, but this…"

Bharta stood, jaw and fists clenched as if he wanted to punch something, but took a deep breath and wrangled himself under control.

"I don't have a memory erasing machine, Mrs. Gannon," he said to Val. "The City knowledge our industrious Mr. Moreno has bestowed upon you is permanent and irreparable, which makes your continued presence in Holtondome an unacceptable risk to the Pact. As much as it pains me… since you actively solicited the information, there is but one punishment."

He looked down at her with genuine sympathy.

"Your injury will be treated by non-Providers until you're coherent enough to submit to an inquiry, where we'll determine if you've spread the contamination, and call additional residents for questioning as necessary.

"Then, as an example to ensure a travesty like this doesn't happen again, you will be summarily and publicly executed."

Val turned her head away, burying her face in Cook's arm, who stroked her hair.

"Sorry, Val," Cook said in a thick voice. "This is all my fault. If I could fix it by trading my life for yours, I'd do it in a snap."

"No, I knew the penalty when I started asking. I didn't care, but I should have. Not for my life, but for yours." She looked up at him, eyes glistening. "Forgive me?"

A tender smile took years from Cook's face. "Always, My Queen."

The touching display was lost on Seg.

Despite everything that had just happened, Val was still going to die.

He looked around for visions that might clue him in to the location and manner of Val's execution, but found nothing. He looked at Fi and shrugged.

Fi gave a subtle nod, confirming that she hadn't seen any visions, either, then settled beside Cook. Her skilled fingers took the shirt-bandage from him and began a more systematic binding of Val's shoulder.

"This is such a heartfelt moment," Fi said. "I almost hate to ruin it."

Val frowned. "Miss Fi?"

Fi ignored her and focused on the wound. "Captain, you can belay your execution order. Assuming she wishes to accept, I formally claim this woman as my apprentice."

A smile twitched Bharta's lips. "A valiant try, Miss Fi, but your claim will be quickly overturned. Adjudicator apprentices require a solid foundation of legal knowledge. My nephew was recently rejected because he didn't have Section 1 memorized to the letter. Clever as Mrs. Gannon may be, I doubt she would even come close to qualifying, which means that not only would her sentence stand, but you would also be charged with obstruction of justice."

"I didn't say I was taking her as an Adjudicator apprentice."

Bharta laughed. "A medical apprentice, then? The same prerequisites apply. But, as I understand, your license has expired, which means you aren't qualified to take on an apprentice anyway."

"Not as a Medical Doctor apprentice, either, though I'm sure she's capable."

"Then, please, enlighten me. Which other profession have you mastered and are qualified to take apprentices for? Automotive mechanics? Agricultural engineering? Software development?"

"All of the above, in fact, but you still haven't guessed. It might be entertaining to see if you can."

Bharta's smile wilted. "Need I remind you that lying to a Federal Officer is an offense."

"Feel free to test my knowledge, Captain. It would be a refreshing exercise. But I'm afraid the apprenticeship I'm offering her would be beyond even your copious experience to probe, so I might as well tell you."

Fi finally met Val's eyes.

"Do you agree to obey and respect me as your teacher, mentor, and master for all things related to your chosen discipline for a period of not less than four years, and to fulfill the duties expected of an apprentice to the best of your abilities?"

Val started to answer, then closed her eyes with a painful grunt and shifted against Cook. "Apprenticeship for *what*, Miss Fi?"

Fi grinned. "For the Mars Program, of course. Which means you'll be coming with me on my next trip to Mars Colony."

Val's shriek made everyone jump. She crushed Fi in a one-armed hug and giggled with a maniacal mixture of elation and agony.

"I accept! I accept! Thank you, Miss—*ouch!*"

"Easy, now." Fi patted her back, then gently laid her down. "Relax until we can properly suture your wound."

"Is that an order, ma'am?"

"I'd hope it's common sense, but if that's what it takes to make you comply, then yes. And I prefer 'Miss Fi,' if you don't mind. 'Ma'am' makes me feel old."

Seg covered his laugh with a cough. *If Val only knew…*

"Yes, Miss Fi." Val settled into Cook's embrace, looking as happy as if she'd been given the world.

"At the risk of bursting your little bubble," Bharta said, "the same problem still applies. Mrs. Gannon has no qualifications for the position. Your agreement will be nullified the moment it hits an Adjudicator council, which it undoubtedly will."

"On the contrary, my new apprentice has unequivocally proven her qualifications for the job. Astronauts often work alone in punishing conditions, where the slightest mistake can cost their own life and many others'. The primary attributes we therefore seek are bravery in the face of insurmountable odds, resourcefulness, integrity, and mental resilience, all of which she has just demonstrated."

Bharta crossed his shiny, white-plated arms. "How so?"

"If you're going to make me spell it out, fine. But remember, you asked.

"In addition to her personal history, which is testament in itself, she defended Seg when his honor was publicly questioned, both verbally and, when that failed, physically. She compromised her safety and social standing simply because she felt it was the right thing to do.

"Then, even under the extreme stress of a shoot-to-kill order, she maintained her wits enough to plan and execute the rescue of two people she felt were also wronged—a plan that may have worked had you not been waiting in ambush."

"But I was, and it failed," Bharta said.

"Her failure was, in my opinion, a reflection of just how far the odds were stacked against her," Fi said. "But my point is that where many would have panicked, frozen, or tried to save their own necks, my new apprentice thought quickly, decisively, and without losing sight of what was most important. I would take someone like that by my side any day over an unproven academic with top scores in their field."

Bharta started to object, then seemed to think better of it and shrugged. "In the end, the decision will be up to the Adjudicators, I suppose."

"You won't fight me on this, then?"

"No."

"Good," Fi said. "Then we can change topics to my driver."

"Mr. Moreno's trial is tomorrow. You'll have a chance to speak on his behalf then."

"Tomorrow may be too late if you want to salvage trade negotiations with Holtondome."

Bharta frowned. "What do you mean? He's an outsider."

"An outsider who helped save Seg's brother, the proverbial Prince of Holtondome. The only reason he's alive is because my driver used the resources at his disposal, at great personal risk, to free him from a malfunctioning three-ton rain collector panel—a panel that had been replaced by City engineers just last season at tremendous cost to Holtondome."

"What precisely are you trying to say, Miss Fi?"

"That you're looking to resolve the trading stalemate. That my driver went above and beyond to help one of theirs. That you've arrested *both* people involved in the much-celebrated rescue. That one of those heroes is now sentenced to die, and the other is facing serious punishment simply because he forgot to hide sensitive technology from the very people it should be benefitting.

"Captain, you're asking these people to sacrifice for the greater good. Not only are you *not* offering any good will in return, you're subjugating those who've tried. What incentive does Holtondome have to bleed for a society they're forbidden to know, and a government who shows so little regard for those who've truly sacrificed on their behalf?"

Bharta stiffened, his face red. "Careful, you tread very closely to breaching the Pact."

"I know where the lines are, Captain. And if a possible breach of Pact is all you've taken away from this conversation, then I've wasted my breath, and you certainly aren't the same compassionate person I spoke with earlier, who had only humanity's interests at heart."

Silence stretched. Bharta started to speak, then again, but each attempt ended with a long sigh. He spent nearly a minute alternating his gaze between Cook and Seg before returning his attention to Fi.

"Even if I wanted to," Bharta said in a measured tone, "some transgressions are beyond my authority to forgive."

"Such as?"

He gestured to Cook. "Though it's definitely flexing the law, I can pardon his passing of forbidden information to Mrs. Gannon because, as your apprentice, the information is no longer forbidden to her—a fact that conveniently pardons them both.

"However, half the population witnessed the technology on Mr. Moreno's car in action. That technology is *explicitly* forbidden. At this point, the witness testimonies are impossible to strike from the records. If I let him go, a review committee will inevitably discover the oversight, and a warrant will be issued for his arrest. Possibly mine as well."

Fi smiled. "Then let me take the blame. The driver was under my employ at the time, which makes me responsible for his actions."

Doohan, who had been quietly watching the exchange, suddenly frowned. "Miss Fi, this whole thing started because you told me that individuals are accountable for breaking the law, regardless of who gave the order."

"Only if someone explicitly charges the offending subordinate instead of their superior." She looked at Bharta. "Are you?"

He considered her for a second. "No."

"Then, if you'd kindly delay my arrest for just a minute, there's somebody I need to speak with." Fi gave a finishing tug on the knot of Val's shirt-bandage, then walked away without waiting to be excused.

Cook's eyebrows rose. "I followed most of that, but just to make sure... am I still under arrest?"

"I've half a mind to charge you for assaulting a Federal Officer," Bharta said. "Especially since it almost cost Mrs. Gannon's life. But doing so would undermine the good will Miss Fi has worked so hard to stage. So, as long as everyone here promises to keep the cause of this little incident between us, I don't think we need to report your involvement in the shooting." He leveled Cook with a stern gaze. "Don't make me regret this kindness. Any further transgressions and you *will* be prosecuted, even if it has to wait until you leave Holtondome."

Cook gulped and nodded.

"I brought Dr. Ven and a stretcher team!" Jen yelled from somewhere outside Seg's limited view.

Seconds later, she and a group of residents rushed in and laid a hand-woven cloth stretcher next to Val. The team rolled her to one side, slid the stretcher under her, then rolled her back and carefully moved her the rest of the way. Val weathered the treatment with scrunched eyes, and didn't open them until the crew lifted her up.

"Wait!" Val gestured toward Seg with her uninjured arm.

The stretcher team obediently moved her closer.

Val gripped a window bar. "I haven't given up on you, Seg. Miss Fi and I will get you out of this mess, I swear." She held two fingers out in their childhood tradition when giving a solemn oath.

Seg hooked two of his fingers around hers, completing the vow. He wanted to give her some encouraging words, like "don't worry about me, just focus on feeling better," but it stuck in his throat. He knew she'd be all right; Fi had confirmed it.

But what about him? Did Seg's visions work on himself? If he stood on top of the dome and scouted the land, would he see the place of his death after he'd been banished?

Fi's visions worked differently. Had she foreseen Seg's death and simply not mentioned it to keep him from worrying? He wouldn't be surprised.

Instead of speaking, Seg tightened his fingers around Val's, swinging the gray pendant he'd fastened around her wrist, and held onto her until the stretcher crew eventually took her away. He hoped his expression had conveyed the feelings of love and gratitude that his mouth couldn't.

Fi returned a few minutes later. "Captain, please check your messages."

Bharta withdrew his own pocket computer screen and tapped it to life. His eyebrows climbed almost to his silver hairline. "This must be a forgery."

"It isn't. The technology my driver exposed is no longer on the forbidden list. The Pact Council had apparently been on the fence about it anyway. A small nudge was all it took to have it removed. A broader announcement will be made tomorrow."

"A nudge, you say?"

Fi shrugged. "It pays to know the Pact Council leader. He owed me a favor."

"I won't ask for what."

"Mm. So, presuming I'm no longer subject to arrest, I'd like a few minutes alone with my client now, if you don't mind."

Bharta glanced at Seg. "I'm afraid I can't allow that, Miss Fi. Mr. Holton's sentence has already been pronounced. He has no need for legal representation."

"He does, because I plan to appeal the ruling to an Adjudicator Council."

"You'll never get one so quickly. Adjudicator Council requests take weeks to process, if not longer."

"Mm." Fi crossed her arms and stared at the pocket screen in his hand.

It beeped.

This time, Bharta's jaw fell. "A council hearing. Tomorrow." He looked at Fi and shook his head. "How on this devastated Earth did you get them to agree to meet before dawn?"

"By saying 'please.' But let me ask you, Captain. If this entire dispute with Holtondome was resolved before then, would you be willing to nullify your ruling?"

"That depends on how complete the resolution was. Despite what you might think of me, I have no desire to kill the boy, but the people of Holtondome *must* understand how critical it is that they participate in trade."

"That's the problem, as you well understand. They don't know, and the law forbids us from telling them. But maybe we can break down some of those knowledge barriers tonight—legally—and let them make a more informed decision."

Bharta's eyes narrowed. "What are you planning?"

"I can't tell you, because then you'd have to arrest me for breaching the Pact," Fi said. "Let's see what the rest of the evening reveals, though, hmm? *After* I speak with my client. Alone."

"I can't leave him unguarded."

"Of course you can. Where would he escape to? Outside of the dome? It would be self-banishment."

Bharta considered her for a second longer, then dropped his eyes. "You can use one of the questioning trailers for thirty minutes. No longer."

"Adjudicator privilege gives me as long as I need, and you know it. But I might be willing to limit our visit to your requested duration if you agreed to let him attend storytime tonight."

"He would have to be shackled and guarded, which would be an uninspiring sight."

Jen stepped forward. "I'd rather have him shackled and with us than locked in a prison." When Bharta hesitated, Jen lifted her chin. "Consider it a gesture of good will toward trade negotiations."

Bharta's lips compressed to a thin line. He arched an eyebrow at Fi. "Thirty minutes?"

"Not a second longer."

He nodded, then gestured to Doohan. "Move the prisoner to Trailer Four. Have a security detail and class-two restraints waiting when he emerges."

"Sir!" Doohan saluted and moved to the back of Seg's trailer.

Fi turned to follow and caught Seg's eye. Insecurity flashed across her face, so at odds with her normal confidence that she seemed a teenager trying to appear brave in front of adults, when all she really wanted was to run to her room and hide.

Seg could only imagine. She was playing a dangerous game with powerful players, from what he could tell. But her gaze lingered on him for longer than he would have expected if her head was filled with worry about her next move.

No, her insecurity wasn't about Bharta or Holtondome. She was insecure about Seg.

He had a sinking feeling he knew why. Fi had wrapped everyone else's predicaments up neatly, but she'd exhausted her bag of tricks. Seg's death sentence might still be carried out.

26

Client Privilege

SEG SAT DOWN ON A stiff bench seat, similar to the one he'd used with Bharta in their earlier inquisition session. Fi lingered at the door of the inquiry vehicle, her eyes downcast, before sitting across from him. She clamped her hands between her knees, burying them in the puffy folds of her opulent blue felt dress. Seg waited patiently while she continued to stare down at nothing.

"You... saw something," Fi said in a small voice, still not meeting his eyes. "Just before our young lady was shot, something terrified you."

"Val being shot was reason enough to be terrified."

"No, you weren't looking at her. You..." Fi swallowed and wet her lips. Her mouth trembled with barely contained emotion. "You were looking at me."

Had he? Everything had happened so fast, Seg could barely remember the sequence, let alone how he'd felt at the time.

She finally met his gaze, tears glistening. "What did you see that made you so afraid of me?"

"I wasn't afraid of you," Seg said, dodging the uncomfortable part of her question.

"Please don't lie. You were upset over the ordeal, but it wasn't until you saw me that you became truly terrified. What did you see?"

"I wasn't afraid of you!" Seg hadn't meant to yell, but the point was important. He took a calming breath and lowered his voice. "I was not— *am* not—afraid of you, Fi. I need you to believe that."

"Why?" Her question was barely a whisper through quivering lips.

She wasn't going to let him get away without answering, no matter how much he wanted to forget what he'd seen. And so, as gently as he could,

251

Seg told her. Uncharacteristically, Fi remained silent through his detailed description of her transformation into the midnight-black creature that, apparently, only he had seen.

Fi sat back after he finished, her enchanting blue eyes haunted. "I always feel... something, when I change people's fate. A coldness throughout my entire body. I just never imagined it was anything more than a feeling."

"How does it work? When you make someone... not die."

"It's like instinct," Fi said. "When the event is about to occur, the vision plays stronger than usual, and I can just tell it's going to be the last one. I concentrate on erasing it. On making it go away."

"That's it?"

"Well, there are the chills I described, and I feel drained afterward, but yes."

"Why did you choose Val's shoulder to be shot? Why not make the bullet miss?"

She leveled him with a familiar stare that said he'd missed something obvious, and that it was up to him to figure out.

Seg considered for a moment. "You erase the vision," he said slowly, assembling the puzzle pieces. "You don't recreate it. You make it go away, which means... you don't control *how* the person's death is avoided, only that it is."

"Right. In this case, your busty lady tripped on her dress, which caused the shot to miss her critical organs. Other instances have been much stranger."

"Such as?"

"One time, a bird swooped down and clawed the shooter. Another time, the attacking Samurai's katana blade came loose from its hilt, an occurrence so unlikely that we all stared in stunned silence, until the Samurai walked away in disgrace. A thunderclap once startled a bowman into dropping his arrow. I even saw a tiger about to attack a child be bowled over by a charging rhino. That introduced a different problem, but we managed to escape with only a few scratches." Fi considered him. "You didn't feel anything similar when you saved your brother?"

"I was in the cold, pouring rain in the middle of a lightning storm, and the only thing on my mind was Troy. Any number of sensations could have passed through me and I wouldn't have noticed."

"Mm. Well, at least you seemed to still be you." Fi wrapped her arms around her middle and shivered. "Your description of the thing I became makes me sound... inhuman."

"I would never use that word to describe you. No more than you would with me."

"Except in this case, you might be right." Fi shook her head and wiped her eyes. "I don't know what I am, Seg. Twenty thousand years on this Earth, and I still don't have any concrete answers, just indisputable evidence that I'm different."

"What evidence?"

"Apart from the information your unique sight has just provided—which I thank you for sharing, because I know it was hard—there's this."

Fi pulled out her pocket computer screen, tapped a complex pattern, and handed it over, but Seg put up his hands.

"Wait... is this something you should be showing me? I'm still in Fed custody."

"Probably not, but at this point..." Her lips quivered again. She sniffled and brushed another tear away. "It's more important to me that you know. I want you to truly understand who—or what—you've chosen to associate with. Understand as much as I do, at least, before it's too late to change your mind about hooking up with your busty lady friend."

Seg grinned. "Your new apprentice, you mean?"

"Mm."

Fi handed the screen to him. Her face twisted in guilt, as if it were a confession to murder, then she clamped her hands between her knees and cast her eyes to the floor.

A shocking computer image of the inside of a human body lit the thin display. Seg was no medic, but he was still able to identify the heart, stomach, intestines, liver, kidneys, and...

Seg squinted at the pelvic region.

The strange organ with the wavy arms must have been a uterus, making this a female body.

"Looks normal to me, I guess, though Doc Ven would be a better judge."

"You're right, it is. I wanted to show you what a normal woman looks like inside, so you'd have something to compare to when you saw this."

Fi reached over and swiped a finger across the screen.

The image that replaced it had a female outline, but the similarities ended there. None of the organs he'd identified in the original image were present. Instead of large organs, smaller, striated shapes ran up and down her body in organized patterns that made the normal woman's anatomy seem chaotic by comparison. He turned it sideways, then upside-down, thinking perhaps the organs he expected to see had just shifted, or were oddly placed, but it didn't help.

Bones aside, Seg couldn't match any of this picture's organs at all with the normal woman's.

Not. Even. One.

"This... is you?" It was the most "obviously" question he'd ever dared to ask Fi, and yet he had to be absolutely sure.

"Mm." Fi seemed to have shrunk in upon herself. Her legs were pulled up tight against her chest, chin on her knees, as if she wanted to fold into a ball and roll away. She remained silent.

The implications were so staggering that, for a moment, Seg couldn't even think. His mind spun without traction, like a hauler with a busted transmission. When it finally kicked into gear, Fi hadn't uncurled from her fetal position, and was gently rocking.

Seg cleared his throat. "Um... w-where's your heart?"

She peeked up at him, then slowly unfolded and tapped three small globs on the screen: one in either side of her chest, and the other in her abdomen.

"I have three, as far as I can tell, though they work differently than yours."

"Can I feel?"

"Mm."

Fi stood in front of him and held out her hand. Her fingers trembled so badly that Seg held them for a few seconds to calm her down. She flashed a grateful smile, but was still trembling when she pressed his hand to her stomach.

Where Seg would have expected the easy rhythm of breathing, or gurgles at most, he felt the unmistakable pulse of... something. It didn't beat with the expected *lub-dub* rhythm, but twisted and writhed like a tiny kitten doing endless somersaults inside of her.

Seg pulled her close and put his ear to her abdomen.

No *thump-thump* heartbeat. No throbbing. Just the quiet whisper of constantly moving fluid.

Her shaking fingers ran through his hair, then hastily withdrew. Fi slipped from his arms and resumed her seat across from him, but wouldn't meet his eyes. Tears streaked her cheeks.

"They say it's not what's on the outside, but on the inside that counts," she said, sniffling. "Well, now you've seen my insides."

Seg stared at the image for a second longer, then cradled the screen to his chest. "Who else knows about this?"

"No one," Fi said softly. "I've never dared show it to anyone before.

Ever."

The revelation splashed through Seg like cold water, leaving a shiver in its wake.

They'd known each other for one day.

One. Day.

Yet, for some reason, Fi trusted Seg enough to reveal a secret she hadn't told anyone else in over twenty thousand years—not her husbands, lovers, or friends.

It was humbling. It was overwhelming.

And it spoke more about her belief that they were compatible than any other evidence he'd seen yet.

Fi had made herself vulnerable, surrendered herself to him so completely that one wrong move from him would utterly destroy her. In her place, Seg didn't think he would have had the courage.

No, courage was the wrong word. Any fool who threw themselves in front of a bullet or charged into a blazing fire could claim to have courage.

What Fi had was faith.

Faith in me.

Faith he wouldn't reject her. Faith he wouldn't rebuke her. Faith he wouldn't betray a secret that would undoubtedly land her on some scientist's dissection table for as long as she was allowed to live. Faith that even though she was different—probably not even human—Seg would see beyond it to what truly mattered.

And, fortunately, that wasn't hard to do.

Seg handed the pocket screen back to her and relaxed on the couch as if she'd just shown him a wonderful drawing instead of her mysterious internal anatomy. "Aren't you worried about carrying those pictures around? That device is probably the first thing the Feds would search."

Fi studied him carefully, as she had when she'd revealed her age. Seg exposed only a warm smile. At long last, she gave a slight nod.

"They wouldn't get far. It's encrypted with a proprietary algorithm. The device will also erase all data after three unauthorized access attempts. And, just to be safe, I've rigged the circuits with micro-incendiaries to make sure the data isn't recoverable."

"Somehow I knew you'd have it covered." Seg rested his elbows on his knees. "How long have you known?"

"I've *suspected* since I was a teenager, but it wasn't until 1895, when x-rays were discovered, that I found out the true extent. The second I heard the news, I was on a ship to Wilhelm Röntgen's lab at the University of Würzburg in Germany.

"You can't imagine how hard it was to get his amazing machine all to myself, even for a few minutes. The resolution was terrible, but enough to confirm what I'd long suspected. Imaging modalities improved drastically after that. The sharper the images became, the more apparent my differences were."

Seg nodded, although he didn't know what an x-ray was. "Must have been a shock."

"Isolating is more like it. Before then, I could at least cling to the hope that I was just a little bit different; a human who had somehow acquired a long lifespan and... other things."

"Like what?"

"Things you already know about, and a few that should probably wait."

More surprises...

Although outwardly calm, Seg wasn't sure if he could take any more shocking information today. He silently thanked Fi for sparing him.

"I can tell you're trying to be brave," she said, calling his bluff. "I've dropped two big ones on you in a single day. I understand if you need time to process."

"Thanks."

Fi nodded, but her gaze fell. Evidently, that wasn't the answer she'd been hoping for. She hugged her knees again and rocked. Her eyes darted around, as if she was seeking escape, but had nowhere to go. And, if she was fretting about what Seg believed she was, he understood the feeling all too well.

She'd confessed her deepest secret yet, and had made no bones about her feelings toward him. Waiting for an answer—for confirmation that he didn't think Fi was the monster she undoubtedly considered herself to be —was a torture she couldn't physically escape.

Seg couldn't stand the thought of putting her through that kind of pain. He *didn't* consider her a monster, regardless of what his selectively blind eye might have seen, or what the pocket screen had shown of her insides.

To him, she was just Fi.

Seg crossed the vehicle and sat next to her so their hips were touching. She didn't look up.

"I forgot to thank you."

"You're welcome." Fi managed to sound even more despondent than she looked.

Seg *tsked*. "So unlike you to fall for such a basic trap. I never said what I was thanking you for."

"The inference is obvious. Saving your busty girl."

"And now you're assuming. I should check for a fever."

"I don't get fevers," Fi said into her knees. "Even bacteria are afraid to infect me." She sulked for a minute, then rolled her head to look at him. "So why did you thank me?"

"Saving Busty Girl *is* the obvious answer." Seg grinned, less because of the amusing nickname than imagining how Val would attack him when he next used it. "But you'd already promised to save her, and I had zero doubts you'd come through. Changing her fate was a kindness I can never repay, and taking her as an apprentice... That was a sacrifice for the history books. I can't imagine she'll be easy to teach."

Fi waved a hand. "I've broken dozens of apprentices who were twice as pigheaded as her. One was a Viking."

Seg laughed, intentionally steering himself away from the hundred questions that sprung to mind about Viking life. There would be time for those later, he hoped. Right now was about Fi.

He wrapped his arm around her and drew her close. Fi stiffened, but soon relaxed into him. He buried his nose in her blonde-green hair, which smelled of golden fields and spring flowers.

"No, what I thanked you for was coming into my life," Seg said.

She looked up at him, hope in her enchanting blue eyes.

"Whatever you are—whatever *I* am... it took me a while, just like you said it would, but I finally get it."

"Get what?"

He leaned down and met her lips, which welcomed his in a tender kiss.

"We *are* compatible."

A smile lit her face, more dazzling than he imagined the shining sun. "Took you long enough. I thought I was going to have to draw pictures."

"Trust you to ruin a perfectly fine moment. You have any idea how hard it was waiting for the right time to use that line?"

"Harder than coming up with it, for sure. I practically gift-wrapped it for you."

He playfully flicked her nose. She graced him with a heartwarming giggle, then snuggled against him.

"Even so, it's nice to hear you say it," Fi said.

They sat in contented silence for a few minutes. But, try as he did to enjoy it, the night's events kept creeping into his thoughts, until he finally gave into them.

"Fi?"

"Mm?"

"Your death visions, they aren't... tied to anything, are they?"

"Talk about killing the mood." She heaved a sigh. "They're tied to the person's fate. But, unlike yours, my visions are free-floating, though they normally only happen when I'm near the subject, or when I'm concentrating on the person. Your brother was an example of the latter."

"No, I mean tied to a physical object, or a type of material. Something the person might wear."

Fi looked up at him. "What are you getting at?"

"Well, I... I think my visions might be linked to those pendants, or to whatever they're made of."

"Why?"

Seg told her how Val's apparition had disappeared when she'd removed the pendant, then reappeared when he'd fastened it around her wrist.

"Not only that," he said afterward, "but from the time she gave it to me until just before she snuck up to my cell, I didn't have any visions of her death at all."

"Fascinating," she said softly, her eyes distant.

"What are they?"

"Things that shouldn't exist."

Figures. "Can you be a little more specific?"

Fi stared at him, as if weighing her answer, and finally nodded. "I suppose there's no point in keeping it from you now. If the Feds question you again, we're both as good as dead."

"I... I'm sorry I put you in that position."

"I didn't mean it that way. I wouldn't have told you if I hadn't been willing to assume the risk." She ran a finger down a fold in her dress. "The pendants are made from a complex material that, I believed until yesterday, had only ever been found in one place." Fi leaned her head against his arm. "Caverns on Mars."

"But... that's impossible, unless the Feds have been lying to us about the Mars missions."

"Oh, they have been, but not about the dates. Your mother claims she acquired those pendants before you were born. The first manned Mars mission was in 2458, a full twenty years before your birth. But the first *return* mission to Earth didn't happen until 2511—just five years ago—and that's when the materials were introduced to this planet. Or so we assumed."

Fi shook her head. "That your family acquired those pendants before you were born shouldn't be possible. Grand Chancellor Chang has an unhealthy obsession with all things Mars. If he learns of their existence and even suspects Holtondome is involved, he will... overreact, in ways that won't benefit the residents here."

Seg opened his mouth, but nothing came out. He tried again with marginally better results. "I... o-okay. First off, how do you know the material doesn't just naturally form on Earth?"

"When I say 'complex,' I mean we still don't have a clue what it's made of, its base elements, or even the physical properties holding it together. To put it unscientifically, the material isn't just from a different planet, it's from a different universe, where the normal rules of physics don't seem to apply."

Seg gulped. His entire life, he and his whole family had been carrying impossible objects of incalculable value around their necks, and they'd never suspected a thing. "So, those strange markings on the pendants that only I can see..."

"I won't even speculate until you've drawn them out for me, but yes, there may be much more to them. And the implications of there also being marks on *me* that only you can see aren't lost on me, either, but again, it's too soon to jump to conclusions."

Too late, Seg thought, his head already spinning with wild possibilities.

"One problem at a time," Fi said, patting his hand. "We need to clear your name and, if possible, make sure Holtondome has what it needs in the process. And we only have about ten minutes left together, so..."

Fi stood. Her suddenly smoldering eyes locked onto his. She reached behind her back. With a few snaps, her dress came loose and fell down around her ankles. She wore no undergarments beneath.

"Last time, I wasn't myself," Fi said, "and I attacked you like a wild beast. This time, if you can resist touching my marks, I'll be in full control. And believe me, you want that."

"But... we only have ten minutes."

She slunk onto his lap and straddled him with a sultry smile. The black marks around her eyes and down the front of her body began to pulse in a sensual rhythm.

"Let me show you the delightful things my unique anatomy and twenty thousand years of experience can do with a whole ten minutes."

27

Storytime

STANDING UP WAS DIFFICULT. FI was already up and around, her dress as perfect as if it hadn't been around her ankles just thirty seconds before, but Seg was still tying his trousers when the vehicle door opened. Fi hadn't been joking about her experience *or* her unique anatomy, this time leaving Seg as the person in need of assistance.

Fi gave him a knowing smile, making him wonder how much of that had been revenge for setting her into a frenzy in the statue room. She extended a helping hand. His legs failed him, causing him to stumble into Fi. She caught him with a gentle pat on his arm and held him until he steadied.

"Thanks."

"Likewise," she said, her breath warm on his ear. She planted a gentle kiss on his cheek, then took a deep breath and strode to the door. "I'm ready to take on the world now."

Careful what you wish for, Seg thought.

The stakes, which had been high to begin with, were now absurd. If Bharta or any of the Feds caught wind of what his family's pendants were —some Martian material that shouldn't have existed on Earth at the time they were acquired—then the Grand Chancellor himself might step in and make everyone wish they'd never laid eyes on the cursed things. Fortunately, all but two were safely hidden in Holly's statue.

Unfortunately, one of those was still around Val's wrist, and she had no idea what it really was.

Probably good she doesn't.

If Val knew she was wearing a material that, in Fi's words, might be from another universe, her fascination would undoubtedly call unwanted

261

attention. He could only hope the Feds didn't feel the need to babysit her in the medical ward while Doc Ven treated her gunshot wound. If one of them even suspected the pendant's origins...

Two armed Feds were waiting for them outside the vehicle. They stepped aside to let Fi pass, but, as Bharta had promised, they fastened hardy restraints around Seg's wrists and ankles.

The ankle cuffs had just enough chain between them to allow half a walking stride. His first few steps nearly landed him on his face when his front foot stopped short of where it wanted to go, but he soon adjusted. Twice he tried to scratch his cheek, only to be foiled by the chain connecting his wrist bindings to the chain between his feet. To reach his face, he would need to bend over, and the Feds didn't seem inclined to stop their march toward the stairs to grant him the opportunity.

Although it felt as if Seg had been locked away for days, many in Tad's Tavern were just finishing the dinners they'd ordered when he'd been hauled away.

Conversation hushed. Seg weathered their stares, as he always did, and followed the Feds to a chair one of them had somehow procured from the packed tavern. The rattle of his chains when he sat echoed in the lull.

Fi glided through the tight crowd like a breeze in the forest. She spared Den and his group of traitors not a glance on her way to the bar, where she grabbed a tankard and began tapping the wooden counter in a steady rhythm. Other taps joined hers. In the space of five heartbeats, conversation stopped, and the entire tavern was filled with the practiced pounding that signaled the start of storytime.

Fi finished the ritual by raising her tankard high—or whoever's tankard it was. Everyone raised their drinks and shouted, "Hey!" Then quiet settled, as if Seg had suddenly gone deaf, with all eyes rapt on Fi.

"People of Holtondome," she said, her voice projecting to every corner of the tavern. "Tonight, the captain has agreed to let me divulge information normally forbidden to Providers. I will stay away from details that may compromise your oath, or impinge on your anti-technology beliefs, but we both feel it important that you have a clearer understanding of how Grand Chancellor Chang the Sixth is shaping the future of the Federated Nations, and how crucial a role that you, the Providers, play in that plan."

Fi meandered between tables. Her enchanting blue eyes met each resident's with intensity and purpose.

"You know I'm an outsider, but what you don't know is from just how far outside I come." She stopped and looked around. "I, ladies and gentlemen, am a Martian."

Gasps rippled through the crowd, but Seg was the only one who nearly fell out of his seat. Fi had just finished telling him that she had no idea if her strange anatomy meant she was a true alien—let alone from Mars—and, either way, how letting her secret slip would be a tragic end to her long life.

So what in Odin's name is she doing?

A sly smile spread across her face. "And by Martian, of course, I mean that I'm one of the few beings on Earth who can also claim to be a Mars Colony resident."

Seg heaved a sigh of relief. How much of that performance had been designed to shock the audience versus giving him a personal heart attack was up for debate.

"Everyone knows about the Federated Nations' incredible achievement of creating a sustainable human habitat on another planet," Fi said. "You also know that, to date, there has been one successful return mission—a feat which far surpasses the first for numerous reasons, and is the only reason I'm standing before you today.

"Those herculean efforts are the focus of today's story. I want you to fully understand the motivations behind the Mars Program, the tremendous time and resources that went into it, and the unimaginable effort and ingenuity required to return just a handful of us to our home soil."

Surprised murmurs filled the room from Holtondome residents, Traders, and Feds alike. Beyond knowing that Mars Colony existed, which was more information than Providers were permitted to know about other domes, they knew nothing of the colony itself, nor how it got there. Second-hand knowledge would have been exciting enough; hearing it from someone who had actually been there was beyond any resident's wildest expectations.

Even Captain Bharta's eyes held a sparkle of interest, which made Seg suddenly wonder just how much the Federated Nations shared with their officers about the Mars Program.

And if they're not entrusted with that, then what else aren't they being told?

The thought also made Seg wonder how much authority Bharta had to even allow this telling, but, judging from the dazzled expressions around the room, no one was eager to call him out on it.

"Throughout history, space programs have catapulted technology and innovation like no other industry," Fi said to her captive audience. "Achieving the impossible requires reaching beyond known limitations;

asking not *if* something can be done, but what measures are necessary to get there. And, of course, having the stamina to endure the countless, inevitable failures along the way.

"But innovation itself was not enough of a driver for such a costly initiative, given humanity's precarious circumstances in 2451, when the manned Mars mission program began. We were over three hundred years into recovery from extinction, yet our planet showed few signs of forgiveness for its abuse.

"It was at this time a new satellite took orbit around Mars, equipped with the most advanced geological survey instruments to date. Its first report provided subterranean maps of unprecedented detail, revealing complex underground caverns of what appeared to be artificial origin."

Til's gasp was the loudest. Had Seg not been forewarned, he would have gasped, too.

"Artificial?" The drink Til was about to give her patron hovered over the table, forgotten. "As in… made by aliens?"

Fi flashed a tolerant smile. "That was the predominant and most hopeful theory, yes. Earth had become uninhabitable to its native population, and showed no signs of healing. Even if it did, by Grand Chancellor Chang's reasoning, there were no guarantees that humanity wouldn't eventually go down the same path that had led it to The Fall, or worse. A single planet just wasn't enough to ensure our survival in the face of our greatest enemy." Fi put a hand on her chest. "Ourselves."

Murmurs and nodding heads. This truth was at the core of the Pact, drilled into every resident from the time they were old enough to talk.

"But now…" Fi swept her gaze around the tavern. "*Now* perhaps humanity had a second chance—a home away from home, left to them by a different civilization from another time. If we could tame the Red Planet, inhabit its caverns as someone else might once have, then the human race would halve its chances of another mass extinction."

A young boy slipped from his mother's arms, dashed forward, and stopped so close to Fi that his toes brushed her hem. Big brown eyes looked up at her from beneath a mop of sandy hair.

"What'd they find in the caverns, Miss Fi? Space aliens?"

Fi hoisted him onto her hip and touched his nose, smiling. "I'll get there in a minute."

The boy pouted but remained silent. She carried him around while she wandered the tavern.

"To discover what the caverns held, they had to first figure out a way to get to them. The caverns were over a kilometer beneath the surface, with no known entrances. Even the most optimistic scientists agreed that any chance of success would require a human presence—a small population who could build and repair excavation equipment as necessary, and modify their tools to meet the inevitable unanticipated setbacks of any operation of scale. And that was the beginning of the Mars Colony program."

Seg suppressed a smirk. The program began over sixty years ago, and he would have bet anything Fi had been involved from the start. He wouldn't have been surprised to learn she'd also been involved in the first Moon landing program over five hundred years prior.

Or aboard Christopher Columbus' ship to America, or with the first Vikings to cross the ocean...

He shook his head to clear the dizzying thoughts and focused on the present.

"Unfortunately, Grand Chancellor Chang's plan was one humanity had been puzzling since before The Fall," Fi said, "made more difficult because of the post-Fall setbacks to science, horrendous weather, and the limited resources our dwindling population could spare for anything not related to daily survival. But Grand Chancellor Chang the First hadn't rebuilt civilization by balking at challenges, and Chang the Fifth wouldn't, either."

Only half-hearted cheers rose, and Seg could understand their lack of enthusiasm. Holtondome's current predicament was supposedly due to a lack of resources. The idea of putting effort into anything other than caring for Earth's existing populace was difficult to support when their own people were already suffering.

Fi beamed as if the crowd had roared approval. "Chang devoted multiple Cities to the effort. He pulled in top minds around the world from whatever projects they were working on, no matter how crucial. He scoured what little information had survived The Fall, and diverted the resources he needed to begin the largest initiative since the domes."

A man near the upstart Den frowned. "That was around 2451, you say?"

"Yes. The very same year of the Mars caverns' discovery."

His frown deepened. "Dates are often lost over retellings, but my dad— rest his soul—once told me of a year similar to this one, where Holtondome couldn't afford the repairs needed to keep the domes running. We lost ten acres of wheat to acid rain that year because an entire section of sun panels collapsed. He was in his early thirties at the time, which lines up."

"Wasn't there also a medicine shortage around then?" a woman next to him said. "Grandma still lights a candle every year for her husband who died from a cough because there wasn't enough medicine to treat him."

"There was a shortage," a man said from across the tavern. "My departed uncle lost an arm to infection as a boy because there were no antibiotics to spare. It would have been around that time."

"Mm." Fi's exaggerated smile never faltered. "Well, I can't legally comment on the economics of it, but, as the Grand Chancellor is fond of saying, great feats require great sacrifices, and this would be among the greatest feats in history."

Bharta's face might have been carved from stone. Seg expected some sort of interruption, given how closely Fi was skirting the law, but the captain remained silent.

In the rear of the tavern, Troy and Gina Teladar had finally ceased their intense conversation and were wholly focused on Fi. Their hands were still joined in a white-knuckled grip. His brother, normally dour, wore a terrified expression, as if he'd just learned the second Fall was nigh. Gina's look of helpless fright wasn't far behind.

Whatever they'd been discussing, Seg was no longer sure he wanted to know.

Fi adjusted the boy on her hip and resumed wandering the tavern.

"So began an intense, three-year effort to design and perfect a means of establishing a colony on Mars. Engineers poured raw materials by the truckload into parts for their enormous rockets, and the facilities necessary to launch them. Every few weeks saw a new test flight. Many crashed and burned, but Chang never wavered. When a rocket blew up, he built another, and another. Twenty-three spacecrafts either exploded or sank to the bottom of the ocean before they declared the program ready."

Len, who had just yesterday goaded Seg when he was trying to save his brother, gawked. "Wait... did you say *twenty-three?* Just how big were these rockets?"

"Huge! The original Saturn V super heavy-lift launch vehicle, which carried us to the Moon in 1969, was one hundred and ten meters tall, weighed almost three thousand tons, and could carry a payload of just forty-eight tons. The new rocket, appropriately named Chang I, would need to carry *two hundred* tons, and successfully land on a planet with sixty-two percent of Earth's gravity, versus the Moon's sixteen percent. That meant more fuel and a sturdier structure. All told, Chang I weighed over *forty-three hundred tons.*"

Len's jaw worked for a few seconds, then he averted his eyes.

"Something the matter?" Fi said casually.

"It's just... well, I'm no rocket expert, but it sounds like an awful lot of time and material went into making just one. And twenty-three of them!" Len shook his head. "We could have built a whole 'nother dome instead."

"Two domes, actually. What's your point?"

Seg checked for signs that Fi was joking, but her face didn't even twitch. The boy on her hip swiveled his head back and forth, watching them each in turn.

Len stared at her, as did the rest of the tavern, then shook himself. "*Two domes*, Miss Fi! That's another ten thousand able hands we could have brought into a world that's already struggling to sustain itself."

The lion twins, seated at a table near the bar, put their drinks down with perfect synchronicity.

The lion sister brushed her sandy mane back with a regal air worthy of her nickname. "Just how many people could this new Mars Colony support?"

"The first mission transported and sustained eighteen colonists."

The twins' expressions darkened, giving Seg the impression of lions about to pounce.

"And how many missions have there been since then?" the brother said.

"Two per year over the last fifty-eight years, each delivering more people, supplies, and materials to help sustain the colony. Not all of them were successful, of course, but enough made it that Grand Chancellor Chang believed it justified the risk."

The lion sister blinked. "One hundred and sixteen launches? How many failed?"

"I feel we're straying from the story, but in the spirit of illustrating how important this program was to Chang, and how brave the first colonists were, I'll answer." Fi turned her attention to the boy on her hip. "Over the course of the program, approximately one in four launches ended in disaster."

Seg did the math.

Twenty-nine! Assuming each launch had eighteen passengers, that means...

"Over five hundred deaths," a woman said aloud.

A vigil-like silence fell over the room.

Fi wandered the tables at a leisurely pace, her focus on the boy. She smoothed back his hair with a smile. "As I said, great feats require great sacrifices, and Grand Chancellor Chang was determined to make Mars Colony succeed."

The lion brother shook his long mane in disbelief. "So they succeeded. What exactly did they find in those Martian caverns?"

A sly smile spread across Fi's face. "There are some details I'm not allowed to reveal, even with Bharta's permission, but with regards to the goal of establishing a human civilization on Mars, they found... nothing."

"Oh, come now!" It was the first Bharta had spoken since Fi's story began. "Surely you're exaggerating. Grand Chancellor Chang wouldn't have invested in one hundred and sixteen missions over the last fifty years if they hadn't found *something*."

"That, Captain, you'll have to take up with Chang himself. I'm already pushing the boundaries of what I'm allowed to reveal. But I *can* tell you that the reason he green-lit so many missions is because Mars Colony was never able to sustain itself as originally planned, and has required frequent supply deliveries to keep the colonists alive. Not to mention additional parts, and fuel for the one-and-only return mission to date."

"Why *was* there a return mission?" the lion sister said.

"Another question I can't directly answer," Fi said. "Let's just say the excavation team found samples meriting the scrutiny of Earth's most talented scientists, many of whom would be unable to survive the seven-month trip to Mars with their sanity intact, let alone perform their duties in the harshness of colony life."

Murmurs filled the tavern. While some held curiosity or wonder, most sounded concerned.

"How many more of these missions are planned?" The speaker was Den, the upstart Seg had punched. His scowl indicated he was none too pleased.

"There is no scheduled end date to the program, which means semi-annual launches will continue for the foreseeable future."

Den collapsed onto a barstool. His scowl melted into shock. "Ten more domes we could have had," he said softly. "A hundred thousand more people we could've sustained here on Earth, helping to make the planet better, instead of the, what... fifteen hundred colonists on Mars who can't even sustain themselves? It doesn't make sense."

"Not to mention where else those resources might have gone," Jen said.

She stepped through the crowd, barely taller than those sitting, but carried herself as surely as if she were two meters high. Her hard eyes swept the crowd.

"New domes aside, how much of our own crumbling infrastructure might have been fixed? For how many *decades* could the materials of *one rocket* and the talent of its engineers have sustained all of Holtondome? How might our productivity have improved? Our quality of life?" Her mouth tightened. "How much more medicine could they have produced for our infirmed if they hadn't been so focused on a fruitless project! How many of our own would have lived? What advances could those brilliant minds have achieved that were *wasted* on—"

"Mrs. Holton!" Bharta marched toward her until he was towering over Seg's smaller sister.

Seg rose to her defense, but a rough hand from a guard sat him firmly back down. He glared at the Fed, who patted his gun in warning.

Godsdamnit...

He bitterly wondered how tough the Fed would act without his weapon —and if Seg weren't bound by his hands and ankles.

Bharta looked down on her. "This sort of speculative... *ruminating* isn't helpful to anyone!"

To her credit, Jen didn't flinch. She crossed her arms and glared at him as if they were of equal height. "I'm only saying what the rest are thinking, Captain—and, if you have a brain in your head, what *you* should be thinking, too."

"My place—and yours—is *not* to question the wisdom of Grand Chancellor Chang, whose family's foresight and wisdom are the only reasons any of us are alive today!"

"I question anything that threatens the well-being of those I hold dearest," Jen said. "And from where I stand, the Mars Program is a losing proposition to everyone, including you. To assume anything else without evidence to the contrary would be turning a blind eye to the truth— otherwise known as *foolishness*."

Bharta's jaw hardened. "I thought 'turning a blind eye' was the cornerstone of Provider philosophy."

"We shun technology, Captain, but don't mistake that for blatant naiveté. We may not know how a harvester works, but we accept that it does because we see its value with our own eyes. Likewise, if someone points a gun in our face, we acknowledge it will kill us, even if we don't understand the mechanics, because we've seen them in action.

"And, most importantly, we know the difference between a harvester and a gun: one benefits Holtondome and the surrounding settlements, and the other has only ever harmed us. I don't think I need to explain on which side of the fence the Mars Program falls."

Bharta trembled with rage. His mouth opened, but Troy interrupted his reply.

"The effects of the Mars Program are worse than you think." Troy's voice carried with authority, desperation, and fear. He stood, intense eyes looking around. "I can't speak for the rest of the world, but the impact to settlements in Wyoming and the surrounding states has been disastrous." He clenched his fists. "No, disastrous is too gentle a word. It's been devastating. Catastrophic! A setback that our species' fragile hold on existence *cannot* afford. And the extent of the damage has been carefully hidden from us all."

Bharta narrowed his eyes. "What do you mean?"

Seg expected a follow-up accusation, questioning where Troy might have received information forbidden to a Provider, but none came. Whatever Troy was alluding to, the captain was genuinely clueless.

"As Providers, we're forbidden literacy, or any sort of written record, which means the details of our trading history have become lost to the ages, either mutated or omitted through telling after re-telling." Troy pointed at Gina. "But the Traders aren't forbidden. Trading is their profession, their livelihood. Their records go back as far as Holtondome's construction. When you pair that with the information I just heard, it paints a clear and terrifying picture."

"Outside trading information is *also* forbidden to Providers," Bharta said. "I'm afraid I'm going to—"

"Section 581.1.6," Troy said over him. "'Outside information must receive Pact Council approval prior to transmittal or other conveyance to Providers, *except* when said information is deemed crucial to the continuing health of a significant portion of the Provider population.'" He crossed his arms. "Funny how that last part is omitted from the yearly Federal Education Program."

"And how did *you* come across it? A little bird told you? They're all but extinct, you know."

"At my request, Miss Fi lent me a spoken version of *Curated Laws for Providers, Third Edition*. It's been very enlightening."

Bharta rounded on Fi with smoldering eyes.

"At ease, Captain," Fi said, hugging the boy so their cheeks pressed. "We've broken no laws. The work is approved for Provider distribution, and Seg's brother will uphold his oath and return my audio player the instant he's done memorizing its contents. Isn't that right?"

"Actually, I'm not sure I will."

Fi mirrored Seg's surprise, which was in itself surprising.

"My oath," Troy said, "and everyone's here, is predicated on *all parties* upholding the Pact in good faith, including Grand Chancellor Chang himself. From what I can tell, Chang hasn't. Why should I or *anyone* in Holtondome keep our oaths to a liar?"

Bharta's hand strayed to the pistol at his side.

Seg's heart nearly leaped from its chest. He'd saved his brother from certain death just yesterday. His time couldn't be up again so quickly, could it?

The Feds guarding him gripped their rifles and advanced. Seg's mind worked furiously, trying to think of a way to help Troy while bound and hobbled, but it was Hap who came to the rescue.

"What have you discovered, son?" he said above the commotion.

"That Chang's Mars Program has done the opposite of ensuring humanity's survival." Troy's hard gaze made its way around the tavern, meeting each resident's in turn. "In fact, over the fifty-odd years since the program started, Provider domes have dwindled to a staggeringly low number."

The tavern broke into worried chatter, but a firm warning from Hap calmed them down. He focused on Troy with rapt intensity.

"Dwindled how?"

"In the beginning, there were thirteen Provider domes in the trader's records in Wyoming." Troy sighed. "Now there are only two, including us. Gina—"

Seg would never discover what his brother was going to say next.

Before anyone could shout warning, Bharta drew his pistol and shot Troy between the eyes.

28

Fallen

SEG WATCHED HIS BIG BROTHER'S body fall, feeling detached, as if he were observing someone else's nightmare. Troy's eyes remained open the entire way down. His head struck the ground with a *thud* that reverberated through the floor, up Seg's legs, and shattered his soul.

Seg's blood-curdling wail joined Gina's, who fell to her knees beside Troy. She grabbed his shirt and shook, yelling incoherently, face contorted in anguish, as if she had just lost her dearest friend. A stream of red flowed out of the hole between Troy's eyes, followed the curve of his ear, and dripped to the floor in a growing pool.

The tavern erupted into action. Some dashed for the stairs, stepping over each other in their haste to escape before the Feds decided to add more bodies to the scene.

Others, such as the lion twins, went on the offensive. The lion sister grabbed the nearest Fed's rifle with both hands. A *rat-tat-tat* sent three shots to the ceiling before her brother caught the Fed from behind in a bear hug and lifted him from his feet. With a roar, the sister yanked it from the startled Fed's grip, then turned the rifle on another Fed, who was aiming at a group of residents and shouting for them to stay back.

The sister put the rifle against her shoulder and bared her teeth. "Drop it! *Now!*"

Seg couldn't be sure what he would have done in the Fed's place, but he *wouldn't* have tried to shoot her.

The Fed made it as far as aiming before three residents jumped him from the sides.

His rifle fired. Someone screamed. And then his weapon was in the hands of a graying Holtondome man. The Fed raised his hands in surrender.

Skirmish outcomes varied. Around one Fed, two residents lay dead or dying. Other groups were still struggling. At least three groups had secured firearms. No Feds appeared to be injured as of yet.

The only Fed not engaged or subdued, strangely, was the one who'd killed Seg's brother.

Bharta looked at the chaos around him in a daze. His eyes slid over Seg as if he were a greased pig.

Slowly, he turned to Fi. Bharta's face became murder.

"*You!*"

Fi didn't appear to have heard him. She was staring at Troy's body with the same look of horror as yesterday, when she'd discovered him alive in Cook's car. Her gaze slid to Bharta, eyes vacant, as if she didn't recognize him.

"I didn't see it." Her words were too soft to hear over the commotion, but Seg could read her lips just fine. She shook her head. "I didn't see it coming. I didn't see it!"

"Lying bitch! You set this whole thing up—tricked me into letting you tell your 'inspiring' story! Now look what you've done. *Look!*"

Fi turned around, eyes sweeping the tavern. Her eyebrows rose as if she'd just noticed she was in the middle of a battle.

The boy on her hip was crying for his mother, holding his ears, face buried in her dress. Fi seemed unaware of his distress.

"It's... it's not possible."

"It's *exactly* how you planned it. Well, I hope you planned for *this!*"

Bharta aimed his gun at her.

Seg leaped from his chair. Shackles around his legs prevented him from running, but it didn't matter.

I have to save her!

He did the next best thing to running and galloped like a horse of legend. Fi was too dazed to dodge Bharta's shot, and too far away to grapple with him. Seg was even farther away. Unless he could catch Bharta's attention, Fi was a dead woman.

"RrrrrrraaaaaaaAAAAAA!!!!!"

His improvised war cry worked. Bharta whipped around. No trace of sanity remained on his silver-haired face, only a rage, now wholly focused on Seg.

Seg's courage faltered. It was one thing to have a gun pointed at him, but quite another to look into the abyssal depths of a barrel, knowing it was the last thing he was likely to see.

Behind Bharta, Fi snapped out of her stupor and… changed. Not into the black creature that had saved Val, but a being of pure light. Her skin became radiant. Blinding. Light rays filled every corner of the room. Her eyes flared to an intensity that made Seg cry in pain, but he couldn't look away. Her brilliance was terrible—a magnificence that radiated power and dread.

Bharta clutched his head, face contorted in agony. He fell to his knees, then toppled over. His pistol slipped from limp fingers, sightless eyes staring forever into Freyja's Green Fields.

The light disappeared. Fi's enchanting blue eyes rolled back into her head. She collapsed on top of the screaming boy, motionless.

29

Fallout

Movement from Fi's bed drew the entire medical ward's attention. Seg was the first to her side, followed closely by Cook, who had been attending Val in the next bed over.

"Fi!" Seg said. "Are you all right?"

"Mm."

She scrunched her eyes and sat up, but Doc Ven gently pushed her back down.

"Easy," Ven said. "Your pulse and blood pressure are erratic. You may need to take it easy for a few days."

"Thank you, doctor," she said weakly. "But I'm sure I'll be fine in a few minutes."

"Said every patient who's ever climbed off that table and immediately collapsed. I'd expect a medical expert such as yourself to know better."

"You know what they say: Doctors make the worst patients."

Ven chuckled. "We do at that. Would you at least entertain the idea of staying put for a few hours? Other patients need my attention, too, and my job will be easier without worrying about you falling on your face when my back is turned."

She looked at him for the first time. "How many?"

"Three Providers injured. One Fed. Their medic has agreed to cooperate, and is assisting with our wounded."

Fi collapsed onto her pillow. "It could have been so much worse."

"It *was*. We lost three of our own in that skirmish, including Troy. It's a shame. A damn, pointless shame."

"Not pointless, doctor." Fi turned to Seg. "Are the Feds secured?"

"We think so."

She arched an eyebrow.

"They didn't exactly let us take a census when they arrived," Seg said. "We rounded up everyone we could find. Hopefully we got them all."

Fi rubbed her face.

"Are you all right, Miss Fi?" Val said from the bed next to her.

"Mm." To prove her point, Fi sat up, her movements stronger this time, and swung her feet over the side of the bed. "Sorry, doctor, but I'm going to be a bad patient after all. Seg and I have to talk, and it can't wait."

Ven threw his hands up. "Do what you want. But if you fall and hurt yourself, you'll be last in queue for a bed, and no amount of whining will move you to the front."

"Noted."

She gathered her billowing felt skirt and stood. After a few tenuous seconds, she took a step. Her legs buckled. Seg barely caught her before she tumbled to the floor.

"Thanks." Fi patted his arm with a smile. "This is the third time today you've made me weak in the knees. It's becoming an awful habit."

Val's jaw dropped. "*Third* time? Seg! When did you—"

"I'll give you all the gritty details you never wanted to know," Fi said. "Later."

Val drew a breath to argue.

Fi leveled her with a stare that would have made the rowdiest child sit obediently—one she had undoubtedly honed over thousands of years to keep her students in line.

Her newest apprentice, apparently, wasn't immune. Val huffed and plopped back onto her pillow. Her face contorted in pain. She gingerly rubbed her wounded shoulder and moaned.

Cook smoothed her hair back. "You can play with the others when you're better. Until then, you're stuck with me."

"If I must."

Despite her casual dismissal, Val took his hand and clutched it to her chest, then snuggled against the pillow and closed her eyes. Seg left them to it.

Outside, Fi seemed to be gaining strength with every step, and soon didn't need him for support.

"Neat trick," Seg said, nodding back to the medical ward. "Val's parents would have traded everything they owned to be able to keep her in line with just a look."

"Mm, I know her type well enough. Establishing authority early is important. Give her an inch and she'll take a mile."

"A what and a what?"

"They're antiquated units of measurement that still slip out every now and then. Sorry."

"I'm surprised that doesn't happen more often."

"I only slip around you. You make me feel... relaxed. Unguarded." Fi tucked her wrist snugly in the crook of his elbow. "How long was I out?"

"Two hours, give or take."

"No longer than usual, then."

Seg stopped her in front of a large stack of apple crates—the same crates he had kissed Val behind earlier. "What happened back there?"

Fi studied him. "Why, what did you see?"

He described the radiant being of light she had briefly become, just before Bharta had fallen over dead. "I assume it's one of those things only I can see," Seg said in conclusion. "Otherwise, the entire dome would be talking about it."

"Fascinating." She patted his face with a smile. "That amazing eye of yours provides no end of insight."

Seg stared at her, waiting patiently for her to answer the question he knew she hadn't forgotten.

Fi sighed. "That was one of my other tricks, a terrible one used only in the direst of circumstances. The blackness was me extending someone's life beyond their predestined fate. The whiteness, apparently, happens when I prematurely *end* someone's life."

Seg paled. "You can do that?"

"Mm. As with saving a life, I can't control the manner of the person's death, only the timing. The captain could just as easily have died from a stray bullet as tripping and impaling his throat on a fork, but in any case, his death was inevitable. In this instance, I'd guess an aneurism took him."

A smile spread across Seg's face. "The power to decide who lives or dies. Ironically, you sound like the Valkyrie Val mentioned yesterday."

"There's no irony about it. The first mention of Valkyries is on a Nordic rune stone dated around 700 A.D., the same period where, in a fit of rage, I had tracked an army down who had butchered my village while I was away." Fi shuddered. "I killed hundreds of them without lifting a hand, and saved everyone on our side that I could. To an observer, it would appear that many simply rose from the dead, while others fell in their tracks." Her voice fell to a whisper. "I rode a brilliant white steed that day. It had been my adopted daughter's favorite before they..."

Fi hugged him tighter, as if afraid he might run.

Part of him wanted to. Knowing the woman on his arm had the power to kill an army with a mere thought was disturbing, to say the least.

But the Fi he knew was conscientious to a fault. In that instance, she had been wounded by the loss of her family and friends. Deeply. Wouldn't Seg have reacted similarly? That she had even been willing to volunteer this dark piece of her history spoke volumes of her character, and of her trust in him.

"I'm surprised you were still upright, if today's demonstration was any measure," Seg said as calmly as he could.

"I wasn't. The effort put me in a coma for a week, according to the villagers who dragged me from the battlefield. But I survived, as I have through every catastrophe, whether I want to or not." Fi shook herself. "Enough cheerful history lessons for now. The captain is dead, which means Holtondome is in deep, terrible trouble."

"That's my biggest question." Seg took her by the shoulders and resisted the urge to shake her. "Why did you change *his* fate to die instead of changing *mine* to live? And why…" Memory of Troy's death choked his throat up tight.

"Why didn't I save your brother?"

Seg nodded.

Her face became haunted. "Because I didn't see his death coming. When Bharta pointed the gun at him, I assumed he was bluffing, or that the wound wouldn't be fatal, or that someone else would save him. I absolutely did *not* expect him to die, otherwise I would have prevented it." She looked at him with sorrow-filled eyes. "Do you believe me?"

The question caught him off guard. "Of course. Why wouldn't I?"

"Well, I didn't exactly celebrate when I found he'd survived the first time. I thought you might suspect…"

"That you let him die on purpose?"

She nodded.

Seg played the events back in his head, as he had dozens of times over the last few hours, but came to the same conclusion.

"No, you were just as shocked as the rest of us when Bharta shot him, and *nothing* shocks you. He was my brother. You knew how much he meant to me. You would have protected him if you thought his life was in danger."

Fi studied him for a moment, then nodded again. "As for your other question, the answer is similar to the first. I didn't see your death coming, but I've been through enough battles to know Bharta was a trained soldier, and that when he turned his pistol on you, it was with deadly intent.

"There was no vision of your death for me to change, but I couldn't—I *wouldn't*—make the same mistake with you as I had just made with your brother. So I did the only thing I could in the fraction of a second I had left to stop him: I changed his fate to die, and hoped it would be enough to save you." She smiled weakly. "Lucky for me, it was."

"Lucky for *me*, you mean."

"You should know by now that every word out of my mouth is intentional." Fi cupped his cheeks and pulled him close for a tender kiss. "I. Meant. Me."

"Would you settle for 'us'?"

"It seems your busty girlfriend isn't the only person in need of a lesson, but in this case…" Fi kissed him again. "I'll bend. Just this once."

"She's your apprentice now," Seg said, grinning. "One of these days, you're going to have to call her by name."

"You'd be surprised. I can be very creative when properly motivated."

Seg laughed, but let the subject drop, along with his smile. "So what's going to happen to Holtondome?"

"If left to its fate… Holtondome is technically in rebellion, to which Grand Chancellor Chang doesn't respond kindly. Word will soon reach him, if it hasn't already. He'll assemble a battalion, breach the dome's non-existent defenses, and cleanse Holtondome of anyone and everyone who participated. And a few more besides, just to make his message clear."

Seg gasped because he'd forgotten to breathe. The Chang taught to them by the Feds was noble and benevolent.

Fi was describing a monster.

"That's horrible…"

"That's how a dictator maintains control," Fi said. "When their authority is questioned, they respond with overwhelming force to squash any hope of future rebellion."

"Did… did you know this was going to happen when you told the Mars Program story?"

Fi shook her head. "I had intended to give Holtondome the leverage they needed to force the Federated Nations to surrender some of their stockpiles, which, ironically, they're holding in reserve for future Mars missions. I felt confident doing so because I'd had no visions of death, which was a strong indication of peaceful resolution. But now…"

Now we're screwed.

Seg's imagination tortured him with visions of troops storming Holtondome, slaughtering everyone in sight.

"Please, is there anything you can do?"

"If you're asking me to kill Feds like I did the invaders who slaughtered my village, I've never done anything on that scale, before or since. I barely remember how I did it the first time. Neither do I relish the idea of taking so many lives when humanity has so few to spare, no matter which side they're on."

"So… we're doomed."

"I didn't say that. Back then, I had only a spear, a horse, and my abilities. Today, I have technology, which opens oh-so-many more doors. *And* I have a direct line to Chang himself." Fi pulled her pocket device out and began tapping the screen.

Seg covered it with a yelp. "Wait! Y-you're going to speak to the Grand Chancellor? Here? Now?"

"Well, I could dunk my head in a bath and try talking to him underwater, but I doubt it would leave a very good impression."

"Hilarious."

"Glad you thought so. Now, unless you have a more constructive idea, stay quiet, and stay out of sight. He bristles like a porcupine when he thinks others are listening."

"Why don't I just…"

Seg started to creep away, wanting to be nowhere near a conversation between a twenty-thousand-year-old Valkyrie, for lack of a better label, and the ruler of the known world. Fi caught his sleeve and tugged him back with a warning glare. Apparently, she didn't want to be alone with Chang, either.

A woman's face appeared on the tiny screen. Her red-painted lips twisted into a smile. "Bureau of Provider Affairs. Is this an emergency?"

"Yes. I'd like to report a Provider rebellion in progress."

Seg and the woman both jumped, although he suspected for different reasons.

This is her strategy? Turning us in?

Seg reached to take the device from her, but Fi evaded like a leaf in the breeze and kept it away from his grasp.

The woman on the screen composed herself. "And how do you know this, ma'am?"

"I'm on site. Residents are holding an entire trade escort at gunpoint."

"I see." Seg heard tapping from the woman. Her expression darkened. "Your location is blocked, which, I shouldn't have to remind you, is illegal. I'm going to have to ask you to unblock it immediately to verify your location. Failure to—"

"Put me through to Grand Chancellor Chang," Fi said over her.

"Excuse me? Who do you think you—"

"I'm risking my neck to provide insider information that can significantly reduce Federal casualties and minimize loss of trade goods. We both know the Federated Nations can't afford any more of either. Connect me to Chang—*now*—or I'm hanging up, and this rebellion will end in a bloodbath, just like the last three."

"I can't! The chancellor will have my job and my *life* if I put you through without even an identity verification—which you've *also* blocked!"

"And if I unblock them?"

The woman's vibrant red lips pressed into a thin line. "I'll put you through. At least then, if you're wasting his time, he'll know who you are and where to find you."

"All right, stand by." Fi fiddled with her device, giving Seg time to think.

Three bloodbaths? Is that why there are only two Provider domes left?

He had been so worried about Fi, and grieved over the loss of his brother, that he hadn't given any thought to Troy's last words.

There used to be thirteen Provider domes. Three ended in bloodbaths. Only two are left, including us.

What happened to the other eight?

"Received," the woman said. "I'll put you through, Miss Ofilia." She stared for a moment longer, shook her head, then her image disappeared.

Seg would have recognized the next face that appeared anywhere. Strong cheekbones, long black hair swept into a ponytail, and eyes so brown that they might as well have been black, Grand Chancellor Chang the Sixth was every bit the confident, imposing authority figure his pictures made him out to be.

"Who is this?" he said by way of greeting.

"Hi, Ty. Sorry for disabling video, but you never know who's watching these days."

Chang's image never flickered, his feelings hidden behind an unbreakable wall. "What was our first meal together?"

"Forty-year-old Scotch Whisky. We drank the entire bottle and joked about how dinner would ruin such a fine experience, so we skipped the meal and went back to your place. Now, my turn. Which Chang rebuked me for not helping him build the Federated Nations into an authoritarian regime?"

"All of them, if I recall, until you finally left me. And I've asked you not to refer to it as 'authoritarian.'"

"A rose by any other name…"

"…still has thorns. Just like you, my Fila." Chang chuckled. "I'll show my face if you show yours."

"Deal."

Fi tapped the screen. A red dot started blinking. At the same time, Chang's image changed. Although his features remained the same, gone was the powerful, stoic leader. In his place was someone Fi's age—in appearance, at least. Smiling eyes gazed fondly, eyes that could have belonged to any person in Holtondome, and a face that Seg would happily have had a drink with over a game of Swaggle.

"My Fila," Chang said, smiling. "It's wonderful to see you again. How many years has it been?"

"A hundred and eighty-three, but who's counting?"

"Who indeed." He sobered. "I assume you haven't called me from a Provider dome—Holtondome, is it?—through an emergency channel just to say hello."

"No. You have another genuine rebellion on your hands. Congratulations."

Chang's jaw tightened. "No need to be snide. So you called to gloat, then?"

"Hardly. I wanted to be the first to tell you so I could also ask you to hold the assault force. I think we can come to a resolution without bloodshed that will leave the Federated Nations' rule intact."

"We've been over this, Fila. Your great Pact experiment has failed. Even in isolation, and with all the wonderful delusions of 'sacrifice for the greater good,' Providers inevitably want more, leaving me with no choice but to take those freedoms away for the good of all."

"It wasn't an experiment. The only reason it failed is because it was severely mismanaged."

Chang's eyes flared, but he took a deep breath and was calm when he spoke. "I followed our plan to the letter."

"That's the problem: it was never intended to be followed to the letter. It was a framework designed to evolve with humanity's changing needs. Well, I have news for you. Humanity has changed, but the laws haven't, which is why the empire *you* clung to is falling down around your head. Civilization was bursting at the seams we'd sewn to get them going again, but once they did, you refused to let them take the needle and thread their own destiny."

"Ah. So this is all my fault?"

Fi sighed. "Not entirely. I… *misjudged* the situation here in Holtondome. The rebellion is my fault."

A muscle on his cheek twitched. "You turned them against me."

"Not intentionally."

"The road to extinction is paved with good intentions, Fila. It's our actions that matter. You taught me that."

"Which is why I called. Actions have consequences, and I'm taking responsibility for mine. Hold the attack."

"Asking a favor of someone over a video call is hardly taking responsibility. There's no effort involved. No personal investment. No risk."

Fi's expression went stony. "What do you want, Ty?"

"For you to call me more than once a century, for one."

"If you insist."

"I do, but that isn't enough. Holtondome is the largest Provider in the Northwest, which means the situation needs to be resolved quickly, or there will be even more unrest. My way is tried and true, and guarantees a speedy resolution. If I'm to risk the Northwest's prosperity on a new scheme of yours, I'll need to be convinced."

"Fine. My proposal is—"

"Not over a video call, Fila. In person."

Fi's face betrayed nothing, but her sunken posture swore like a farmer with her hand caught in a harvester.

"And since Holtondome is such a critical settlement," Chang said, "I'll need to hedge my bets and get the army moving, in case your tactic fails. But don't worry. It'll take a week at least for them to arrive, which should give you plenty of time to enjoy the sights on your way here."

"On two conditions," Fi said.

"You aren't in a position to bargain."

"And you wonder why I call you an authoritarian. The moment you feel challenged, you resort to threats instead of listening to reason."

Chang took a deep breath. "What are your conditions?"

"First, these people need relief. Harvest is the lowest it's been in two centuries. They need medicine, repairs, a new hauler, and they can't wait until next season to get them."

His brow furrowed. Seg thought sure Chang would refuse, but he eventually nodded.

"Send me the list," Chang said. "I'll approve it personally—but just this once."

"Thank you. As for the second condition, I'll be bringing a representative from Holtondome to speak on their behalf."

He grimaced. "I was hoping for a more intimate presentation. We have so much to catch up on."

"There will be time for us, I promise. But for formal negotiations, it's only fair they have one of their own represent their interests."

"And is this 'someone' special? Your pet of the decade?"

"He's Seg Holton, from Thorn's direct bloodline. And no, he holds no interest to me beyond his value as an emissary."

Chang's smile held no humor. "A pity. What will he do when you're done with him? I can't allow him to return to the dome."

"Seg is resourceful. He'll have no trouble adapting to City life."

"Or a life of labor, depending on how well I like your pitch."

"There you go with the authoritarianism again. What about making your decision based on the *merits* of our pitch, rather than your personal mood?"

Chang blew a wistful sigh. "I've definitely missed you, Fila. You were never afraid to speak your mind. I was crushed when you left."

"I left because you stopped listening, which doesn't seem to have changed."

"All right," Chang said, clenching his jaw. "Your new pet has my permission to leave his cage. I hope for his sake he understands your propensity for wagering dangerous bets with other people's lives. But he couldn't, now, could he?"

"He understands that his people's lives are in grave danger. That's reason enough for him to make any sacrifice. And you're right that he doesn't understand the true risks. Perhaps you'd like to explain to him how, if he says something to displease you, he might become a prisoner in one of the forced-labor camps you've turned the *other* domes into who've rebelled? I'm sure that would make the negotiations go so much better."

"I've agreed to your terms," Chang said, his voice deadly soft. "Don't push me."

"Pushing you is what you loved best about me, and look where it got you. Have faith in me now, Ty. Let yourself be pushed, and see where it takes you next."

Chang's dour expression melted into a thoughtful smile. "One week, Fila. I look forward to picking up where we—"

To Seg's shock, Fi ended the call before the grand chancellor finished his sentence.

"Um, won't that just aggravate him?"

"Everything aggravates him," Fi said. "He's used to getting his way, and has forgotten what it's like to be challenged. He's truly become the dictator I feared."

"Just how long have you known him?"

"Over three hundred years, before he became Chang the First."

Fi wrapped her arms around him and buried her face in his neck. Scents of ancient fields and fresh breezes filled his nostrils. She hugged him tight and sighed.

"I'm afraid I made him."

30

New Dawn

FI BECAME MOROSE AFTER HER call with Chang. She gently rebuffed Seg's attempts to pry into details of the conversation, which had left more questions than it answered. He soon took the hint that she didn't want to talk about it and escorted her back to their room for some much-needed rest.

Instead of climbing into bed, Fi grabbed her medical bag and headed back down to the ward, where she spent the next hour treating Val's shoulder. Any attempt at conversation, including Doc Ven trying to shoo her away from his patient, was met with either silence or her signature, "Mm."

As soon as Fi finished, Val fell right to sleep, looking more comfortable than she had even before her injury.

Fi ignored Cook's profound thanks, packed her bag up, and headed back to their room. She allowed Seg to tuck her into bed. When he tried to leave to give her some privacy, she caught his hand, pulled him down into bed with her, and wrapped his arm around her like a blanket. He kissed her shoulder, relishing her wonderful scents that hinted of the world she was born into—an ancient Earth he would never see.

Her breathing calmed. Minutes later, she was fast asleep.

Seg debated sneaking out. There were so many things he needed to do before he left. So much he wanted to say to his family, who were hurting from Troy's loss. His father, his mother, Jen and her boys... they had just lost a family member.

Now they were about to lose another. He had to talk to them, do what he could to ease their worry and pain. Let them know that, despite his surliness, Seg cared about them enough to march into the gorgon's lair on their behalf without so much as a pointy stick to defend himself.

That Fi had volunteered him without asking was irrelevant. Seg would have done it regardless, which she knew.

Fi always knew.

But then he imagined her waking in the middle of the night and finding herself alone. Fi hated being alone. One of these days, she'd tell him why, he was sure, but tonight it didn't matter. Tonight, Fi needed him near.

So that was exactly where he stayed.

Seg woke to the sound of the shower running. Rubbing the sleep from his eyes revealed an empty closet and two stuffed suitcases on the opposite bed, which made him wonder what exactly he would pack for the trip. And, more pointedly, what he would pack it in.

He'd never traveled more than a few kilometers from Holtondome. No one had, so luggage wasn't something they had a use for. The closest he owned was a wood-and-leather storage trunk at the foot of his bed, which doubled as a seat when he dressed in the morning.

It would have to do. He only hoped it would fit in the back of Cook's car with the rest of the luggage.

Seg stretched his muscles, stiff from being in one position all night, and poked his head into the bathroom. "I'll be right back. I'm going to pack a few things."

"Hold on, I'll be out in a minute."

He started to argue, then shook his head.

She doesn't like to be alone.

Seg plopped into a chair and waited patiently while Fi toweled and dressed into comfortable-looking brown leather pants and a loose white blouse. Even her travel outfit made Seg's finest seem like country patchwork.

She followed him upstairs to his room. Seg opened his trunk and began emptying it, but Fi shook her head.

"One outfit should be enough, and there's plenty of room in my luggage for that. We'll buy more when we reach the City."

"Buy?"

"Mm. Providers are forbidden to use currency, but Cities reverted to it centuries ago."

"Gee, that's not hypocritical at all."

"You don't know the half of it. But you will." Fi rummaged through his drawers and pulled out a moderately-worn work outfit. "I suggest these for your audience with Chang."

"Seriously? Peg wouldn't let me attend storytime in those rags. They hardly seem suitable for a meeting with the Grand Chancellor."

"As I've said, Chang's forgotten his roots, and has surrounded himself with people who reflect only what he wants to see. This will be a stark reminder for him and his entire staff about who exactly is the backbone of his empire, and where the true power lies."

Seg nodded, although he couldn't help feeling that the reminder—*him*—wouldn't be received well.

Minutes later, they were back in their shared room, packed and ready to go. They each carried a suitcase downstairs, despite Seg's insistence that he carry both. She was still a guest, after all, but Fi wouldn't hear it and had left the room in mid-argument with the heavier bag in tow.

Most of the dome's residents were downstairs when they arrived, all dressed in solemn black. His mother, Peg, gasped loudly when she saw them. Her surprise quickly turned to anger, and she bustled over to them.

"Seg Holton! I can forgive you sleeping in after last night's ordeal, but this!"

Peg curtsied to Fi, a move so unlike the usually grease-stained mechanic that Seg rubbed his good eye to make sure it was actually her.

"Apologies, honored guest, that we've disgraced ourselves with such violence during your visit. Let me at least try to atone by fetching someone to help you with your bags. We'll also have food and drink prepared for your trip home."

"What I saw last night wasn't disgraceful, Mrs. Holton. It was courageous and civil. Your people diffused a hostile situation with minimal casualties, and showed your aggressors a leniency they wouldn't have shown you. If the rest of humanity was more like you, The Fall would never have happened."

Tears welled in Pegs eyes. She pulled a cloth from her sleeve and dabbed her face. "Thank you for your kind words, Miss Fi. If it wouldn't inconvenience your departure, we were about to hold a service for those whose lights were extinguished last night, on both sides."

"Including your son's," Fi said.

Peg started to reply, but her lips closed with a stuttering quiver, and she simply nodded.

"He was among the bravest men I've ever met, Mrs. Holton, and I don't say that lightly. I'm deeply sorry for his passing."

The tears Peg had been holding spilled over. Fi wrapped her in an embrace.

"I would be humbled to attend," Fi said. "Would it be inappropriate for me to say a few words during the service?"

"O-of course not," Peg said, sniffling. "Troy would have liked that. He admired your no-nonsense spunk."

"And I his."

Fi led her away, arm-in-arm. Seg surreptitiously took the bag from her, deposited it next to Cook's vehicle, then hurried back to join everyone, who were gathered in a huge crowd around Hap.

Unsurprisingly, the service had a larger turnout than usual, but Hap conducted it like he did any other. Dressed in his finest black, he spoke at length about each of the departed, even about Bharta and the other Fed, who he had evidently received details about from those who worked with them.

Hap's voice broke when he reached Troy. Seg weaved through the crowd as fast as he respectably could and stood next to his father. Hap gave a grateful, teary nod, then stepped aside.

Talking about his brother was hard. Not just because he was dead, but because they had never seen eye to eye growing up. Even as adults, he and Seg had rarely agreed on anything. They kept each other's company only during family gatherings, which he relayed to the gathered crowd in the kindest way he could.

"But one thing we did well, as Doc Ven will tell you, is fight," Seg said, projecting his voice as far as his constricted throat would allow. "I fought because I didn't know how to handle being different, and Troy was a willing target. Troy, however, fought because he believed he was helping me. He took the punches when no one else would—so no one else had to. I think that sums him up better than anything else.

"What killed him last night was the same thing that kept him going day after day. Holtondome was in trouble, so Troy rolled up his sleeves, stepped into the arena—knowing he might be outclassed—and fought with everything he had, taking the weight of the world upon himself so others could live free. It's…" Seg's quivering lips ceased cooperating. He wiped his eyes and stepped away, hoping he'd made his point clear enough.

Wet faces all around told him he had.

Then Fi was beside him. She swept her enchanting eyes around the crowd. Her voice projected like a trained professional.

"Last night was a tragic event. Blood was shed. Lives were lost. And, whether you realize it or not, your long, honorable journey as Providers came to an abrupt end."

The crowd broke into commotion, but Fi's firm voice quieted them down.

"Don't take that as failure. Holtondome has upheld the Pact for almost three hundred years, a feat which only one other dome in the Northwest can claim. It's an absolute testament to the temerity and integrity of its inhabitants.

"But those days are gone. The veil has been lifted. Once you've seen the truth, returning to a life of ignorance is impossible."

"What truth?" an older woman shouted, bordering on hysteria. "That we've been lied to? That humanity is doomed? We've broken our oath, if ever there was a Pact to swear to!" She began sobbing. "Was there truth behind anything we sacrificed for? Anything at all?"

Fi made her way to the woman and took her hands. "More than you can imagine. Come, I'd like to show you something."

The crowd followed in silence. Fi led them to the center of the dome to a dark storage warehouse filled with empty crates and other supplies, which she and Seg had visited just yesterday.

"Wait out here, please. I'll be just a few minutes."

Fi disappeared into the darkness.

Murmurs of "where is she going?" and "why are we here?" echoed through the gathering. Val and Cook caught up to Seg, looking as confused as everyone else.

"What's she up to?" Val whispered.

"Wait and see," Seg said.

She eyed him, then punched his shoulder.

"Ow!"

"Don't 'ow' me. You know what's going on, and you're not telling. Spill it!"

"I don't!" It was mostly true, anyway. There was only one thing it could be, but Seg had no idea why Fi would ask everyone to wait out here. "Hang on... you punched me with your injured arm!"

"Oh, yeah." Val rotated her arm in a wide circle. "Whatever Miss Fi did last night worked miracles. Doesn't even feel like I was shot." She sobered. "I, um... saw you with Miss Fi's bags earlier. You'd better not be leaving without me."

"Well, she's not leaving without *me*," Cook said, "unless she knows how to hot-wire a state-of-the-art Kavsky Class M. And I'm not leaving without you, so I'd say no, he's not. Right, kid?"

"Right. Fi took you on as an apprentice, Val, and treated your wound even though she could barely stand. I don't think she'd leave without you."

"Good." Val relaxed and sidled next to Seg, then dropped her voice to a whisper. "So what's her excuse for getting *you* out of here?"

"Long story. You'll have plenty of time to hear the whole, messed up tale once we're on the road."

Or as much as Fi feels like sharing, anyway.

Seg was the only person in whom she'd ever confided her secret. If even the Grand Chancellor didn't know—who she'd created, whatever that meant—he wasn't sure how much information, if any, she would entrust with her new apprentice and hired driver.

Val cocked her fist and punched him again.

"*Gah!* What was that for?"

"For almost getting shot. I heard about your little rescue attempt. It was pure luck that the stress of battle caused Bharta to die of a massive stroke just before he pulled the trigger." She rubbed his arm, then looked up at him. "Don't do it again, okay? That dumb luck of yours won't hold forever, and I don't want to be attending your funeral service anytime soon."

"Says the woman who *was* shot, and only by *dumb luck* tripped and avoided a fatal heart wound."

"That was… different."

"Mm-hmm."

Seg itched to tell her that it wasn't different at all; their "dumb luck" had a name. Fi had saved them both, twice over, whether Val knew it or not: once with her ingenuity, and once with her strange Valkyrie abilities. He had a sinking feeling it wouldn't be the last time on either count.

A loud *snap* drew everyone's attention to the center of the dome. Another *snap* followed, then two more.

With a roaring *crash*, the inside wall of the storage unit folded in half lengthwise, then collapsed upon itself, blasting splintered crates across the room. Three more crashes assaulted Seg's eardrums, throwing dust everywhere.

When the air settled, Holly's statue gleamed bright and clear. The walls hiding it had collapsed, giving people from all sides a glimpse of the precious artifact Fi had just yesterday explained couldn't exist.

Fi began clearing a path to the statue through the debris. Everyone jumped in to help. In no time, there wasn't a single obstruction within thirty meters of Holly. People crowded and awed at the sight, but only Fi dared climb on its pedestal so she and Holly were the same height. In her right hand, Fi held a book Seg recognized.

The handmaiden's journal.

Or, rather, hers.

"As you can see," Fi said over the crowd, quieting them, "Holly's statue is real, as was the woman herself, and her conviction of how crucial Holtondome is to humanity's survival. If you ever doubted the importance of your oath, or the worth of your sacrifices over the last three hundred years, listen now to a passage from her handmaiden's journal, and judge for yourselves."

Fi opened the worn, leather-bound notebook to a round of awed whispers, and read in a clear voice.

> While washing my dear mistress' back tonight, she said something so profound that I abandoned her to her towel so I could rush back to my quarters and write it down before it escaped me.
>
> "Ofilia," she said to me, "the world is in chaos. Our food supplies dwindle while our freshwater reserves are one-by-one contaminated by acid rain, or run dry by desperate and thirsty people. Bandits take what they will, caring only for their needs of today, without a single thought of how their pillaging and destruction will finish off what little of us survived The Fall."
>
> "Our greatest and perhaps only hope is the Domes Initiative—and of them all, if Thorn wins the election against Revon, ours will be the shining example. Thorn is a good man and will attract the most upstanding people, for it is only through civility and faith in our fellow survivors that any of us can hope to thrive."

Fi closed the notebook and looked out over the crowd.

"Civility and faith. Ladies and gentlemen, time has proven Holly right on several points.

"You *are* the shining example. You upheld your oaths where so many others reneged and fell to ruin, forcing Chang to strip their freedoms. You've maintained civility to yourselves, to your guests, and even to those who eventually became your oppressors, acting with integrity and faith when neither were deserved, simply because you knew it was the right thing to do.

"But times change. People change. Governments and circumstances change. Technology has evolved beyond pre-Fall achievements, but the benefits of that technology haven't been equally shared with those who deserve it—with the backbone of the Federated Nations, who are the only reason any of us are alive today." Her intense gaze swept the crowd. "You."

Fi paused while the residents chatted among themselves. Seg could tell from their tones that her message had been received.

"As other Providers have fallen, so your importance to the Federated Nations has risen. Free people are productive people, and only two free Provider domes remain."

Fi's voice was regal. Powerful. Seg imagined her holding not a book, but a spear, sunlight glistening from her armor while sitting atop a magnificent steed.

"The time for isolation and the simple life you all swore to has passed. Your voices need to be heard, your own needs acknowledged and prioritized as partners in our great effort for collective survival—not as slaves to someone else's fancy. That starts with recognizing your worth and standing up for yourselves. If you don't, Troy's noble sacrifice, and that of the others last night, will fade to oblivion, along with the freedoms you've all enjoyed to date."

"How?" a man with a full mustache shouted. "Who will listen now? Captain Bharta is dead! We hold a dozen Feds at gunpoint. And even if we wanted to beg mercy from the Grand Chancellor for our egregious acts, we have no way of contacting him."

"Wrong," Fi said. "As an act of good faith, Grand Chancellor Chang has granted temporary respite in the form of medicine and repairs, so you may rest easy this season. As for the future and your new standing in the Federated Nations, he's agreed to personally hear your case, and I'll be there to make sure you're treated fairly."

Sighs of relief sounded all around. Their eyes then turned to Hap, who, in an uncharacteristic move, shrugged.

"This is the first I've heard," he said.

"That's because your representative has already been chosen." Fi pointed directly at Seg.

The weight of the entire dome pressed down on him.

"One Eye!" another man shouted. "No! Send Hap. Or Me. Anyone else! He'll take a swing at the Chancellor and sentence us all to death!"

"His name has already been submitted to Chang himself, and I doubt anyone else will be permitted to leave Holtondome until negotiations have been finalized." A smile twitched Fi's lips. "Seg Holton is now your best chance for prosperity, so I suggest you stop calling him childish names and use what little time remains before our departure to ensure he properly understands your needs."

More than a few moans greeted her. Several moved away from Seg, their disgust clear, but even more rushed in, babbling advice and demands in an incoherent stream, until Seg finally raised his hands.

"Enough! Hap, Jen, and I will each setup a table in Tad's Tavern. Choose which of us you're most comfortable with, and come prepared with a *brief* summary of issues you'd like addressed. We'll consolidate everything into a concise list of concerns before I leave that I'll present to Ty—er, Grand Chancellor Chang, and we'll see how it goes."

The crowd erupted again.

"That's the best I can do in the time we have left! If you have concerns, bring them upstairs. Now, if you'll excuse me…"

Seg pushed his way through the clamoring throng, several of whom followed him all the way up to Tad's.

Jen slipped in next to him and helped arrange the tables in a more crowd-conducive manner. She didn't speak a word to him, but she didn't have to.

Her proud, misty eyes said it all.

31

The Road

IT WAS LATE AFTERNOON BY the time Seg came downstairs. His head was ready to explode from the deluge of information dumped on him, and from the intense consolidation and cram session afterward. Fortunately, Fi had taken detailed notes on her portable screen, which she promised to read to him later, temporarily taking the immense pressure of having to memorize everything off his knotted shoulders.

Their sending-off party was small, but everyone Seg wanted to say goodbye to was present. He hugged his mother and father. Hap was teary but silent, as opposed to Peg, who cried amidst a babble of how proud she was of him, how she'd miss him, and if he was sure that packing one outfit was enough. She relaxed some when he told her he'd packed three pairs of undergarments. She then backed away so Jen's twin boys could body-tackle him against the car with a pair of hugs.

Jen came next. Her hug was firm but brief.

"Do us proud, Seg," Jen said in a thick voice. She cleared her throat and stepped back, standing as tall as her tiny frame would allow. "And don't take no for an answer. We have the food, which means we have the power. Don't let Chang forget it."

"I won't."

Not for the first time, Seg wished Jen were going instead of him. Her diminutive backbone had always been stronger than his. He could already imagine the Grand Chancellor reeling from her razor-sharp tongue.

Jen nodded and stepped aside.

To Seg's surprise, next in line were the lion twins.

The brother shook his hand in a firm grip. "Be strong."

Seg nodded, then shook hands with the sister, whose grip was equally firm.

"Listen to Miss Fi," the sister said. "The dunderheads here don't know what they're talking about, but her... she's seen things. She knows."

"And she's a fighter," the brother said. "Follow her lead, and Holtondome will come out on top."

"I will."

The last two people to see him off were Tad and Nin. Tad gave him a firm handshake and a hearty farewell, while Nin wrapped him in a warm embrace and handed him a basket of fresh pork pot pies for their trip.

With the last of their farewell party gone, Seg joined his traveling companions by Cook's car. Their bags were already inside. Fi was leaning against the rear of the vehicle, staring at the ground, while Cook and Val stood near the driver's door, having what appeared to be an intense debate.

"But I told you, my shoulder is better," Val said to Cook. She stretched it up and down, then side to side. "See? So you have no reason to not let me drive."

"Miss Fi said you need at least another day before it's fully healed," Cook said. "Expired medical license or not, I trust her opinion more than yours. Especially when my baby's involved." He patted his car with a smile.

"I thought *I* was your baby."

"You're my Queen. There's a difference."

"But your *Queen* is asking you to let her drive."

"Queens don't drive, they're driven. That puts you in the back seat with Fi, who I'm sure is eager to start instructing her new apprentice."

Val's face turned bitter, as if she'd just chewed an orange rind.

"She should heal before my instructions begin," Fi said without looking up. "My lessons can be... intense. And if she re-injures herself, that's more work for me, so I'd prefer to wait."

"Well, that puts Seg and Fi in the back," Cook said, "with no one to look after my Queen. Unless..." He turned to Seg with a grin and opened the driver's door. "How about it, kid?"

"What... *me?*"

"Sure. You drove that hauler all over the place, right? My car's even easier to drive, and a hell of a lot faster. I'll even let you open it up when we hit the freeway."

"Well, if you're sure..." But Seg was already moving for the driver's door.

The luxurious leather seat hugged him when he climbed in. The slick steering wheel felt as good in his grip as he'd ever imagined. No, it was better, as if it were custom made for his hands alone.

Fi settled into the front passenger seat and patted his hand. "Happy?"

Seg grinned from ear to ear. "Where to, my lady?"

She arched an eyebrow at the formal reference, but a slight smile ruined her annoyance. Fi reached into her pocket and pulled out five dark-gray pendants, dangling from leather necklaces of varied wear.

"The merchant who sold the last of these to your sister just a few years ago claims he found them in some old City ruins about eighty kilometers from here. Our audience with Chang is in six days, giving us plenty of time for a detour to investigate."

"Fine by me. Which way?"

"East."

It didn't take long for Seg to find the car's "on" switch. Instruments flared to life, bombarding him with foreign symbols. But, true to Cook's word, he didn't need to be able to read them to put the car in gear.

Cook's baby responded like a dream when Seg depressed the accelerator pedal. It glided through Holtondome as if on a cushion of air.

Kilometers later, when they reached the highway, Seg asked which way he should turn, but really, he didn't care.

For the first time in his life, the world and all its wonders were wide open to him.

32

Mother Doom

JEN HOLTON STARED OUT THROUGH Holtondome's eastern entrance, slack jawed, along with a hundred other residents. She tugged at her long, black ponytail, teeth clenched in frustration.

One week!

Seg and Fi had claimed that Grand Chancellor Chang's assault force wouldn't arrive for *one full week.*

Yet here they were, just three days after Fi and her younger brother had left to negotiate Holtondome's fate with the ruler of the known world.

Jen stared at the rows of armored personnel carriers scattered among the sharpgrass like giant metal boulders. Twenty vehicles at least, each holding a dozen armed soldiers or more.

Even scarier were the tanks: sleek, white vehicles with long, thick barrels that looked as if they could blow a hole through one side of Holtondome and out the other.

Had Seg misunderstood Chang's message? Jen doubted it.

More likely, the grand chancellor lied.

"Maybe they're just here to talk?"

Jen spun to find her twin sons standing behind her.

"Back to your room," Jen said, trying to keep the hysteria from her voice. "I'll tell you when it's safe to come down."

"Yeah," Jak said, "but has anyone tried talking to them yet?"

Tom's hand shot into the air. "Oh, pick me! I'll go!"

"You'll do no such thing," Jen said. "Grandpa Hap is out there right now to find out what they want. Until he does, back to your room!"

"But—"

"No buts! Move it, or I'll—"

"Mom, look!"

Jen spotted the object of Jak's attention immediately. The blood drained from her face.

Fifty meters away, a soldier walked Hap into the middle of the road at gunpoint. Hap spared Jen a glance—small, fleeting, heartbroken—before the soldier slammed the barrel of his rifle onto Hap's shoulder, driving him to his knees. His weathered face, which for as long as Jen could remember held the strength of their entire dome, turned hopelessly down.

"No..." Jen whispered.

She could see the terrible tragedy about to unfold as sure as a coming storm.

"Hap! Daddy! *Daddy!*"

And then she was running. Jen screamed to him with shrill desperation.

Thirty steps from her goal, the soldier's weapon recoiled with a crack of cruel thunder. The ground beneath her father turned crimson. Hap jerked once, then fell to the dirt, unmoving.

Jen's anguished wail drowned all of the resounding cries behind her combined. She collapsed onto the road, crying so hard she couldn't breathe. Dirt covered her face, coated her mouth. She didn't care.

Her father—Holtondome's leader—was dead, murdered in cold blood.

She also knew without a doubt the killing wouldn't stop there. Holtondome had rebelled, casting aside the oath they had faithfully upheld for four-hundred-years where, apparently, other Provider domes had long ago failed. It was a different world now, Fi had claimed, that didn't at all resemble the picture the Federated Nations had painted.

Grand Chancellor Chang had been lying to them, squandering the few precious resources Earth had left for a dwindling population so he could support some ridiculous Mars Program, instead of trying to fix the planet he was on and providing for its people.

Seg and Fi had set off to negotiate Holtondome's future. Unfortunately, Chang had decided the outcome before talks had even begun.

The entire thing was a sham, Jen thought, her tears driven by a new grief. *Chang never intended to treat us as equals.*

Her brown eyes swept the ungodly display of military might before her. Holtondome had maybe twenty rifles they'd captured during the uprising, wielded by farmers who, until a few days ago, had never held a modern weapon, let alone fired one.

The Feds had tanks.

Tanks!

How can we possibly stand against them?

The answer was simple: They couldn't.

And Chang knew it.

Jak. Tom, Jen thought miserably, bringing a fresh round of tears.

Life at Holtondome would never be the same. Survivors would undoubtedly be treated like slaves, forced to work the same agricultural jobs they had for centuries, except without even the limited, isolated freedoms she had enjoyed up to now.

My boys... I failed you. I'm sorry. So very, very sorry.

Boots crunched in the dirt ahead of her.

The Fed who had killed Hap was now coming for Jen.

A cold calm swept through her. Running back to the dome would do no good. If the Feds wanted her dead, they could gun her down on the run almost as easily as if the barrel were pressed to her head—except if she ran, a stray shot may injure someone else she cared about. One of her boys, perhaps.

Wiping her face, Jen locked her grief and terror deep inside, where she kept the rest of the doubts and fears that she refused to let hamper her responsibilities, then stood on unsteady legs. Although she was over a head shorter than the approaching soldier and probably weighed half as much, she lifted her chin with pride. Jen was a Holton, for Freyja's sake, descended from Thorn himself. She would damned well act like one.

The world tilted sideways. Inexplicably, Jen found herself falling in entirely the wrong direction, as if gravity itself had shifted ninety degrees to her left. She flailed through the air, narrowly missing a clump of sharpgrass that would have sliced her open in a dozen places. Her mind stumbled over the dichotomy of what her eyes and stomach were experiencing, leaving her dizzy, confused, and nauseous.

A black, funnel-shaped hole appeared not two meters above the ground directly in her path, as if someone had punctured reality itself, revealing a great void of nothing beyond. Rocks and dirt streamed toward it from all directions, pulled by the same force that drew Jen through the air. The flying debris disappeared into the funnel, eaten by the blackness within.

Jen screamed in helpless fear.

Against the steady stream of ballistic debris, the cosmic funnel spat out a woman onto the ground, covered in armor that couldn't seem to pick a color and almost hurt to look at. Rocks flying in the opposite direction clanged against her protective covering loud enough to make Jen's ears ring, but her armor appeared undamaged.

The hole closed in an instant.

Like the flip of a switch, the unnatural gravitational pull abated. Jen and the strangely armored woman tumbled through the dirt on a collision course, limbs flailing, and collided with a mutual, bone-crunching "Oof!"

After the world stopped spinning, Jen cracked an eyelid. Color-shifting armor lay across her face, attached to the woman's arm. The colors shifted so quickly that it threatened to bring up Jen's lunch.

Jen tentatively flexed her legs, feet, hands, and arms. A sharp pain in her side told her she'd probably cracked a rib, but, miraculously, nothing else appeared broken.

The strangely armored woman was another matter. Her right elbow, Jen realized with horror, was bent entirely the wrong way.

"M... *meme*," the woman said with a pained gasp. *"Ko mu tyufki?"*

The words sounded like no language Jen had heard before, not that she had much experience. English was Holtondome's only language, smattered with the odd Nordic phrase that had somehow managed to survive the centuries without censorship, which hardly made her a linguistic expert.

"I... I have no idea what you're saying, but your arm appears broken."

The poor woman must be in shock from such an ordeal. I surely would be.

"We have to get you in to see Doc Ven. He'll fix you right up."

The woman stared at her, blinking.

Jen gently patted the woman's arm. "Arm. Broken." She pointed back to Holtondome, where the crowd had thankfully scattered, then mimed moving the woman's arm into a more natural position. "Holtondome. Doctor. Fix arm."

Eyes the color of a gentle, cozy fire lit with understanding. Jen had never seen anything like them.

Do human eyes even come in that color?

"*Tyœ shpü ko mütfa,*" the woman said, flashing a reassuring smile. She glanced meaningfully at her arm and nodded. "*Tyœ sa ghœsto chi, ghifa.*"

Jen looked at the woman's broken arm. Bile rose in her throat. "You... want me to move it for you?"

The woman stared at nothing. For a terrifying moment, Jen thought another innocent person had just passed to Freyja's green fields, but her fire-orange eyes soon focused back on Jen.

"Yes. Fix move, please."

Although heavily accented, Jen understood well enough to feel suddenly faint. "I-I'm not a doctor. We should really get you back to the dome so Doc Ven can take care of you."

Staring and silence again, then the woman chuckled. "Doctor need no. Move arm now. Be okay will. Please. You help, I help. Okay?"

It wasn't okay; it was ridiculous. The injured woman was clearly delirious from pain and had no idea what she was talking about.

At least, that was what Jen's rational mind wanted to believe. What she saw in those eyes and bruised face inside her helmet, however, was calm, cool, and collected, backed by a confidence that made Jen's mouth fall open in awe.

Almost without thinking, Jen obeyed. She grabbed the woman's forearm, braced her palm at the crook of her elbow, and, with a shuddering breath, pushed.

Bone crunched against bone. The woman's scream lanced Jen's soul. Jen instinctively hugged her close, rocking her back and forth while they lay tangled on the ground, whispering soothing words into her ear, like she had for her boys when they were still small enough to fit in her lap, instead of the other way around.

The woman calmed quickly, much sooner than Jen would have. She leaned back and, to Jen's surprise, wore a smile on her sweat-dappled face.

"A thousand thanks. Hard on you was. You okay?"

"Me?" Jen did another mental check. Apart from her aching ribs, her dead father, the army at Holtondome's door, and the woman that the universe appeared to have spat into her arms, everything seemed in order.

Am I losing my mind?

The last three days had been stressful, yes, but Jen wasn't prone to hallucinations. Her brother Seg might have spun a story like this. Jen was firmly grounded, however, and always had been.

Still, she touched the woman's face just to make sure. Her skin was warm and soft, as she expected, with high cheekbones and a rosy complexion.

The woman laughed and tipped her head. "O'Kel'Anaran named am. You?"

"J-Jen." She cleared her throat, the heat of embarrassment flaring her cheeks at her lapse in manners. "Holtondome welcomes and protects you, brave traveler. I'm Jen Holton, at your service, and shall ensure your needs are attended to during your stay."

Again the woman stared at nothing, then her smile returned. "I, O'Kel'Anaran, Straala of Aeczan, accept." Her expression turned grave. "Jen of Holtondome, I need help yours more. I someone seek. Straala. Very important. Female, like me appears. O'Fi'Liara."

Only one person Jen had ever met looked like this woman. "You must mean Miss Fi."

Her face lit with delight. "Maybe. Here?"

"No, she and my brother—"

Jen startled when a white-helmeted Fed stepped around a clump of sharpgrass, followed by two others, their rifles at the ready. If they hadn't just murdered her father, she would have pleaded with them to help O'Kel'Anaran back to the dome for medical treatment, but she doubted they would grant any such mercies today.

"I'm afraid our usual hospitalities may have to wait," Jen said to her new guest. "Can you stand?"

"Yes, stand can." O'Kel'Anaran took the soldiers in with a casual glance. "Trouble?"

"Most certainly," Jen said under her breath.

She helped O'Kel'Anaran to her feet. The woman kept rising and rising until she towered over Jen—a full two meters tall at least, with legs that seemed to stretch for kilometers. She was, if Jen remembered right, even taller than Fi, and that was saying something.

Jen straightened, giving her own small frame as much height as she could, and rounded on the Feds. "This woman is injured. Under the Laws of Hospitality, I ask that you lower your weapons so that we may offer her shelter and aid her recovery."

"Holtondome stands charged with violent insurrection," the Fed in front said. His voice inside his visored helmet sounded younger than Jen expected. "The Laws of Hospitality no longer apply."

"Don't waste your breath," a female Fed next to him said, sounding almost bored. "She's probably one of the ring leaders. Smoke 'em both and let's go. We got more to thin out inside."

"But the taller one—"

"Is guilty by association. Our orders are clear. Now, rookie, unless you want to stand out here all day, I said *smoke 'em and let's go!*"

"Ma'am!"

And like that, Jen's fate was decided. She had no say, no trial, despite Chang's promise to peacefully negotiate Holtondome's future in the Federated Nations.

Standing behind her, O'Kel'Anaran rested both hands on Jen's shoulders, as if the arm Jen had just crunched back into place had never been broken, and spoke with calm authority. "Who charges makes?"

The soldier in front hesitated, half-lowering his rifle. He looked at the woman who was obviously his superior. She sighed and faced O'Kel'Anaran.

"Grand Chancellor Chang himself. Now unless—"

"Accused agree do?"

"No!" Jen said, watching their weapons as if they were live vipers about to strike. "The accused do *not* agree. And neither did Chang, to our knowledge. There was violence, yes, but we kept it to a minimum, and have treated the surviving Feds well."

"Trial?" O'Kel'Anaran said.

"Not as such. Miss Fi had a conversation with the grand chancellor, as I understand, and they came to an agreement."

"See." O'Kel'Anaran's fiery eyes swept the area, taking in the large tanks, personnel carriers, and array of armed and armored troops. "Holtondome weapons has? Defend?"

"No," Jen said through clenched teeth. A tear rolled down her cheek at the thought of what this overwhelming force was about to do to the people she loved—the only people she'd ever known. "We have a few rifles, but that's it! We're farmers. *Farmers!* They're going to slaughter us!"

The female Fed shook her head and turned to her male subordinate. "Told you it was a waste of breath. Next time, follow orders, or it'll go on your record."

With that, she raised her rifle at Jen and O'Kel'Anaran and pulled the trigger.

Jen couldn't even scream. She simply closed her eyes, said a silent apology to her dear, rambunctious boys, and waited for the end.

Instead of a gunshot, Jen heard the female Fed swear. She cracked an eye to find her fiddling with her rifle.

"Trigger's jammed." Her finger shook with effort, but the tiny sliver of death metal refused to budge. She nudged the first Fed. "Do it this time, or I *will* report you."

"You not will," O'Kel'Anaran said to him. "Finished not have. Fair trial Jen Holton received not has. Neither you listen. Without compassion kill. Without understanding murder. Power abuse. Like Phezath are."

"You don't know a goddamned thing," the female Fed said. She redoubled her effort to move the stuck trigger, but to no avail.

"Plenty know. Your kind many times seen. Bullies. Weak. Corrupt. Complicit. Harm spreading when preventing should."

O'Kel'Anaran didn't move. She didn't need to. The command in her voice should have been enough to bring the entire army to their knees.

"I, O'Kel'Anaran, Aeczan Straala, judgement proclaim. Your weapons down lay. Peaceful leave, or sentence I pass will. No other warning give. Acknowledge."

"Ugh! I'm sick of this self-righteous bitch," the female Fed said. "Someone shoot her. Now!"

"With pleasure." A large Fed stepped around her, took aim...

...and exploded in a fountain of red gore.

For a moment, time stood still. The Feds stared at the falling remains of their companion, their shiny white armor dotted with his blood, minds working like Jen's to process what had just happened.

The first Fed yanked his helmet off and wretched.

"K-k-kill them," the female Fed said, retreating as fast as she could without taking her eyes from O'Kel'Anaran. "Kill them now! Fire! *Fire!* Everybody f—"

The female Fed erupted in a fountain of blood, too, covering the ground around her in sickly red. Her empty armor clattered to the ground in a heap.

Then all Hel broke loose. Gunfire erupted everywhere, assaulting Jen's eardrums like a thousand tiny thunderclaps. She cowered against the taller woman, wishing she could somehow crawl inside her multi-colored armor to share its protection.

All around them, soldiers fired in a constant roar, muzzles belching angry dragon fire. A tank barrel leveled and shot directly at them, louder and scarier than Jen's most terrifying nightmare.

None of it connected. Bullets and tank shells burst into fine gray dust approximately ten meters around them in all directions, as if disintegrating against some invisible circular wall.

Then, horrifyingly, Feds began exploding in series, each erupting into a crimson nova. Tank hatches blew open one after another, where red mist spewed up from the tops like demonic geysers. The stench of iron and entrails filled the air, worse than any pig slaughter Jen had ever worked at Holtondome. That conditioning alone was the only reason she didn't empty the contents of her stomach right there.

And then it was quiet. Only the wind and the residual ringing in Jen's ears disturbed the unholy silence in the aftermath that would surely haunt the rest of Jen's nights—however many she had left.

Jen slowly looked up at the woman who still held her gently by the shoulders.

O'Kel'Anaran looked down and stroked Jen's hair like a child. "Told them, but no helping was. Sentence passed. Holtondome safe.

"Now, we move must. Find O'Fi'Liara before too late is."

ACKNOWLEDGMENTS

Writing a new series after *The Z-Tech Chronicles,* in a different genre with brand new characters and a reimagined Earth, gave me cold shivers when I first conceived the idea. Only the unwavering faith and support of my friends, family, and amazing beta readers propelled me forward. I can only hope this final work makes them proud.

To my mom, as always, for being the first eyes on all my works, a solid measure of readability, and a bottomless font of encouragement.

To my wife for gifting me the space to write. Your patience and sacrifice has not gone unnoticed nor unappreciated.

To Jiné and Laura, who supported this manuscript with every shred of their souls. You are my friends, my team, and my inspiration.

To José for effortlessly bringing my imaginary world to life with yet another dazzling cover.

To Keri for your boundless enthusiasm and wealth of ideas. Your creativity and curious mind helped bring reality and detail where I would have faltered.

And to Brandon, Kelley, Liz, Josh, and Jo for taking the time to provide your valuable feedback and make Holtondome the best book it could be. The confidence you instilled is immeasurable. Thank you!

ABOUT THE AUTHOR

Ryan Southwick decided to dabble at writing late in life, and quickly became obsessed with the craft. He currently lives in the San Francisco Bay Area with his wife and two children.

His technical skills as a software developer, healthcare experience, and lifelong fascination for science fiction became the ingredients for his first series, *The Z-Tech Chronicles*, which combines these elements into a fantastic contemporary tale of super-science, fantasy, and adventure, based in his Bay Area stomping grounds.

Find out more by visiting ryansouthwickauthor.com.

Subscribe for a monthly newsletter filled with interesting fiction articles, blog posts, artwork, and upcoming events in the science fantasy world:

ryansouthwickauthor.com/newsletter

You can also show support by following Ryan on social media, including TikTok, Goodreads, Facebook, and Instagram. Find these links and more on LinkTree:

linktr.ee/RyanSouthwick

Find other works and more on his author website:

ryansouthwickauthor.com